ALESIA PRESS LLC

ALSO BY JOHN PEARCE

Treasure of Saint-Lazare
Last Stop: Paris
Lauren (a short story)

Finding Pegasus is the third in the Eddie Grant thriller series

The full-length audiobook, narrated by **Adam Barr**, is available from Amazon or Audible.com.

Finding Pegasus is a work of fiction. The names, characters, places and incidents portrayed are the product of the author's imagination. Any resemblance to actual persons, living or dead (with the exception of certain historical figures) is entirely coincidental.

Copyright © 2018 John Pearce
All rights reserved.

Published by
Alesia Press
539 W. Commerce #481
Dallas TX 75208

Publisher@alesiapress.com

ISBN-13: 978-0-9859626-8-5

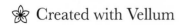 Created with Vellum

For Jan

1

PEGASUS AND ICARUS

MIAMI

The ruby dot of Mark McGinley's pointer circled an old stone church, dark but for the dim yellow glow cast by the lighting in its parking lot.

Icky Crane, the entire audience for this private showing, leaned forward in his chair at the other end of the conference table. To his right Kate Hall, the sole additional employee of McGinley Engineering and editor of the video Mark was narrating, watched it as though she were seeing it for the first time instead of the twentieth.

"This is an old Episcopal church on the north side of town," Mark said. "It's late at night, well after the street lights go out. The pastor is an ex-Navy officer like Kate, which made it easy to talk him into letting us do this test. He's a techie and couldn't drag himself away until we were finished, *and* he suggested that we try to sell it to the CIA. I mumbled something vague – I forget what – because I sure didn't want to tell him you'd be here today.

"It's three o'clock in the morning. The camera and I are perched on top of a rental truck."

The video panned across the church's bell tower. The afternoon before, its ancient gray stone walls gleamed in the summer sunlight, but after midnight they were cold and unwelcoming.

"Keep an eye on this gargoyle," Mark said. The camera zoomed in on the medieval rainspout projecting from the tower as his pointer traced circles around the dragon's head. "Our six-prop drone, Icarus, will fly in close. It's an important part of this test. First we'll swing over and watch Kate launch Icarus, but we'll come back to the church."

The camera panned across the street to a single van that sat in front of a dimly lit park.

"This is where we begin. Watch the back of the van closely and you'll see Kate launch Icarus. Don't blink."

Kate picked up the narration.

"That murky silhouette at the back of the van is me. The blue halo is something we put in during editing so you can follow the drone's path."

As the blue cloud rose she said, "Watch closely and you'll see the actual drone. I put a light on it for an instant – actually, we timed it later and it was two-tenths of a second. This will be your only chance on this run."

The brief flash of light revealed a small, spiderish black helicopter, accelerating rapidly as its six propellers pulled it away from Kate.

"This is your introduction to Icarus. This demonstration shows a few of his abilities, but he has many more."

"The name fits," Icky said. "Just don't send him too close to the sun."

Mark said, "The first time I met Kate, she told me both pieces of this project needed names. We chose Icarus in honor of the Greek myth of the boy who flew too close to the sun. The other half, which you'll see in a couple of minutes, we christened Pegasus, after the winged horse."

"How about the sound?" Icky asked.

"Almost silent," Mark said. "The blades are carefully machined and turn at relatively low speed. From a hundred feet away you wouldn't hear anything."

The camera followed the blue cloud as it approached the church.

"How are you controlling it?" Icky asked.

"It's autonomous. That's its most important feature. We basically told it to find St. John's Church, go there, drop off a package in a specific place, then come back to where it started. It has to figure out the rest. We had to show it what a gargoyle looks like, but before long it will be able to find that out by itself."

The blue cloud stopped halfway up the tower, then ascended and hovered above the gargoyle for a few seconds before it retraced its path and settled behind the van. Kate's shadowy figure lifted it inside and closed the doors.

"And then we drove back to the shop," Mark concluded.

Kate spoke up. "We wanted to run this test in Paris, at Notre Dame. It would be really dramatic to see Icarus against that background. But my friend Aurélie Cabillaud told me it would be far too dangerous. Her father, the *commissaire,* told her it would be crazy and we'd probably spend a couple of days in jail, even with his help. So we dropped that idea."

"Her judgment has been good so far," Icky said. "Somehow she knew you and Mark would be a good fit after he fired his last engineer."

"She was dead right about that," Mark said. Then, trying to bring the discussion back to his presentation, he continued, "Now let's change the vantage point and see what Icarus saw as he approached St. John's. I want you to see the details of his little donation to the gargoyle, so I've turned the light intensifier up as high as it will go. The image is pretty grainy."

"This is the south tower," Mark said. "Icarus miscalculated the altitude and came in a little too low, but corrected. You'll see it stop, reorient itself, then ascend. It made that calculation in milliseconds."

The wall loomed closer, then stopped. The camera rose until it reached the row of gargoyles and paused above the closest one. A robot arm reached into the frame from the left and gently placed what looked like a stone in the water channel leading to the gargoyle's mouth.

Mark said, "Icky, I know you have some suspicious colleagues who'll say all you saw is a fake blue light. But this is the proof – when you open that little package, it will do away with any doubts."

Icky asked the obvious question. "How do you know it's still there?"

"It's stuck in the channel pretty well and there hasn't been much rain," Mark answered. "And the package has a location sensor in it – a sort of Find My Phone. I checked a couple of hours ago and it's still there. Now let's look at the other member of the team, Pegasus."

The screen went blank, then switched to an image of a wooden worktable where a long, cigar-shaped object lay, covered by a white cloth. A hand pulled back the cover to reveal a black cylinder that looked like a torpedo, except that it had stubby wings and a bulbous front end.

"Icky, I told you this package has two parts. Here's the other half. This is Pegasus, our fully autonomous self-driving submarine. Software completion is still a few weeks away, but soon we'll be able to put the sub into the water miles away from its target, tell it to deliver Icarus and wait, or sail off and do something else for a while, then meet up with him somewhere.

"Here's a short video of an open-water test we did a couple of weeks ago. We can't really demonstrate the autonomous control very well because most of that is done underwater, but we did make it do a trick that may amuse you."

The camera showed a picture of blue, open water, with the faint smudge of land on the horizon.

"We're on a remote spot on Biscayne Bay, standing on a rickety old pier. Kate has just launched Pegasus, and in a second you'll see them come into view from the left."

The sky above was not the savage blue that northern tourists love in winter, but the milky azure of a hot August, with puffy rain clouds in the distance and streaks of cirrus far overhead.

As he spoke, the sleek black silhouette came into the picture, low in the water, with a figure in a dark wetsuit riding it.

"That's Kate. She's steering the sub manually now, using a control panel set into the top of the hull – an iPhone in a military case. There's an adapter kit that provides a sort of saddle and stirrups, so she can ride it either submerged or surfaced. Now watch."

The sub stopped. Kate raised one hand dramatically, extended a finger to press a button on the iPhone, then slipped off the saddle and swam quickly toward the shore.

As Pegasus rocked gently on the swells of Biscayne Bay, a hatch at the front of the submarine opened and Icarus rotated into view. It flew off, the hatch closed and the sub moved swiftly away. They caught a brief glimpse of one stubby wing rising out of the water as it banked and sank out of sight.

"Watch carefully," Mark said. "The sub will do a three-sixty and surface about where you saw it last. If you listen carefully you may be able to hear the motor accelerate. It needs a lot of speed for what it's about to do."

The camera followed Kate as she climbed from the water, took off her mask and shook out her short dark hair, then turned back toward the bay. The distant sound of a powerful turbine revving to high speed came through the speakers and the submarine broke the surface. It sailed fifty feet in a graceful arc, pointed its nose down, and disappeared into the water with hardly a splash. "A dive as sweet as any you'd see at the Olympics," Mark told Kate on the video. "Nice work."

Pegasus surfaced again fifty feet from the end of the pier and moved quietly toward them, like a friendly black dolphin. The hatch opened as Icarus floated down from their right and settled gracefully onto its landing pad. The top of its hull closed and a corona of foam surrounded its stern as the propeller reversed to brake its momentum. Kate reached down to clip a mooring line to a ring at the end of its left wing.

WHEN THE LIGHTS CAME ON, Mark turned to face Icky. "Together, Pegasus and Icarus are a highly sophisticated espionage package, well suited for the rivers of Europe. And thanks to some engineering Kate did a month or so ago, we've been able to build in the ability to do short sprints at very high speeds and jump over an obstacle like a submarine net, which could help it escape from a tight spot. Icky, I hope it's what you need.

"We realize autonomous subs are already in use here and there, for duties like ocean floor mapping or searching for sunken ships or lost airliners, but as far as we know this is the first time something this small and smart has had its own air force."

"You're right. We do have some, but they aren't this flexible. It's a long step in the right direction," Icky replied. "There are days I look at the newspaper and think the 1930s are back. A lot of the old Soviet satellites are turning into small-bore dictatorships before our eyes, and we desperately need ways to stay abreast. Pegasus and Icarus would be a big help.

"Anything you do from here on will have to be

classified. I'll send the security people down in a few days to look at your setup."

He turned to Kate. "Everybody involved will have to have security clearances. Is that a problem for you?"

"Hardly. I used to root around in the engine rooms of nuclear submarines. I'm top secret code-word, although you may have to reactivate it."

Mark said, "Now that we've gotten this far I'd like to know more about what you have in mind. If we know more, we can probably build in some useful features."

"I think you're entitled to that," Icky said. "Our big concern now is Eastern Europe, where it seems there is a new wannabe dictator every weekend. We need a more advanced close-in listening post, or a lot of them.

"But there are other threats out there as well. The Russians are building small subs that could carry nuclear bombs into harbors. We'd like to have some way to defend against them, and another sub, smaller and smarter, might be just the ticket. As we have more ideas I'll send them to you."

Icky looked at his watch. "I promised my very pregnant wife I'd try to be home for dinner. If I leave now I can catch an earlier plane to Dulles and I might just barely make it, traffic willing."

MARK AND KATE stood side by side on the parking lot, watching as Icky drove out of the industrial park.

"We made a good presentation today. Thanks," he said with a smile. He did not smile often.

"I thought we both did well. It's a good product and will do what it's designed to do. Icky is a tough customer but he respects you. Respect always helps."

"He and I get along fine. He'll send some other people down to ask a lot more questions, and some of those may be touchy."

"Icky's wife is Aurélie's friend, isn't she?" Kate asked.

"More like the friend of her husband, Eddie Grant."

"Friend?"

"Very close friend. Before Aurélie. Or, according to Icky, between times with Aurélie." He looked at his watch. "I have some paperwork to do before we leave."

"And I need to get back to the motor. Icky is going to put a lot of pressure on us, and on Pegasus. He needs to go faster. I'm tweaking the hydrogen injectors, but we need to keep looking for another trick, too."

2

A KILLING ON THE SEINE

PARIS

Six time zones to the east, Sophie Leroux stood calmly, smoking a cigarette as she waited for a bus at a shelter across the street from the Café Le Mistral. Even at mid-afternoon, every one of its outdoor tables was filled.

She inhaled deeply, exhaled slowly and watched the smoke float downwind on the gentle breeze that follows the Seine past Notre Dame Cathedral.

It's a lousy habit, she told herself one more time. Dirty, expensive, bad for her and everyone around her. Then she reached into her shoulder bag and pulled out another one.

ONCE UPON A TIME chic *parisiennes* wore black, which

turned out to be a habit much easier to break than cigarettes. Black was the fashion statement that separated them from their country cousins, but as summers became warmer and then manifestly hot, their frocks faded.

Not Sophie's. As her friends went dull, she went bright. Even in black, she stood out from the crowd, but in the tailored red number she wore now on the bustling corner overlooking the Seine, she was a robin among sparrows, and the sparrows noticed.

A dozen of them, all with long dark hair and perfect but almost invisible makeup, strode purposefully down the sidewalk or waited impatiently for the light to change. A few flirted casually with their companions, many of whom stole a glance at Sophie. A stout German guide hoisted her parasol and commanded her charges to stop and admire the sweeping view stretching from Notre Dame on the left to the Eiffel Tower in the distance on the right. The Left Bank stretched away on the far side of the river.

Sophie stepped back from the rough stone wall separating two booksellers' stalls. The electronic notice board above the bus shelter told her the next one would arrive in three minutes, but it was wrong, as she discovered only after she lit another cigarette. The 72 stopped two minutes early to disgorge its cargo of chattering *écoliers*. Her eight-year-old son Lucas jumped out as soon as the back door opened.

The cigarette, unsmoked, went into the bin attached to the shelter.

"How are you, *mon petit?* Did you do well in school?" She smiled down at him and ruffled his raven hair, then took his hand and began the walk across two bridges and the Île de la Cité, the island where Paris first became Paris well before the Romans arrived. It was a tradition they had followed for Lucas's first two years of primary school, but now that the third had started he was already lobbying to make the walk alone. The idea made her nervous, and she suspected he wasn't all that convinced, either.

The walk across the Île de la Cité is one of the most famous in a city of famous walks. It never bored Sophie and Lucas seemed to enjoy it more every day, as she had at his age. The walks of her childhood were a deep cultural memory, one of the many experiences that had turned her from just another schoolgirl to a true *parisienne*, with a feel for the city and its monuments that she knew would be hers forever. No one could take it away.

Sophie's world was bordered by Châtelet and its bus stop, Notre Dame, the Place Saint-Michel, the French Institute and the Louvre. She was convinced her personal stretch of the Seine bordered the most beautiful square mile in the world and saw little reason to wander very far away.

The Seine was Sophie's home. She had lived on

the river for every one of her thirty-two years and, little by little, had become one of those contented Parisians who view their *arrondissement* as their own small village and live happily in it, venturing out of it only when absolutely necessary.

They turned their backs on the twin theaters bracketing the Châtelet fountain and headed across the Pont au Change, dodging pedestrians and tourists with the aplomb that comes from long practice. On the Île itself they steered to the east side to avoid the lines of tourists hoping to enter Sainte-Chapelle before it closed for the day.

Thronged with visitors, dense with imposing stone buildings, the Île de la Cité has two main populations: police and tourists. Most of the buildings belong to the National Police and the courts, and the sidewalks belong to the tourists.

On the façade of one building, the city had mounted a display of old photos of soldiers returning from World War II, where Lucas always insisted on stopping so he could search out his grandfather once again.

Lucas knew Sophie's father only from her stories, but the picture of him as a young soldier with a luxuriant walrus mustache was the icon Lucas depended on to connect with the family's past. They both would be sorry when the traveling exhibit moved somewhere else.

"UP OR DOWN?" Sophie asked as they started across the second bridge, the ornate Pont Saint-Michel. Its south end, on the Left Bank, lay across the broad intersection from the tourist restaurant where she worked as a hostess six days a week, first at lunch and again through the dinner hour, stopping only for the afternoon break, when she met Lucas at the bus. On school days she delivered him into the caring hands of Madame Westerhof, her downstairs neighbor, where he would stay until her workday ended at nine thirty. Madame Westerhof was pleased when Lucas stayed overnight, as well.

"Down," Lucas burbled. He pulled his little hand free and dashed in and out of the pack of commuters headed for the suburban trains that met below the street, one to run alongside the river, the other to cross under it.

Her nose wrinkled at the thought of the secluded staircase that connected the street to the Saint-Michel RER station and, further down, to the riverbank. It was an unofficial haven for a handful of hardcore homeless men, and the smell of urine was ever-present.

She held her breath and dashed down the stairs, then took a deep breath of the fresh air gusting down the Seine. Lucas stood under the massive stone arch of Saint-Michel Bridge staring with intense curiosity at the flotsam whirling in the eddies around its massive pilings. At those moments he reminded Sophie of her own father, whose curiosity about anything and everything had remained sharp until the end of his life seven years before.

They turned away from the bridge to walk downstream. She had measured it one day – from Pont Saint-Michel to Pont Neuf was 500 paces on her long legs, many more for a small boy, although Lucas had more than enough energy to compensate.

He darted ahead, his feet hardly seeming to touch the large cobbles that made her low heels risky. After a hundred yards, he stopped and turned back to her.

"Maman, why are those men fighting?" he asked, pointing ahead to two men sitting with their legs hanging over the heavy granite edge of the quai. The river flowed only a couple of feet below, unlike other stretches where the drop was much longer. As a result, this was a favorite spot for couples to share lunch or doze idly in the sun. Now and then one rolled the wrong way and had to be pulled out by the fire department, whose station and boats were just a hundred yards downstream.

Sophie saw one of the men push the other away from him and try to stand. He's trying to get away, she thought, but then the other man grabbed hard for his belt and pulled him back, then raised his arm and threw a hard punch to his midsection. It ended the fight.

As she watched, the attacker rummaged in his victim's trouser pocket and pulled out a wallet, which he put into his own pocket. He walked back toward them, stumbling once on the large cobblestones and almost falling on Lucas. As he passed her, Sophie saw his eyes dart around. He's just robbed a man and he's afraid, she thought.

She watched him turn into the odiferous staircase. The homeless man hunched in the corner of the first step put out his hand in fruitless appeal as the man bounded up the stairs and disappeared around the corner. She could not tell if he had gone into the RER station or continued up to the street – in either case, he was gone.

When she turned back, the second man was lying on his side. From her vantage point a dozen yards away he looked like any of the other tired office workers she'd seen dozing in the sun, but the terrified "*Maman!*" from Lucas told her it was something else.

"*Maman!*" he cried again as he wrapped his arms tightly around her legs. "That man is bleeding."

She gently pulled free from his grip and approached cautiously. From the back the man looked normal. But when she got close enough to look at his face she saw a gusher of blood flowing down the granite wall into the Seine. The handle of a large knife protruded from his chest.

She screamed.

SOPHIE'S PANIC lasted only a few seconds. She wasn't timid, and she'd seen bodies before – just last month a tourist from Indiana had collapsed during his cheese course and fallen out of his chair, sightless eyes staring into the afternoon sky.

She reached for her phone and dialed 112. As calmly as she could, she explained what she'd seen. The operator told her to wait, and by the time he came back on the line she could hear the distinctive two-tone siren of the fire department's high-speed rescue boat coming upriver toward her.

"The *pompiers* are on the way, madame," the operator said formally. "Please wait for them and for the police, who will be only a few minutes behind. And please don't touch anything. I gave your name and number to Commissaire Cabillaud. He will have questions."

"Philippe?" she shouted at the operator. "Philippe is nothing but questions." It calmed her to know that the policeman was one of the regulars who walked across the bridge for their afternoon coffee. She did not normally have much use for policemen, but Philippe was different. He was kind and had gentle eyes. So what if he had a daughter her age?

Its blue light still flashing, the firefighters' boat nudged the stone wall. The driver revved the engine to hold it in place while two fit young men jumped from the bow onto the granite river bank. Bystanders had gathered in a tight knot around the body but backed away now, leaving only Sophie, Lucas, and a young doctor who had been reading a book next to Pont Neuf when Sophie's scream interrupted his plan for a quiet lunch. He found no pulse.

Lucas's fascination with the firemen drove all thoughts of the corpse from his mind. The bleeding had stopped, leaving an ugly brown stain on the quay. It would remain until the city's ever-present cleaners brought a pressure washer.

The taller of the firemen pressed his gloved fingers to the dead man's throat.

"*Mort*," he said flatly. His partner picked up the man's legs and stretched him out to his full length. Together, they turned him gently on his back. A sandwich wrapper lodged under the body blew free. One of the firemen followed it for three steps before giving up and watching it float down the river.

The boat's driver handed up a tightly folded white plastic sheet, which the two spread over the body. A large sheath knife, still stuck between the man's ribs, held the sheet up like a tent pole.

A small ambulance approached from the Pont
Neuf traffic ramp and parked a dozen yards away.

"Now we wait for the police," one of the
firemen told Sophie. "The commissaire and a
doctor are on the way from the Quai des Orfèvres."
He indicated with his head toward the police headquarters directly across the Seine. She could see the
line of blue vans that carry crowd-control police to
the many street demonstrations Paris sees each
week.

Sophie spotted Philippe as soon as he left the
stairs. "Here he is," she said to the firefighters.

"Of course they would walk," the taller one
replied. "They should keep a boat over there. If he'd
called us we could have picked them up sooner and
by now we'd be back at the station."

She recognized Philippe first by his hat – the one
that looked like an Australian outback hat, made of
light, butter-soft leather. He'd placed it in the chair
next to him many times when she'd shown him to a
table. The other man carried a small black bag.

The two firemen shook hands formally with
Philippe and the doctor, who pulled back the sheet to
look closely at the body. Like the fireman, he tested
for a pulse.

"*Rien*," he said to Philippe. Nothing.

"This lady found the body and thinks she saw the
killing," the taller fireman said to Philippe, who
looked at the witnesses for the first time.

"Sophie!" he said in surprise. "Shouldn't you be at work?"

"It appears Lucas and I are your witnesses. I was walking him home from the bus like I do every afternoon. We had just come down the stairs when Lucas spotted the two men arguing. The robber walked right by us and up the stairs."

"You're sure it was a robbery?"

"I saw him take something brown, like a wallet, out of that man's pocket." She pointed toward the still shape lying on the stones.

"So you got a good look at him?"

"I would know him again."

Philippe crouched so he could look her son in the eye.

"Lucas, my name is Commissaire Cabillaud and I see your mother sometimes at her work. Can you tell me what you saw?"

Lucas repeated the story he'd told his mother. Philippe nodded and thanked him gravely, one grownup to another, and stood up.

"Sophie, the doctor and I have some things to do but I need to talk to you some more. Would you mind waiting on that bench?" He escorted her to a granite bench against the wall and asked a young couple to move. They got up grudgingly and walked away.

By then Philippe's driver had arrived with another policeman. The doctor had pulled the sheet completely away and was inspecting the body carefully for other wounds, pulling the man's white t-shirt from side to side.

"Nothing," he said, standing up. "One knife thrust. It went between his ribs and into his heart, and probably severed his aorta. I'll know more after the autopsy, but I suspect he was unconscious within seconds and died almost immediately."

Philippe put on gloves and expertly rifled the man's pockets, finding a dirty handkerchief, which he dropped into the bag his driver held open.

"No ID, no money, no métro pass. But there should be a wallet or some money."

"Maybe he was just forgetful and left his wallet at home," the doctor said.

"Sophie saw the killer take it."

Philippe leaned over to photograph the man's face with his iPhone, then took a picture of the gaping wound. He raised an eyebrow and the doctor shrugged as if to say, Whatever you want, and pulled at the knife. It resisted at first but by twisting it he was able to withdraw it, holding it only by the guard so he would not disturb the fingerprints both of them hoped were present. He placed it on the stone so Philippe could photograph it as well, then the driver put it into another evidence bag.

"It stuck between his ribs," the doctor said. "I suspect the killer tried to get it out but couldn't, and panicked."

As the ambulance pulled away, Philippe turned to Sophie. "Now I need to know what you saw. You may be the only witnesses, unless we get really lucky and find a tourist who was taking video at the time."

"I'm already late for work," Sophie said, clearly pleading for his help. "I was gone too long once last week and Alex got very angry."

"This is going to take some time," he replied. "I'll call Alex right now so he won't worry." He found the number and summarized for the restaurant owner what had happened to Sophie.

In very few words, he told the boss she would be away for several hours. The man on the other end of the line, whom he'd known for several years but didn't count among his friends, seemed to resist.

"Alex, this is not a request. I did not say please. It's police business. There has been a murder and Sophie was a witness. I know you'll do the right thing, especially since her sunny personality is a big part of the reason you seldom have to face a health inspector. And why my colleagues and I visit you instead of your friendly neighbor across the street."

He ended the call and turned back to Sophie. "You live on the quai, don't you?"

"Yes, at the corner."

"Then we'll go there, to the bistro. It would take too long to go to the préfecture. I can talk first to Lucas, then you can take him to the sitter. Does he stay in the building?"

"With Madame Westerhof, two floors down from me."

———

SOPHIE'S BUILDING was one of a row of massive stone piles lining the sidewalk not far from the Mint, at the corner where Pont Neuf ends at the Quai des Grands-Augustins. The busy street was named for a long-defunct order of monks whose property had once dominated the neighborhood but whose only surviving relic was the fine arts academy nearby.

"This is the best place," she said, leading him into the Bistro Augustin. At mid-afternoon it was dark and as quiet as any pub on a major thoroughfare could be.

"I need to talk to Lucas alone for a few minutes. Why don't I bring him up to you when we're done? You can take him to Madame Westerhof and then we can talk. After that, you can go to work and make Alex happy. I'll even take you back there myself."

She knelt before Lucas. "You need to stay here with the commissaire and tell him what you saw, and then we'll go see Madame. Can you do that?"

"*Bien sûr, Maman,*" he said, not entirely convinced. "Where will you be?"

"I'll be at home. Philippe will bring you there."

She turned to Philippe and said, "Fifth floor on the right."

Philippe picked a table in the corner. When the waiter came he looked suspiciously at Philippe and said, "I know Lucas well, monsieur. But who are you?"

"Very observant. Good for you," Philippe said, and showed his ID. He ordered an orange pressé for the boy and a glass of Bordeaux for himself.

They each took a sip of their drink, then he said gently, "Now, Lucas, will you tell me what you saw on the quai? Please don't leave anything out. You may be our most important witness."

SLOWLY, Lucas recounted how he first saw the two men arguing and then, as he drew closer, one appearing to reach for something on his belt.

"I thought he was giving it to the other man, but he pushed it pretty hard."

"Show me," Philippe said. He pulled his chair around next to Lucas and asked, "Is this how they were sitting?"

"The man with the knife was on the other side. He used his right hand." Lucas extended his right hand to show he knew the difference. "Maman taught me."

They switched sides. "Now show me what the man on the right did."

"First they argued, then he reached down to his belt…" Lucas put his hand to his waist.

"On that side of his body?" Philippe asked.

"Yes, sir. Then his hand came up with something in it. He said something loud, then that's when I thought he'd handed something to the other man. Then he got up and left. He walked right past me."

"Could you hear what he said?"

"It was loud, but I didn't understand. It was in some other language. I have a friend at school who talks like that and I can't understand him, either, but he's learning French."

"Where is your friend from?"

"Hungary. That's where Professor Westerhof is from, too. He speaks that way sometimes."

THE QUESTIONS WENT on for another ten minutes, until Philippe said, "You've done a good job, Lucas. Would you like to be a policeman one day?"

"My grandfather was a soldier."

"Was he?"

"His picture is on the wall of the préfecture, behind General de Gaulle."

Philippe thought that unlikely because those pictures had been made seventy years before. All the old soldiers who had served with the sainted general were either dead or very, very old, and it was unlikely that any of them had a daughter Sophie's age.

"You and your mother must be proud of him. Now let's go find her and you can visit Madame Westerhof."

The boy clapped his hands in glee. "She promised to make a gâteau. But don't tell Maman."

"I won't. Boys should have a little cake from time to time, and there's no need for their mothers to know everything."

Philippe took the boy's hand and started toward the front door. The bartender stopped them with a polite, "Monsieur le Commissaire?" and pointed toward a half-hidden door at the end of a hallway, past the stairway that led downstairs to the toilets. Philippe thanked him gravely and they stepped out into the lobby of Sophie's building.

It was, he thought, a very nice fringe benefit for both the residents and the bistro.

THE BUILDING WAS one of tens of thousands built to Baron Haussmann's design in the second half of the nineteenth century. Emperor Napoleon III gave him a free hand to raze large sections of the old medieval city and construct grand thoroughfares lined with elegant seven-story apartment buildings, which still housed many of the two million Parisians who live inside the perimeter traced by the old city wall. Haussmann set the design firmly: the façades must be built of cut stone, with iron balconies on certain floors, so that the entire block looked like a continuous building. The design gives Paris a feeling of elegance and formality.

As a side effect, entirely intended, the broad avenues offered uninterrupted fields of fire if the population got too restless. The nineteenth century had been a raucous one. The memory of the brutal Commune soon after the American Civil War was still fresh in peoples' minds.

Sophie's lobby, like many Paris buildings of the epoch, showed a faded elegance. It was dominated by a grand central staircase, which narrowed as it approached the next floor. Uncounted feet had hollowed the stone steps to thin crescents.

Lucas pulled Philippe away from the stairs to a tiny elevator whose shaft rose in the center of the spiral. To Philippe, it looked like it had been added between the two world wars and updated since for self-service. He opened the century-old scissor door and Lucas immediately pulled the threadbare operator's seat from the wall and sat down. Ceremoniously, he pressed the button for the fifth floor.

When the old car rattled to a stop, Lucas dashed toward the door to the right, key in hand. He pushed the door open with a loud, "Maman! I'm home!"

Philippe hung back until Sophie appeared and invited him in. She asked Philippe to wait while she took him down to Madame Westerhof.

As Sophie had said to the police operator, Philippe had nothing but questions. He grilled her closely for a half-hour and, just as she thought he would never quit, he did.

"We should get you back to work," he said as he stood to leave. "But your sitter – was her husband the professor there when you took Lucas?"

"I didn't see him today, but he spends most of the day locked in his study, and he travels to Hungary quite a bit for politics. He was at home yesterday. Do you know him?"

"I met him once at a party, but I have an American friend who was his student years ago and knows him very well. I asked because Lucas said the killer spoke Hungarian.

"I've wanted to ask ever since I walked into this great apartment. How long have you lived here?"

"All my life, quite literally. I was born in the master bedroom over there." She pointed down the dark-paneled hallway toward the rear.

"So you inherited it?"

"Fortunately. I can barely afford to maintain it, and I certainly couldn't buy it now. My grandfather bought it right after World War One. My father inherited it when he was a young captain just out of the army and beginning to make a career in the de Gaulle government."

"So Lucas was right? I had my doubts that someone of that generation could have a daughter your age."

"His first wife left him in the sixties. He married my mother in the eighties. She died when I was a child.

"When I married, he called in an architect and had the back of the apartment separated into a smaller one-bedroom place with access from the back stairwell. He lived there the rest of his life, which was only a couple of years. That apartment is a lifesaver for me. With the income I get from it and what I earn at the restaurant, I get by."

"And Lucas's father?" Philippe asked, hoping he wasn't intruding too much, but he thought it odd such an attractive and personable woman would live alone.

"He left just about the time Lucas started to walk, right after he found out the apartment was the sum total of my father's estate. Last I heard he was operating some sort of tourist attraction in Biarritz. He was a bad decision."

"The marriage decision is usually either good or bad. I did about as well as you, I think." He closed his notebook and stood. "I'm done. Are you ready to go now?"

"You don't have to accompany me. I'm a big girl."

"I also know Alex and I knew his father before him. Their business is very profitable, but they are really tight and not always pleasant. I'll just be sure he does the right thing by you."

In twenty minutes they arrived at the restaurant. Alex walked with a scowl to the podium, where Philippe waited with Sophie.

"Alex, the police thank you for allowing Sophie to help us today. A man was murdered down by the river and she gave us very valuable information. I'll be sure my friends know of your generosity. It's not every owner who would pay her for the time she missed helping the police."

Alex stammered and finally was able to force out a few words. "It was my pleasure, Monsieur le Commissaire." He didn't notice Philippe's conspiratorial wink at Sophie.

PHILIPPE HUNG the hat on the chair across the small table, ordered an espresso, and sat back under the red awning along the pedestrian street separating the restaurant from the boutique next door. The sound of the city was in his blood; the chattering of the bright young things flitting from shop to shop didn't break his concentration any more than the bewildered conversation of the tourists trying to figure out how to get to Notre Dame (they were walking the wrong way).

He was tempted to go back and try to see André Westerhof but decided it would be better to use an indirect approach. Westerhof was closely tied to one of the centrist political parties of Hungary, and in fact had received death threats from people who openly identified with the collaborators who had done the Germans' bidding during the war. Every country had its hidden history, often alluded to but seldom brought into the light for examination. France was no exception.

It amazed him every time he ran across someone whose politics were driven by something their grandfather had said or done three-quarters of a century ago. He occasionally discussed it with his daughter Aurélie, a history professor, who invariably told him to stop worrying.

"You'll never change the blood-and-soil types," she told him. "They will always – always – carry their grievances and grudges. We're lucky our politics aren't that chaotic, but remember that we've been at it a lot longer than the Eastern Europeans, and we've had our moments. The Hungarians lived under the

Russian boot until just yesterday, as the history of nations is measured. We got rid of our Germans seventy years ago."

"With a little help," Philippe interjected.

"With a *lot* of help. But look at how much better off we are having the Germans as friends. It will be a long time before the Hungarians and the other Soviet satellites get to the same point with the Russians.

"My big concern," she added, "is that they will go the other way and decide the strong man is the best man to govern the country. Of course, the Russians would welcome them back with open arms, plus a little armed encouragement. Look at what's happened in Ukraine."

So, Philippe mused, I'm not the guy to have a discussion with André Westerhof. I just need answers to police questions, like has he ever seen the dead man, just in case Lucas was right that he spoke Hungarian. This is a job I should leave to Aurélie or —

Easy. There was only one man for the job. He picked up his phone to call Jeremy Bentham.

———

"C'est Jeremy. Bonjour." The voice sounded exhausted, and Philippe realized he'd caught Jeremy during the run he did three or four afternoons a week, after his partner Juliette Bertrand had gone to work.

"I forgot about your run. This is Philippe. Should I call you later?"

"Lord, no. I've been looking for an excuse to sit down for the last mile. You called just as I spotted an empty bench right on the edge of the canal. Hold on a minute."

Philippe heard a sigh of contentment and conjured up an image of Jeremy planting himself firmly in a cool spot under the trees along Canal Saint-Martin, near the townhouse he shared with Juliette.

"Much better," Jeremy said. "What can I do for you, Monsieur le Commissaire?"

"We had a bizarre one this afternoon. A man was stabbed as he sat on the edge of the Seine just across from the Quai des Orfèvres. No ID. There are two witnesses, a woman and her eight-year-old son. It's a small world. The woman works at a restaurant at Saint-Michel and leaves the boy with a sitter, who happens to be the wife of your old professor, André Westerhof."

"Sophie and Lucas. Quite a coincidence," Jeremy replied. "But what could the professor have to do with it?"

"The victim looks like a Slav, and Lucas heard the dying man say something in a language he thinks was Hungarian – he has a schoolmate who speaks the language. It's a long shot, but I remembered that the professor is into Hungarian politics, and anybody who reads the newspaper knows how nasty things are now. It's possible he might know something, maybe even know the victim, and I thought you might get a better response than I would."

"I'll be glad to try," Jeremy said. "Dr. Westerhof was a terrific professor at West Point and he helped me considerably with one of my books, but I don't see him much anymore. I'd like an excuse to get back in touch with him. Did Sophie also see what happened?"

"Mainly Lucas. Sophie was a little farther away. You know them?"

"More. She and I dated a few times just before I met Juliette. It wasn't going anywhere, but she is interesting; she likes to stay out late, and she likes older men. You should talk to her. She might be just your type."

She is attractive and smart, Philippe reminded himself. She's also younger than my daughter.

"Some other time. The thing is, if Lucas is right about the dying man being Hungarian, perhaps Professor Westerhof could help us. Would you mind talking to him?"

"I'm certainly willing to try," Jeremy replied. "A lot depends on what mood he's in. At the best of times he can be a little rigid. Email me what you'd like me to ask and I'll call him tonight. No promises."

PHILIPPE HUNG UP, then raised his hand for the waiter but saw him disappear around a corner into the kitchen. Sophie came to take his order instead.

"I didn't know you and Jeremy Bentham were friends," Philippe said.

"Friends? You could say that. We had a nice relationship for a month or two until he met the TV star, what's her name? Juliette. Juliette Bertrand. And I think it was your daughter who introduced them."

"I'm just a little surprised, that's all. I know Aurélie would be unhappy if she hurt you."

"I think I saw my father in him," Sophie replied. "My father was never a general, but he was a very serious man. Jeremy is like that, and he writes books. I like to read them but I can't imagine ever writing one.

"Anyway, I like older men. They're solid and they're kind. They've had all the children they want. And they're not at you all the time.

"I'll get your wine. It's Bordeaux, isn't it?"

———

PHILIPPE TEXTED his picture of the dead man to Jeremy, asking him simply to find out if André Westerhof recognized him. There was nothing suspicious about a man speaking Hungarian in Paris, a polyglot city of immigrants, tourists, and citizens from all over the world. It was, Philippe had to admit, a bit unusual to hear anyone shout in any language as he committed murder in one of the most heavily trafficked tourist areas in the city, one where he knew his daughter would walk alone without concern for her safety.

Violent crime, a one-on-one attack, was almost unheard of in the upscale parts of the city, which added to his suspicion that this was either political or organized crime. In either case, he needed to find the source of the infection and stamp it out, quickly and thoroughly.

DESPITE HIS GERMAN-SOUNDING NAME, the man Jeremy had always known simply as "Dr. Westerhof" was a Hungarian patriot to the core, a sentiment that had grown during his last years teaching in the United States. Years earlier, after he had been Jeremy's history professor at West Point, he had moved to a large university in the Midwest.

For the same reason, Major General Bentham had retired early from the army – disapproval of the impending American invasion of Iraq and fear it would do nothing positive in the Middle East and might arouse a perfect storm of jihadis and suicide bombers – Dr. Westerhof had retired and returned home to Budapest, dragging his reluctant American wife Emma with him. They had bought a small apartment in the hills on the Buda side of the Danube, overlooking the city, but Emma spent as much time as she could in Paris, at the old apartment they had bought soon after they married.

He knew the professor had a habit of two or three glasses of strong, spicy Villány red wine in the evening, so he allowed time for two and part of a third before he called.

"We haven't talked much since you were researching your books," the professor said. "I read them all and I compliment you on them. But tell me what prompts this call."

"Thank you again for the help you offered.

"I'm calling because a man was stabbed on the quai this afternoon, just a few hundred meters from you. Sophie and Lucas witnessed the killing."

"That's terrible! She didn't mention it to Emma when she brought Lucas."

"Lucas thought he heard the victim say something in Hungarian just before he died. He has a schoolmate from Hungary and thinks the language he heard was the same one his friend speaks.

"Philippe Cabillaud sent me a picture of the dead man, on the slim chance you might have run across him in the expat community. Could I send it to you?"

"Of course, but I don't know every Hungarian in Paris. Far from it."

"I understand, but Philippe thinks this was no ordinary street crime, that it might have been political. After all, it's not every day that a murderer sits down with his victim on the edge of the Seine and then walks away as though nothing had happened."

Jeremy went silent as he prepared to send the picture.

Dr. Westerhof said, "What you say about politics could be right. You would not believe how disorganized and miserable the politics of Hungary have become. The Jobbik Party thinks our right-wing government is insufficiently right-wing, and that's dangerous enough, but most people haven't heard about the splinter Jobbiks, the little outfits that are fighting with each other to gain seats in parliament. Then there are the neo-Nazis, who come from all over the world, including your country, and think they've found a home in Hungary. It's pitiful.

"Aside from the imported crazies, the Jobbiks and their little brothers have a couple of things in common. They want to leave the EU but they want to keep the subsidies. If Russia would give them the same money they would happily take it, but the Russians are broke and everybody knows it.

"The other is their view on Jews, and as a Jew I'm sensitive to that. Worse, both the governing party and Jobbik get funds from Moscow, some of it in ways that benefit their leaders directly. These are people whose fathers and grandfathers fought the Russians in the Second World War, then lived under the communist boot for forty years. It's inconceivable!"

They both heard his phone chirp as Jeremy's message arrived. "Wait just a minute and I'll look at the picture," the professor said.

Dr. Westerhof was silent for a long minute, then Jeremy heard him say, "My God! It's Vasily."

"So you do know him?"

"Do I know him? He came to Paris two days ago specifically to see me. We talked all day yesterday and again this morning, until nearly lunchtime. We were supposed to go see a man together this afternoon but Vasily didn't show up."

"Who was he?" Jeremy asked.

"He is – was – deputy general secretary of my party. He ran the party in effect, because the general secretary is an old man and has turned very inflexible as he's aged. The plan was for Vasily to replace him at the end of the year, in plenty of time to organize the next parliamentary elections." He was silent for a moment, then continued in a faltering voice, "I don't know what we will do now. This is a blow, and a bad one."

"I think Philippe would like to talk to you about this. Could I bring him over later, say in an hour?"

"Yes, but even later will be better. Sophie picks

up Lucas at nine thirty, so if you can wait until then, it would be good. I'll tell you everything I can."

PHILIPPE WOULDN'T CONSIDER WAITING. "Wait? *Wait?* This is a murder investigation, not a tea party. Call and tell him I'll be there in a half-hour. Can you come, too? It might help."

"Sure," Jeremy responded. "There's a café on the ground floor. I will meet you there as soon as I can, but it won't be in a half-hour. More like twice that."

Philippe arrived in forty-five minutes and was surprised to find Jeremy sitting at the same corner table where he'd interviewed Lucas. He had a notebook out and was outlining what he knew about modern Hungarian politics, which he'd studied before writing his last book about post-Soviet Eastern Europe. Philippe signaled the waiter for a coffee and pulled out a chair opposite him.

"Hungarian politics is a little like American politics," Jeremy told Philippe. He had drawn a chart showing a group of overlapping circles and used it to illustrate how the right-wing parties were becoming more influential in both countries, and their anti-democratic branches were gathering strength as well.

He drew a circle in the center of the page. "This is André Westerhof's party, which they call The Center, a signal that it's not extremist in either direction.

In the United States it would be slightly left of the Democrats. In France it's somewhere to the right, but not very far.

"It would be unfair to say Hungary is a neo-Nazi state, but in reality there is a hard core of voters who are so upset by the changes in European society that they want a strong man in power.

"A lot of people think the current prime minister is strong enough, but not the hardcore revanchists – they dream about someone like the Turkish leader, Erdogan. Most of them have settled in the Jobbik Party and a bunch of small factions on its right. This murder could be a squabble between parties."

THEY TOOK the elevator to Professor Westerhof's floor and knocked on his door. Lucas answered.

"Mon Général!" he said briskly to Jeremy. "Maman is not here now."

"I know, Lucas," Jeremy answered. "Have you met Commissaire Cabillaud? He is another friend of your mother."

"He was at the Seine this afternoon."

"Good. Would you please tell the professor that we are here?"

Dr. Westerhof looked only mildly annoyed that they had come early. He invited them into his bedroom, where a small suitcase lay open on the bed.

"I have to fly back to Budapest tomorrow morning," he told them. "Vasily's death is going to cause big problems in the party and I need to be there to help. Do you mind if I continue packing while we talk?" He did not wait for a reply.

Under Philippe's questioning, he told about the political changes he thought might have led to Vasily's murder.

"Vasily was a mild man," he said. "Not everyone in Hungarian politics is. If I had to guess, it will be something personal or it will be politics; probably politics because he led a very quiet life otherwise. There are some people on the right who are afraid Vasily would be a much stronger leader than the man who is retiring, which is not saying much."

"The current leader is being pushed out?" Philippe asked.

"He knows he isn't up to the job anymore," the professor said. "He's not happy to leave but he knows the time has come. Hell, my time has come, too. Emma and I spend almost the entire year in Paris now, mainly because we think it's time for a new generation to take over.

"But no, it's not someone in the Center Party. You will probably find it's someone in a small right-wing party who sees an opportunity to make progress at our expense. And mainly at the expense of poor Vasily.

"If I were you, I wouldn't expect much help from the Hungarian police."

"Did he have a family?" Jeremy posed the question but Philippe nodded in approval.

"There's an ex-wife and a couple of children, but they moved to Germany, where she works in a hospital. I don't think he had talked to her in a couple of years, although he did send small gifts to the children. One of the reasons he could afford to work for the tiny salary we can pay is that his former wife is a very successful doctor. She doesn't support him, but she gave him some money when she left and sends a bit every few months. I think it's the price of his absence."

"Where did he stay when he was in Paris?" Philippe asked. Professor Westerhof had closed his suitcase and was clearly ready for them to leave. "Maybe we can get some information there."

"There are a couple of one-star or no-star hotels down in the fourteenth, near the Catacombs. He liked the area and could always get a room in one of them. I don't know which one he was in this time, but there are only two or three. We tried to get him to stay with us but he wouldn't."

As they left, the professor said, "There's one more thing. I've kept in touch over the years with a man named Viktor Nagy, who was a security agent for the Hungarian government before the Wall fell.

"I saw him a couple of weeks ago because,

frankly, I was trying to get him to make a donation. At first he laughed at me. He said we were old and out of date, too far behind the times, and he was thinking of shifting his support to a new party. It is so new it doesn't even have an official name yet, but for now it is called Arrow Cross."

"Arrow Cross!" Jeremy was aghast. "That was a Nazi organization, or pretty close to it. Why would anyone choose that name?"

"To send a signal. They will change it well ahead of the elections next year, but it's code, what you Americans call a dog whistle. It's to tell their members that their policies will be very nationalist. Marine Le Pen, who borrowed Russian money for her presidential campaign, is a piker next to these Hungarian parties. A lot of them are wholly owned subsidiaries of the Russian government."

Jeremy, baffled, asked, "Is the Arrow Cross party an old party in a new suit of clothes, or is it something entirely novel?"

"It has been organizing for almost a year, and its personalities don't seem to want a lot of personal publicity. I have done some checking around, and the money behind it is American, from a Hungarian émigré who made his first fortune in Silicon Valley and his second by buying into the insurance industry in a big way. I know nothing about him, and I think Viktor Nagy was a little concerned because he knew nothing about him, either. Or said he didn't."

"Do you have a name?" Jeremy asked. "We can probably find out something."

"Viktor says the man's name is Max Molnar. I called some friends in Budapest and they tell me he's been more and more visible there lately. It makes sense – Viktor was the foreign arm of the Hungarian intelligence services, and they don't play fair. A tough, authoritarian politician would appeal to him, especially one with money.

"I don't think this Molnar has fully convinced him. Viktor didn't close the door to us completely. I asked him if Vasily could come talk to him further, and he consented, although I could tell it would be uphill. That was the appointment for this afternoon.

"Emma made him a sandwich because he enjoyed taking a late lunch and eating it along the Seine, where he could watch the barges and cruise ships go past. He must have been having lunch when the killer found him."

"Who knew about these lunches?" Philippe asked.

"Anybody and everybody," Westerhof said. "He loved Paris, and he'd talk about it to anyone who would listen. He made a lot of new friends just sitting on the riverbank talking about the city. My guess is that he thought he was just chatting with a friendly stranger, not the man who would kill him.

"Emma and I thought about going with him today, but she didn't want to take a chance on missing

Sophie and Lucas. I wish we had. Things would be much different now."

"Maybe," Philippe said, "but maybe not. You might have been stabbed, too."

Westerhof nodded gravely. "That's right," Jeremy added. "There's no telling what the killer might have done."

Philippe continued, "Viktor told you about Max Molnar. Could he have told Max Molnar, or someone else, that you and Vasily had been to see him?"

"Viktor was and probably still is a spy. If he thought it would serve his purpose to tell Max Molnar who his competition was, he would do it. But it wouldn't be out of friendship. It would be a tactical step in a very complex game of political chess."

As THEY RODE down the elevator Philippe said, "I'd like to take the métro and go see what we can find at those hotels. Do you have time to go with me? I can get an officer if not."

"I have time," Jeremy replied. "It's only eight o'clock, and I can't pick up Juliette for another two hours."

They walked the quarter-mile to the Saint-Michel station. Jeremy stopped to run has finger down the menu of Lapérouse and pointed out a famous and complicated veal dish.

"Juliette would like that," he said, then turned to catch up with Philippe.

The walls of the immense Saint-Michel station are the original steel caisson that was dug into the Seine riverbank to keep the work dry. Jeremy and Philippe walked down three flights to the track level and waited to catch the Line 4 train, which they rode for ten minutes to Denfert-Rochereau, the stop serving the Catacombs and the big Montparnasse Cemetery.

"Let's start with the Idaho. It's just around the corner," Philippe said.

The block would be dark in another hour, when the sun finally set, but now it was bathed in the softening pre-sunset light the French call the *crépuscule* – no longer full daylight but far from night.

As THEY WALKED from the métro stairs past two sidewalk cafés filled to overflowing, Jeremy said, "This is turning into an international affair, or at least it might. I saw Icky Crane a couple of months ago and he asked me – all of us – to send him a signal if we saw or heard anything about Russia and the EU, or Brexit. His people know the Russians are trying their best to stir chaos in European politics. He'd already talked to Eddie.

"While we were on the métro I was thinking that we have a new name – Max Molnar – which may be important. I'll tell Eddie about it later and he can work it into what he already knows. He and Aurélie are probably at dinner, but this won't be the first time."

"Okay," Philippe said. "But I didn't hear a word of what you just said."

EDDIE GRANT and Jeremy Bentham's complicated relationship had begun in the eighties, when Eddie was a freshman ROTC cadet at West Texas State University and Jeremy, then a lieutenant colonel, was the ROTC commander. They had met again in 1991 when Captain Grant was a Special Forces company commander in the first Gulf War, Operation Desert Storm, and then-Colonel Bentham was his commander three levels up.

Jeremy had retired from the army as a two-star general ten years later, concerned that the pending invasion of Iraq would lead to the deaths of thousands of Americans and reduce the Middle East to chaos. As plain Dr. Bentham, he had gone back to West Texas State as chairman of the history department and begun working on the first of several books about the former Soviet satellite countries in Eastern Europe, one of them Hungary.

At the same time, he and his wife Pat had bought and renovated an old townhouse in the Canal Saint-Martin district of Paris, which at the time was far from gentrified. When Pat had fallen ill, she and Jeremy had moved permanently into the townhouse and Jeremy had renewed his relationship with Eddie. After Pat died, he and Eddie had become occasional teammates in intelligence projects for the CIA through their friend Icky Crane, who had been Eddie's executive officer during Desert Storm.

When both were soldiers, Jeremy's stars had made him the unquestioned leader, but Eddie had had a closer relationship with Icky. When he left the army, he had moved back to Paris and become both prominent and successful – and had married Philippe's daughter Aurélie Cabillaud, who was well known in parts of Paris's intellectual society both for her skill as a professor of history at the Sorbonne, as an author — and for her striking beauty. She turned heads everywhere. As a couple the tall, ash-blonde Aurélie and the dark-haired Eddie were even more noticeable.

"ON SECOND THOUGHT," Jeremy said, "I'll text him. They're probably just sitting down to a candlelight dinner somewhere and this isn't a super-hot issue right now." He sent a message asking for a call, not urgent.

"I wouldn't be surprised if they were at dinner a hundred meters from us," Philippe said. "This is one of their favorite parts of Paris."

A WAITER in the iconic uniform of white shirt, black trousers, and many-pocketed vest signaled to invite them to a table on the back row, but Jeremy shook his head and they walked on.

The Idaho was no different from hundreds of other Paris buildings that had sprung up in the construction boom just before World War I. Its Art Deco façade set it off from its less distinguished neighbors and the grimy stone was mute evidence that the ten-year cleaning required by the city was long overdue.

A row of well-used bicycles stood in a rack under the windows. Next to them a half-dozen middle-aged men smoked and chatted noisily in Arabic but fell silent as Philippe and Jeremy passed.

The peeling front door refused to budge. Jeremy reached out to press a doorbell button to its right. Through the dirty glass panes they saw the night clerk look up from his small TV set, then reach under the counter. The door buzzed and they pushed their way through.

"*Bonsoir, Monsieur,*" Philippe said, taking out his police identity card. The clerk looked at it without interest and after a few seconds said, "Yes?"

"We are trying to find the hotel where a visitor stayed in the last few days," Philippe said. He took out his iPhone and turned the picture toward the night clerk.

"Do you know this man?"

"Is he dead?" the clerk asked, startled.

"Yes," Philippe said. "I need to know if he was a guest here last night."

"He was here for two nights. He checked out this morning but asked me to keep his baggage. Another man came looking for him but he had already left."

"Was this other man also a Hungarian?"

"No," the clerk said. "I figured he was Russian."

"How did this other man know he was here?"

The clerk glanced from side to side, seemingly looking for a way to escape, but finally said, "He came last night and asked me if I knew this dead man, Vasily. I said I did, and he asked me to call him when Vasily came in."

"How much did he give you?"

"A hundred euros."

"So one hundred euros was the price of his life," Philippe said. "Your conscience will have to carry that burden, but right now I need to see the man who paid you. Please show me the pictures from that camera on the wall behind you."

THE CLERK LIFTED a gate in the counter and led the way through a door marked "Security." What passed for a security office was cramped and airless, more a closet than a room. A desk on the right side held an old Dell computer whose screen showed the lobby as viewed from the camera above the check-in desk.

"He was here about this time," the clerk said. He entered the time on a keyboard and the image of the lobby rewound rapidly.

The picture went forward and back as the clerk looked for his visitor, and finally he stopped it.

"There," he said, pointing to a single figure standing at the check-in desk.

Philippe leaned into the screen and photographed it with his phone, and Jeremy did the same.

"You are to keep that file," Philippe told the clerk. "Someone will come for it tomorrow, along with the luggage Vasily left with you."

"I can give you a copy now on a thumb drive," the clerk said.

"Do that."

"You won't meet Juliette for a while yet, and I have no particular desire to go home and cook," Philippe said. "Let's go around the corner for a coffee. Or something."

"Café Daguerre," Jeremy said. "A favorite."

3

FIRST DATE

MIAMI

As Philippe and Jeremy paid the waiter two hours later, Mark McGinley was bringing the day rapidly to a close. He pressed the send button on the last email of the day and closed his laptop, but he wasn't free to leave just yet. There was still the matter of the daily update he and Kate gave each other, and then there was the discreet chime that sounded to signal that someone had entered the cramped reception lobby.

Why the hell didn't I lock the door? he asked himself, but it was too late. A thin, casually dressed man waited on the other side of the security window.

He was dressed like a golf pro — pink knit shirt, gray Dockers, a belt with golf clubs and flags embroidered all around. He introduced himself as Frank Matthews, a patent lawyer from downtown.

"I'm sorry to come so late on a Friday," Matthews said in a rush. "I hope I'm not being a bother, but I ran into Raul Gutierrez last night and he told me you're making a small remote-control submarine. I'm always on the lookout for new products for some of my clients, and this sounded like it might really fit. Can we talk about it?"

His friend Raul's name made Mark more willing to listen, but not for long. He was ready to leave, his patience worn thin by Icky's inquisition, and he wanted to be sailing on Biscayne Bay.

Matthews offered a business card, which Mark took by the edges. It looked genuine, identifying Raul as a U.S. Customs officer, one of the cover identities he used to hide his main role as the CIA's chief case manager in South Florida. Mark turned it over and saw his own name and address written on the back.

"Where did you meet Raul?"

"At a reception for one of the new police captains the county just promoted. I suppose he works with them. Another police captain is a neighbor of mine and invited me to tag along. I sometimes find clients at affairs like that, but I thought last night was a zero until I met Raul."

Mark thought for a few seconds. "I don't think it's going to be anything for the commercial market, at least not for a while. I have thought about ways to convert it if my main market doesn't work out."

"You mean the government?"

"Yep. Like the sign on the door says, I'm an engineer, but I'm also an inventor. The government has bought several gadgets from me, most of them for the military, so I built my sub using milspec components. As you can imagine, it's very expensive to do that."

"Do you think you'll be able to convert it?"

"Probably," Mark answered. "But I wouldn't start working on a civilian model until the government turns it down, and it can take months to get a decision. And even a civilian model will be very expensive."

The man paused, then asked, "Could I look at it?"

"You could have if you'd come yesterday, but today the government put an official classification on it. Up until now it hasn't been classified, although we don't talk a lot about it in public. Raul must have thought you have an honest face."

"My wife says I do."

"Wait here for just a couple of minutes," Mark said. "I've set the alarm for the shop. I need to disarm it or we'll hear from the police, and I don't want to annoy them any more than I have to."

He was dissembling. He had not set the alarm, but he was suspicious enough to go back to his office and flip the switch on a new video system that used a half-dozen thumb-sized cameras spaced around the offices. The CIA friend who had recommended it said its image quality was good enough to use in facial recognition systems.

Back at the window he said to his visitor, "Give me a new business card, please. And I'll need your driver's license again. We're not officially a secure site, but some of my customers want us to be very careful anyway."

"That's no problem," Frank said. He pulled a wallet out of his back pocket and extracted a Florida license and a card, which Mark took back to his office and photographed with his phone. He kept the card to look at later, then pulled the interior door open and handed the license back.

"Come into my office and we'll talk a minute. I'm sorry I can't take very long, though."

Mark offered Frank a seat and sat opposite him at his desk, then spent ten minutes turning away questions about how it navigated itself – that was the secret sauce and he had no intention of giving it away for free, especially to someone he knew little about. He said nothing about the helicopter.

"Why don't you call me in three months or so?" he said, standing to signal that the conversation was over. "I should have a decent idea of whether the government will want it, and if they don't I'll be looking for a buyer."

LIKE MARK, Kate was ready for some time off after the crush of the last ten days. Editing a video had been something new and very time-consuming for both of them, and there were a hundred small tune-ups and tweaks to be made before they could chance demonstrating the real Pegasus and Icarus to Icky.

She snapped down the rear engine hatch, satisfied that it made a solid *clunk*, like a Mercedes door closing. She stood for a minute with her hand on the sleek black hull, almost like a fond caress, and looked contentedly up and down its length.

She wiped off the engine oil, first from the hatch and then from her hands, before going to wash up in the bathroom in the corner of the shop.

As she let the warm water run, her mind wandered back to the day she first met Mark, a Friday afternoon like this one, almost exactly a year before. It was her first job interview since high school, and she was nervous.

He needed a competent engineer, and soon. Three weeks after he had fired the last one he was making no progress, and his search for the perfect candidate had been set back when he was knocked on the head by a burglar. He and the police were confident it was an effort to steal the submarine, but so far there had been no arrests and no progress. And no engineer.

From her chair across the desk she could see the large bandage on the back of his head.

"You'll have to pardon me if I wander a bit," he told her early in the conversation. "I'm still a little woozy from getting whacked on the head last weekend, but it's better every day. By next week I should be in top form."

She remembered asking him, "Shouldn't you take a little more time off? Concussions can be dangerous."

"Can't. I have a product, my competitors have a product, or at least I think they might. I can't afford to lose this race. That's why I need someone good, and now."

Mark began to go through the routine questions of a job interview and made clear he had time for complete answers. "We can send out for pizza if we have to," he said.

"I've spent a little time in Maine," he told her. "Not as much as I'd like, but I haven't run across any Mickelwaites. Are there many of you?"

"That's not my name. At least, it won't be much longer. In an eternity of stupidity I took my husband's name, and when my divorce is final in a few weeks his name will go with the marriage, and good riddance. Let's just start off with me being Kate Hall."

She talked about her childhood as the mechanically precocious and prematurely mature daughter of a successful lobster harvester and his wife, who'd become a mother late in life at considerable cost to her own health. Her heart had failed the summer before Kate entered high school, leaving her father bereft and concerned about leaving an adolescent daughter alone all summer just as her friends' hormones were starting to make their presence known.

"My father was going to have none of that. And luckily, neither was I. In fact, I wasn't particularly interested in boys, because even then I knew I wanted to do something that would require more education and I'd seen too many promising girls get pregnant.

"He handled the problem the only way he knew how. He made me his sternman, or maybe I should say sternwoman – anyway, I was the deckhand in the back end of the boat. I was already fairly strong, but by the end of the summer I could handle pulling the traps and stacking the crates as well as any hung-over twenty-something, which is what most of the other deckhands were.

"My body was almost completely developed by the time my mother died. She kept me in shapeless school dresses, but even then I filled them out pretty well, and in shorts and tee-shirts during the summer I was a danger." She noticed his eyebrows go up slightly but otherwise he didn't react. She was glad she'd worn a long, modest blue skirt and white blouse and put her long gray-flecked auburn hair up in a Navy bun.

"From that day until I went away to Annapolis Prep, I was on the boat every day I wasn't in school. I learned how to harvest lobsters and how to keep the books. I learned how to service diesel engines and all the gadgets on board, and I got my dad interested in better navigation. All of that made me certain before I left high school that I wanted to be an engineering officer.

"He also got what he wanted. When I left Portsmouth I was still a virgin, the only one among my friends. That didn't last long, though. Don't get me wrong – I'm not promiscuous."

Mark replied, "Your life is your life. You're an active young woman so there are probably men in it. The only thing I can promise is that sex is not part of anybody's job description at McGinley Engineering."

Chastened, she could only say, "I understand," and hope she hadn't crossed a line.

DURING THE UNCOMFORTABLE pause that followed, Mark's portable phone rang. When he saw Icky Crane's name on the screen he asked Kate, "Would you mind if I take this? It's an important customer. There's no need for you to leave."

"Hello, Ick…" Mark said before he leaned into the phone to listen intently.

Hearing only his end of the conversation made it hard to follow, but she tried.

"So you think it would be okay?" he asked, then

waited as another burst of static came from the phone.

"And those people. Are they sound?"

A pause.

"That's good."

HE PUT THE PHONE AWAY. "Let's go look at the shop, shall we? I think I've asked everything I need to ask."

"But you haven't asked me anything about what I did in the Navy."

"I know you're an Annapolis graduate and you spent eight years as an engineering officer, that you have a propulsion specialty and know radar and high-frequency communication, and that you have good discharge papers. I know you had a bad marriage and decided the only way to get away from your husband, the admiral, was to leave the Navy and make a new life, and that now you have a doctorate in engineering.

"I don't know yet if I have to call you Ma'am, since you're a lieutenant commander and I was only a chief petty officer, but we can sort that out." He smiled to let her know he wasn't serious. "Let's go see the hardware, then decide where to go from there. How would that be?"

She had come to him from the engineering dean at the University of Miami, where she had just finished her doctorate. It was the capstone of her career and would certainly have led to high rank and honors in the Navy if the mess in her personal life hadn't pushed her out of the service. It was a reminder of what her father had told her time and time again: your decision to go to Annapolis is an important one, but the most important choice you'll ever have to make is your husband.

She'd made a bad choice.

THAT WAS the first time of hundreds Kate would walk down the corridor from the front door of McGinley Engineering to the secure door, its retina scanners guarding the entrance to the shop.

"This isn't at all what I expected," she said as the automatic lights came on. "When you said shop, I expected something like an auto repair shop. This is more like an operating room."

The submarine itself sat shrouded on a wooden stand in the center of the room, the little helicopter next to it on a rolling table, and both walls were lined with workbenches. On the left, the long bench was a metalworking shop. On the right it was an electronics lab. The high ceiling made the room look larger than it was.

"A hundred people ... no, a thousand people could have built the submarine and the helo. My design is good, but the secret sauce is in the software and controls. Tom Farkas was valuable because he'd made iPhone apps in California, and he was good at it, when he wasn't drinking. Eventually, that was never."

"May I look at it?"

"Sure." He stripped away the white sheet covering the submarine. Its black paint glinted in the strong white light from overhead, marred here and there by scratch marks from the assembly tools. The bulbous forward section reminded her of her work on aircraft carriers, whose immense elevators carried warplanes from the landing deck to the hangar deck below. This, though a miniature, seemed to be the same thing.

"So the little helo fits in that chamber?"

"Yep. It's tight but it works. Right now the sub has to surface in order to launch it, but by version two or three we'll have everything waterproofed so it can just pop to the surface. It will give the sub a whole lot more security."

"This is really elegant metalwork."

"Thanks. I plan to sheath the second or third version in fiberglass, but for now it's easy to bend sheet metal in the shop, and the bends can be adjusted. We do a lot of that."

"What are their names?" Kate asked.

"Names? The sub is Sub, the helo is Helo. Do they need anything more?"

"Mark, you're developing something no one has ever built before. They need memorable names, ringing names that fit their design and their duty. Nobody will ever remember Sub and Helo. You've studied World War Two history – hardly anybody could tell you today what an F6F was, but everybody of a certain age remembers the Hellcat."

She stood for a few seconds and rubbed her hand against her head, pushing a few unruly strands back into place.

"I know. Let's name the sub after Pegasus, the mythical horse that carried the hero into battle. I wish we gave our ships warlike names like Repulse or Vengeance, the way the British do, instead of naming them for politicians, but nobody ever asked me. Pegasus will make the point.

"Of course, there's only one name for Helo. We'll call him Icarus. We just won't let him get too close to the sun. Or overconfident."

"You're right. They do need names, and those are good ones." He swept his hand over both tables, palm down. "I dub thee Pegasus and Icarus," he intoned.

MARK OFFERED HER THE JOB.

"But do you think you know enough about me? I mean, you've talked to the dean, we've spent an hour together. I'd like the job. In fact, I need the job, but I want the fit to be right."

"It will be right. That phone call I took was the last piece of information I needed."

"Who was it?"

"Have you met Icky Crane?"

She looked puzzled for a minute, then shook her head. "I don't think so, although I could have run into him. Who is he?"

"For one, I hope he's going to be our customer for the s… for Pegasus and Icarus. He's high up in the CIA, and he gave me your name at about the same time I first called the dean."

"Where would he know me from?"

"He didn't. But a friend mentioned a bright young engineer who was planning to bail on a Navy career because of an abusive husband, who also happened to be a two-star. The friend thought it was shabby. Icky knows the admiral, and also thinks it's shabby. I asked him to ask some more questions, and that's why he called me back today.

"You and he share a friend in Paris named…" He opened a desk drawer and took out a notepad. "Aurélie Cabillaud."

"Aurélie! She saved my life in New York a couple of years ago when my husband was being even more of a jerk than usual."

"Aurélie's husband Eddie Grant was Icky's company commander in Iraq during Operation Desert

Storm," Mark said. "They were college classmates and went to Special Forces together, then Icky went to the CIA while Eddie went back to his family's businesses in Paris. I thought it was a little odd that a Frenchman would be in the Special Forces, but it happens."

Kate replied, "Oh, Eddie isn't a Frenchman." She paused. "Well, he's a French citizen, but he's also as American as you or I. His father was a famous American military spy during World War II, behind the German lines with the French Resistance. His mother is French. The two of them met in a forest shortly before D-Day when she was little more than a child, younger than I was when my mother died, and Eddie's father was there as a middleman between the Resistance and the Allied forces.

"She only met him that once, but she waited years for him to come back to her. It's a very romantic story.

"They were married for more than fifty years, until he was murdered the same year as Eddie's wife and young son. Eddie and Aurélie set out together to track down the people who had him killed. They don't talk about the details, but I do know that one sad old man in Florida is the only one who survived, and he's in prison."

Mark said, "I'd like to know more of that story. I've never met Aurélie, but based on Icky's recom-

mendation and what you just told me, I know everything I need to know. When can you start?"

"I get some of my best work done on weekends,"
Kate said. "How about tomorrow? Eight o'clock?
Seven?"

ON ANOTHER LATE afternoon fifty-plus Fridays later,
as she pushed through the shop door toward Mark's
office for their daily wrap-up, she reflected that she'd
been in this building almost every weekend for the
past year, and now she wouldn't have it any other
way. It had given meaning to her life at a time when
she was adrift and unhappy. Now she was neither,
and she burned with the desire to succeed.

"FINALLY," Mark said aloud as he locked front the
door behind the visitor. He sat down at his desk one
last time just as Kate walked through the open door
to his office.

"He's gone. I'm going to wrap up. I don't want
homework to interfere with sailing."

She sat on the edge of his desk, crossed her legs,
and pulled her dark blue skirt over her knees.
"Who?"

"A downtown lawyer named Frank Matthews. He

heard about the sub from a friend of mine in the CIA and supposedly has a client who wants to buy it. A toy company thinks it can sell them for gifts, fancy ones like the stuff Neiman-Marcus used to feature in its Christmas catalogs. But that sounds bogus to me – it's more likely that he represents a small defense contractor. Miami is full of them."

"Are you interested in selling?"

"If the government doesn't buy it we'll have to find someone else, but it's early for that. I think Icky will take care of us."

It was the first time Kate had heard him talk about the project as theirs together, and she worked hard to keep from smiling.

She said, "I thought a friend was coming to town this weekend, but she texted me this morning and cancelled, something about a new boyfriend. I never even met the last one.

"The weather looks good, so I'm ready to sail. Where will we go?"

"I haven't thought about it much," Mark replied. "We ought to celebrate our own success anyway, so why don't we go to dinner? Maybe one of us will have a brilliant idea. Somewhere French, downtown, with white tablecloths?"

"That would beat the hell out of a hamburger on South Beach."

The invitation was a surprise. From the first, Mark had shown little sign of interest in her as a woman, with the single exception of a memorable scene in the shop one day shortly after she had arrived. Sometimes it seemed she might as well be a robot, smart and willing to work hard but not much in the way of company. He paid her well enough that she'd never looked for another job, never even followed up on unsolicited calls from headhunters. Besides, his submarine project – now *their* project – excited her. Her eight years in the Navy had been spent as a marine engineer, but as one of many working on big ships. The high-precision duo of Pegasus and Icarus gave her a chance to prove what she could do by herself.

Mark had been a one-man band when they'd met, although not by choice. Kate's predecessor had been a heavy drinker whose productivity had dwindled week by week until it finally disappeared entirely. Mark had let him go and stepped up the time he spent in the shop, sometimes spending the night.

She'd watched him take the little submarine from a bare framework to an almost-finished work of elegance and efficiency. Within a month, she knew she was where she belonged, and so had Mark: he had returned to the part of the job he'd marked out for himself, writing the software that would make the little sub and its intelligent helicopter control themselves.

She also knew she wanted more of Mark. He had initiated one clumsy makeout session a couple of months after she started work, and without thinking she had responded eagerly to his unexpected kiss. When he had unhooked her bra to stroke her breasts she was ready and willing to follow him straight to the sofa in his office, but he had broken it off without explanation and hadn't repeated the approach.

He'd apologized awkwardly the next day and she had tried to respond in a way that would leave the door open for him to try again, but for months he'd kept his hands to himself – until today. If this was an approach, it was too early to tell.

She looked down at him appraisingly and saw a man settled into his 40s, not quite six feet tall and solidly built, thinning brown hair cut short and going white around the temples. Half a cauliflower ear and a nose that kinked slightly to the right were the legacy of younger days when he fancied himself a fleet boxing champion. A life with Mark, at least as she imagined it, would be much different from her past. The thought brought a feeling of deep comfort, combined with an unexpected surge of desire that made her squirm on the hard surface of the desk.

WHEN KATE HAD MOVED to Miami she'd bought a condo in South Beach. She loved its Art Deco ambiance and downtown vibe and treasured her walks in the park and along the beach, but after her thirty-fourth birthday passed, she found that being surrounded by much younger singles had lost its charm. She'd dealt with loneliness the first year by immersing herself in her engineering doctorate, and the second by working punishing hours for Mark. She was ready for the next stage.

"CAN I pick you up at seven?" he asked. "That will give us time to change. I don't think I should wear a golf shirt and khakis to La Provence, do you?"

"We can both do a little better, especially if we're going to one of the best restaurants in South Florida. I should at least wear something without a grease spot on it. Seven will be fine."

MARK TOOK Kate's hand at her door and they walked together down the corridor. His unexpected touch gave her a thrill; the evening had serious potential.

Her building didn't have full-time doormen but did offer after-work valet service by a group of clean-cut college students. He'd given one of them a too-large tip to watch his BMW, which now stood waiting at the curb, its top down.

Kate was ready for a nice evening out. She'd changed from her standard work outfit – a deep blue skirt, or sometimes jeans, paired with a dark top that

showed neither grease spots nor much of her figure —
into a jaunty and very expensive silk dress with large
red poppies on a white background. She'd saved it
for an occasion just like this and intended it to be
eye-catching. She couldn't tell if it was the dress or
the two buttons she'd left undone that kept Mark's
attention. She hoped it was the buttons.

"This feels like an event already," she said.

"It is. I have a feeling tonight is going to be the
capstone to a perfect day." He paused. "Is that what
you had in mind?"

"Mostly."

He pulled away from the curb, the car's powerful
engine purring, and turned to take the bridge to the
mainland.

They hadn't talked much of personal matters
since her first interview, but on the bridge she began
to probe.

"Mark, do you do anything but work? You're
there when I leave, and I don't leave early, and when
I come in on weekends you're there again. There is
obviously a lot about you I don't know, such as when
you have time to do anything but work."

"I've been like that forever. I know I should take
more time off, and I will when Pegasus and Icarus
are finished and sold. You've been good for my san-
ity. Just our weekend sails are a great mental health
break."

She wasn't shy. The second week on the job,

when Mark had told her he was going sailing on Saturday so wouldn't be in the office, she had invited herself along. An hour on Biscayne Bay showed him she was an experienced and passionate sailor. They began taking his 32-foot Morgan sloop out at least twice a month, but always returned to the marina by sundown.

Sometimes they would have a sandwich at the snack bar, which frustrated her because there was no way she could convince herself it was a date. She had turned down offers from several interesting men because they would have conflicted with her work and the sailing, and eventually they had stopped calling.

After their first outing, she sailed the boat at least half the time and was ready to take it over completely if Mark let down his guard.

"It's always fun being on the water," she replied. "Maybe we should enter a race or two. Or take a longer cruise. I'm not a natural landlubber. I belong on the water."

AT THE RESTAURANT, the wine steward recommended a smooth red from Burgundy, and after two glasses they were exchanging confidences like old friends. Kate told him about her life as an admiral's wife but at first avoided questions about the details of her divorce.

"I needed a new life. I was thirty-two, a naval officer and Academy graduate – everything I'd ever
wanted. That is, everything except I had an absolute
prick for a husband.

"I met Henry during my third year at Annapolis,
when he was a guest speaker. We were pretty involved almost immediately, in a platonic way. He was
married, and I never, ever went out with married
men. But when I graduated things changed. By then
he was separated from his wife, which was an enabler
of sorts for me, and he was a handsome, virile, com-
manding guy, just what I thought I was looking for."

She looked away and stopped talking. "Boy, was I
ever wrong." Then she wiped her eyes and
continued.

"He was fine in the early years, but when my first
tour ended he wanted me to quit and be a full-time
admiral's wife. I told him nicely I wasn't cut out to be
a housewife, and besides, the Navy had been really
good about giving me time to make the diplomatic
circuit with him.

"It didn't matter. It wasn't long before he started
treating me like I was his mess steward. He started to
pick up some strange ideas, more like fixations, until
finally I couldn't take it anymore. He got involved
with some questionable people in some shady deals.
He wasn't the man I married."

Mark hesitated. "I never told you this because…
well, just because. I served on his ship for six months,

and based on how he treated his mess steward, I don't know how you stood it as long as you did. That was before you married him, but people don't change much, deep down."

Kate said, "He hid it a long time. When I met him no one could have been more attentive and romantic. The Navy suspected I'd broken up his first marriage, and they don't like divorce anyway. Before long he started to believe the divorce was holding his career back. His efficiency ratings started to slip and he got even more hostile and abusive to the people who worked for him. He'd always kissed up the ladder, but now he began to kick down it.

"He blamed all his problems on the divorce, and then he started to take it out on me as well as the officers and sailors under him.

"It came home to me one really bad day. We hadn't had a real marriage in years, then one Sunday he insisted we take a business acquaintance out to dinner. We had a little wine and both of them started saying suggestive things, until this man, who was much older than my husband, finally propositioned me, right in front of him."

Mark was aghast. "Was he really trying to pimp you?"

"It sure felt like it. The man was his partner in a couple of business deals I had serious doubts about, and Henry wanted to get him involved in a cockamamie real estate deal in Europe." She gave an involuntary shudder. "He was so smarmy.

"Anyway, I shot down the idea and threw in some choice words for both of them, then I got a taxi. He came home drunk and we had a screaming fight, one of many. He had to leave next morning for an inspection tour of bases on the West Coast, and that week gave me the opening I needed."

"Did he ever hit you?"

"Once. I gave him a black eye."

Mark raised his eyebrows. "You're at least six inches shorter than I am but I've seen you lift impossible things in the shop. I wouldn't pick a fight with you," he said. "So what did you do while he was out of town?"

"First, I put in my papers. In retrospect it was probably stupid, but I'd had enough of his kind of military. I was already on leave, so I spent a couple of days gathering things up and packing, then set out for Miami. I stopped at every interesting place I found. It took me two weeks to work my way down the coast.

"I'd been thinking about leaving for a long time and knew about the engineering school here, so I decided I'd just wait until I could get in. As it turned out, that only took a couple of months. I spent a year finishing my doctorate, and you know the rest."

"Did he come looking for you?"

"He sure did. I left the name of a childhood

friend in Maine as a forwarding address. He even went up there to look for me, but her husband is a tough lobsterman like my father, and he told Henry I had gone camping in the forest. I did that a lot as a teenager.

"It took him six months to learn I was in Miami. I can put a date on it because after that I got stopped by a cop every couple of months, just as a reminder. I never got a ticket, just the silent reminder."

Mark asked, "How can you be sure he's behind that?"

"There's a detective here he's known for a long time, a guy who got kicked out of the Annapolis police when the evidence locker came up short. Henry got him a job somewhere in Central Florida, and probably the job in Miami as well. It would take an admiral lying for him to get past the black mark he's been carrying since he worked in Annapolis."

"Wow," Mark said. "I know you've heard it before, but you've had an interesting life."

"I haven't told the whole story to a soul since I got to Miami," Kate said, smiling and touching his arm. "Thanks for being a good listener.

"I don't think there is much more he can do because I have a pretty full dossier on him. My divorce lawyer showed it to his and the police stops came to a screeching halt."

"I HAD BETTER luck on the marriage front," Mark told her when he was almost finished with his veal chop.

"I'm an Appalachian, just in case you couldn't tell. My parents moved to Miami from West Virginia in the seventies, looking to get away from the farm. They had a hard life but loved the city, just as I do. Especially the Latino influence.

"Like most of my friends, I got married right out of high school. I was happy, and she was as happy as any woman can be when her husband is gone more than he's home. We bought the house and started renovating it as time and money allowed. She did a lot of the work.

"She waited patiently for me while I was sailing around the world on active duty, but it was only a month or two after I retired that her pains started. We saw a half-dozen doctors and finally found one who figured it out. Pancreatic cancer. She died three months after the diagnosis.

"I spent three months driving around the West, seeing places we'd never been able to see together, then I came back to Miami and started my new business and my new life. I got lucky with my first project."

"What a sad story. That first project – was that the gunsight?"

"I got the idea talking to some Marines on ship one day. They were complaining about the sights on their tanks and how they were dependent on spotters to find targets over the horizon or behind the hills – this was before drones. I was already working on that sort of technology in my spare time and thought I could find some way to combine an optical sight with the GPS system and give them what they wanted."

"But GPS is just good for line-of-sight." She was back in curious-engineer mode.

"Normally that's true, but I found I could jigger it some by using indirect signals. A lot of my proto-types failed, but I finally figured it out." He lowered his voice. "And, by accident, I think I discovered a way to use it underwater. That will be our next big improvement for Pegasus."

"It worked, and then you sold it and moved on to the next challenge, the sub?"

Mark paused, then decided she might as well have the whole story.

"It took a long time and almost all the money I had. The first lawyer I hired to help me find a buyer turned out to be completely incompetent. It cost me a lot to work my way out of his mess."

"I don't understand. I'd think the only legal buyer for something like that would be the U.S. gov-ernment. Were you looking elsewhere as well?"

"The government had to be involved, but it's a hydra-headed beast. I was amazed to learn how many agencies there are that might be prospects, but none of them want to buy something like that from a shoestring operation like mine – they want it to come from an established military contractor, a reliable supplier."

"That sounds like the bureaucracy I knew and hated."

"That's the one. After the first effort fizzled I found another guy, this time one who lives and works in Washington. He found the right people in the army right away, and with their support I wound up making the sale to one of the big technology companies for a cash and royalties deal. As part of the process I ran into Icky Crane again. I hadn't seen him for years."

She asked, "Now I understand why he's so enthusiastic. And that contract financed the sub?"

"Entirely. But now I need more help from the CIA. Your paycheck is safe, but I'm not willing to put everything I have into the project.

"Now that we've shown them a product that works, I'm pretty sure Icky will find us some development money. In fact, when I talked to him last week he said he really needed the sub, but he wouldn't tell me for what, and I'm sure you noticed he didn't tell us much in the shop.

"He may need us more than we need him. This is an entirely different thing from the gunsight. That was old warfare, this is new warfare. It's the future, not the past. Icky lives in the future."

She lifted her glass and looked at him in a way he

hadn't seen before, like there was a new and secret bond of some sort between two damaged people, finding consolation in each other's secrets. "Here's to the future, then. It starts now."

"I've been thinking," he said slowly, and then paused.

"What about?" It wasn't like him to hesitate. "Penny for your thoughts?"

"More than that, I hope."

She put down her fork and sat back against the banquette. He put his large hand on her small one. She sensed something important was about to happen and put her other hand on his.

"Would you like to make the sail this weekend an overnighter?"

He started to add something but she lifted her finger to his lips. "You don't have to sell me on the idea. I'd love to."

THEY RODE in silence most of the way back to South Beach. On the bridge over Biscayne Bay she looked back at the city behind them and said, "I'm learning to love Miami. I came here because there's a good school and because it's as far as I could get from my ex, but now I'm seeing its charms. It looks like you might be one of those, too."

He walked with her up the two flights of stairs,

then down the long and ornate yellow-and-green corridor to her door. She pushed the door open a few inches.

"Should I come to your house about noon?" she asked.

"You can leave your car there." He turned to leave.

"Mark," she said, reaching out to touch his arm. "If we're going to do this new thing…"

He turned again and took her in his arms. "I know. Wouldn't it make sense to start now, right here?"

"Inside," she whispered.

***

THE NEXT MORNING, Kate insisted on driving herself to Mark's house. She didn't know yet where the affair with Mark was headed – she hoped it would last, but it was too early to be sure. She could choose to stay with him or go back to her own place, depending on how the weekend sail went.

Traffic across the bridges was light and she was early, so Mark's doorbell chimed long before he was ready. He came to the door with a towel wrapped around his waist.

"You're a fit-looking bugger," she said as she put her arms around his neck for a kiss. She kicked the door closed behind her, then stepped out of her shoes. She backed off for another look and the towel fell away. "Wow," was all she said before he took her hand and pulled her toward the bedroom.

A half-hour later they lay quietly with her head on his shoulder. She smiled as he ran his fingers idly over her breast.

"That was great," he said. "We'd better enjoy the AC while we have it, because the rest of the weekend is going to be sweaty."

Her laugh was a musical peal he hadn't heard until months after she started work.

"Y'know, I never heard you laugh until the week you got back after your divorce. And you really surprised me a few days later. I was walking down the hall and heard you singing through the shop door. It was something from before your time. ABBA, I think."

"Old-fashioned. ABBA is one of my favorites. I like any music that has a melody, from rock to opera. I guess I was pretty transparent, but I was sure happy. I always enjoyed the job, but my personal life was a wreck. Maybe now it's back on track." She caressed him gently.

They lay for a minute longer, and then he shifted toward the edge of the bed and said, "Now come with me. It's shower time."

Feigning reluctance, she let herself be pulled into the bathroom. In one corner he had installed an immense shower, big enough for a party of two.

"You choose the temperature." She fiddled with the controls until the water streaming down from the oversized head was hot, far hotter than he liked, but Kate's enthusiastic caress drove the thought from his mind in seconds.

He picked up a bar of almond soap made by an ancient order of monks in rural France and began with her shoulders, working his way down her back to the curve of her hips, where he lingered.

"You're done on that side," she finally said. "Now start on the front. Then it's my turn."

———

BACK IN BED A HALF-HOUR LATER, Kate rolled to her side and asked, "Are we ready for a sail?"

"A little recharge time would probably be a good thing right now."

He dropped a half-dozen Diet Cokes and three bottles of pinot noir into a cooler, topped it with ice, and tossed a bag of chips into a carrier bag. Then they got into his BMW and headed toward the marina a half-mile beyond downtown Coconut Grove.

"Why don't you run into Fresh Market while I start unbuttoning the boat?" he asked, holding out two twenties. "And stop at the dockmaster's shack and tell him we'll be out overnight."

"My pleasure. Sushi or chicken? And I'm buying."

"In that case, both. And ice cream. It's a hot day. We'll need it. And something for tomorrow."

MARK HAD THOUGHT many times of moving the boat to a less expensive slip, but finally decided the kick he got from spur-of-the-moment day trips outweighed the money he would save. Today made that decision seem an even better one.

The sailboat was not young, but fiberglass ages well. Many hours of hard labor had kept it pristine and sparkling, and painting the hull the color of the deep ocean had taken years off its age. A sign-painter friend had carefully applied its name, Gunner, in gold on the stern.

By the time Kate arrived with the groceries he had the sail cover off and the cabin open. A solar-powered exhaust fan struggled to pull out the heat, with little noticeable effect. It was still too hot for humans down there, but when they got under way the open foredeck hatch would scoop air inside and make it more comfortable. In the meantime they could enjoy the breeze in the cockpit.

He took the grocery bag and the small tote she used instead of a purse on their sailing days and reached through the cabin hatch to place them next to the stack of swim towels. Then he held out his hand to steady her as she stepped over the gunwale.

She caught him admiring her long, tanned legs but said nothing.

"I hope you like pistachio," she said. "It's my favorite, strawberry is my second choice. So I got both. Into the cooler they go."

Mark cranked the two-cylinder engine, Kate took in the last mooring line and they began the hour's trip toward one of their favorite lunchtime anchorages, the shoals just off West Point, where the shallow water brought out kiteboarders by the dozens. If that was too crowded they could sail a few miles further down the coast and anchor off a park. There, the boats were always comfortably far apart and well away from the main routes of powerboaters.

They picked their way carefully through the field of mooring buoys, then turned down the Dinner Key channel into the bay. Only then could he kill the engine and winch the heavy mainsail to its full height, while she pulled the roller-furling jib open and tightened its sheet. As he set a course for Key Biscayne, Kate stepped down the short ladder into the cabin to change.

"Do you like this?" she asked, holding up the brilliant multi-hued swimsuit. "I bought it this morning, just for you."

"It's beautiful – it looks like the peacocks that prowl all over Coconut Grove," he replied.

"I hope I won't be as noisy as a peacock. Although, based on my short experience, I can't guarantee that."

She was just stepping into it when he called down to her, "You'd better get that on quick or I'm going to throw out an anchor and come take it off."

With a smile that matched his, she stepped to the hatch and slowly, tantalizingly, pulled it over her breasts. "Too late now, buster. Maybe you'll get lucky later. In fact, I'm pretty sure you will."

She took over the wheel while he went below to change, then she went to lie in the bright sun on the foredeck, where she could wait for her first view of the dozens of kiteboarders tacking back and forth in the shallow water – more of an underwater beach.

"How about here?" he asked when they reached a spot a quarter-mile from the kiteboarders. The water was shallow enough to make an easy anchorage and they were far enough away from the beach and the nearest other boat to be free from prying eyes.

"Let's watch for a while then go further south," she said. "It will be too exposed for an overnight stay."

She raised the blue canvas sun shelter over the cockpit and settled back to watch the colorful kites fly. Mark released the sheets and dropped anchor, freeing the boat to turn gently with the wind. He rolled in the jib, then when it was out of the way he came back to join her in the shaded cockpit.

"Sunscreen?" He held up a bottle of SPF 50.

She turned over and pointed to her back, above the plunging vee. "There. I can't reach all of it."

"This is what I'm good at," he said as he squeezed a dollop onto her bronzed skin and spread it over her shoulders, then moved his hand further down her back. When he got to the bottom of the suit's deep vee he stopped and added more, then slid his hand under the suit to cup her bottom.

He kissed her shoulder, then pushed her hair aside to kiss the back of her neck. Her breathing became shallow. He slipped one strap down, then the other, and then turned her over so he could kiss her breasts. When he raised his head she took in both her hands and pressed his lips tightly to hers. "Now," she said softly.

He went down the cabin ladder first, then reached up to grasp her around the waist and place her bare feet gently on the teak cabin sole. She pressed his hand to her breast, then peeled off the rest of the suit, finishing the job he'd started in the cockpit. She grasped the drawstring of his shorts and pulled. They dropped to the floor.

She sat down on the narrow starboard bunk.

"It's a good thing it only has to be wide enough for one," she said, then smiled at her own wit as she lay back and pulled him slowly into her.

TWENTY MINUTES later she whispered in his ear, "Let's take a swim before dinner. Can we go in like this?"

"Don't see why not. We're far enough away from land to be pretty much out of sight. Other than the random boat coming by, no one but me should see your lovely body." He smiled in anticipation.

They dropped into the cool water and made three laps around the boat before stopping at the swim ladder mounted on the stern.

"Ladies first."

"Sure. I like keeping you interested."

When they were dressed again, Mark reached into the cabin for the grocery store bag. "There's a surprise in the cooler bag," Kate said. "I told you about the ice cream, but …."

"I can't wait." Mark reached into the bag and pulled out a bottle of chilled rosé. He opened it quickly and filled two glasses, then took out a plate of sushi and one of fried wings.

"This will be a feast."

"I hoped you'd like it. Let's eat."

To a boater passing a civilized distance away, they were just another sailing couple out to watch the kiteboarders glide to and fro on the zephyrs off Key Biscayne.

MARK PULLED another bottle from the bucket to refill her glass but Kate held out her hand to stop him. She sat up on the seat and moved away.

"Mark, before we get so deep into this we can't get out of it there are a couple of things I need to tell you, and I want to do it before we fall completely into the next bottle."

"Sure." He pulled himself upright. "Shoot."

"At dinner last night I told you my ex-husband was getting strange. You knew he wasn't normal from when you served under him, but this is different. I just want you to know what might lie ahead."

"I think I have an idea, but tell me."

"Henry Mickelwaite is a vindictive man. He let the divorce go through without contesting it because he didn't want me telling stories that would hurt his career, and I didn't want any of his money. But I'm afraid that when he finally retires, and that will be soon, he'll come back for me one way or another."

Mark asked, "Why would he do that? As much as I loved my wife, I sure wouldn't have chased after her if she decided to leave me. People have to be free to live life in their own way."

"He's different. First, he's an admiral, and they don't think the way civilians do. Worse, he's convinced he's the heir to a great Eastern European dynasty going back to Vlad the Impaler or some such nonsense. In fact, his family did once own a castle on a mountaintop in Hungary, but they lost it before

World War Two, then moved to the States and changed their name. Henry was born here, so it's not like the castle is his long-lost home. It's more a revanchist dream.

"One time when he was in Berlin for a NATO meeting he went to see it and fell in love with it, or at least the idea of it. It's a ruin now, and a quarry for the locals. He decided then and there to buy it and rebuild it to its former glory. And he also fell for the tales of how the Nazis left treasure buried all over the area in their scramble to get out of the way of the Russian army, although I think he's decided those are just local rumor."

"Did you go with him?"

She nodded. "It was a command performance. I've seen pictures, and the old castle was an impressive place once, but it would take an incredible amount of money to restore it. It took almost all our savings to buy it in the first place, so I don't know where he'll get the rest of the money. He was looking for sponsors when I left him but I don't know if he found one. Not every rich man wants to own a cold and drafty castle in the Carpathians.

"The guy he tried to pimp me to was a prospect, but I don't know if it led anywhere."

"Why should this affect us?"

"Because he thinks the lord of the manor must have his chatelaine. I don't know why he doesn't hook up with some local countess, real or imagined.

"You must remember what a drab little wren I was when I came to our first interview. The whole thing – the hair, the clothes – was my effort to keep my head down."

Mark remembered. After a big buildup from the engineering dean, he had been surprised to meet a nervous woman, graying hair in a bun, wearing a long plain skirt and a simple blouse. He had had serious doubts that she had enough self-confidence to do the job.

But she had shown immediately that her engineering skills and imagination were keen, and it wasn't long before Mark had found the Navy officer hiding under the drab exterior.

The old Kate had disappeared completely by the time she returned from a week in Washington, where her divorce was made final. The vibrant woman who came back to work, with a new name and dark hair carefully styled into a sophisticated Cleopatra, was nothing like the one who'd left. And, for the first time, she had laughed in his presence.

It was only then that Mark had realized what a powerful woman she was, and how much the last years must have taken out of her. It was then that their weekend sails had begun to hold new possibilities for him.

"I HAVEN'T HEARD anything from him," Mark said. "How do you suppose I escaped?"

"I threatened him. He called me after I went to work with you. I told him you were my boss, nothing more, and I liked the job. I told him if he bothered me or you I'd go straight to the Pentagon about him and that I would never under any circumstances go back to him. When we hung up, he knew I meant it."

"Well, things are officially different now," Mark replied. "If somebody's watching there won't be any doubt about what's going on. But he lives more than a thousand miles away. Who could be watching us?"

"Those Miami policemen, I think."

"This is like something out of a psycho movie. We have to deal with it." Mark moved across the boat and took her in his arms.

"Kate, we have something good. I can tell that already, and I'm not going to let some half-deranged former husband interfere with us, even if he is a brass hat."

"Thank you for that." She threw her arms around his neck and gave him a lingering kiss.

"Let them take a picture of that."

A DEAD SOLDIER stood bottom up in a bucket of tepid water.

The day went silent, awaiting the coming sunset.

Kiteboarders straggled off toward home or the beach bars, wherever they planned to start their nighttime rounds. The small armada that had gathered around Gunner drifted away. Kate followed Mark out of the cabin and sat on the starboard cockpit seat. He bent to kiss the top of her head.

He said, "Let's go further south. Down to the park. It will be a quiet stop for our first overnight. There will be too many drunk powerboaters this close to the Key."

"You look like the cat who's just finished off the canary," she said, smiling up at him. After a year working closely together in Mark's little engineering company they had learned to anticipate each other's thoughts. "Somewhere quieter would be good. And we both need a rest."

"That last time was one or two over my limit. I could use some recharge time."

She raised the anchor while he cranked the mainsail winch, then she tightened the jib sheet and moved to the wheel. An hour later they stopped a quarter-mile off the beach of a small state park. It seemed secure. The anchor light on the mast far above them cast a dim white glow, but without the quarter moon rising to the north, over the Miami skyline, the deck would have been completely dark.

They dropped the anchor a dozen feet to the sandy bottom and secured the sails for the night.

4
A VERY CLOSE CALL

Midnight. They lay entwined on the narrow bunk, exhausted and searching for sleep as the boat rose and fell on the swells rolling into Biscayne Bay. Atlantic breezes that had been gentle all day were just beginning to stiffen, but it wasn't yet cool enough for them to need cover.

She lifted her face from the hollow of his neck just long enough to kiss him gently on the cheek and say, "This has been an outstanding weekend, Mark, certainly my personal best. Now go to sleep." She caressed the fouled anchor tattooed on his bicep, fading with age.

He mumbled, "The best ever." He moved his hand to circle her nipple slowly with his thumb.

"That makes me crazy," she said. "Quit it." But there was no urgency in her voice.

Their breathing slowed and fell into the same re-laxed cadence. Mark was no longer aware of any-thing but the gentle movement of the sea under him and her pleasant weight on his chest.

SOMETHING HIT the hull and the boat jerked. Mark slipped out of the bunk and was standing with one foot on the cabin ladder when she asked, "What was that?"

"Anchor dragged, I think. It'll just take a minute. Want to go?"

She closed her eyes. "Call me if you need me. Be careful. We've had a lot of wine."

As an afterthought he reached for the slim life vest he'd hardly ever worn and strapped his iPhone, in its waterproof case, to his left arm. He might go up without his shorts, but never without his phone.

In three quick steps he was on the cabin top, carefully avoiding the winches and other hardware toe-stubbers that lie in wait for the inattentive sailor.

The cloud cover was heavier than an hour be-fore, making the anchor light seem brighter as it carved white circles in the indigo sky. The rising wind hadn't yet kicked up whitecaps but would soon. All in all, he told himself, it should be a good night for sleeping.

He knelt and pulled hard at the anchor line. To

his surprise, it held. He tugged again to be sure. So what had caused the bump?

With a shrug, he turned to piss over the rail. The old sailor's saying, "One hand for yourself, one for the ship," ran through his mind unbidden as he reached for a shroud.

His eyes swept the horizon, surveying the half-dozen boats sharing the anchorage with Gunner. The closest, a sport fisherman, was a hundred yards away. As he watched, a silver flash broke the surface close to it. It could have been a fish jumping, a bird diving, anything, but to him it looked like the brief flick of a diver's fin, which he did not expect to see at one o'clock on a Sunday morning. It filled him with a deep sense of dread and told him instantly what had bumped the boat.

He turned toward the stern, shouting, "Kate, get out now! Go over the side!" He knocked hard on the cabin top, then dropped through its open hatch, ignoring the ladder. She was sitting up in the bunk with a befuddled look when he pulled her arm hard and forced her up and through the hatch into the cockpit.

"I think a diver put a limpet on the hull," he said urgently. "Get over the side, now. Swim as far astern as you can. I'll be right behind you." Her eyes widened and she looked around anxiously.

As she put her leg over the thin rail they both heard the unmistakable sharp click of a timing fuse.

Time stopped. An immeasurably tiny fraction of

a second seemed to stretch into eternity. He picked her up like a medicine ball and tossed her as far out as he could. "Swim!" he shouted. "Don't wait! I'll be right behind you! And get underwater! Go deep!"

He was in mid-vault when he heard the sharp crack, the sound of a rifle shot, as the initiator blasted first through the fiberglass hull then the gas tank, spraying its contents into the bilge and vaporizing enough of it to create one of the most lethal explosives known to man, a fuel–air bomb. A quarter-second later it went off.

WHEN MARK HEARD the metallic click he was certain he was a dead man. By the time the rifle shot came he was beginning to believe he might escape, but it would be a very close call.

He vaulted over the starboard rail, clearing it just as an angry yellow fireball mushroomed from the hatch. The cabin top exploded into a thousand fiberglass shreds and an expanding bubble of incandescent gas, the angry color of the sun, passed close overhead just before he hit the water. He pulled hard toward the bottom, trying to escape from the immense blast wave he knew was coming in less than a second.

The cool water of Biscayne Bay saved him. Just as his left hand felt the packed sand a dozen feet down, the gas cartridge in his life vest fired, jerking him upright. Then the blast wave sent him tumbling once again, scrambling his sense of direction.

The boiling flames on the surface were a beacon. He put them behind him and pulled away, using the frogman breast stroke he'd learned in the Navy more than twenty years before.

By the time his head broke water the boat had already burned almost to the waterline and the hulk was beginning to capsize. Like a slow-motion nightmare, he saw the mast tip toward him and swam as hard as he could away from the danger zone, but he couldn't move fast enough. He escaped the mast but felt one of the stainless-steel shrouds fall hard on his outstretched left arm. A sharp pain ran up to his shoulder.

A few yards further away and well out of range, he did a quick inventory. He was upright and breathing, so he wasn't dead – yet. The salt water brought stabbing pain to the back of his head, so he was burned, but it was nothing he couldn't handle. His back felt a little questionable.

He couldn't lift his left arm. Broken, he thought, and when he reached around with his right hand he could feel that all the hair on the back of his head was gone. Not that he'd had much.

"Mark! Mark!" Kate's voice called from the darkness. She was only a dozen yards away, and when a swell raised him enough, he could see her face in the yellow light of the fire, wide-eyed with surprise but showing no fear.

"Swim toward me," he told her. "My life vest inflated and it'll support both of us until help arrives." He reached around to test his left forearm and cried out briefly from the pain. "My left arm's broken. Try not to grab me there."

He unclipped the iPhone carefully from his injured arm, shook the water off its case, and dialed 911. The woman who answered was terse and professional. She asked if they needed medical help.

Kate stopped a few feet away and began to tread water. He asked the 911 operator to wait while he asked her, "Did you get hurt anywhere? Burned?"

"No, surprised and now mad. I sure as hell didn't expect to need my Navy training on a lazy overnight sail."

"She's okay," Mark reported back to 911. "No injuries. I have some burns, nothing too bad, and I think my left arm is broken."

The 911 operator kept him on the line until he saw the blue light of a fire department boat in the distance. As he disconnected, he heard the sound of another boat coming from the direction of the anchored sport fisherman he'd noticed just before the explosion.

"Hello." The voice of a young man came across the water. "Is there anybody there?" Silence for a moment as the boat circled the burning wreck. "I see your light. I'll be right there." The voice had an accent Mark could not place.

"We're okay!" Kate called out to him.

"We called 911," Mark added. His subconscious told him it was important to say that. "Thanks for coming to check on us but I can already see the fire department boat."

THE RESCUE BOAT throttled back and its siren died away.

"Mr. McGinley, Ms. Hall?" A burly fireman standing on the foredeck of the rescue boat pointed a blinding searchlight at them. Mark turned away from the light and caught a glimpse of the sailor in the sport fisherman, also covering his eyes and hiding his face. He looked like a Slav, maybe a Russian, and had a military air – short hair, bulging biceps, a little younger than Kate.

"I have a broken arm and some burns, not too bad. Kate thinks she is okay. Take her first, since she's not wearing a life vest."

She added, "And I'll need a blanket. I'm not dressed for a boat full of firemen."

Kate swam the dozen feet to the rescue boat's boarding ladder and scrambled aboard. A fireman wrapped her immediately in a coarse woolen blanket. A diver splashed over the side and swam to Mark.

"Where are you burned?"

"My head, mainly. And my left arm's broken and hurts like hell."

"Can you climb up the ladder if I give you a boost?"

"I'm pretty sure I can. I practiced it in the Navy a lot of years ago."

Between the burns and the stress, not to mention his broken arm, Mark had seriously overestimated his strength. He struggled slowly up the ladder but collapsed on the deck. Kate knelt next to him and covered him with her own blanket. A fireman gently put another over her.

"Can we get him to a hospital soon?" she asked.

"You bet," the driver said. "My partner just needs to finish getting the other fellow's ID." Within seconds the small boat was zipping toward the flashing light of an ambulance waiting at the dock.

Time is fluid, Einstein said, but that was concept, theory. In Mark's real world, time had gone from glacial to frenetic, pushed by the pain of his burns and his fractured arm.

He lost track, but Kate told him later they were in the water only twenty minutes before the first help arrived, and a half-hour after that he was in the hands of the emergency room doctors at University Hospital.

MARK LAY on a rolling bed in one of the ER examining rooms. A technician x-rayed his arm and the nurse slipped an IV into the back of his good hand, mainly to deliver a painkiller, then offered Kate a set of blue scrubs decorated with yellow daffodils.

"You're lucky," the nurse told them. "The doctor just told me the break is a pretty simple one. He'll set it here and put it in a soft cast. He wants you to stay at least overnight to see if you have any lingering effects of the explosion."

After she left, Mark beckoned to Kate. "Come closer," he said softly. "Kate, I'm really sorry I got you into this mess."

She touched her finger to his lips and gripped his hand tightly.

"Stop it. I wasn't drafted for this cruise. I won't hear any more of that."

Mark said, "I'm pretty sure that other sailor planted the limpet then swam back to his boat underwater. He made the mistake of bumping us, and then he swam too close to the surface. And he got to us almost immediately after the bomb went off.

"I'd guess his job was to be sure we were dead. We would be, too, if he hadn't known the firemen were on the way. But why blow up the boat? Why didn't they just break into the shop and take what they wanted?"

Kate said, "I think there's more going on than we think. I wouldn't be surprised to learn my ex-husband is somewhere in the background."

"Really? I know he's a mean bastard. We called him Captain Queeg. But this sounds like a lot for a jealous sailor, even if he is an admiral."

"It's just a feeling. That sailor had an Eastern European accent, and my husband's family was from Hungary. I know it's far-fetched, but it's just a feeling I have. You're right – your work is more likely, and I'm just being paranoid, but it's not paranoia if someone is really out to get you.

"What should I do next?"

"The other sailor may come back after us, so you need to move," Mark said. "Use the Uber account on my phone. Go home to get some clothes and some money. Most important, a weapon of some sort. Do you have a gun?"

"No, but I have a Ka-Bar fighting knife, and I was once very good with it. It's a serious throat-slitter."

"That will work. Then go to my place. In the kitchen, in the bottom drawer to the left of the sink, there's a thick envelope behind a fake panel. Bring that with you. There's a gun in the envelope, but it's a little one. Your knife may be better in a tight space.

"Then drive over to the shop and see what you can see. For God's sake, if there are any strange cars there don't go in. And don't call the police. If Pegasus and Icarus are gone or damaged there are others who need to know first."

SHORTLY AFTER KATE had begun working for Mark, he had asked her to replace the existing lock on her condo door with a high-security passcode version, just in case someone got the idea of looking there for information about the submarine. The condo board had put up a fight, but now she was grateful she had won, because the few keys she carried had gone down with Gunner.

While the car waited, she changed into a dark running outfit and black sneakers and retrieved the few hundred dollars cash she kept hidden in a drawer, along with her spare keys. She went to a cabinet near the front door and pulled out her Navy fighting knife, the one she'd been awarded when she finished close combat school in Georgia and had kept sharp and oiled ever since. As an afterthought, she stuck her passport into her purse, along with a handful of strong cable ties she'd brought from the shop, intending to use them to fasten a loose leg on her kitchen table.

She stood on the shell driveway outside the stone wall Mark had built around his house until the car disappeared around the corner, then keyed in the combination and the gate swung open. Another combination opened Mark's front door. She found the envelope just where he said it would be, but hidden behind several years' accumulation of small, old-fashioned kitchen tools. "Junk drawer," she said to herself. "Good place. A little obvious."

She hefted the package. "Outstanding."

THE EARLY-MORNING TRAFFIC WAS LIGHT. In fifteen minutes she arrived at the small industrial park that housed McGinley Engineering, a single bay in a multi-tenant building near a Metrorail station on the edge of Coral Gables.

The industrial park was a well-kept island in a grubby neighborhood of auto repair and paint shops, surrounded by a sturdy fence with razor wire running along the top. Mark's office and shop – *her* office and shop – stood at the end of a row of five cookie-cutter entrances and looked like dozens of others within a few miles, except that all of his fellow tenants were working to develop new gadgets or software for the government, usually the defense department. The center was an incubator for projects that were still in their early stages, most of which would fail before they ever became usable, so security wasn't tight.

As Kate drove toward the entrance it appeared dark and empty. Her parking pass had gone down with Gunner, so she punched in her access code, drove through the security gate, and parked at the far end. She wedged an umbrella in the door to keep it from slamming and tiptoed the length of the front, taking care not to scuff her rubber soles on the sidewalk. When she arrived at McGinley Engineering she stopped and peered around the corner into Mark's office. Nothing.

The next stop would be the most critical – the back door, the only one large enough to roll the sub through. She continued around the side, staying close to the building's rough concrete surface, and paused when she reached the back corner. Taking a deep breath, she gripped the knife and looked around the corner.

"Damn!" she said under her breath. She could have driven straight to the door blowing her horn and no one would have heard, for there had been burglars, but they were long gone.

The back wall of the shop was a pile of rubble, its concrete blocks torn down so that Pegasus, Icarus, and their custom trailer could be towed through the gap. The guilty tool, a backhoe she had seen digging pipe trenches for a new building a hundred yards down the street, stood mute near the damage, its engine still warm. Behind it, the chain-link fence had been pushed down to give the backhoe a way in and the trailer a way out.

She looked carefully through the gap to be sure

no one remained inside, then stepped into the ruined and vacant shop. Mark didn't want her to call the police, so she wouldn't, but she did need to be sure the door to the offices at the front was locked and the alarm was still set. It would at least slow down anyone who wanted to get into the offices.

IT SEEMED clear that the plan was to eliminate Mark and steal the sub. Someone must have known the CIA was interested and decided to stop a small problem before it could blow up into a big one. But who would have known?

If the boater in the sport fisherman was the killer, which seemed more and more likely, both he and his master would be anxious to finish the job. She needed to get back to the hospital.

MARK HAD LEFT a message giving her his new room number, B435, on the fourth floor, south wing.

She parked as close as she could to the hospital entrance, talked her way past the off-duty policeman idly standing guard, and walked up the stairs into the dim and silent corridor. She paused to listen outside the door and then, just in case the attacker was already inside, shoved it open abruptly. Relief washed over her when she saw Mark's chest rise and fall steadily.

What was the best way to defend the room? She decided a straight chair in the dark space behind the door would be the hardest for an intruder to see. She took off her shoes and laid the unsheathed knife on the seat next to her, then picked up the package she'd retrieved from Mark's kitchen. It was about seven inches square, and heavy.

She peeled off the top layer, which felt like oilcloth sealed with duct tape. Inside was a gallon-sized plastic bag, with duct tape over the zipper for added protection, and inside that was a white cardboard box.

She carefully pulled off the top of the box. Inside she saw a passport clipped to an envelope with a black metal clamp, and under it was a formless cloth package tied with string. She picked up the familiar odor of light gun oil. Mark had foreseen this kind of problem, and this was his escape kit.

She hefted the gun, then her knife, and decided her chances would be better with the knife. For the ultimate backup, however, she chambered a round in the pocket Glock and placed it carefully beside Mark, where he could reach it easily but it wouldn't be visible to an intruder coming through the door. She knew if she got into a fight with a killer she wouldn't have time to pull the pistol from her belt.

Then there was nothing to do but wait.

The clock on the far wall ticked past four o'clock. Was it only three hours ago that they were swimming frantically away from the flaming wreckage of the sailboat?

Time crawled. She fought the urge to sleep and even considered waking Mark to ask him to stand a watch, but decided against it because the painkillers might slow his reaction time. The risk would disappear near sunrise, a little after 6 a.m. The dangerous time was now.

5

THE SAILOR'S RETURN

AT 5:15 THE DOOR OPENED SLOWLY, surreptitiously, not at all like a nurse would open it. Kate stood and pressed her back against the wall, knife in hand, as a burly man walked in, dressed in black from his running shoes to his watch cap. She couldn't see his face, but his build looked a lot like the sailor's.

He stepped silently across the room to stand at Mark's side, then from his pocket he took what looked like a length of wire with a short handle on each end – it was a garotte, a silent strangler used by soldiers who need to overpower a sentry without raising an alarm.

As he formed the wire into a loop and started to bend over Mark, she took two quick paces and wrapped her arm around his neck, hard. She pressed the tip of the fighting knife into his back. She wanted him to feel it in his skin, to understand that he would be dead if he didn't do exactly what she told him.

"Drop the garotte NOW," she said, her voice low and hard.

"You!" he snarled. "Bitch!"

She anticipated that he would react quickly, but with her arm tightly around his neck and the knife point pressing hard between his ribs she was confident she could control him.

She was wrong. He used his elbow to strike fiercely at the arm that held the knife. The blow knocked the knife away, dragging the tip across his skin and spraying his blood on her, but she managed to hold on to it. He turned and slipped the garotte around the back of her neck, crossed his arms deftly, and started to pull on its handles. She had only seconds. She raised the knife to slip it inside the tightening loop of cable but she saw at once that he could pull it tighter and force her own blade into her face, so she pulled it away again and pressed it instead to the side of his neck, hard enough to draw blood. He jerked and tried to circle away from her but she grabbed the front of his shirt and stayed close.

The noise woke Mark, who looked around in confusion.

"Kate!" he shouted.

The sailor started, giving Kate the time she needed to press the blade home again.

"Count of two and I cut your throat from ear to ear, and enjoy it," she hissed. She heard her own voice as though she were standing outside her body, watching to see if this surprising and unknown Kate would rise to the hardest task of her life or die trying. "One! T…"

"Okay. Okay," the killer said, and put his hands behind his head. The garotte clattered to the floor.

"On the floor! On your face!"

He obeyed quickly. She pulled a cable tie from her pocket and cinched it tight around his wrists, then used another to secure both wrists to his belt. Then she tied his ankles together, reached up to press the nurse call button lying on Mark's bed, and sat back on the floor to catch her breath.

Mark pushed himself to a semi-sitting position and stared down at the intruder. "You… you… you're the guy!" he sputtered. He had found the pistol, and held it loosely, his finger off the trigger.

"They just sent me to deliver a message," the man on the floor said. Mark now recognized the accent he'd heard on the Bay. It was Russian, or from one of the old Central European satellite countries that spun off when the Soviet Union collapsed. "I didn't mean you no harm."

"Of course you didn't. You just used a warning bomb, and now you come in here with a warning garotte. Don't bullshit us."

KATE HAD to talk fast to convince the 911 operator that she was the woman they'd rescued from the burning boat only a few hours before. Finally, her call was transferred to the same agent Mark had talked to from the water, who quickly took charge. The police, she said, would be on the way immediately, and she'd contact a detective as well.

"They thought the boat was an accident or some sort of trick, maybe for the insurance," she told Kate. "I didn't think so, and I told them that. This will put an end to that idea. Is Mr. McGinley doing okay?"

"He is," Kate said. "I'm here in his room, and the bomber is lying on the floor, trussed up like a roast chicken."

The woman gave a low whistle. "Good work! I'll stay on the line with you until the officers get there. It shouldn't be too long."

The duty nurse came through the door as Kate ended the call. She sized up the situation instantly and called hospital security, which sent a beefy guard to investigate. His only concern was that it was against rules for Kate to have the knife, and he tried unsuccessfully to take it from her.

"No, I'm keeping the knife," she told him in a voice much sweeter than she felt. "It would be really good if you would stand watch outside the room in case this fellow has a partner." The guard blanched.

They could hear his footsteps receding down the hall.

"Not a cop who rides to the guns, is he?" Mark asked with a droll smile.

THE NURSE KNELT beside the trussed sailor to look at the cuts Kate's knife had inflicted. She put a bandage on his neck, then cut away his jacket and bandaged his back.

In a few minutes they heard footsteps running down the corridor. Two policemen in blue knit shirts came through the door, guns drawn.

"I don't think you'll need the guns," Kate told them as she placed the knife carefully on a table. "He's docile as a baby right now.

"He tried to kill Mark with a garotte. There it is." She pointed at the wire contraption, which seemed to be simply a three-foot length of marine cable, each end attached to a handle fashioned from a bronze deck cleat.

The older officer looked at the garotte, then surveyed the room suspiciously.

"We'll have to take that knife, ma'am," the older one said.

"If you have to," Kate replied. "But I want it back."

"Detective Lieutenant Willimon will be here in a

few minutes. He'll do the investigation. In the mean-time, can I get some facts?"

"Not yet, Officer." Mark signaled with a shake of his head that he didn't want to tell the prisoner any-thing he didn't already know. "Could we wait for the detective while you deal with this guy?"

The patrolman understood. "Sure. It won't be long."

He bent over and put his handcuffs on the man on the floor, then told the second policeman to go to the nursing station and get some scissors so they could cut the plastic ties Kate had put on him.

"That was foresight, to have that flexicuff," he said, looking first at Mark, then at Kate.

She replied, "It's just a cable tie. We use them all the time, so I stuck a few in my pocket just in case."

"Were you expecting him?"

"Oh, yes. His job was to kill us. We knew he'd be back to finish what he'd started."

The door swung open to admit a man in a rum-pled brown suit and white shirt, with a narrow black tie knotted loosely under a wrinkled collar. Mark figured him to be about sixty years old. Kate correctly thought he was five or six years younger but had lived a hard life and not a happy one. She wondered who had en-couraged him to grow the ridiculous walrus mustache.

"You two have had a night full of adventure," Willimon said in a friendly way.

"We have," Mark said. "I hope this is the end of the problem."

"So do I. We don't often have boats blown up, unless it's by somebody who puts gasoline in the bilge while they're filling up, and those usually burn right at the marina. This was obviously something different."

"It sure as hell was," Mark said. His head had begun to hurt again. "This guy planted a limpet on the outside of the boat just where it would blow through the fuel tank and ignite the vapor. It made a perfect fuel–air bomb, and it's just blind luck that he bumped the boat while he was planting it. If he'd done his job right, we'd be dead and he'd be collecting his reward somewhere."

"How do you know about limpets?" the detective asked.

"Ex-Navy. I'd like to know how he fastened it to the fiberglass. Military limpets are magnetic, but our guy here probably used an underwater adhesive. I'd guess a wave hit just as he was attaching it and pushed him into the hull."

Willimon knelt next to the man on the floor. "How about that? Is that the way it happened?"

"Somethin' like that," the man muttered. "I ain't talking to you."

The detective stood up and said to the two patrolmen, "Get him out of here. We'll start with a charge of attempted murder and work out from there, but that will keep him locked up for now."

They pulled him to his feet. Just inside the door he turned to Mark and said, "They'll get you yet."

Mark ignored him.

"Don't forget this," the detective said. He reached for the garotte and placed it into the evidence bag the younger patrolman held out to him. He turned back to Kate and Mark, took out a worn notebook and opened it to a fresh page.

"I have your names from the fire call this morning, but they haven't passed us any more information yet. Can we call the roll? You first, Mr. McGinley."

"Mark McGinley. I'm an engineer. My company's office is in Coral Gables."

"What's your company?"

"McGinley Engineering LLC."

"I know of it. Mainly defense department work, as I understand. You invented a super gunsight for tanks?"

"That's the kind of thing I do. Small stuff that I can build myself. I'm mainly an inventor."

He turned to Kate.

"Commander Mickelwaite?"

"Not anymore. My name is Kate Hall, and I'm an engineer for Mark."

"I heard you weren't married to the admiral anymore, but not that you'd changed your name."

"I should never have taken his name in the first place."

He looked at her neck. "Did he get the garotte around your neck?"

"Yes. I gave him two seconds before I cut his throat. He made it by a half-second."

"Quick thinking," the lieutenant said. "Navy knife training?"

"I always did well in hand-to-hand. If I hadn't been confident I wouldn't have given him the warning, but this way you have another suspect to question.

"One thing about it was weird. It seemed like the minute he saw me he lost all interest in Mark."

WILLIMON MADE notes for a full minute before he asked his next question.

"Umm. I have to ask this. Are you a couple?"

She looked at Mark, who shrugged.

"We're trying it out," Kate replied. "The first day got pretty bad at the end. We'll try again soon, I hope."

Willimon turned his attention back to Mark.

"Mr. McGinley, is it true you're working on some sort of super-secret submarine?"

Mark was surprised he know about Pegasus, but

he knew the story had made the rounds of the competitive fraternity of weapons entrepreneurs.

"I wouldn't call it super-secret, although as of last week it's classified. We don't talk about it. People know I develop things for the government, and it wouldn't be out of the question for me to be working on something like a sub."

"Can you tell me more about it?"

"Not just yet, but I understand you'll need to know more. I just have to get the go-ahead from some people in Washington, and they'll probably want to have someone present when you and I talk about it, more to check what I say than what you ask."

Kate stepped into the conversation. "There's nothing much we can do right now. Whoever burgled the place tore down a wall and wheeled everything out. The sub is gone."

"You should have told this to 911," Willimon said. "The sooner we get on the case the better our chances of recovering it."

"I had some other stuff on my mind, like the guy you just took away."

"I suppose that's right," Willimon said. He did not look mollified.

"One more thing. Can you think of anybody who might want to hurt you? I mean, stealing your submarine is pretty serious, but bombing your sailboat is in a different class altogether."

Mark replied, "I do my best to fly under the radar. No publicity, no rivalries with other contractors. The only other unpleasant experience I've had was a year ago, when someone found a way to get into the shop and hit me on the head with a two-by-four. The concussion laid me up for a couple of weeks. The officers who investigated it suspected an engineer I had to let go because he kept coming to work drunk, but he didn't leave much of a trail when he left town. Whoever it was knew how to get through the burglar alarm and reset it when he left, and Tom Farkas is the only employee I'd ever had until Kate came aboard. We installed the alarm ourselves, so there was no contractor to plant a Trojan-horse code."

Kate added, "And whoever tore down the wall also knew how to bypass the alarm."

"Tom Farkas." Willimon wrote the name in his notebook. "Do you have any idea where he is now?"

"None, although it looks like he may be in Miami right now. He used to work in California so he might have gone back to Silicon Valley, but that's just a guess on my part. I really have no idea and not much interest. He was a true pain in the ass."

Willimon turned to Kate. "Do you know this Farkas?"

"He was gone before I arrived."

WILLIMON FLIPPED THE NOTEBOOK CLOSED. "That's all I need for now. You'll probably be here another day, Mr. McGinley, and by then you can contact your man at the CIA or wherever. Call me and I'll meet you and him."

He slipped out as smoothly as he'd entered, raising a hand in a mock salute to Kate. "Jerk," she muttered, just loud enough for Mark to hear.

"You already know him?" Mark asked.

"He's the detective I told you about at dinner, the one who was cashiered in Annapolis. He's probably already on the phone with my ex."

Mark's eyebrows shot up. "That certainly adds seasoning to the story. We'd better bring Icky up to date. May I have my phone?"

As he searched for Icky's number in his list, she said, "I need to get another phone myself, but I'll wait to see what Icky says."

"He'll probably send Raul Gutierrez to babysit. After he gets here you can go, if the stores are open by then." Mark replied. "My arm still hurts but my head feels better, so maybe I can get them to let me out today."

"Tomorrow is more likely. I'll wait around for a bit."

"It's Sunday. And it's the middle of the night." He turned to look out the window at the brightening sky. "Well, it's very early in the morning. He won't be there," Mark said ruefully as he poked at the screen with his one good hand. And he was correct – Icky's voice message said simply that he was away, but "Leave me a message at the tone, or press zero to be connected with the duty officer." Mark punched zero.

After two rings a man's voice said, "Mr. Crane isn't in the office now. How can I help you?"

"This is Mark McGinley in Miami. I have an important message for him."

"Please hold a minute," the voice said. When he returned, he asked several identification questions.

"Thank you, Mr. McGinley. You are on Mr. Crane's list for immediate response. Please wait and I'll try to connect you."

The line went silent. As he waited, Mark covered the phone's mic and told Kate, "Something's happening. Icky put us on a special list of high-priority callers."

After two minutes he heard Icky's distinctive New England twang. For an instant he sounded like a man wakened from a sound sleep, then he was fully awake.

"Mark! This can't be a social call. Tell me what disaster has befallen us."

"A couple of them, actually. Somebody tried to kill me and Kate. They blew up my boat with a limpet. We barely got away in time. And someone – probably the same people – stole Pegasus and Icarus from the shop."

"Shit! Are you hurt?"

"Kate is fine, but she's really pissed. The killer came to the hospital to finish us off and she nearly had to cut his throat, but she left enough of him for the police to question."

"I have a broken arm and some burns. I ought to be out of the hospital tomorrow."

"That was serious. Do you have any idea who might be behind this?"

"The obvious choice is Tom Farkas, but that's so obvious it's probably not true. Otherwise I'm stumped, but Kate has some thoughts."

She took the phone. "My ex might be in this mix somewhere. I came to Miami to get away from him. I think he's at the Norfolk naval station now, waiting out the last few weeks before retirement. He had some problems and got put out to pasture."

"Oops," Icky said. "Admiral Mickelwaite. I know him, but not well. I wouldn't want to be married to him. Put Mark back on, please. And, Kate, I'm really glad you weren't injured. Mark depends on you." He waited while Kate handed over the phone and Mark fumbled it back to his ear. "Mark, have you seen a limpet mine used anywhere other than in the military?"

"I haven't been paying attention, but no. Even when the French sank the Greenpeace ship a few years back it was the government's security service that planted the mine."

Icky said, "I think you're right. This has the fingerprints of some government at some level. I don't believe we can count on anyone official outside our own group until we have more info, and that includes the police.

"I'm going to ask Raul to come sit with you. You'll have to talk to the police, so just tell them Raul is your cousin or something. We don't want a turf fight."

"A detective came by a little while ago. He knows about the sub and wants to see the shop tomorrow. He expects someone from the CIA to be there, so there shouldn't be any reason to hide Raul's identity."

"What was his name? Maybe we know him?"

"Willimon. Kate says he has a history with the admiral that's not all that savory."

"I'll check. Now stay put until you hear from Raul. Don't ever be alone in the room." He hung up.

———————

TEN MINUTES LATER, Raul called from the interstate. "I'll be there in less than a half-hour, and I'll knock four times in a row, three then one, like the V for victory signal. Icky says please don't let anyone in until I arrive."

"You don't need to worry about that," Mark said.

"It would be a brave man who came to our door right now."

KATE ANSWERED RAUL'S KNOCK. She told Mark later she was amazed to see him for the first time – a powerfully built man with broad shoulders and immense hands, but in miniature. He was only an inch or two taller than five feet. When he shook her hand, though, his grip was crushing. Don't jump to conclusions, she told herself. You're not Arnold Schwarzenegger, either.

He pushed the door tightly closed, turned the lock, and pulled up a chair.

"We are very concerned about this. Obviously not as intensely as you are, since you're the target, but Icky just called me to say he's found some connections that bother him.

"For starters, Detective Willimon is not someone I know, either because he only arrived here a few months ago and our paths haven't crossed, or because he's dodging me. But Icky found some background.

"For the last couple of years he was a patrolman in one of the tiny little jurisdictions we have in Dade County. But before that, he spent a long time as a detective in Annapolis, Maryland, and left under quite a cloud. I'm not sure what the problem was, but there are signs there was political influence involved."

He chuckled. "Of course, there would never be any politics in law enforcement."

Kate stopped him. "Willimon was caught taking cocaine from the evidence locker. My ex-husband got him the new job."

Mark said, "He sure didn't act like your close friend."

"I don't think anybody ever accused him of being a bad detective," she replied. "Just a crooked one. He was a weak man who got into trouble. I suspect my ex made it very expensive for him to stay out of jail."

"I'll mention that to Icky," Raul said. "On the way up I stopped to see the night manager. I needed to identify myself anyway, because I'm carrying a weapon. Places like hospitals and courthouses get a little nervous about people in plain clothes being armed.

"She told me the doctor wants you to stay another night. They're going to move you to another room and it won't be listed on the telephone directory. Sometime overnight we will leave the hospital and go to your house. By that time a colleague of mine will have arrived to give us a little more firepower, and both of you will be ready to go wherever you're needed."

Kate asked, "Where do you think that will be?"

"None of us will know until the last minute. Icky

is on the way to his office and will bring in a team. They will spend the next few hours trying to figure out where the submarine went. That will determine where you go. As of a few minutes ago, they haven't found anything, but Icky told me it will almost certainly be somewhere overseas.

"And by the way, I need your house keys. Did they survive?"

Mark replied, "All my locks are electronic, and so are Kate's. We'll give you the codes."

"Good. We were going to re-key all the locks anyway, so that will make it easier. Icky is arranging for the Navy to send a counterintelligence team to do a sweep of your office at the same time."

Kate said, "So you think it might be bugged?"

"We don't know yet. I sort of hope it is, because that would explain how they knew you were going out overnight. Otherwise we have to do more detective work."

"It could be as simple as casing the marina," Mark said.

"Yes, but I know you don't ordinarily go out overnight, so somebody else could know that, too. They could have stolen the sub while you were out during the day, but to sink you at night they'd have to be waiting, or have some way to track your movements."

Raul stood up and set the straight chair back behind the door, where Kate had waited for the would-be killer.

"Neither of you has had any sleep, and tonight is going to be active, just like tomorrow will be." He turned to Kate. "Try to sleep for an hour, at least until they find a new room for Mark. I'll keep watch here. Kate, you take the easy chair."

She passed by the single window to pull down the sunshade and darken the room, then stretched out in the recliner with a sigh.

Raul pulled his pistol from its holster and sat up straight to wait for the call from the nurses' station. Kate seemed to be already asleep. He couldn't tell about Mark.

6

THE HOSPITAL

MARK WASN'T ASLEEP. FOR THE FIRST TIME SINCE THE explosion his mind was working again, sorting through the possible reasons behind the attack and theft. Why steal the submarine in the first place? Pegasus was still very much a beta model and wouldn't be ready for its first real wet test for another two or three weeks, even though they'd rushed it for the video Icky wanted. It might take even longer than that, because Kate was still tweaking its high-torque turbine.

Why steal it at all? Mark knew of at least three companies like his that were working on similar drones. Their work wasn't even officially secret, although the agencies that were their prospective buyers wanted them kept quiet – no press releases, no shouting – and they had been known to turn off the development money if the rules weren't followed.

Unless Mark's little sub was different – or would be when it was finished. Unlike his competitors, his target market wasn't the Navy. His very interested prospect was the CIA, because the sub would offer an entirely new approach to a drone program that was already well established.

And while it could do the same sorts of things as any other mini-sub, including carry weapons, it had the little helicopter, an add-on of unknown value, but potentially a very useful one indeed.

But even taking Icarus into consideration, there was something in the story he couldn't quite understand. He decided to let it go for now and let his subconscious work on it. He'd learned that a lot of his best ideas came to him when he least expected them, like a bluebird landing on his shoulder. He hoped this one wouldn't crap on him.

RAUL'S PHONE CHIRPED GENTLY. "At the nurse station," the text said. "Ready?"

He clicked out the answer using the only way he'd learned, one character at a time, poking his large index finger at the tiny letters on the tiny keyboard.

"Come in. Quiet. They're asleep."

In two minutes the door swung slowly open and an immense head peered around it. It was a sailor in dress whites, minus the traditional Dixie-cup hat, and carrying a large briefcase.

"God, you get bigger every time I see you," Raul said in a whisper.

"Something about the uniform, bro. But when Icky called I was on duty. I offered to change but he said forget it, that helping you was more important. Did somebody really try to kill both of them?"

"With a fuel–air bomb made out of their boat's own gas tank. Would have, too, if the diver hadn't been careless and bumped the boat. It woke them up. He threw her over the side just in time." He looked at his watch and said, "Come over here. It's time to introduce you."

Raul stood, walked to Mark's side and touched him on the shoulder to wake him. Mark mumbled something rude and tried to turn away, but when his broken arm touched the bed the pain jolted him wide awake.

He sat up and pulled the little silver pistol from under the covers, leveling it at the new face. "Who the hell are you?" he asked, with no effort to be polite.

"Petty Officer First Class Antoine Washington, at your service. I'm a friend."

Mark looked up at the immense black man towering over him and smiling broadly. "Sorry. I wasn't going to shoot you, especially since Raul said he had a friend coming in to help."

Raul turned away from the bed and bent to whisper in Kate's ear.

"Wake up, Commander. Reinforcements have arrived."

Kate was sound asleep, dreaming of the Saturday afternoon she'd spent on the boat with Mark, mainly the time she'd spent in his bed, but she still had the Navy officer's skill of coming fully awake in the blink of an eye. She pushed aside the light blanket and stood up.

"I'm Kate," she said, extending her hand to Antoine. "Thank you for coming to help us out. I have a feeling we're going to need it."

He took her hand. "You're welcome, ma'am. Did I hear Raul address you as Commander?"

"Used to be a Lieutenant Commander. Now Reserves. I was on active duty after Annapolis, but I resigned to go back to school and now I work for Mark. Call me Kate."

"I'm here to help," Antoine said. "Raul, what's the drill?"

"We don't know yet who is on our side and who's not, so for now it's us against the world. I've made arrangements for Mark to get a new room, one that's on the inside of the building and has a locking door, but I don't know yet where it will be. They already have more patients than they can handle here.

"As soon as I hear from the nurse, I'll take Mark and Kate. We'll walk, and we'll have to move fast because I want to get us into the new room with the door locked before word gets around about where he's gone."

"So I'll hang back just to see if anyone shows too much interest?"

"You got it," Raul said. "Icky said you were really good at that kind of thing."

"I met him in my SEAL days. That was a long time ago, but I should be okay if we're dealing with civilians.

"He said I should bring you a scrambler cell phone, and you should keep it. It works anywhere in the world." He opened the briefcase and pulled out a plastic box the size of two paperback books.

THE FOUR WERE SOON CHATTING EASILY – Mark and Antoine compared notes about the jobs they'd had in common, which were many since they'd held the same rank. Kate listened and learned more and more about Mark, and liked what she learned. From time to time they broke off to include Raul, who had joined the CIA right out of college and never served in the military. She was not surprised to learn he was a weightlifter by avocation.

Raul had told the nurses to text him the new

room number when they had it, and under no circumstances to come into the room. But the shift had changed and the new nurse hadn't heard the instruction, so when she walked in Raul jumped up, gun in hand.

She was surprised and frightened. "You can't have that in here."

"Federal officer, Nurse. Do you have a new room number?"

Her breathing slowed and she handed him a slip. "Here – Room C658. You can follow the volunteer who will be here in a few minutes with a wheelchair." She beat a hasty retreat.

Raul looked out to be certain she had disappeared.

"Show time," he said. "Mark and Kate, follow me. Antoine, hang back for an hour to see if anyone comes in. I'll text the number to you."

Antoine made a face. "I heard her, man. I'll be there." As he spoke, he was fashioning a roll out of all the extra blankets he could find.

"This is for the bed. If somebody comes in I want him to see this and think Mark is still here. If he's distracted he'll be less of a problem."

Raul stuck his head out into the corridor and looked left and right.

"All clear," he announced to the others. "The nursing station is down the hall to the right, around the corner, with the elevator beyond. The wheelchair is a smokescreen -- we're going the other way, to take the stairs up two floors."

Antoine watched until the stairway door closed behind them. He pulled the sheet back and placed his dummy in the center, then pulled up the covers and positioned the straight chair behind the door. He opened his briefcase to retrieve his service pistol, a long-barreled 9mm automatic, clicked the safety off and on, then sat down to wait and listen.

He didn't have to wait long. In less than twenty minutes he heard a soft rap on the door and stood up, pressing his back against the wall.

It opened slowly. Through the gap between the hinges he could see an elderly woman push on it, a wheelchair waiting beside her.

A volunteer, he thought with relief. Not another thug. He let the gun fall to his side.

He was premature. A deep, threatening voice said, "I'll take it from here, lady."

"This is my job, young man. I'll move Mr. McGinley like I was told to do. You go find someone else."

"We'll see about that, lady," the man said. Antoine peered back through the gap just as the man grabbed her by the shoulders and tossed her aside. She went sprawling across the hall like a rag doll and he heard her head hit the wall. He saw the man pull a silenced automatic from his belt.

Antoine raised his own gun and waited. It only

took a few seconds for the thug to walk into the room and fire two quick shots into the blanket rolled up on the bed. Antoine heard the second bullet ricochet, but it rebounded off the floor and the far wall, then embedded itself harmlessly in the ceiling.

Antoine stepped forward and brought the butt of his gun down hard on the shooter's wrist. The pistol clattered to the floor, bounced once and stopped under the bed.

The fight ended without ever really starting.

Antoine was almost a foot taller and fifty pounds heavier than the intruder. With his free hand, he grabbed the man by the neck and pulled him fully into the room, tossing him face-first onto the ruined bed. He placed the muzzle of his gun at the point where the man's skull met his neck.

"Fight over," he said with a growl. "Next quick move earns you a shot in the head, no warnings. Do you understand that?" The man nodded.

The automatic and its silencer went into Antoine's briefcase and a roll of gray tape came out. He fastened the hit man's ankles together, then wrapped the duct tape around his right wrist and stretched it to the foot of the bed, where he wrapped it several times around the steel frame.

He took the other arm and stretched it out toward the head of the bed and gave it the same treatment, then pressed the nurse call button.

He propped the room door open and went out to

look at the injured volunteer. The entire episode, tape and all, had taken less than two minutes.

A nurse had heard the noise and knelt beside the volunteer, who lay crumpled against the wall. Antoine reached down to show his ID as he dialed 911.

The nurse touched the volunteer gently and told her, "Miss Rosalita, you lie just where you are while this man gets some help for us."

"I'm sorry to tell you that you need to send the officers back to the hospital right away," Antoine said into the phone. "The man they took away earlier today had a partner. We have him trussed up and waiting for you." He returned the phone to his pocket and turned to the nurse.

"We had another attempt on Mr. McGinley's life. He put a couple of bullets through your bed, but I've immobilized him until the police arrive.

"There's something else very important you should know. The police are going to want to know where Mr. McGinley went. They think it's a local criminal investigation, but they're wrong. It's become a serious federal matter.

"It's critical that you not give anyone, and that includes the police, his new room number. They can get it from me or from my CIA colleague, Raul Gutierrez.

"Is that clear enough?" He smiled, but the smile didn't reach his eyes, which were dead and flat.

"Yes, sir. I'll tell the others. I noticed his new room isn't in the computer, either. Did you do that?"

"Agent Gutierrez spoke with the hospital manager, who was very cooperative."

Miss Rosalita stirred at Antoine's feet.

"Mister, can I go sit in the wheelchair?" she asked. "I think I'm okay."

"You sure can." He put his ham-sized hands under her arms and said, "Now you just relax."

He picked her up and placed her gently on the blue seat cushion, then clicked the chair's brakes into place.

"Who was that man?" she asked. "And what was he trying to do? Nothing good, I wager."

"You'd win that bet. He was up to no good. I have him tied up on the bed, so he isn't going anywhere before the police arrive. They'll be here soon."

They chatted amiably until two orderlies arrived and helped her lie down on a gurney. They told him Miss Rosalita had been one of the nursing staff's favorite volunteers for years, then turned and wheeled her toward the elevators. As they left, they passed Detective Willimon, accompanied by two patrolmen in blue summer uniforms, walking toward him with guns in their hands.

"You won't need the guns, officers," Antoine said. He pulled out his Navy ID and showed it to the lieutenant, making certain to maintain a grip on it.

"Petty Officer First Class Antoine Washington,

NCIS," he said. "Another intruder entered Mr. McGinley's room and tried again to kill him. You'll find him inside the room, taped to the bed."

The detective looked in. Frustrated and exhausted, the attacker had quit struggling but kept up a stream of insults, most of them racial.

"How did NCIS get involved? I thought this was a CIA operation?" Willimon asked.

"It was, and is, but we got an emergency request for help from a very senior man in Washington.

"Anyway, Mr. McGinley and Commander Mickelwaite – Ms. Hall – have been moved to a safe place. I hung back just in case, and sure enough, this fellow came through the door shooting."

"Was anyone hurt?"

"He pushed an elderly volunteer pretty hard. She just passed you on that gurney, on the way to the ER. I think she'll be fine, though."

"What about the shots?" Willimon asked.

"He fired two shots from a suppressed automatic. Both hit the bed – there was a decoy roll in it. I suspect you'll find both the cartridges and the bullets. I'll give you his pistol. It has a very expensive suppressor, a kind I've only seen once before, when I took it off the leader of a drug gang."

As they spoke, the two patrolmen were pulling the duct tape away roughly, ignoring the man's curses and cries of pain. Then they cuffed his hands behind him and cut the tape from around his ankles.

"Will you have Mr. McGinley call me later?" Willimon said. "He'll probably be released in the morning. I'd like to talk to him and see his shop. I suspect the sub is long gone from my jurisdiction, but I want to help him get it back. And we'll need him as a witness against these two goons."

"I've just met him this one time, but I'm sure he'll be available. I'll pass on your message."

THE DOOR of C658 opened a crack and Kate's face appeared.

"Antoine! We thought it might be the police. Did you get bored?"

"Not really. Another goon came to visit, this one with a gun. The bed did not come out well, but he did worse."

The door closed behind him. Raul and Mark looked up from a small table. The scrambler cell phone lay on it.

Raul held a finger to his lips, then talked to the phone. "Icky, Antoine just came in. He says there was a second attempt. It looks like he's okay."

Icky's voice came tinnily from the phone's small speaker.

"Antoine, first, thanks for stepping in to help. Second, are you in good shape, not hurt?"

"I'm fine. The intruder was not as heavy as me

and not as tall as you, but big enough to be trouble. He came through the door and put a couple of bullets in what he thought was Mr. McGinley, but he didn't know I was there. I disarmed him and called the police."

"Thanks for doing that with your usual style," Icky said. "Can you help us out for a day or two?"

"Sure. I have a couple of cases going, but my C.O. will be fine with it. I'll call him first thing in the morning."

"Perfect. Raul, go over the plan one more time, please."

"Sure. First, you'll fly in late this afternoon and rent a car."

"Right. I don't want any of you to leave until I get there. We'll go together," Icky said.

"Then we'll all go to Mark's shop."

"Right again. Antoine, could you get a couple of forensics people over there in the morning?"

"Consider it done."

Icky continued. "Kate will go to her home, with an escort, to pack a suitcase just in case we have to follow the sub somewhere. Then we'll all go to Mark's house and look it over, and he can pack."

"How long should I pack for?" she asked.

"A week or two. If it goes longer you can buy stuff. From what I hear the two of you travel cheap, now that you don't need but one room."

Kate reddened slightly. Mark looked at her, smiled, and shrugged.

"It's our patriotic effort to save the government a little money," he said.

THE DAY PASSED SLOWLY. The chief of nursing on the wing had spent twenty years as a Navy nurse and was anxious to help. She told them conspiratorially that she'd make sure they were fed, and promised with a wink that it would be better food than the typical patient ate. The club sandwiches she brought in for lunch lived up to her promise.

She sent an orderly with salve for Mark's burned head and shoulder, but Kate sent him away and kept the salve, which she was applying very carefully a few hours after lunch when Icky ducked through the door, barely clearing the top of the frame.

He explained that his team had learned some of Willimon's background, but it turned out that Kate knew more than he did so she completed the briefing.

As soon as the sun had set, Raul alerted the hospital's security chief that his group would leave in an hour. To help them, the chief assigned a young policeman who worked days for one of the village departments scattered through Miami-Dade County. He would stay with them until they left and make certain there were no misunderstandings with the security or medical staff. And he was excited to get a chance to work with the CIA, because his main career goal was to be an FBI agent.

"Nice guy but God only knows why he'd want to work for those clowns," Raul lamented, out of the man's hearing. Friction between the CIA and FBI was a standing joke in both services.

Icky's rented SUV, a huge Cadillac, stood close to the loading dock. The hospital guard checked the few parked cars that remained in the area and found them empty. Mark and Raul rode with Icky directly to McGinley Engineering. Antoine took Kate and they headed across Biscayne Bay to her condo. Raul would pick up his car later.

"Mark, do you have any idea who might want to steal the sub?" Icky asked as they drove up I-95.

"Not really. Of course it could always be some local guy who's looking to ransom it, but he'd have to be pretty unaware, because the sub itself is still in beta. In six months it would be worth a lot bigger ransom."

Icky thought a minute. "That local kidnapper probably wouldn't try to kill you and Kate, would he?"

"Not unless he's profoundly stupid," Mark said. "Right now all of the final software changes are in my head, and hers. A competitor might think he could finish the job, but I doubt it. I wouldn't be willing to take on somebody else's project at the stage where ours is right now. The engineer I fired would know a lot of it, but he's been gone a year and we've made a lot of changes since then."

Icky thought for a minute. "So I guess what I'm saying is that it's probably somebody big. A major defense contractor would just come in and offer you so much money you couldn't refuse, so it's probably not one of those.

"My guess is that it's a foreign government, or somebody working for one. They would assume you wouldn't ever sell it to them, at least willingly. The thugs who came after you had the odor of Russians, or maybe Eastern Europeans. At least the first one did."

Mark added, "It might even be somebody completely outside the defense industry, like the man Raul gave my name to, Frank Matthews."

"Who?" Raul said.

"He came to see me Friday and said you'd told him at a police party Thursday night he should see me about buying the sub for commercial users. I told him that wouldn't happen unless the government turned it down, which would take a long time."

"I wasn't at a police party or any other kind of party Thursday night. I was watching a Russian mafioso in South Beach, starting at sunset and going well past midnight."

"Well, there's our first key clue. Mark, did you get some ID?"

"I photographed his business card and driver's license and turned on the high-res cameras in the office, so we should have a good picture."

"Good. And even though he's been gone a while, we need to assume that your former engineer is involved somehow. I presume he could finish up the software work if you were out of the picture?"

"A lot of it, but there are changes that I'd never even thought of until Kate came on board," Mark said. "His brain was so pickled the last couple of months I wouldn't put a lot of money on how much he remembers."

Icky said, "As soon as you called I brought in a team to start looking. One of the first things they did was check private jet departures around the time your boat blew up. I'll know more about them within a few hours, but I'd bet next month's paycheck that your gadget is somewhere in Europe right now, probably on a Gulfstream that left around three a.m.

"One of the places the Gulfstream stopped was Paris, or more precisely Saint-Yan, a smaller airport an hour's flight from Paris. It wasn't the only stop they made, but if I were going to sell something in Europe I'd want to set up shop in either London or Paris, and the plane didn't stop near London.

"I think Paris is where we start."

Mark asked, "Does that mean I'm going there?"

"That's the obvious choice. Of course, we'll be looking for web and other chatter that might give us another lead. We can relay things to you for help with deciphering. No one could do that better than you two. And we might find something that would point us in another direction."

Icky took the expressway exit while Mark tried to pull together everything that was going on.

He broached the question directly. "I just need to understand something. Two weeks ago you'd only heard the outline of my project, basically what we talked about at the beginning. Even now, Kate and I aren't sure the sub itself would pass our tests, much less yours. So why are you throwing all this effort and money at a beta project, rather than just ask us to build a replacement?"

Icky glanced at him and asked, "And how long would that take?"

"A year, tops. The first one took two years, but I was inventing as I went along."

Icky looked at him. "I thought so. Mark, I don't have a year. We have problems that are small now but are going to get bigger soon if we don't do something about them, and your brilliant combo is just what we need. In all honesty, I don't have a choice."

"Then I suppose I don't have a choice, either. Can Kate come, too?"

"Not 'can.' Must. She's lived in France, she

speaks some French, and she can be very polished when she has to be."

"How do you know all that? She never told me any of it."

"You know she was married to an admiral. Even if he turned crazy at the end of his career, which he did, he was a very important figure in his prime. She's seen the inside of more embassy receptions than anyone should have to put up with. She'll go. If I read her correctly, she won't let you go anywhere without her."

INSPECTION TOUR

From the street, Mark's house showed no sign of entry. He opened the outside gate, then led the way up the nineteenth-century staircase to the broad porch, where he used a different code to unlock the front door.

"Let's go check the entry log," he said, and walked into the office off the wide entrance hallway.

On a control panel attached to the wall, he entered his access code then scrolled up as one short line after another appeared on the small screen. "Nothing," he said. "There were no entries or attempts after the time Kate and I left to go sailing, except for her visit last night. There was a two-second power blip after she left, but other than her, nobody's been in here."

HE PACKED A SMALL BAG, then directed Icky the few blocks to the shop, where he put the bag next to the yellow case containing Kate's wetsuit. In the half-hour before Kate and Antoine arrived, he led a careful tour, looking for signs that might point them to the burglars.

"They knocked the wall down, rolled Pegasus into its trailer, probably with Icarus in it, and drove out with no one the wiser. They knew we were asleep on the bay and the street in front doesn't get a lot of traffic, so all they had to do was steal the backhoe and tear down a wall. Whoever did it knew the alarm system, so we've narrowed that down. Wherever this road ends, there we'll find Tom Farkas or one of his friends."

Icky asked, "Didn't you change the codes when he left?"

"Of course. But in his shoes, I'd have put a Trojan horse in place when I started to get in trouble with the boss. There's always some way to do an inside job."

"We think they drove it to an airport, put it on someone's bizjet, and flew away," Icky said.

"We're suspicious of one flight in particular. It was an insurance company's Gulfstream V, one of the few business jets big enough to carry the sub in one piece, and it left Fort Lauderdale Executive Airport in the early hours yesterday. It made four stops in Europe and could have dropped the cargo at any one of them. Or it could be a complete dead end.

"I suspect we've found the right one. The problems we're having are in Eastern Europe. I think that's where our burglars will try to sell it, if they're the kind of people I suspect."

"What kind is that?" Mark asked?

"The Russians are stirring up the old European nationalists. Putin found, after he swallowed Crimea and invaded Ukraine, that he'd bitten off more than he could chew. The sanctions we and the Europeans put on Russia are crippling their economy at the time when they can least afford it. Putin plays a long game and might have been able to withstand all that, but he didn't foresee that the price of oil would collapse."

"So he might have had it stolen?"

"I don't think so, but I'd be surprised if someone no more than two or three levels below him isn't at least aware. There's a lot of unrest along the western edge of the old Soviet Union. The nationalists are very unhappy about the flood of refugees from the Middle East, and they're using that to turn their own governments into near-dictatorships.

"I can imagine a situation where an Eastern European country wants to beef up its military and use something like this to spy on its own people, or where it wants to use it as a bargaining chip, either with us or with the Russians. Maybe with the European Union.

"Or maybe it's some sort of splinter group trying to make trouble. Either way, the market is in Eastern Europe, and the gateway to Eastern Europe, the place where everybody with money wants to go, is Paris."

———

"OUR NEXT STOP has to be Langley," Icky said after Kate and Antoine walked in. "I'll have a Company plane pick us up tomorrow somewhere away from Miami, but for now we need a safe place to stay tonight. We shouldn't stay here at the shop any longer than we have to, and we definitely shouldn't go back to either Mark's or Kate's places."

"How about NCIS?" Antoine responded. "The ready room is secure and has bunk space. It's nothing grand, but it's a safe place, and you can leave in a couple of our cars. They might be on the lookout for yours."

"Good idea." Icky said. "Let's get out of here, pronto."

In a half-hour they pulled through the gate of the Navy's massive operations center on the coastal highway. Antoine led the way to a three-story annex inside the complex and ushered them into a big room lined with bunk beds two deep.

"This is the ready room," he said. "It's only used when we have an operation going, or when we need to staff up for a hurricane or something like that. You'll find cold drinks in the refrigerator and a few snacks in the cabinet, but I can't guarantee how fresh they are."

Icky finished a call and put his phone back into his pocket. "The plane will arrive around noon at a little airport on the edge of the Everglades, about a two-hour drive from here. We need to leave at ten o'clock," he announced.

"I'll get the cars set up," Antoine said.

"We have time for a few hours of shut-eye. It's been a long day. Lights out."

TWO BLACK SUBURBANS with heavily tinted windows picked them up, still groggy from too little sleep, and two hours later stopped on the apron of Palm Beach International Airport, on the Atlantic coast north of Miami.

Raul and Antoine stayed in Miami to find out more about the two men who'd tried to attack Mark and Kate in the hospital. Two armed sailors took their places for the ride to Palm Beach.

"I wanted an airport that was close enough to Miami that we could drive it in a reasonable time, as well as one that had enough routine business jet traffic that one more Gulfstream wouldn't look out of place," Icky said. "The pilot suggested this one. It's far enough away from Miami, so there probably aren't any watchers around."

A SMOOTH TWO-HOUR flight took them directly to Dulles Airport, where two more Suburbans waited for them outside the business jet terminal.

Icky asked the Navy guards to ride in the first car. He got into the second with Mark and Kate.

"You'll only be here one night. We'll have documents ready for you tomorrow, then you'll fly commercial to Paris and meet Eddie Grant. I don't have any reason to think we have a leak inside the Company, but Admiral M. has a lot of contacts and I'm told he's saved up a lot of dirt on some of them, so just in case we'll keep our heads down. For the same reason, I'm going around the Paris station manager."

"So Eddie will be our contact?" Kate asked.

"I will ask him to meet you. You may or may not know that he's a volunteer, what we call an unofficial, which is good because we need an outsider for this. Aurélie works closely with him on everything. They live in each other's pockets.

"You'll also meet a man named Jeremy Bentham. Eddie and I served under him in Desert Storm. He's a retired two-star and a well-known scholar of

Eastern Europe who's lived in Paris since he retired from the army.

"Eddie is a pretty well-known businessman with a real knack for making money. And there are a few other people he works with from time to time, including the guy who was our top sergeant, Paul Fitzhugh. You'll meet all of them eventually, but I don't know exactly who will be at the airport."

THE SMALL CONVOY turned off the Beltway onto Georgetown Pike. Five minutes later it pulled up to the back door of a four-story building whose sign announced the Hotel Langley. The private elevator had only two buttons – ground and fourth. Icky touched an ID card to the reader on the keypad and it ascended to the top.

"This is where we put out-of-town guests to get them ready for travel. That way we can skip the super security at headquarters and give you a little more privacy, not to mention the chance to go out to a restaurant if you want. You can also call for room service, which comes in from a pretty good place across the Pike. Tonight I'd like you to stick with room service."

Their suite was large, dominated by a king bed and an immense television set and sofa. Next to the bed was a door that led to a small conference room.

"We're going to issue you official passports, which don't give as much protection as diplomatic ones, but they're the best I can do right now, and you probably won't use them anyway. In a couple of hours the photographer will come to take your pictures and get the other information we'll need. After that, I suggest you call in dinner and relax.

"By tomorrow I'll know more about where the mystery plane went and will give you an update. Your plane leaves Dulles around eight."

"A COUPLE OF HOURS," Mark said as he took Kate's hand and pulled her toward the bed.

"Plenty of time," she said, grinning. "But what are the odds they'll be watching?"

"Close to a hundred percent. We can stay under the sheet if you'd be more comfortable."

"What the hell? Why should we change now?"

"LUNCH," Icky announced proudly as Kate opened the door at one o'clock the next day. "We have pizza, plus some really great hamburgers from a joint down the street, and some Diet Cokes. Let's get to work."

He spread the food on the desk. Mark reached for a cheeseburger, Kate for a slice of pizza.

"Pepperoni is my favorite," she said. "But I will only have one slice. You guys eat the rest."

Icky took a hamburger and opened a Coke.

"Let's see what we have here," he said. He reached into his briefcase and pulled out two brown envelopes.

"Kate, this one is for you," he said, handing it to her. He gave the second to Mark, who cleared away his burger wrapper, opened the envelope and dumped its contents onto the desk. A maroon passport and a fat letter-sized envelope fell out. Kate slit her packet open and extracted a passport and similar envelope.

"Each of you now has an official passport," said Icky. "You need to keep your regular passports, too, since the official ones are for use only when you're traveling for the government. The image we want to present for now is that of businesspeople trying to get back their stolen property. If you get into trouble the official passports may be a help, though.

"The smaller envelope is money and your boarding passes. You each have eight thousand euros in a variety of bills, which comes to just under ten thousand dollars at today's exchange rate. The finance people insisted we keep it below the level that interests the IRS. It's yours to use as you need, but do keep some records in case I get audited.

"And there's a debit card for each of you on HSBC. It's a big international bank that seems to be in trouble with the government all the time, but they have branches everywhere. Another ten thousand euros will always be available. And Eddie will have French cell phones for you when you arrive. He will be the lead on this case.

"Is there anything you'd like me to keep for you? Raul said you had a gun…"

"That's right," Mark said. "TSA wouldn't approve." He rummaged in his small suitcase for the Glock and handed it to Icky.

"The police took my knife but Antoine got me a new one. I'll hold on to it. In checked luggage it should be OK," Kate said.

"Then this is the last time I'll see you. A car will come to get you around five o'clock, and at eight you'll be on your way to Paris. Give my regards to Eddie and Aurélie, and good luck. We really need your sub back."

8

LUXEMBOURG GARDENS

Paris

A slim man wearing a faded blue golf shirt crouched just inside the worn and weathered boards outlining the *pétanque* court. With a smooth underhand, he flipped a palm-sized steel ball toward his target, a little collection of identical balls clustered around the smaller white target, the *cochon*. It glinted as it spun in the afternoon sun but landed far short, the backspin kicking up dust. His three friends jeered, but gently. "Your turn to buy," one of them said.

"I think that's our cue," Eddie Grant said to Aurélie Cabillaud as the game came to an end. He stuffed their sandwich wrappers into a sack and stood up from the green bench. "Ready?"

Eddie and Aurélie had been coming to Luxembourg Gardens at least once a month since their marriage two years before, joining hundreds of other Parisians out to enjoy the fresh air and the beauty of the impeccable landscaping. Today, an August scorcher, was an especially good time to luxuriate in the cool shade of the trees and watch a few games of *pétanque* or tennis.

Parisians since birth, they normally looked forward to the brisk half-hour walk from the Left Bank to the Right, skirting Aurélie's office at the Sorbonne. But a ninety-degree day, far hotter than Paris had seen in years and twenty degrees above normal, made their decision easy. Eddie called an Uber.

A FEW MINUTES LATER, Eddie and Aurélie settled into the back seat of a white Renault Mégane. It pulled away from the curb, made a U-turn and headed down Boulevard Saint-Michel toward the Seine.

Eddie's iPhone rang. He looked suspiciously at the screen, then at Aurélie, and said, "Icky. I should take it." She nodded.

Eddie and Icky Crane – born Thomas Jefferson Crane but nicknamed Icky because of his height and gaunt frame – had met as ROTC cadets in Texas. They'd each left the army when their tours ended, and Eddie had returned to Paris, where he'd been born and lived until college. Icky had gone into the CIA.

"Hello, sport," Icky said. "How's everybody?" Icky's usual telephone manner was abrupt almost to the point of rudeness, and he almost never opened a call with pleasantries. Eddie knew the signs. He was about to hear a big ask.

"We're both fine," Eddie replied cheerfully.

Aurélie added, "Hi, Icky. Jen doing well? When's she due?" They had slipped effortlessly into English.

"Two months," Icky replied.

They leaned close together so both could hear his side of the call. Eddie turned down the volume so the driver wouldn't be able to overhear, although he seemed completely absorbed in a complex rap.

"Eddie, I need some help and have to apologize in advance for the short notice. I thought about asking Jeremy, but he and Juliette have gone to Provence. Are you going anywhere this month? I thought everybody in France went to the beach in August."

"We're going to stay around town," Eddie said. "Paris is nice in August. Don't believe the propaganda about everything being closed. The restaurants even spread their vacations around so there's always something."

"Here's the story," Icky began. "I was impressed with the video Mark McGinley and Kate Hall made a couple of weeks ago. They have a little autonomous sub, with a built-in helicopter, that I really need. Their setup would be perfect for sailing up the rivers of Eastern Europe to troll for stuff we can't easily pick up by satellite. There's been a whole new flowering of autocrats in that part of the world, and too many of them are cozying up to Russia.

"You saw what happened in Crimea and the rest of Ukraine. We can't afford to have that happen to a NATO country."

Eddie stopped him. "Of course I'll be happy to help, and I have some time, but—"

"Somebody stole the sub," Icky interrupted. "We think they flew it to Paris, although it could have been two or three other European cities, but Paris is the best guess right now."

"Wouldn't you be better off talking to the police? Philippe doesn't like the Russians much."

"Political problems. There's another wrinkle. Whoever stole the sub tried to kill Mark with a limpet mine while he was anchored out with Kate last Saturday night. Damn near succeeded, too.

"We think Kate's ex-husband's fingerprints may be on this somewhere, either because of politics or because of jealousy."

"My God!" Aurélie interjected. "I thought she was rid of that guy."

Icky replied, "Her divorce is final but he's persistent. And since you and I pretty much set her up with Mark I think we need to help get her out of it.

Not that she can't do that by herself, but this may be touchy.

"All of that is a long way of saying I don't want to do anything using official means until I know more about that. I'm already borrowing manpower from the Navy in Miami."

"Jeez. No wonder you're so friendly today. This could be a nasty mess," Eddie said.

"Just your sort of thing," Icky said with a chuckle.

Eddie raised a questioning eyebrow at Aurélie. She shrugged, the signal that she was ready.

"Sure. We'll look at it. What's first?"

"I have to get Mark and Kate out of harm's way. We got them outfitted with new passports, official ones, just in case they get in trouble. Tonight we'll put them on Air France to de Gaulle. Can you take it from there?"

"How long do you think they'll be here?"

"No idea. Is Aurélie's apartment free?" She had owned an apartment since her student days at the Sorbonne and rented it to tourists from time to time.

"We'll have to ask the agent. If not, we'll find something," Eddie replied. "That's a small thing. Aurélie and I will pick them up at CDG in the morning if you'll text me the flight number and arrival time."

Aurélie interrupted. "Sorry. I have class in the morning. Can you take Paul?"

"Correction," Eddie told Icky. "Aurélie has to work. Paul and I will do it."

THE DRIVER TOOK Pont Royal across the Seine, then ducked into the tunnel that passes under the Tuileries Garden at the end nearest the Louvre. They went around the block to Rue Saint-Roch, where they stopped in front of the old stone building housing the Hotel Luxor. A porter stopped polishing its discreet brass nameplate and opened the door for Aurélie.

As the elevator rose toward their apartment on the seventh floor, Aurélie said, "Poor Kate. We should do everything we can. I think my place is open. I can call the agent. But let's invite them to stay here at least one night, so they can relax a bit. Paris can be intense for Americans who get dropped in without warning. Will they need one room or two?

"They were overnighting together on the sailboat. That's pretty cozy, so my guess is one room."

9

WHO IS HE AND WHO'S BEHIND HIM?

MIAMI

Raul and Antoine stood on First Street, two blocks from the courthouse. The address on Frank Matthews' card was a lime-green one-story frame relic that seemed to tilt a bit to the right. A peeling sign said "DUI? See Frank." An arrow outlined in red lights, half of them dead, pointed to a sagging screen door. Antoine had to duck to clear the door frame.

It looked nothing like a lawyer's office. They stopped at what had once been a reception counter but was now covered with old newspapers and file folders stacked in haphazard piles just a strong breeze away from tumbling onto the floor. A bell in the back chimed and a man's voice said, "Just a minute. Have a seat."

The only chairs they saw were covered in papers so they stood, backing a safe distance away from the stacks.

The man who came through the door was definitely the one whose picture was on the driver's license Mark had photographed, and in the pictures from Mark's specialized cameras.

"I'm sorry the air conditioning is off this afternoon, but they have to order a part," he said. Raul figured he'd made the same excuse all summer.

Antoine extended his ID card and introduced himself.

"We're investigating a marine problem and thought you might be able to help us. We'd like to ask about your visit to McGinley Engineering last week."

Matthews looked confused. "I think you're looking for somebody else. I don't know anything about engineering."

Antoine reached into the black file folder he was carrying and pulled out the picture Mark had made of the driver's license. "Will this help refresh your memory, sir?" He showed it to Matthews.

"That looks like my license, but I lost my wallet a couple of weeks ago. Anybody could have it."

Raul fidgeted impatiently, but Antoine gave him a look that warned him to back off.

"Maybe this one will make it easier for you, sir," he said, pulling out a print made from Mark's own surveillance camera. "This man looks quite a bit like you, I'd say."

"I haven't done anything illegal," Matthews mumbled, flustered.

"We're not here to accuse you of anything illegal," Antoine told him gently. "We just want to know why you went to see Mark McGinley. When we know that we'll leave."

"It's just like I told him at the time. I met one of his friends at a party a day or two before, and he told me Mr. McGinley was building a drone submarine. I went to see if it was something I could maybe sell to a toy manufacturer or one of those fancy catalog stores that sells expensive gadgets."

"This person you met. Who was he and where did you meet him?"

"At a party over in the courthouse. It was a police affair. One of my neighbors invited me to go, and he introduced me to this customs agent, Raul Gutierrez. Raul gave me his card with Mark McGinley's name written on it, so I decided to try. That's all there was to it. Honest."

By then, it was obvious Matthews knew he was in deep, and both of them wanted to bring his charade to a quick end. Raul cleared his throat as a signal and Antoine took a step back to let Raul continue the questioning.

"Mr. Matthews, can you describe Raul Gutierrez to us?"

"Not really. He was a little taller than you are, but I'd had a lot to drink by that time and wasn't focusing real well."

"Taller than me covers basically everybody. Did he maybe look a little like me?"

"He could have."

"Maybe more than just a little? The game you're trying to play has gone on long enough. You're a lawyer, so you know you've already committed a felony by lying to a federal officer. But what's worse, you've been stupid. You see, I'm Raul Gutierrez, and I definitely didn't tell you anything about Mark McGinley because I was nowhere near that party, if it happened at all.

"Would you like to tell us the truth now? It's pretty important to your future."

"What do you want to know?" Matthews' shoulders drooped.

"Let's go back to the first question," Raul said. "Why did you go to see Mark McGinley last Friday?"

"A man called and offered me a lot of money to do it, a thousand dollars cash. You don't get that kind of money from my clients, so I took it. He told me what to say and what information he wanted. I didn't get much, because I never got to see the sub itself — the government classified it that day, my bad luck."

"Who hired you?" Antoine asked.

"He never gave me his name. He called me Friday morning and said he had a two-hour job that

was worth a thousand dollars, and that he was of-
fering it to three lawyers. It would go to the first one
to say yes.

"I told him he could stop looking, because I'd
take it. He said he'd see me in a half-hour with the
stuff I'd need to pull it off, and he was as good as his
word."

"But he never gave you his name."

"He told me names didn't matter, but I could
call him Mr. Smith if I wanted. He gave me an envelope with ten fifty-dollar bills and the business
card, and told me where to go and when to go
there. I was to go late in the afternoon, near closing
time. Then I was to come back here at six-thirty
and deliver my report and get the rest of my
money.

"He wasn't happy that I didn't see the sub, but I
repeated what Mark McGinley told me and that
seemed to satisfy him. He gave me the rest of my
money. He seemed surprised to hear the government
had classified it."

"The guy who paid you the thousand dollars,"
Raul said. "Give us the best description you can."

"He was 'way better dressed than most people
you see on the streets of downtown Miami – a very
expensive blue suit. He was really turned out, very
formal, and that's the way he talked, too.

"But it was his hair that I noticed. It's jet black,
and it's curled into tight ringlets. It looked like he

just stepped out of the beauty parlor. He came across as pretty tough, and he looked really fit for an old guy.

"I wouldn't want him looking for me. He had really mean eyes. And he had a very slight accent, like he was born somewhere in Europe and came here young."

Raul and Antoine looked at each other, puzzled. Frank Matthews was no white-shoe lawyer. He was a drunks' lawyer and the disarray of his office hinted that he might once have been his own client. Both he and the mysterious caller had taken care to see that there was no paper trail of his visit to Mark, even though his front office looked as though he'd kept every document he'd ever seen.

Antoine asked, "Could we see the fifties he gave you?"

"They were gone the next day." Matthews stared at the floor.

Raul blew out a breath, willing himself to hold onto his patience. "Is it possible your phone kept a record of this guy's call?"

"It might have." Matthews rooted around the stacks of paper on the reception desk until he found a telephone and pulled it out. "This one and mine are on the same line. If the call hasn't rolled off into the trash, the number will be here."

His index finger sought out a button marked with a down arrow. The calling number appeared on the left of the small screen, the date and time on the right.

"Here we are. Friday," he said, and the pace of his button presses slowed until he stopped.

"Found it. It's local."

Both Raul and Antoine wrote down the number.

Raul said, "We're going to try to find your mysterious benefactor. It will be better for you if he doesn't hear about us in advance."

"Don't worry about that. I hope I never see him again. The guy scared me."

———

"TURN ON THE AC, man, and quick," Antoine said as soon as they were back in Raul's black government Impala. "Miami in August is no place to be outdoors, and that dump of an office was hell."

Raul ran up the engine speed and turned the AC to max. "So what do we have?"

"Quite a bit," Antoine replied. "We know who Frank Matthews is, or at least part of who he is, and we have a lead on who sent him. We should be able to pin that down before lunch.

"The next guy up the chain of command will be a harder case. He'll be smarter, and he will know he's in danger. If Frank's intuition is right, he may be a threat, too."

"Let's reverse-engineer the number. We might get

lucky and find out it's a business." Antoine said. "I'll try whitepages.com; you try another one."

Antoine turned to his phone and keyed in the number. Before Raul had even found another service, Antoine said, "I got a hit. It's an insurance company with a really odd name –Budapest Re."

"Bingo," Raul said. "That's the company that owns the Gulfstream. They are a reinsurer, an insurance company for insurance companies. Big insurance companies buy insurance to spread their risk. A lot of them are overseas, and a lot of them are very big businesses, even if we peons hardly ever hear of them. And Budapest is in Hungary. Where is their office?"

"Not far. They're just across downtown, near the university. We can be there in ten minutes."

BUDAPEST RE WAS on the third floor of a low office building built of blue brick – "*Very* Miami," Antoine said. Raul pulled into a parking lot down First Avenue and paid the attendant, then they walked back and stopped at the lobby directory.

"Whoever came up with the idea of having a First Avenue and a First Street in the same downtown?" Raul groused.

"Welcome to Miami, and a bunch more Florida cities," Antoine said. "Anyway, they're by themselves on the third floor. That should make it easier to find him. I was chasing a guy in a building like this once and he dodged from suite to suite and slipped out the back door. Fortunately, my partner was waiting for him in the stairwell."

"Should I do that?"

"Not this time. This guy could be a zero, or he could be Mr. Big. That's not likely, but in any case both of us should be there if we get a chance to ask him some questions."

They stepped out of the elevator in front of a glass wall with the name of the company in gold leaf. A receptionist in a short skirt sat behind a plexiglass desk, looking at a computer monitor.

"Looks like Fox News," Raul said with a chuckle.

"I don't know, man. I stay away from bimbo TV."

Antoine presented his identification to the woman and gave her the description of the man they were seeking. She looked puzzled.

"That doesn't sound like anyone here," she said. "Nobody here wears suits, anyway, and there's hardly anybody over forty except Mr. Jonas, the manager, and he's been on vacation for the last ten days."

She thought for a minute. "Excuse me," she said, and went into a glass-walled office close to her desk to talk to another woman, whom Raul took to be a supervisor. The heavy glass blocked most of what was said, but by pretending to talk quietly to each other they could focus on the conversation and make out much of it.

"Wasn't Mr. Molnar here last Friday?" the receptionist asked the other woman, who immediately turned to look at Raul and Antoine. She turned back and waved her finger and her head at the receptionist. She lowered her voice, but Raul thought he heard her say, "We're not ever supposed to say when Mr. Molnar is here. Don't tell them anything." The receptionist's frown told them all they needed to know about her relationship with the supervisor.

The receptionist sat back down at her desk. "I thought there might have been somebody fitting your description visiting the office last Friday, but I was wrong. Sorry, but I can't help you." She glanced toward the window.

Antoine said. "We understand, and thanks for checking. Tell me, does each phone have its own number or do you use a central switchboard?"

The young woman looked at him with pity.

"I'm twenty-five, and I've heard of a central switchboard but I've never seen one. Of course every phone has its own number."

"Could someone else have used Mr. Jonas's number last Friday morning?"

"Absolutely not," she said with certainty. "We all know not to go into his office, and anyway it's been locked the entire time he's been on vacation."

"Does anyone else have a key?"

"I don't think so," the young woman said. It was clear she was getting tired of the questions and wanted them to leave. "The company runs entirely in the cloud. Mr. Jonas and all the agents have their laptops and work almost exclusively out of the office. They report to different people at the head office in California.

"The only other person who ever uses Mr. Jonas's office is the owner of the company, who comes to Miami only a couple of times a year. We have some offices for visiting agents and he usually uses one of those, but last Friday those were full. I thought he might have been here but I guess not."

She inclined her head toward the woman still visible through the glass wall. When the supervisor looked away, she lowered her voice to a whisper. "He is never here more than a day. Someone told me he had a late flight to Paris. He spends a lot of time in Europe."

"And what is his name?" Raul asked, holding his breath.

"He is Mr. Molnar. Max Molnar."

"Why do you think she told us?" Antoine asked as they walked back to the car.

"My guess is that supervisor is a real dragon," Raul responded. "Anyway, Icky has already been looking at

Max Molnar. He's originally from Hungary but made his big money in Silicon Valley and now invests it in businesses all over the United States and Europe, mainly France. He's part of a network of old Eastern European families who had money before World War Two. Most of them supported the Germans and had to leave the country when the Russians took over after the war. Max's father was one of those. He escaped just ahead of the Russians with Max and an older son. His wife died giving birth to Max just a month or two before.

"Icky is looking at him because he supports one of the new pro-Russian political parties in Hungary, and some dangerous Americans have been going there to get involved. And he has political connections."

"Jeez, don't you guys ever deal with anything that's straightforward? You know, like a garden-variety burglary or something like that?"

"The CIA can't do domestic, so we're always looking at things that have an overseas angle, like this one. Icky will get us involved officially now because Mark's sub was doubtless flown out of the country. In fact, we'd better bring him up to date on what we just found. He'll need to tell Mark and Kate about Molnar and that lawyer. Icky has dealt with Molnar before, but I doubt he's seen this aspect of his personality.

"You drive," he said, handing Antoine the keys.

"Let's head down to that fire station on the Inter-coastal, where the rescue boat that picked up Mark and Kate is docked. We need to find out who else was at the scene. Then let's circle back and see that detective, Willimon. Maybe he's identified the two guys who tried to kill Mark in the hospital."

As Antoine steered the Impala down I-95, Raul dialed Icky and left a detailed summary in his voice mail.

THE FIRE STATION stood on the edge of Biscayne Bay, nestled in among a collection of fishing marinas and fast-food restaurants. Antoine pulled into its tiny parking lot, which was paved with crushed seashells packed tight by time..

"The boat's not here," he said, pointing through a rusting fence at the empty dock where it would normally be tied. "There will be a station master, though, and he should have an incident report that will give us some information."

They were lucky. When they stepped into the small room that served as office, kitchen, and crew gathering area, they found a grizzled firefighter just finishing lunch.

Antoine identified himself and told him they were trying to find out the identity of the man who had been in the third boat the night Mark and Kate were pulled from Biscayne Bay.

"We were hoping we might talk to one of the firefighters who made that run, or maybe see the incident report," Raul said.

"This is your lucky day, Chief. You get both, and from an ex-seaman at that. I was driving the boat, and we have a copy of the report here. I was supposed to mail it off to the police today but we had to rescue a boater from New York who managed to capsize his Sunfish, God knows how."

"Wouldn't you always keep a copy here?" Raul asked.

"Yup. But on this one the police want to keep it all in their hands. Do you know the detective on the case, Lieutenant Willimon? He's kind of a strange duck, but effective. He called me yesterday and asked for the original of the report. I couldn't get approval from the county until this morning.

"When I told Willimon that, he said he would pick it up himself later today. So your timing is good."

"We're glad we caught you," Raul said. "What can you tell us about the man in the other boat?"

"Nada. His driver's license was fake, according to Willimon. The only thing helpful we got was the ID number of the boat, and it's a rental registered to a marina up the coast. The guy's license must have been good enough to get a rental, or that's what Willimon thinks, anyway."

Antoine read the report carefully.

"An eighteen-foot sport fisherman with big engines? How many of those do you see anchored out overnight?"

"Not many," the fireman said. "I'm sure there are some, but I don't remember seeing them."

"Did you see scuba equipment on the boat?"

"I didn't, but my partner said there was a stack of something on the cockpit floor, covered with a tarp. It could have been anything. We don't have search powers and we weren't suspicious of him at the time. We thought he was a Good Samaritan trying to rescue a fellow boater."

Raul said, "I can see that. Did anything strike you as strange about him? Could you tell if he was a local?"

"He knew his way around a boat, I'll say that for him. As for local, I don't know about that. He had a little bit of an accent, but not one I could recognize. Of course, if it's not Spanish I probably wouldn't recognize it anyway. The only time I been out of Florida was when I went to the Navy.

"Do you want me to tell Willimon you was here? I don't have no reason to tell him anything, so I won't if it matters to you."

"We're not hiding from him, and we're really looking for different things," Raul said, "But if you don't mind, it might help keep things simpler if he didn't find out just yet."

"I can keep a secret. I helped the FBI bust a Cuban spy once up at Norfolk."

As the door closed behind them, Raul saw the fireman pick up the phone.

"See that? We probably shouldn't depend on him keeping our little secret."

"I never thought he would," Antoine said. "The county guys really hate it when we take a case from them.

"Let's drop by the marina and see if they can shed any light on the guy who rented the boat. The fake ID will make it harder, but somebody might have seen him before."

YEARS OF STANDING in the South Florida sun had faded the marina's sign to a pale, ghostly blue, and Raul drove past it. He turned around in a shopping center parking lot, found the sign, then followed a rutted gravel road for the quarter-mile drive to a remote section of the coastline, halfway between the shopping center and a residential subdivision. It was at least a thousand feet from each, isolated by dense vegetation.

"This doesn't look like a Miami suburb, does it?" Antoine asked.

"Not yet," Raul replied. "But look how close the houses are already. In twenty years it will be solid condos. They'd probably be building now if the recession hadn't shut down the real estate business."

The dockmaster's office was a rickety wooden shack with a tin roof set just inside a chain-link fence. It was empty, but a man gassing up a boat midway down the wooden dock signaled with a wave that he would be there in a minute.

"Look over there," Antoine said, pointing to the chain-link fence. It ended at the water's edge, a few feet behind a garish plastic doghouse, which looked unoccupied.

"Maybe he didn't rent the boat. Maybe he came out here after closing time, stepped around the fence, and helped himself. He could have returned it within a couple of hours."

The dockmaster, meanwhile, had walked over to join them. He was a wizened man of an uncertain age, certainly more than 70, wearing oil-stained jeans, a t-shirt that had once lauded the merits of outboard motors and a faded red baseball cap.

"What can I do for you fellers?" he asked, then spat tobacco into the weedy grass patch along the fence. "You lookin' to do some fishin'? It's been pretty good today."

"Not today," Antoine said, showing his ID. "We're federal officers, and we need to ask you about one of your boats."

"My boats? Did you boys catch somebody shaggin' on one of them?" He looked straight at Antoine and emphasized "boys."

"Nothing that simple, sir," Antoine said. He showed the ID number they'd received from the fire department.

The old man leaned in and peered at the photo. "That one. It's a good, fast sport fisherman but it hasn't been out in a while."

"Can we see it?" Raul asked. "And may we go aboard and look around?"

"Sure. It's the last one on the left, down at the end of the dock."

Antoine said, "And while we're at it, would you tell us who had it rented Saturday night and Sunday morning?"

"Nobody. Like I said, that boat hasn't been out in quite some time, maybe two weeks. I'm thinking of selling it. Costs too much to keep."

"I SEE one of his problems with it," Antoine said. "It's filthy. Would you rent something this dirty?"

"I wouldn't know. I can barely even swim. But what does your sailor's eye tell you?"

"For one, it tells me this marina does more than rent out fishing boats. That old guy doesn't have enough of them to make a living, and all the ones tied up here are just as dirty as this one. I wouldn't be surprised if some strange boats dock here from time to time, maybe carrying stuff they shouldn't be carrying."

They stepped carefully into the boat and looked around. "Our guy didn't leave his scuba gear behind," Raul said. "And the key is on a lanyard tied to the steering wheel, so anybody could start it.

"What's that brown mark on the other side?"

Antoine leaned closer to the gunwale. "My guess is that it's blood, but it's not fresh. On the other hand, it's not real old, either. And it's a gunwale." He pronounced it *gunnel*. "Boats don't have sides."

They took pictures, then walked back to the dockmaster's shack.

"Find anything?" the old man asked.

"Not really," Raul said. "By the way, do you keep records of your gas pump every day?"

"Nah. The state says I'm supposed to but it's too much work. When it gets low I just call and the truck brings another load. Easier that way."

"So there's no way you could tell if someone snuck in here at night and gassed up this boat?"

"It'd be a brave man that did that. I have a really mean watchdog that keeps an eye on things for me, a big Doberman bitch. Or I had. She ran away."

"And when was that, sir?" Antoine asked.

"Saturday night, I guess. When I opened up

Sunday morning she was gone. She's done it before and she always comes back."

Raul and Antoine glanced at each other.

"How did she get away?" Raul asked.

"Damned if I know. When I leave I move her chain from the doghouse over there and hook it to the dock. This Sunday both dog and chain were gone. I used to tie her to a concrete block but she towed that sucker a mile down the highway one time. I figured she could never pull the whole dock."

10

CHASING WILLIMON

As they compared notes in the car, Antoine said, "Now we know how he did it. The poor dog is on the bottom of the bay, wrapped in her own chain. He must have killed her with a knife on the boat."

"He was brave to take on a Doberman, but I don't see any other explanation. Maybe the police will test the bloodstain on the gunwale."

"Do you get the feeling the police are AWOL from this case? This is the second place today they should have visited well before we arrived."

"Maybe they figure they have two men in jail and are working on them to find out more," Raul replied. "But I do think it's odd. There could be a lot of explanations, ranging from lack of resources to some pretty unsavory ones, up to and including police complicity."

"Oof," Antoine said. "I wasn't thinking that far ahead."

"Now that you mention it, though, how could we check on it without stirring up a huge mess?"

"Icky is probably our best bet there. If there's a plot it won't have started here, and it will be better if he's the one to ask those questions."

"Maybe not," Raul replied. "He's tied up with the Paris end of things. How about we pay a call on the lieutenant? We can tell him it's just because the sub was stolen and the killer sounded like a Russian, so he won't feel like we're stepping on his toes. We're only interested in the national security end of the case, but we might get a little idea of why he's been so slow getting off the mark."

"Do you know him at all?"

"I do, but when I met him it was under pretty strained circumstances. Last year we got a lead on a Cuban spy who was working as a cook in a Russian restaurant on South Beach. Supposedly the county and the federal prosecutor coordinated things, but Willimon was in charge and he barged into the kitchen before the judge signed the warrant. It took some fancy footwork to keep the case from being thrown out."

"So he's a hothead," Antoine said.

"Big time. He's worked three or four places. I heard he moved to Florida from Annapolis five years ago after a stash of cocaine went missing from the evidence locker. He worked in a small department somewhere else in Florida until this job came open, but I'm damned if I know how he got it, with the Annapolis rap hanging over him."

Raul looked at his watch, then put the car in gear. "Willimon's office is in the downtown station. Let's try to catch him there. I'd rather walk in without warning."

FORTY-FIVE MINUTES later they were still waiting for him, seated in uncomfortable plastic chairs in an uncomfortably cold waiting room. When Willimon finally arrived he was not friendly.

"I know we probably have to work on this together," he said, "but you snatched my main witnesses and now it looks like you're trying to hijack the investigation. Pardon me if I don't welcome you with open arms."

Raul tried to pacify him, with little success.

"The decision to put them out of sight was an important one, and it was made for their safety," he said. "Anyway, it looks like you have the guy who planted the bomb and the one who tried to finish off Mr. McGinley. Solving the bombing is a lot more important than the theft of a submarine."

"But neither of them is talking. I need to know if they can identify either one of the sailors. It's hard to do that, whether they're in Washington or some-where overseas, or just in a safe house in Orlando."

"Have you been able to identify either one of them?"

"Their IDs were fake, no surprise. The one we think did the bombing is a Russian, we're pretty sure. The other one probably is, too. We're circulating their pictures and we'll eventually find them. They aren't going anywhere, and I plan to interview both of them again before I leave tonight."

"Let me ask you this," Raul said. "How did you know Mark McGinley was working on a submarine?"

"What do you mean?"

"When you questioned him in the hospital you asked about it. It wasn't a classified project at the time, but we're curious about how the word got around. That's all."

Willimon replied, "It was an accident. One of the other businesses in that park had a burglary a month or so ago. I asked the owner about his neigh-bors and he mentioned Mr. McGinley's submarine. It seemed to be pretty common knowledge. I didn't get more information because I was running behind and needed to get to another interview. I could prob-ably find his name for you."

"Maybe later. Right now one submarine is more than enough."

Antoine stepped into the conversation.

"The Navy forensic team tells me no one's been to Mr. McGinley's house. Are you planning to look it over soon? Of course, we'll share anything we've found."

Willimon had been looking down at his desk, but his head snapped up at the suggestion he wasn't doing his job.

"I've had two murders since I got this case," he said archly. "My main witnesses have been taken where I can't get to them, we have the perps in custody, and the submarine is gone, probably out of the country. I figured you were working on that, and I have live suspects but no arrests in my two murders. And we're short-handed.

"I was planning to get to the house tomorrow, and I'm going to pick up the fire department's report later today. That's all I have the resources to do.

"And now I'm busy. Call me any time."

"FIRST TIME I was ever kicked out of a cop's office," Raul said wryly as they walked back to the Impala.

"Can't say it's ever happened to me either," Antoine said. "I can understand why he's a little pissed, but if I were in his shoes I wouldn't want to make us mad. Anyway, we still have time to run down to the marina in Coconut Grove and see if we can find out how the killer knew Mark and Kate would be on the boat overnight."

THEY LEFT the car in the parking lot of the grocery store where Kate had bought dinner and walked down a passageway decorated with a fanciful enamel sculpture of a smiling peacock, its tail fanned into a still life of fruits and flowers.

"The harbormaster has a shed over that way," Raul said, pointing vaguely to the left. "It's close to the Coast Guard hangar."

They walked down the sidewalk, past a sailboat for sale, and found the harbormaster, a young man with close-cropped blond hair, patiently explaining to a couple that they could not dock in someone else's spot. They would have to anchor out and take their dingy or the water taxi in. The news was not well received.

The boaters stalked off toward their trawler.

"Hi, guys," the harbormaster greeted them. He gazed back up the dock, shaking his head and smiling. "Those two just haven't docked in enough busy marinas to understand how things work. What can I do for you?"

Antoine showed his ID. "We're looking into the boat that blew up in the bay last weekend," he said.

"We thought you might know something about the owners."

"Not really. I've known Mark McGinley a long time. He used to sail by himself, but a while back he started bringing Kate with him. Now her I'd like to know better!"

"Really? I think she's almost old enough to be your mother."

"Yeah, she is, but still…" He grinned.

Raul showed his ID and stepped in before the conversation got any more specific.

"What we're looking for, Mr. …. What is your name, by the way?"

"Just call me Jack."

"OK, Jack. What we're trying to find out is how somebody found out Mark McGinley was going out overnight, for the first time in a very long time if not forever. Can you help us with that?"

Jack dropped his voice. "You guys are Feds, right? So we're all on the same side?"

"You bet," Antoine said.

"I've been helping out the police all summer. They have a contract with the CIA to protect Mark because of some super-secret work he does, and the CIA doesn't have enough people to watch him like they'd like.

"Mark always tells me where he's sailing, and he probably wouldn't tell the cops. Nobody likes to think he needs a babysitter.

"Then a cop comes around mid-afternoon on Saturday and I tell him what Mark told me. No big deal. This time it was Kate who told me they'd be out overnight. Lucky guy, Mark."

"Is it always the same police officer?" Antoine asked.

"It's usually one of the guys who works out of the Coral Gables substation. That's just a mile away or so. But they report downtown."

"Any idea who they report to?"

"Sure. A detective. He's even come by once or twice to check. His name's Willimon. He told me he used to be a Fed just like you guys."

11

PICK-UP AT CDG

PARIS

Eddie waited outside the frosted glass doors of the customs area at de Gaulle. Paul Fitzhugh stood to his right holding a sign with "McGinley" printed on it.

"I dunno about this one, Eddie," Paul said. "A drone submarine sounds a little flaky, even for Icky."

"Mark McGinley is a genius, according to Icky. He designed some sort of super gunsight for battle tanks and it made him semi-rich, then Icky asked him to come up with something to gather intelligence in European cities. He figured out pretty quickly that one of the easiest ways to get into those is through the rivers. You could do it with barges but they're huge, ponderous things. As I understand it, this sub is so small and so smart that it would be extremely hard to find. And it drives itself."

Paul interrupted him. "I think that's them coming through the door right now. He's in his forties, she's in her thirties, he's losing his hair, she has a whole lot and it's black. I wish I were younger."

Kate spotted them immediately. She turned and tugged at Mark's sleeve, then pointed to Eddie and Paul.

"THIS IS PAUL FITZHUGH," Eddie said. "Together with Aurélie, we'll get you squared away in Paris. Have you spent much time here?"

Mark answered for both of them. "Other than that one brief trip, I've only been here for a three-day vacation. Kate has seen more of it. I hope we can spend a little time as tourists."

Paul and Eddie each took a suitcase and led them to the Peugeot sedan Eddie and his mother shared. Eddie climbed into the passenger seat.

"We won't do a tour now. You've had a long flight and most of the trip is on the highway. By the time we get downtown it will be time for lunch. Aurélie has classes this morning and can't meet us until later, so we'll grab something on the way. We would like for you to spend tonight with us, then tomorrow we'll find you more permanent quarters."

"We don't want to put you out. Aurélie's already helped me out of a jam more than once. I don't want it to be a habit," Kate said.

"We're looking forward to it. Aurélie really wants to catch up, and both of us need to know more about the problem we're trying to solve. Besides, it will be much easier to communicate if we're under the same roof."

AURÉLIE WAS WAITING when the elevator door opened. "Welcome to *chez nous*," she said with a smile, as she bent to wrap her arms around Kate in a warm embrace. "I am so glad to see you. The story about your sailboat really frightened me. Are you sure you're all right?"

"I'm angry but otherwise fine. Let me introduce Mark McGinley, who tossed me off the boat just in time but couldn't get completely away before the mast fell on him and broke his arm."

Mark extended his hand but Aurélie enfolded him in the same embrace she'd given Kate.

"Welcome both of you to Paris and our home."

TEN MINUTES later the four sat under an awning on

the eastern terrace looking across the rooftops at Notre Dame.

Mark carefully put ice cubes in his glass of chilled and fizzy mineral water but Kate took it without ice, the way Eddie and Aurélie did.

"I see you know the custom. You've been here more than once," Aurélie said to her.

"I've been to a few diplomatic and military receptions, some of them not that far from where we are right now."

Mark was burning to ask about the Luxor. Turning to Eddie, he said, "Captain, could I ask you one question? How did you wind up living in a hotel?"

Eddie looked around, miming a search for the missing captain. "You can ask Eddie anything you want. *Captain* ended a long time ago. We are one hundred percent civilian here."

"Hallelujah!" Kate said quietly.

"The hotel," Eddie said. "Years ago, I was looking for a place to live. At the time this was a once-grand place that had fallen on hard times. It needed renovation.

"I bought it partly because it had this top-floor add-on. There's no way the city would let us build it now, but they're fairly tolerant as long as you don't block anybody else's view, so I got away with it."

"It was sure worthwhile," Mark said. "Notre

Dame on one side, the Eiffel Tower on the other. It's really terrific." He paused. "Eddie."

AURÉLIE WAS fond of socializing and, as a prominent Sorbonne professor and the author of a series of surprisingly popular French history books, she had social duties to fulfill. Eddie faithfully went to everything she was invited to, but she had not succeeded in getting him more comfortable with the shallow chitchat of the cocktail circuit.

He sat impatiently through the small talk as Aurélie tried to put Mark and Kate more at ease, but finally he asked, "Would you like to fill us in on the background? Icky told me some of it, but I'd feel better if I heard it all directly from you. We could wait until tomorrow, but Aurélie has a class and then office hours, so you'd wind up having to go through it twice."

"I'm ready," Mark said. "We need to find the sub."

Eddie said, "I think we should discuss this behind closed doors, so let's go into the living room. It's cooler in there, anyway."

Kate looked up, surprised. "I thought Paris apartments didn't have air conditioning."

"Most don't. The hotel has had it since the renovation because that's what tourists expect. Aurélie and I grew up without it, but it seems summers get hotter every year, so we installed it in our apartment just after we were married. Pretty soon the whole city will need it."

In the living room, he pulled four chairs together around a coffee table, and Aurélie put fresh bottles of water in the center.

Eddie said, "Just start from wherever you need to start. We can take as much or as little time as necessary for this, because I'm sure we'll have to go over it more than once."

"I'VE KNOWN Icky for twenty-plus years," Mark began. "I was Chief Petty Officer on a carrier off Kuwait at the invasion of Iraq in 2003, and Icky and a few other CIA people used it as a headquarters in the early days of the invasion. I understand you and he served together in the first Gulf War twelve years before that."

"That's right. Icky and I went to college and then the army together. Paul was our top sergeant in Desert Storm," Eddie replied.

"Icky knew I wasn't completely happy in the Navy, and he asked me to join the Company," Mark said.

"I'd had more than enough of big bureaucracy for two lifetimes, but I really wanted to stay in the

Navy long enough to qualify for my retirement, so I told him I would wait a while. I also told him I was working on a couple of projects on the side that might interest him. It took me a few years – actually quite a few – but after I retired one of them turned into a special gunsight for battle tanks. He helped me sell it to a big military contractor.

"We lost touch after that, but then one day he called me, real urgent, and said he needed something that would provide a listening post for cities in Eastern Europe. I went to Washington and we chewed it over and later decided a little submarine would be best. But to make it work it would have to operate almost completely without guidance – it would be like setting the GPS for a trip but having the car drive itself, without failure and in secret.

"The problem with a sub is that you can't get much in the way of radio signals to it or from it because it's under water, so we needed something to be the tip of the spear. I had the idea of another piece, a little helicopter that looks much like the toy drones people buy to look over their neighbors' fences, or the TV networks use. But it wouldn't be a toy. In fact, it turned out almost like the full-size drones the military already uses, squeezed down. Theirs are usually fixed-wing craft while ours is a helicopter, but we've managed to incorporate most of the sensors and cameras that you find in the larger ones.

"That's the background. It's been moving quickly

since Kate joined me – that was a very important step forward. The last couple of weeks have been really critical. Icky called and more or less demanded that I show him where things stood, so we set up a demonstration we thought would impress him and invited him to Miami.

"We showed him the video last Friday and he liked it. He classified the project, and we decided to go out to dinner to celebrate. First time we've ever done that."

"Our first date," Kate added.

"And one hell of a date it was. Then we decided to go on our first overnight sail, which should have been a walk in the park, but instead here we are. In Paris, Pegasus and Icarus stolen, and me with a broken wing." He held up the blue sling for emphasis. "The only good part is that we're in Paris."

12

DINNER PLANS AT THE LUXOR

AN HOUR LATER, MARK SAT BACK IN HIS CHAIR. "And that's our weekend so far.

"There are parts of it I'd love to do over, but the last two days were something I hope never to go through again." He looked at Kate and smiled as he patted her hand.

"It was awful," she said. "I thought I'd lost him just a few hours after I found him."

Eddie stood up. "It's mid-afternoon, and you two are probably exhausted. Why don't you take a nap? I'll try to reach Icky to see if they've found anything at that end, then we'll have dinner. Mark, will you need a doctor for the arm?"

"I don't think so. It only hurts if I move it wrong and the doc in Miami said that would go away in a week or so. I was lucky. If the mast had landed on my head the outcome would have been much different."

"Dinner will be carry-in," Aurélie interjected. "I have homework before my classes tomorrow."

They followed her down the hall into a guest room she had decorated much like Paris apartments of the nineteenth century, except that heavy red brocade had been replaced by lighter fabrics and the wood was blonde rather than dark mahogany. She flipped a switch and a crystal chandelier in the ten-foot ceiling brightened the tan walls. Eddie had already put their suitcases on racks, ready to open.

Kate opened a floor-length window that looked onto the wooded courtyard below, protected only by a steel bar and an ornate panel whose ironwork repeated the profile of Notre Dame behind it.

"Watch out for that window," Aurélie said. "Until we added the grill last year there was only the bar between us and eternity."

"But the view is so calm and it seems so cool. Who would believe a block in the center of Paris would have a park like this in it?" Kate said. Mark moved to her side and put his good hand on her shoulder.

"A lot of Paris blocks have green space at their centers," Aurélie said. "At one time most of them did, but apartments and office buildings have been built in some of them."

She looked at her watch. "It's now four. Dinner

will be at eight thirty. Should we knock around seven thirty?"

"No need," Mark said, holding up his iPhone. "I'll set an alarm and we'll come out a little before eight thirty."

"Good. We'll have an apéritif."

AURÉLIE FOUND Eddie in the small bedroom he'd converted into a secure office. She closed the heavy soundproof door and sat down on a small sofa as he read intently from the screen of his laptop.

"Anything new?"

"Email from Icky. It looks like Kate may be on to something when she suspects her ex-husband. They weren't even on the plane to Paris before the admiral called Icky's boss, on the warpath about his ex-wife being put in danger and demanding that Mark be arrested for it." He turned the screen so she could read it.

"Is there any chance that's true?"

"Almost none. The fire department's investigation agreed with what Mark told Icky, and that agrees with what he told us. They raised the sailboat and found a hole in the hull next to the gas tank, just where it would have to be, and the tank itself blown out from the inside. Kate said herself that Mark didn't leave the boat until after he'd pitched her overboard. And they found the remains of an old Navy limpet mine on the bottom near the boat.

"No, it was clearly somebody else, not Mark. He wasn't trying to kill her. I'm confident about that."

He looked at her. "Are you comfortable? There's always some danger when Icky comes back into our life."

"There's danger every time we cross the street. Still, I'd say go for it," Aurélie replied. "It makes me angry when people try to do things like that, and if we can help make it right we should.

"I'll help you all I can, but this time you may have to depend more on Paul. I have a heavy schedule this year and I'm already committed to some projects that will keep me busy this month."

She reached out and put her hand on his. "I'd rather be there with you. Please watch out for yourself."

"I'll be careful," he replied. "And if it turns out to be something sticky I'll ask for help. Let's call Icky."

ICKY ANSWERED on the third ring.

"Hang on a minute," he said.

Four o'clock in Paris is ten o'clock in Washington, the time Icky normally finished his morning staff planning session. On the speaker, they heard the sounds of papers being picked up, chairs scraping back from Icky's conference table, and feet shuffling out the door. In a few seconds they heard a door close and Icky came back on the speaker.

"Is everything under control?" he asked.

"It's fine. They showed up on time and Paul and I brought them back to the Luxor. Aurélie just settled them in the guest room, and I presume the next time we see them will be dinner. We'll stay in tonight.

"We've read your email. What's your take on the admiral? Could he just be jealous of Mark?"

Icky replied, "It's obvious he's going to be a problem, but I don't know yet how serious it will be. My boss is a standup guy, but he's Navy through and through. He thinks Admiral Mickelwaite has a screw loose and treated Kate really badly, but ..." He paused. "It's clear we made the right call in getting the two of them out of the way, but anybody who knows me will have a pretty good idea they may have come to you, so we probably need to bury them a little deeper until we decide what to do next. Raul and Antoine are turning up some interesting things in Miami, but they haven't found the man behind the bombing and the attempted murders in the hospital yet."

Aurélie said, "Icky, I know you've been thinking about using my apartment as a safe house, but I've had it a long time and it would be easy to figure out that's one place they might be.

"How about we do it the simple, straightforward

way and rent them a place on Airbnb? We could use one of the corporate credit cards and keep their name off it entirely. They could stay as long as it's safe and then move on to another one."

Icky agreed. "Short of a formal safe house I can't think of anything better. I say we do it."

They talked for another ten minutes, a long conversation by Icky's standards, then agreed to talk the following day and not to put the address of the apartment they chose in email.

"I really need to go to the office for a couple of hours," Eddie said as he hung up the phone. "Would you set up the apartment?"

"Sure. And I'd better call for dinner. Do you want anything in particular?"

"Steak frites plus anything else you think they might like. We'll give him an introduction to bistro food. On the way home I'll get a pinot noir and a Chardonnay out of the cellar. We won't hit them with real Bordeaux the day they arrive. It would put them to sleep right at the table."

"That will be a good menu. Go easy on the frites, though. We need to start running again, and soon." She reached to pat his stomach, then gave him a kiss.

EDDIE'S OFFICE was at the headquarters of Gran'Langue, a chain of language schools he had started when he left the army. He had first purchased a single school in Paris, and in twenty-five years had expanded it into the largest network of schools in France, with faculty in every major city and some smaller ones. He also owned and ran several other businesses, some started by his father and now owned by his mother, plus some he owned with Aurélie. It was only in recent years that he had found capable managers to run them on a day-to-day basis, leaving more time for his extracurricular work for Icky.

Gran'Langue, the crown of his empire, taught French to thousands of expat corporate employees and tourists, many of them American, and English to a smaller but significant number of French corporate employees and government functionaries. It was extremely lucrative, but it was not the main source of Eddie's immense wealth — that was his inheritance from his father, a descendant of the founders of Norway Steel, which had furnished steel for the expansion of American railroads after the American Civil War. His French grandmother, widowed by World War I, had returned to Paris after the war, bringing with her the young son who would grow up to be Eddie's father, Artie Grant.

When Eddie had bought the Paris school he had left its office in the classic Haussmannien stone building on Avenue de l'Opéra, the wide and elegant avenue that leads to the original opera house, the Palais Garnier. The office was only a ten-minute walk from the Luxor, past the landmark church of Saint-Roch, where Napoleon Bonaparte had made his reputation with an artillery attack on protesters during the Revolution. The marks of his cannon fire were still visible in the stone facade.

When he had a few extra minutes, Eddie would sometimes walk down Rue Saint-Honoré to the foot of Avenue de l'Opéra, just so he could look in the elegant shop windows and walk up the avenue with its view of the gilded old opera house in the distance.

As he passed a *pâtisserie* whose prices were so high Aurélie refused to pay them, he reflected on the French term for window shopping, *lèche-vitrine*, or window-licking, because the displays did look good enough to eat. He didn't stop with looking, however – he had been known to buy the occasional pastry, to be savored on a bench in the magnificent Tuileries Garden, and always finished before he got home. Aurélie was clearly correct that he needed to get back to running.

***

DINNER WOULD COME from the Bistro Maxim, an old-style Paris establishment with wood-paneled walls, brass sconces, and a collection of wine bottles that stretched entirely around the dining room on a narrow shelf ten feet above the floor.

The bistro was the Hotel Luxor's main source of room service meals. The chef, Maxim Barrotte, knew that much of his success depended on satisfying Eddie's guests, not to mention Eddie and Aurélie themselves, who frequently asked him to cater their dinner parties. The only other employee was the waiter, Alexander, a middle-aged man of Russian heritage who had worked in a half-dozen good restaurants in Paris and the provinces. Alexander was friendly and efficient, so Maxim usually chose him to deliver the food the twenty yards to the Luxor and set it up for the guests, which he invariably did with dramatic flair.

Maxim took Aurélie's call himself. She decided on escargot for the first course, figuring Kate would like the succulent garden snails in garlic butter As a backup, in case Mark just didn't like them, she ordered a rich potato soup.

The best fish that day, Maxim said, was Mediterranean *loup*, sea bass, which he'd just received that morning, so she told him to send two orders of that and two of steak frites, and they would sort out at the table who ate what.

"And Monsieur Grant will have his frites extra-crispy as usual?" Max asked. He had no doubt Eddie would claim one of the steaks.

"Let's not forget that," Aurélie replied with a laugh.

For dessert she ordered Maxim's yogurt with

raspberries and cream. She would make the coffee, and Eddie was taking care of the wine.

As an afterthought she asked, "Can Alexander bring it exactly at eight forty-five?"

"I'm very sorry, Madame," Maxim replied. "Alexander is ill today. He has sent me his cousin, who is a server at a very good place in Nice and is visiting for his annual holiday. He has substituted for Alexander before, and he did very well at lunch today. But if you would prefer, I will bring your dinner myself."

Aurélie took a second to recall the last time Maxim had made their delivery, wearing the tomato-stained apron he wore every night in the kitchen. "If you trust him that will be fine."

13

SUBSTITUTE WAITER

ALEXANDER, THOUGH, WAS NOT FINE.

At 12:30 that morning, exhausted from an eleven-hour split shift, he climbed wearily up the stairs of the Convention métro station in the far reaches of the 15th arrondissement and started the six-block walk to his one-bedroom apartment on Rue Saint-Lambert. As he did every night, he gave thanks for the elevator that would take him to the fifth floor – his feet hurt.

A man got up from a bench across from his front door. The street lights were dim, but the red glow of his cigarette made him impossible to miss. It was his cousin from Nice, whom he'd expected to meet at the restaurant hours before.

"Boris, where the hell have you been?" Alexander growled.

"I missed the train." Boris had moved to France only five years before and spoke French with a marked Russian accent. He was not a true cousin but the son of a close friend with a mildly checkered past who had trained Alexander to be a waiter. Boris himself was "known to the forces of order," as the newspapers phrased it, for a half-dozen small property crimes committed mainly when he was out of work and hungry, although there were rumors that he had killed a man during a burglary in Moscow, and Alexander was inclined to believe the tales were more than rumors. He knew better than to leave money or valuables in view.

"Look," Boris said, holding up a plastic bag. "I've brought vodka."

"How much is left?"

"More than half. There will be plenty for you, as little as you drink."

"Come in, then. I'm beat and have to get to bed. You can have the pullout bed in the living room and watch TV if you want."

Boris asked, "What time do you have to be at work tomorrow?"

"Eleven o'clock. How long will you stay?"

"Just two nights," Boris replied. "That's unless I find a woman tomorrow. Then only one night."

Alexander keyed in the door code and led the way to the elevator. In the tight space it was immediately obvious that Boris had started drinking long before he'd bought the new bottle of vodka.

"You need sleep, too," Alexander said as he pushed the elevator door open. "Let's call it a night. Tomorrow we can celebrate."

Alexander's apartment was Spartan. He rented it furnished, as many Parisian working people do, and the French legal definition of what constitutes a furnished apartment includes a minimum of furniture. In the five years since he'd moved in Alexander had filled in some of the gaps, but it lacked a woman's touch and his last partner had moved out a year ago.

"You know how to pull out the sofa bed," Alexander told him. "I'm going to take a shower and turn in. There's some food in the refrigerator if you're hungry. I'm going to set my alarm for nine o'clock."

Alexander was in and out of a hot shower and in bed within ten minutes, sound asleep a minute later. Even the TV couldn't keep him awake.

HE SLEPT SOUNDLY until just after dawn, when the door flew open and Boris leapt into the room. Before he could react, handcuffs clicked tightly around his wrists, first his left, then his right. Then Boris flipped him onto his stomach, so that he was resting on the cuffs and immobilized.

"I'm sorry to do this, my friend, but if you do what I tell you all will go well. Do not shout or make any loud noise.

"A very important man in America wants something done. You will have only a small part in it, and when it is done you will be released without harm. Is your boss at his restaurant now?"

Alexander nodded. "This is the time he arrives."

"Good. You are going to call in sick and tell him I will substitute for you today. He likes my work so he will not object. When my shift is over I will free you, and then I will leave Paris. Do you agree?"

Again, Alexander nodded.

"Good. You are being smart about this." He picked Alexander's phone from the nightstand, an old one connected to the wall with a cord, and dialed the number from memory, pausing before the last digit.

"Remember. You are sick, but I am staying with you and will work in your place. If you get it wrong you will suffer." He pressed the last number, then put the receiver to Alexander's ear and moved close so he could hear.

The phone rang for a long time, but just before it would have gone to voice mail, Maxim picked it up.

"Monsieur, I seem to have picked up a stomach bug last night. I did not feel well when I came home but thought it would be better by now, but it is not.

My cousin Boris is visiting me and will be my substitute today. Will that be satisfactory?"

Maxim grudgingly accepted the inevitable.

"Of course, Alexander. Try to come back tomorrow."

"I will be there tomorrow."

Boris told Alexander to turn over and raise his arms over his head. He unlocked one of the cuffs, ran the chain around a bar on the headboard, and relocked it. The ankles were next – he strapped them tightly to the foot of the bed with duct tape. Alexander could move, but not enough to escape.

Then Boris went to the shelves where Alexander kept his clothes and found a clean sock. "Open your mouth," he commanded, and Alexander did as he was told. Boris tore a long strip off the top sheet and used it to tie the gag in place.

"Now I will wait until it is time to go to work. Don't make any noise," Boris said. Leaving the door open, he went and sat down in the living room.

At 10:30 Alexander heard Boris leave and lock the door. He waited fifteen minutes, then tried to rub the duct tape away from around his ankles, but only succeeded in tightening it. If he could free his feet, he reasoned, he could slide up the bed to reach the gag with his hands and remove it, then call the police. But Boris had used many layers of the tape and it held fast.

In an hour he had accomplished nothing. Both

his wrists and his ankles remained as tightly bound as ever, which left only the gag.

Boris had wrapped the sheet around his head several times and tied it in back. Perhaps the knot would come loose if he rubbed it against the bedding. He tried for a half-hour to no avail. Boris, he recalled, had been kicked out of the Russian Navy, but had learned his knots well.

The only other solution he could think of was to make the bed jump on the floor and rouse his nosy downstairs neighbor, so he began moving his hips up and down until he finally got the rhythm. The foot of the bed bounced off the wooden parquet floor for a half-hour until she shouted "Quiet!" from the window below.

He bounced some more and she shouted again. Then he heard her door slam and hoped she was going in search of the concierge. But when another half-hour passed and no one came knocking at his door he realized she had just left her apartment to escape the noise. He settled back on the bed, tired and disappointed, to wait until she returned.

By the time she returned the sun had moved below the open window. His bedside clock was half hidden by a table lamp, but he could see the hours. It was after 8 o'clock – surely someone would hear him and respond this time.

Help came from an unexpected quarter. The couple who lived across the hall got off the elevator and heard the racket. He was Jerôme Fontainebleau, who spent his days inspecting apartment buildings for the city and had no fear of getting involved in a neighbor's affairs – it was what he did for a living.

He stood at Alexander's front door listening and finally was able to identify the source of the noise.

"It's the bed," he said to his wife with a malicious grin. His magnificent salt-and-pepper walrus mustache twitched at the thought. "He must be having a real good time in there."

But as the noise continued he began to change his mind and went to knock on the door.

Alexander heard the knock and stopped. Then he bounced again, twice, hoping to send a message. Jerôme knocked again, Alexander responded again.

"Something's wrong," Jerôme said. "Let's go find Madame Laroudie and ask her to check."

"You know she doesn't like being bothered after five," his wife said cautiously.

"If it's just noisy sex, then I'll apologize to her. If it's not, Alexander may be in trouble. We need to find out."

His wife was right. Madame Laroudie, the live-in combination janitor and building manager, thought her day ended at five and she did complain vociferously about being dragged away from the evening news. But she couldn't decide whether she was dealing with Jerôme the building inspector or Jerôme the resident of her building. She decided to go with the safer option.

She wiped her hands on her apron, then took a master key from a hook behind her front door and led the way officiously to Alexander's door. Behind her back, Jerôme grinned at his wife.

She knocked. The bed responded.

"Monsieur. Do you need help?"

The bed bounced twice.

"Give me the damned key," Jerôme said brusquely. He opened the door quickly and ran into the living room, then to the door of the bedroom.

"Mon Dieu," his wife said, looking over his shoulder. "Poor Alexander is tied up like a Christmas goose."

Jerôme bent over Alexander and carefully untied the gag, then pulled the sock from his mouth.

"Thank you," Alexander said. He could hardly speak, his mouth was so dry. "I didn't think anyone would ever hear me."

"What happened?"

"My cousin, Boris – he's up to no good. He took my shift at the restaurant today and said something about a rich American wanting something done. He's a dangerous man, and he runs with dangerous men. But we must be careful. He could hurt my *patron* or someone in the restaurant, and then I wouldn't have a job."

If you still have one after this, Jerôme thought

doubtfully. "What could he possibly be planning? He's certainly not going to work all day just to stick up the restaurant.

"This is something for the police. But we don't want the riot squad barging in. We need someone with more finesse. I know just who to call."

He looked at the clock. It was 8:40.

PHILIPPE CABILLAUD WAITED while his dinner guest slid into the *banquette* facing Rue Daguerre, then sat down to face her across the small round table.

"Monsieur le Commissaire, would you or madame like a kir to start?" the waiter asked. Tonight, as always, the waiter was René, the restaurant's owner. Philippe had been his customer at several different restaurants for a dozen years, but Bistro Augustin was the first one René had owned himself, and Philippe was pleased to be a small investor in it.

He looked across the table at his friend Margaux Grant and raised an eyebrow.

"Of course," she said.

The instant Philippe said "Make it two," the iPhone in his jacket pocket rang. "Merde," he said. Then he looked at the screen and said aloud, "Jerôme Fontainebleau. Why on earth would he be calling me at this hour?" He considered sending it to voice mail but something made him hesitate.

"Would you excuse me?" he said, getting to his feet. "I hardly ever talk to this man, but when he calls it's important." He pressed the phone to his ear as he walked toward the front of the restaurant and out on to the street, away from the curious ears of other diners.

"Hello, Jerôme. I'm guessing this is important. I'm just sitting down to dinner."

"I think it is, Monsieur le Commissaire. I just found my neighbor Alexander tied up in his bedroom. He tells me his cousin left him there this morning and went to take his shift at Bistro Maxim. The cousin is a known Russian hood from Nice and told my neighbor he's here on some sort of mission for a rich American. He specifically said an American, and I wouldn't think the Russian Mafia would normally be doing American work.

"But Alexander told me one of the restaurant's big clients is your daughter's hotel. The bistro is right down the street from the Hotel Luxor, and one of Alexander's main jobs is delivering to the chichi people who stay there.

"So I asked myself, whom should I call?"

"You did the right thing," Philippe replied, his mind racing through the alternatives. "I'll let you know what happens."

He looked at the time: 8:45. Then he placed a call to Aurélie.

AURÉLIE WAS DOING her best to lighten the mood. Mark and Kate had been through enough problems, including the detailed and intrusive questions she and Eddie had asked, and she wanted dinner to be a social event, a chance for her to catch up with Kate. Eddie wasn't entirely convinced but agreed to go along.

Kate and Mark had come to the living room looking relaxed and scrubbed, smiling from the shower they'd shared. They sat close together on a sofa that faced the unlit fireplace and Eddie handed each a glass of champagne.

"We hope you got rested," Eddie said to them. "Dinner should be here soon."

"I'm guessing this is not going to be Chinese carryout," Kate said with a smile.

"It could have been, but this is from Bistro Maxim, which is just down the street and provides our room service. If this were a normal night we'd take you out somewhere, but Icky wants you to stay out of sight until he knows a little more. Even then you'll have to be careful. And we wanted to start you off with a real French meal."

Eddie got up to answer the house telephone. "Send him up," he said. "Did you give him the elevator code? ...No, of course not. For a while we don't want anyone to have it, especially someone we don't know."

He turned to the room. "The waiter is on the way up with dinner. Mark and Kate, will you please go into the bedroom until he leaves?"

"WAS THAT NECESSARY?" Aurélie asked.

"Probably not, but I have a feeling this is going to be more of a mess than we first thought. We don't know anything about this new waiter, even if Maxim is okay with him. If I'm being too suspicious, none of us is out anything. If I'm not, we might be heading off a problem."

Eddie opened the front door when he heard the elevator door open. The waiter was shorter and looked more Slavic than Alexander. Eddie thought he saw him adjust the cover on one of the plates just as the door slid open.

"Please just roll it inside the front door, and thanks to you and Maxim for being prompt," Eddie said, handing him a twenty-euro tip.

With Boris gone, Aurélie summoned Kate and Mark from their bedroom and said, "Let's finish the champagne. Dinner will stay hot for a few minutes."

In ten minutes Aurélie asked, "I bet our two guests are ready to eat. It's late for Americans, but you'll need to get used to it. In Paris the restaurants don't open until around eight o'clock. I hope the food will make up for it."

"I guarantee I'm ready," Mark said.

Kate nodded in agreement. "In the Navy we eat even earlier than the civilians. I got used to that change, so I'll probably be able to handle this one, too."

"Maxim's food is usually very good. Our first course will be escargots, which I hope everyone likes." Mark looked doubtful.

"We have some important choices to make. I didn't know who likes what, so I ordered two fish and two meat. The fish is *loup*, or Mediterranean bass, which Maxim does well. The meat is steak frites. It's a dish that's almost as common as hamburger in the States, but Maxim has his own special touches. It's one of Eddie's favorites."

"Mark likes fish," Kate said. "When we're busy we bring in fast food, and he orders fish tacos at least half the time. So unless I miss my guess, Mark will have the sea bass." She waited and looked expectantly at him.

"When I was aboard ship I hated fish, I guess because there was so much water around. But when I got back on terra firma I developed a real taste for it."

Aurélie passed a plate of sautéed sea bass, its skin crisp, on a round of herbed polenta, covered with a sauce of tiny vegetables, across the table to Mark.

Kate and Aurélie flipped a coin and Kate won the steak.

Eddie said, "Tonight we'll start the wines the classical way, white with fish and red with meat. After one glass, you can do it any way you want. I drink red with almost everything."

Aurélie was placing Mark's escargots in front of him when the phone in her purse rang.

"That's Philippe's ring. Édouard, would you mind getting it?"

He stood up, but by the time he got across the room to the purse the ringing had stopped. "He will call back if it's important, or he'll leave a message." Immediately, the phone in his pocket rang.

"So it must be important."

Philippe didn't give him a chance to say hello. "Did you order dinner from Maxim tonight?"

"Yes, it …"

"Have you started to eat?"

"We just sat down."

"Listen to me. This is important. Whatever you do, don't eat anything from that restaurant. Back away from the table immediately. If you've touched anything that came from the restaurant, don't touch anything else with your hands. Nothing else. Don't go to the bathroom, don't blow your nose, don't eat or drink anything. Don't touch anything but your own clothes. Those will have to be destroyed anyway."

"Hold on," Eddie said, and turned to the others.

"Philippe says we may have a problem – the food might be poisoned. Push back from the table now and don't touch anything with your hands."

To Philippe he said, "Are you on the way here?"

"I'm in a cab with your mother. We were at dinner when I got a call, which I'll tell you about later. I'm going first to the restaurant to meet several officers. Two officers and the on-call doctor are on their way to you."

"Margaux is with you?"

"We hadn't seen each other in a long time and thought this would be a good evening for it." They had an occasional relationship that went back a decade.

In the background, Eddie heard Margaux say, "Do what Philippe says, Édouard. We are crossing the Seine now."

BISTRO MAXIM WAS A SMALL PLACE – a dozen tables, only two of them occupied now. Philippe walked through the front door and was greeted by a short and Slavic-looking waiter whom he took to be Boris, who gave him a table on the wall near the spiral staircase that led down to the kitchen and restrooms, a feature common to many old Paris restaurants.

Philippe asked for a glass of Burgundy and a

small bottle of San Pellegrino mineral water. He put the menu aside and asked, "Les toilettes?"

"Downstairs, Monsieur. On your right."

At the bottom of the staircase, Philippe turned left instead of right and walked quickly into the kitchen, where he found Maxim delicately plating an order of sea bass. He placed it in the dumbwaiter, then asked, "May I help you, Monsieur?"

Philippe showed his identity card. Maxim looked at it closely and said, "Commissaire Cabillaud? I have a client by that name."

"She is my daughter, Maxim. Please tell me quickly, is the waiter upstairs named Boris, the Russian sent to you by Alexander?"

"Yes, Commissaire. Is there a problem?"

"We will know soon enough, but for now there is great risk. He tied Alexander to his bed this morning just so he could work this shift, and said he was doing a job for a rich American. He did not say what job, or which American, but he wanted very specifically to work at your restaurant at this time. I don't know why, but I suspect he planned to poison someone."

"Mon Dieu! He delivered dinner to your daughter."

"I called and stopped them before they ate the food, and a police doctor is on the way. Now we have to deal with Boris, who might be armed. No matter. The *gendarmes* waiting outside will handle him.

"Tell me, does he have a locker here, or any-where he could store a small object?"

"Yes, there is a locker behind the door beyond the toilets, where we put our coats in winter."

"Show me."

Maxim led the way across the basement, between the enclosed stalls and the washbasins, into a tiny room with three lockers against one wall and a bench in front of them. Philippe looked carefully in each one and found nothing. Then he took out a small radio and said to the policemen outside, "If he has a bottle it is on him now, or already thrown away. Put on your gloves and try not to touch him any more than you have to. I will push him into your arms in one minute or less."

To Maxim, he said, "Your clients are going to be very concerned in a few minutes. I will talk to them, but you will need to make them happy some way, perhaps with a free meal later."

"Can they not finish their dinners?"

"The food may be dangerous. It probably is not, but you will have to close immediately and you may be closed for a day or two."

Experience had taught Philippe to carry latex gloves with him day and night. He put them on, ad-justed the 9mm Sig Sauer that rested high on his right hip, and started up the stairs.

When he reached the dining room, Boris was standing before a couple, just placing the fish on the table. He straightened, holding a champagne glass, and turned toward the dumbwaiter. At that moment Philippe took two quick steps toward him. Boris saw the gloves, dropped the glass, and bolted for the open front door – directly into the waiting hands of two beefy policemen, who caught and held him at arms' length as he twisted and struggled. It was an uneven contest, and Boris quickly gave up, but not before shouting enough well-chosen curses to attract a small crowd.

One of the gendarmes handcuffed him to a bicycle rack and stepped back. Philippe approached him and said, "I am going to search your pockets. If you move toward me or try to touch me in any way you will be shot."

There was nothing in the white apron Boris wore, but in the right pocket of his trousers Philippe felt a short cylindrical object. He reached in and pulled out a glass bottle about three inches long with a rubber stopper. He first held it up to a streetlight and saw it was empty, then dropped it into the plastic evidence bag one of the officers held out.

"What was in the bottle, Boris?"

"Mouthwash. Vodka. None of your business. Piss off."

"I'm afraid it is my business. Talk if you want, or not. We will find out." To the gendarmes, he said, "Bag him up like hazardous waste."

One of them reached into a large briefcase and

took out a zippered bag much like a body bag, except that it did not cover the head. He cuffed Boris's ankles, then released his wrists and wrapped the bag completely around him.

As he pulled the zipper to Boris's neck the policeman said, "Now you're bagged up like the shit I pick up behind my dog. Try getting out of that."

"The wagon will be here in a few minutes," Philippe said. "Take him in for attempted murder. Keep him segregated. I need to go to the hotel."

A GENDARME STANDING guard at the door of the Hotel Luxor straightened and touched his cap as Philippe entered.

"Has the doctor arrived?"

"Yes, Monsieur le Commissaire. He went up a few minutes ago."

To his friend M. Dupont, the front-desk manager, Philippe asked, "Is the code still 6161?"

"M. Grant had me change it last week. It is now 5043."

The apartment door was open when Philippe arrived. Aurélie stood to greet her father, but he waved her away. The doctor, a cadaverously thin but very tall man who reminded Philippe of Icky Crane, was taking swabs from everyone's hands and from the food.

"How long will it take to get results, doctor?" Philippe asked.

"It used to take hours, but we have a new test for the most common poisons that will give a good indication in less than an hour. They did not eat any of the food, so the risk is low. I hear you called just in time."

Philippe said, "We only found out because Jerôme Fontainebleau was suspicious enough to challenge the concierge of his apartment building. He found the real waiter tied up in the bed. We arrested his cousin downstairs just a few minutes ago.

"Now, Eddie and Aurélie, will you introduce me to your guests?"

"Of course," Aurélie said. "Mark McGinley, Kate Hall, this is my father Philippe Cabillaud. He's a policeman who has never been able to retire because something keeps coming up. This is not the first time he's pulled my chestnuts out of the fire."

They did not shake hands.

THE DOCTOR HAD SET up a rack of test tubes. He put each of his swabs in one, then added a solvent and a freeze-dried pellet and waited to see if the color of the liquid changed.

After a half-hour he interrupted the conversation. "I have a preliminary result, and it seems pretty certain. The fish was poisoned with a large dose of ricin. There's no way to tell how sick it would have made you, but it would have been very uncomfortable and possibly even worse. It looks like the steak got less, just a tiny amount."

"Could it have been a fatal dose?" Eddie asked, looking anxiously at Aurélie and Mark.

"It's possible. Ricin isn't always fatal, but there's no antidote and people who get it suffer the results for years. It's what the Bulgarians used to poison Georgi Markov, a Russian defector, a couple of decades ago. But then, they injected him using an umbrella with a poisoned tip. He died very painfully.

"An oral dosage has to be much larger to be fatal, but it's nasty stuff and the smallest amount is too much."

Aurélie asked, "Did we get it on our hands? I think I'm the only one who touched the plates."

"You have some traces on your hands, probably from powder spilled off to the side of the food, and some on your dress. You need to take a long, soapy shower, or a couple of them. To keep from spreading it your clothes will have to be cut off and put in a double-sealed plastic bag."

"Cut off?" she asked. "This is a brand-new dress."

"We'll get a new one," Eddie said. He got up and walked toward the kitchen. "I'll get the scissors and meet you in the bathroom."

"Let me," Philippe said. "You shouldn't touch anything.

The doctor added, "Everyone else should change clothes right away and put their clothes into the wash. If they can't be washed, put them with Madame Cabillaud's and we will dispose of them. Run the washer a couple of times, take a thorough shower, and you should be safe."

"Everybody to it, then," Philippe said. "Doctor, thank you very much and I'll look for a report before noon tomorrow."

Philippe closed the door behind the doctor and turned to say, "Unfortunately, Bistro Maxim is going to be closed for a couple of days for a thorough cleaning. Margaux and I didn't even get to our kirs tonight, so I suggest we all go somewhere close for dinner. Whoever sent Boris has no way of knowing he failed, so it should be safe to go out tonight. Let's try the new Japanese place over near Eddie's office, once you get scrubbed."

14

THEIR OWN VIEW OVER PARIS

AURÉLIE FOUND A ONE-BEDROOM APARTMENT IN the Montparnasse area, on the Left Bank a 20-minute métro ride from the Luxor. At breakfast the next morning she showed the pictures to Mark and Kate and they agreed that it looked like a good spot.

"It's a great neighborhood," Aurélie told them. "There's a bus stop in front of the building and it has a view of the cemetery across the street, which is a giant green park – much better than looking into a neighbor's bedroom window. And it's just a block away from Rue Daguerre, which is full of restaurants and shops and is a lot of fun to walk in. Eddie and I like that district a lot."

"What arrondissement is it in?" Kate asked.

"The fourteenth. It's not fancy like the areas closer to the river, but it's quieter. And because it doesn't get as many tourists as the first, where we are, you'll have more chances to practice your French. Eddie told me before he left that he's going to enroll you in classes.

"Philippe is working to find out if Boris has any more friends lurking around Paris. If he doesn't, it's probably safe for you to walk around, as long as you keep both eyes open. Philippe will try to find out who sent him and head that off at the source. We have quite a problem with Eastern European criminals, especially on the Mediterranean coast, which is where this guy came from."

AT ONE O'CLOCK they met the owner of the apartment, a hardworking thirtyish man with a ring in his nose who designed web pages during the day and drove for Uber at night. He showed them around and then left them to it, closing the door quietly behind him as they stood at the bow window looking out over the broad Montparnasse Cemetery. To the left, in the distance, they could see the Eiffel Tower and ahead of them, high on the hill of Montmartre, Sacré-Coeur Cathedral gleamed white in the afternoon sun.

Mark put his arm around Kate and pulled her close. "Do you like it?"

"I've stayed in some nice places in Paris, but

nothing with a view like this one. This will be a vacation," she replied.

"At least until Icky figures out what happened to Pegasus and Icarus and where the problems are coming from. At some point we'll have to go to work, but for now let's just enjoy Paris."

He bent to kiss her. "Are you thinking what I'm thinking?"

"It's not huge, but it's wider than the bunk in Gunner," Kate said as they stood in the tiny bedroom. He pulled the heavy red curtain closed, then turned and began to unbutton her blouse. He pulled down her bra straps one at a time and very slowly and seriously kissed each breast.

"Now," she said urgently, tugging at his belt buckle. In less than a minute they collapsed onto the bed.

"I DON'T THINK the shower here is going to do the job," Mark said. "It's a bathtub with a curtain. We'd probably fall out of the damned thing and break our necks. Do you want to go first? And if so, can I come watch?" He grinned. "Then, let's go get some lunch. I'm starved."

A half-hour later, Mark called up the map on his iPhone and pointed them toward the south, away from the cemetery and toward Rue Daguerre.

"There are dozens of places to eat on Rue Daguerre," Kate said. "Aurélie said there's an especially good traditional bistro on the second corner after we turn left. Let's try that, if they're still serving lunch. If not, there are some outdoor places a few blocks further down the street toward the big underground station where three subway lines cross."

They arrived at the bistro a half-hour before its kitchen closed for the afternoon. Each ordered a glass of pinot noir and the fixed-price lunch, which was leek soup followed by a hanger steak with fries and a small salad, dressed with a sharp vinaigrette.

"So this is the steak frites Aurélie wanted me to try last night," he said, pleased with his choice. "You sure handled that menu well. I had no idea you spoke French like that."

"I have a tourist vocabulary," she said. "I can also manage some diplomat-speak but once I get away from food I have a very hard time."

"D'you suppose Eddie's school can teach us the language of making love?"

"I'm sure he can, but it's better in braille."

———

DESSERT WAS a small raspberry tart with a tiny dollop of whipped cream. As they finished, Mark said, "It sure seems that the portions are smaller than I'm used to. Is it like that everywhere?"

"Pretty much. They say that's one of the main reasons French women don't get fat. Nor do the men, for that matter. Now let's go down the street for our coffee. It's a great day for a walk and we should see as much as we can."

They crossed the street into the pedestrian area of Rue Daguerre and crisscrossed from side to side looking into shop windows and reading restaurant menus. But before they had walked a hundred yards Mark's phone rang in his shirt pocket.

He looked at the screen. "It's Eddie," he said as he answered the call.

"I know you're trying to be tourists, but can you come down to my office right away? There's someone here you need to meet."

Mark turned and mouthed to Kate, "OK to go see Eddie?" She nodded.

"Sure," he said into the phone. "Home or office?"

"Office," Eddie replied, and gave him the address on Avenue de l'Opéra. Mark plugged it into his phone's map, fumbling the unfamiliar street name the first time, and replied, "It looks like the best way from here is the bus."

"I don't say this often," Eddie said, "but get a cab this time. There's a stand there next to the RER, across the square from Café Daguerre. Use cash, just in case."

THE CAB DROPPED them at the shopping-center entrance to the Louvre, on Rue Royale a couple of
blocks from the Palais Royal.

"I don't know if we're being followed," Mark
said, "but I'd rather walk a couple of blocks than get
blindsided. The street is one way and we need to
walk upstream to meet Eddie, which will let us take a
look at anyone who shows too much interest."

Kate replied, "We'd be lucky to pick anyone out
of the crowd unless he was wearing a clown suit, but
it's a good plan. Just in case."

They walked two blocks against a solid stream of
cars and buses, then sprinted across Rue Royale
during a brief gap, barely ahead of a green-and-
white city bus clanging its warning bell angrily. It
gave them a chance to duck onto the shopping ar-
cade and stop between two of the stone arches,
where they couldn't be seen from across the street.

"I thought that bus driver was going to blow a
gasket," Mark said. "But he gave us great cover. Let's
wait here just a minute and see if anyone followed us,
then we go to the right – but you know better than I
where we go. What do you think is our best route to
Eddie's building?"

"Why don't we go through the Palais Royal? It's a
great old building, and it's not usually all that
crowded. Colette had an apartment there until she

died." Befuddlement clouded Mark's face. "She was a famous French writer, not to everybody's taste. Never mind."

TEN MINUTES later they pushed open the ten-foot oak doors of Eddie's building and took the elevator to Gran'Langue on the fourth floor, where a receptionist directed them up a spiral staircase.

Eddie waited at the head of the stairs. He had taken off his jacket in deference to the heat but his tie was still tightly knotted.

"Icky called while you were checking in at your apartment. He wanted me to meet a man who lives in Paris, and who has something to tell us, or so he says. He's a Hungarian-American who made a lot of money in Silicon Valley but in his later years has become more and more involved in Hungarian politics. I don't know if you've been following, but the Hungarian government has turned very authoritarian recently, but not enough for this man."

Kate stopped him. "Max Molnar!" she said.

Eddie's eyebrows went up. "That's right. Icky is not at all sure how much of what he says can be believed, but we need to listen to him. He may or may not be able to tell us something about last night, and we're also Icky's eyes and ears now. Shall we?"

Eddie led the way into his spacious office, which

was decorated much like his home – the eighteenth century rendered with modern materials.

Max Molnar stood up from the guest chair in front of Eddie's desk.

"I'm glad to see you again, Kate," he said, smiling. "It's been a very long time."

The diplomat in her had taken over and she responded coolly, "It has been a while. I hope you are well." She clearly had no such hope and did not offer to shake hands.

The smile stayed on his skeletal face. He extended his hand to Mark and said, "I'm Max Molnar. I heard very good things about your engineering skills – both of your engineering skills – when I talked to our mutual friend Icky Crane yesterday.

"I'm here to apologize for the problems you've had recently and to assure you they won't be repeated. You and I probably will not be on the same wavelength, politically speaking, but there's no reason we can't have a civilized relationship. After all, Paris has always welcomed and absorbed refugees and people of very different views."

Eddie said, "Max and I don't know each other well, but we run into each other from time to time around Paris. He holds both American and French citizenship and lives here almost all the time…"

"And Hungarian, as well," Max interjected. "May I?

"Kate, Mark, it's no secret that I'm unhappy with

the direction of the Hungarian government. I left as a child but went back for quite a few years, and now I have some things I want to get done and I have to get on them before it's too late."

Kate interrupted, "So you're involved with my ex-husband?"

"Yes, my dear, I am. But my involvement is limited to helping finance the reconstruction of the old family castle in the north of Hungary.

"He was so looking forward to sharing it with you, and when that chance disappeared I'm afraid he started to do some rash things. I'm not here to tell you things that would get him involved with the police, either here or in the United States, but I can assure you that he is no longer in either place and he's been told that my financing depends on his good behavior.

"It's important to me because the castle will be the national headquarters for a new political party I plan to start soon. I can't have anyone doing stupid things and bringing me negative attention. I'm not one of those who believe all publicity is good publicity."

Eddie asked, knowing what the answer would be, "So he bombed the boat and tried to poison all four of us last night? Is he completely crazy?"

Max held up his hand, palm out. "You know I can't give you a yes-or-no answer to the first, but as for the second, let's just say—"

Mark spoke over him. "And just where the hell is our submarine?"

"That, unfortunately, I can't answer. Not because I don't want to, but because I just don't know. It's clear to everyone that the theft of the sub and the bombing of your sailboat were connected, and I have reason to believe my company's Gulfstream may have been used to bring it somewhere in Europe. But the plane was on a trip that stopped at five airports and I have no idea where the sub was unloaded, or even if it was loaded in the first place. It could still be in Miami.

"In any case, I just learned about the theft of the sub yesterday, from Icky Crane. I didn't know about the poison until Eddie told me this morning. I am so glad to see you weren't hurt.

"I wasn't involved, because I would never have let myself be pulled into anything violent like that. I might eventually learn something, but I have to be honest and say I can't promise to tell you everything.

"Eddie, should I get back in touch through you if I learn anything interesting?" He stood to leave.

"That would be best," Eddie said.

Kate interrupted. "Mr. Molnar, there's one other thing you should know. I've told this to my former husband, or most of it, but I have assembled a pretty extensive file on some of the things he's been involved in, including corrupting the police in Miami and God knows where else. He had the Miami police stop me from time to time, until I had my lawyer show my file to his lawyer. That stopped it.

"I already knew you were involved in funding the damned castle, although I didn't know until now exactly why. I also know about a couple of procurement deals you and he participated in while he was in the Pentagon, neither of which was completely honest. And now, of course, it's obvious that you're at least an accessory after the fact to attempted murder in Florida and possibly in France, and you know the police here don't screw around. They arrested the former president of France on suspicion of bribery and kept him in jail overnight. You can imagine what they would do with an American carpetbagger who wants to turn back the European political clock to the 1930s and get in bed with the Russians at the same time. And now … Hungarian politics.

"If anything happens to either of us, or to Eddie, or Aurélie, or anybody connected with them, all this information goes to the FBI and to the French police. I can promise you that if any of us had been poisoned last night, you would already be in a French jail."

"But… but… I had nothing to do with that."

"Then you have nothing to worry about, do you?" She bared her teeth in an insincere facsimile of a smile. "I'm sure you'd just tell that to the Examining Magistrate and he'd let you go. Or do you think maybe not? You do know, don't you, that if you're charged with a crime in France you're held in prison during the trial, even if you've made bail?"

"He was right about you. Good day," Max said through clenched teeth as he stalked out.

"THAT WAS QUITE A PRESENTATION," Mark said after a long silence. "I sure don't want you for an enemy."

"You didn't believe any of that crap about him not being involved in the bombing, did you? I've heard about him for years. He's an absolute shark and he's convinced anything he does is by divine right, mainly because he's rich. He's an authoritarian through and through, and he responds only to force. And that's what his friends say. By the way, they also say all those tiny little curls are the most ridiculous hairdo they ever saw on a man."

"Hold on just a minute," Eddie said as he picked up his iPhone and sent a rapid text. His face, like Mark's, was dark with rage. "There. I asked Paul to find out who Max sees next. That could be interesting."

Then, to Kate, "Do you really have a dossier like that?"

"I didn't promise a single thing I can't deliver," she said. "It's in a lawyer's safe in Washington and there's a copy hidden in my Gmail account. In fact,

I'd like to send it to you. Can you put it in someone's hands for safekeeping here?"

"Sure, or if you want to play hardball we could just send it to Aurélie's father."

"No, not yet. We should do what we say we'll do. If he upholds his end of the bargain and helps us get the sub back, we can put this all behind us. If not...."

"My ex always had an irrational respect for people above him, or anyone very rich, so he's probably doing exactly what he's been told to do: supervising the renovation of his damned castle with Molnar dollars. I'm pretty sure Max will keep him under control for now.

"But can you believe it? He's going into Hungarian politics? Politically, you can't slip a playing card between the Hungarian authoritarians and the Russians!"

Eddie said, "Hungarian politics or any politics aside, your ex tried to kill us. His goon put a deadly poison into your food and Aurélie's. I'm not a very forgiving guy – just ask anybody who knows my past. He will pay for it, I guarantee."

"I'm with you," Mark said angrily. "This has gone on long enough. Let's light a fire under Icky and get on with it."

"It's already lit," Eddie said. "Raul and Antoine are turning over rocks in Miami and finding some interesting stuff – they know Max Molnar was behind the so-called patent lawyer who visited you Friday evening.

"Icky says they hope to have a good idea how the bombing got set up, and by whom, within a couple of days. You two should take that time to be tourists."

15

A DAY IN PARIS

"Where do we go from here?" Mark asked. They stood again on the sidewalk in front of Eddie's building. He was still flushed with anger at the way Max Molnar had treated Kate, but at the same time proud that she had clearly come out on top.

"You leave that to me," Kate replied with a broad smile. "First, we're going to finish what we started at the Café Daguerre, but this time we're going to a place just a block or two up the avenue. We can sit there and watch the sun bounce off the opera house while we hold hands under the table."

She took his arm as they crossed the avenue to claim a tiny round table nestled into a corner of the café's terrace. The opera house lighted up as the sun played on the gold leaf on its pediment and statuary.

"I can't tell you how much I love this view," she

said. "I spent a month in Paris the summer after high school, before I started Annapolis prep school. I found this place by accident and came here almost every day, even though I couldn't afford it."

She took his hand and pressed it hard into the warmth between her legs. "This will be the best time of our lives. I can see it coming."

A waiter stopped two tables away to make change. "What are you drinking?" Mark asked. "I think red wine would be best, don't you?"

"It seems to me that's going to be our favorite, judging from one night on the boat. Red wine it is. You OK with pinot noir?"

"Is there any other kind?"

"You have no idea."

"Madame, Monsieur, what may I offer you today?"

"*Deux pinot noir, s'il vous plaît,*" she replied.

"You really do speak it," Mark said after the waiter had left.

"Like I said, just in restaurants and places that aren't very demanding. I'd like to learn more, and you should, too. I'm looking forward to going to school."

They sat for an hour, content to watch the unending stream of passers-by on the broad sidewalk.

An old woman approached them. In the universal sign language of tourism, she persuaded Mark to buy a rose for Kate, but the waiter chased her away before he could get his hand out of his pocket.

"Tough luck," he said. "I'll find one for you somewhere else."

"Don't try to get out of it now. There's a shop at the bus stop near our apartment. You can get a whole bunch of them, and I plan to hold you to it." She smiled again at him and stroked his cheek lightly.

"You're good for me, Mark," she said. "You make me smile, and I've hardly done that for years. Thank you."

He squeezed her hand in response and smiled, then looked quickly away, but she was happy. She'd worked with Mark long enough to know he would have a hard time expressing his feelings. For now, his words were unimportant; the honesty of his feeling was clear to her.

"Let's walk further up the street," she said impulsively after they had paid the waiter. "We can look closer at the opera house, then I'd like to walk by the big department stores, Au Printemps and Galeries Lafayette. They're wonderful."

"Walk by?"

"Well, I won't keep you long. I'm guessing you're not much of a shopper, so I can come back by myself some day or you can park yourself in one of the cafés."

Arm in arm, they promenaded slowly up the avenue, stopping to look in the window of every third store, or so it seemed to Mark. Twice she said, "Wait here for me. I'll just be a few minutes" and then disappeared into a shop. Both times, she returned empty-handed.

Finally, they stood on the sidewalk in front of the opera house.

She said, "Did you know the last emperor, Napoleon the Third, commissioned this building but never got to see a performance in it? He lost a war with Prussia and was deposed before it was completed. Around to the left there's a carriage entrance built just for him."

They walked the two long blocks to Galeries Lafayette. The sidewalk outside the store swarmed with shoppers crowded around booths the store had set up to sell scarves, purses, and gadgets of all sorts. Mark and Kate let themselves be swept to the next entrance and found themselves in what seemed to Mark to be an entire store of women's handbags. There were purses of all sorts and colors, all with one thing in common. They were expensive.

The store's elegantly perfumed air smelled wonderful to him.

In fifteen minutes they were back on the street.

"I think I'm done now," Kate said.

"Do you want to go back to the apartment? I could probably do with a nap."

"A nap or something like that. Let's go back on

the bus. It's a good way to get a quick tour. There's probably a transit app on the phones Eddie gave us."

Mark scrolled through the app icons and found the one issued by RATP, the bus and métro system. "We want to go from here to where?" he asked.

"Our stop is Denfert-Rochereau. From there it's a short walk from the flower shop I mentioned."

Mark plugged in the destination. "Magic. It's just a couple of blocks to the bus stop."

MARK HAD Kate's pants down to her knees when her telephone buzzed.

"Damn!" she said in frustration.

Mark reached for her purse. "It's Aurélie," he said.

Kate closed her eyes tight to hold the mood.

Mark pressed answer. "Kate's tied up right now, Aurélie. Can I help?"

"There's someone you should meet. He's back from a trip a day early and is coming for dinner tonight. Can you join us? I promise it won't be as eventful as last night."

"Sure. When?"

"Early. We need to start at five thirty. One of the guests is a TV news announcer and has to go to work. We'll talk business after she leaves."

While Mark was negotiating the dinner hour Kate kicked her pants to the other side of the bed.

"Now come to me," she said, and then clapped a hand over her mouth as she realized he hadn't disconnected the call.

He grinned. "Don't worry about it. She knows what's going on."

16

JEREMY BENTHAM

A TALL MAN OPENED THE DOOR AND SAID, "YOU must be Mark and Kate. Welcome. Aurélie and Juliette are in the kitchen and Eddie is on the phone, so I've been drafted as doorman. My name is Jeremy Bentham." He held out his hand, then led them back into the living room.

"And by the way, Aurélie asked me to tell you that she's preparing everything from scratch tonight, so you won't have to worry."

He paused and frowned. "Sorry. I don't mean to make light of your close call. I will probably do it again, though, so I'll apologize in advance now. Juliette says I have no tact."

Kate tried to put him at ease. "Don't worry about it, General Bentham. We all came out OK and the poisoner is safely locked up, I presume. We should be able to joke when things turn out well. Mark and I can do with a laugh or two after our weekend."

"Call me Jeremy, please. Eddie told me something about your weekend. It's a hell of a story, and I want to hear more about it tonight, but now I'd like you to meet Juliette Bertrand."

Juliette was a smiling woman with, Kate mentioned to Mark later, "a hundred-dollar hairdo."

"I'm sorry to make you have dinner so early," she said. Her English was not completely fluent but was easily understandable. "Since we came back early I volunteered to do the broadcast tonight, so I worked hard today to catch up so I could come to dinner.

"I have to work at seven thirty. We can chat until I leave, and after that I know you have serious business things to discuss."

Jeremy matched the description Icky had given them in Washington. His manners were smooth, like her husband's had been before his behavior had gone strange, but he was friendlier, which Kate thought might be because he had retired earlier. She had heard the story behind his retirement – he'd objected to invading Iraq and taken early retirement before the war started, only to see the dire consequences he'd predicted come true.

Icky had also told them the story of his whirlwind romance with Juliette, several years after his wife died. They had met at dinner, introduced by Eddie and Aurélie, and were inseparable from the beginning. Within a few weeks she had moved into his old house near Canal Saint-Martin. Normally, he met her at the end of her newscast and they went to dinner, taking the métro to a restaurant in a different part of Paris each night.

This discussion tonight must be important, Kate thought, to make Jeremy change his routine, and to have returned early from a vacation on the Riviera.

During their lunch in the Hotel Langley, Icky had explained that Jeremy's expertise and doctorate were in post–World War II Europe, especially the Soviet satellite countries. After he retired from the army he had become a history professor and written three books on East Germany. Now he was thinking of writing another about how the satellites had fared when their governments turned democratic. Icky had convinced him the case of the missing submarine might help with his research.

Juliette turned out to be a vivacious story-teller, full of barbed tales about politicians who stumbled over their own pretensions. In a half-hour they had forgotten her weak English in the pleasure of hearing her stories.

"Juliette's known as a pretty well-prepared interviewer," Jeremy told them. "She spends most days holed up at home going over the background for that day's newscast, and no small part of that is finding things politicians don't want anyone to remember. As she reminds me from time to time, news is what your subject doesn't want talked about. Everything else is publicity, and she doesn't do publicity."

"Nooo…" she said.

Eddie got up to pour a second glass of wine for everyone but Juliette, who demurred and said, "One's just right, but two's too many before the newscast. I remember your Dorothy Parker's poem about martinis."

AURÉLIE SAID, "Everyone to the table. I promise dinner is safe – I made it with my own hands so there's no ricin in it. Escargots for everyone to start, steaks for all, and a fruit tart for dessert." The joke had seemed funnier when Jeremy told it.

Mark and Kate took turns telling the story of building the submarine and of their close call the previous weekend. Juliette studiously avoided asking questions.

Jeremy said, "You think your ex was involved? That would be a remarkably hostile thing to do."

"I don't think he placed the bomb," she said. "I have trouble believing he would do that to me, but he is a jealous man. He really thought I was going to go back to him and move to a drafty castle on a cliff in Hungary. When I turned him down for the last time it made him the angriest I'd ever seen him, and that's saying something. And about that time he did some other things I found very offensive.

"I moved to Miami shortly after that and hid my tracks as well as I could. I only heard directly from him once, but from time to time I'd get a little reminder. For example, I got pulled over by the local police several times on a pretext. I never got a ticket, just a subliminal warning that someone was watching."

Eddie jumped in. "You mentioned when we saw Max Molnar that you thought your husband had corrupted the Miami police. Is that what you're talking about?"

"My ex-husband." She emphasized the ex.

"Sorry," Eddie replied. "Your ex."

"Yes, there was a policeman in Annapolis. As I heard the story, Henry helped this guy out of a jam and helped him find a job somewhere in Florida when he was fired from the Annapolis force."

"What on earth had he done?" Jeremy asked.

Kate said, "The evidence locker came up short some cocaine. It does happen from time to time, but I gather he was caught red-handed."

"And is he still in Florida?"

"Until this week I had never seen him, even in Annapolis. But he was the detective who came to the hospital after the boat was bombed. His name was Willimon, and there can't be too many policemen with that name. And he knew me."

Eddie sat bolt upright.

"Raul and Antoine are working on this right now. They've already interviewed him once. I'd better give them a heads-up.

"Excuse me for a minute. I'll send a quick email." He left the table and headed down the hall to his study.

———————

JULIETTE LOOKED at her watch and said, "You'll have to excuse me. It's seven o'clock and I must leave. Jeremy, there's no need for you to go with me."

"I'll at least see you to the street," Jeremy replied. "I'll be right back."

While he was gone the others moved in front of the dead fireplace. In five minutes he came back through the door and said, "She's off. It's an easy ride from here. She will be there on the dot."

"How long does it take to learn your way around the métro?" Mark asked. "I haven't even been on it yet."

"A lifetime," Aurélie said. "But now most people have the apps that tell you exactly how to get where you're going and when the next train or bus will arrive."

"We have a car," Jeremy said. "Actually it's Juliette's. She used to live in the suburbs and drive it to work, but now we keep it in a garage and use it maybe once every couple of weeks. It's a money pit."

"We've never had one," Eddie said. "Now and then we use my mother's car, but we ride the bus more than anything else. Some people are a little nervous about it because of the terrorist attacks, but the odds of getting hurt are pretty low."

"Juliette said something about waiting to talk business until after she left. What was that about?" Kate said.

Eddie opened his mouth to speak but Jeremy interrupted him.

"You have to remember that Juliette is a journalist, and a rather prominent one. Some of the things Eddie, Aurélie, and I do for Icky might be – shall we say – of professional interest to her.

"She and I reached agreement early that she wouldn't ask and I wouldn't tell, and it's worked."

EDDIE SAID, "Let me bring you up to date on Max Molnar.

"When he left us, he went to an apartment building in the sixteenth arrondissement. We can't be sure who he visited there, but it isn't a large building, and one of its occupants is a man named Viktor Nagy, who was high up in the Hungarian security apparatus before the Berlin Wall fell. He was a pro-

Soviet hardliner and was very much opposed to opening the borders, not to mention converting his country to a democracy.

"In fact, he said if he was going to have to live under capitalism he'd rather do it in Paris, where the food was better. He moved here and, as far as we can find out, has never lived in Hungary again. Icky is looking at his extracurricular political activities."

"What does Icky think might be going on?" Kate asked.

"He doesn't know, but it's becoming more and more apparent to me that your missing submarine and his concerns about Eastern European politics are tied together.

"Oh, and Paul got a quick and not very good picture of Max's driver. He's not familiar to me, but you should look."

He handed his phone to Kate, who said, "He's a stranger to me" and passed it to Mark.

Mark looked at the picture closely. He turned the phone on its side, then back again, then said, "I'm almost certain this is Tom Farkas, the engineer I had to fire a couple of months before Kate joined me. If it's not Tom it's a relative, and a close one."

Eddie said, "That would explain a lot. I haven't been able to figure out why they tried to kill you, but if they had an engineer who was already familiar with the submarine, they might think they didn't need you. It also strengthens a feeling I've had since this morning that Max Molnar is behind all the dirty tricks."

MARK PICKED up the bottle of Cabernet Sauvignon. Aurélie signaled she'd had enough, but Kate and Jeremy each took another glass and he poured one for himself and one for Eddie.

"Now tell me about the engineer," Eddie said.

Mark said, "I hired him two years ago. He'd worked for an aerospace firm in Germany, then moved to Silicon Valley, where he developed smartphone applications. That's what I needed most because I was using an iPhone to control the sub.

"It didn't take me long to find out he had a drinking problem. At first he would only show up with a hangover, which kicked hell out of his productivity, but by noon he was usually working pretty well. But it got worse, week by week, and eventually he started coming in drunk. He'd go into his office and close the door.

"Eventually he became completely useless. I had to let him go. It was a shame, because he understood what I was trying to do."

Kate picked up the story.

"When I came for my first interview, Mark was still recovering from a bad knock on the head. Somebody attacked him in the shop one night, and it had

to be someone who knew how to go around the burglar alarm."

Mark added, "I heard the back door open and
went to check on it. No sooner had I stepped through
the shop door than the lights went out. I woke up an
hour or so later in a pool of my own blood, with a
splitting headache. The police think I interrupted a
burglar, who hit me with a two-by-four. He was ap-
parently trying to steal the sub but didn't have time
to finish."

Aurélie interrupted, a quizzical look on her face.
"A two-by-four?"

Eddie said, "It's a size of American lumber used
in construction. Each board used to be two inches by
four inches. Like candy bars they're smaller now, but
the name stuck."

"Sort of like jumbo eggs that are really very
small?"

"That's about it."

Mark continued, "The doctor pulled splinters
out of my scalp for an hour. I had to stay in bed for
a week and move pretty slowly for a couple of weeks
after that. I didn't see who hit me, but I have a
vague memory of an SUV backed into the overhead
door. They probably intended to hook up the trailer
and drive it away, but got spooked when I
showed up.

"Anyway, after that things started looking up. I
asked Icky if he knew any good engineers, and he

sent me Kate's name, which he got from Aurélie. Small world.

"I asked the dean of the engineering school at about the same time, and he came up with Kate's name, too, because she was one of his prize doctoral students. My luck that week went from terrible to terrific." He smiled at Kate. "When we met I was still pretty woozy, but she was a big help and we're back on track – ahead of schedule, in fact, although we're not moving fast enough to satisfy Icky."

Mark asked Kate, "Where did you and Aurélie meet?"

"In New York. I was taking a master's course at Columbia while she was a visiting professor. We were both taking the sun on the library steps one day and got to talking. She was even nice enough to put me up for a week while I was having big problems at home, and we saw each other from time to time for the next couple of months.

"In fact, I think it was Aurélie who first heard about my plan to leave the Navy and move to Miami. Maybe that helped lead me to Mark."

"It was my pleasure," Aurélie said with a big smile. "Eddie was in Paris, the New York house was too big for the two of us anyway, and I discovered you were a really good cook."

"You told me about the great food," Eddie said. "I was sorry I missed it, and I really appreciated the company for Aurélie."

"You were lucky. If your burglar had used a wrench or a steel angle iron instead of wood, we wouldn't be having this conversation and the sub would have a new owner," Eddie said. "Now we need to find it. Icky doesn't know anything more about the Gulfstream than he did before, but we know it was Max Molnar's airplane, and the odds are close to one hundred percent that it was carrying the sub. He's told us all he's going to, but we know from Icky's men in Miami that Max was behind the efforts to buy your sub."

He outlined a plan of action for trying to find out, at least in general, where the sub had been taken.

"I suggest that we start tomorrow, and that Mark, Kate and I go to the airport and see who we can find who might have seen the plane land. We might get lucky.

"Jeremy, your part is a harder ask. Can you call in favors from some of the ex-communists you interviewed for your books? Wear your stars.

"Then can you go to Hungary and see what you can learn about the castle and the area around it — what's going on now, who's been seen there, that sort of thing. A couple of days should do it."

"Just where is this castle?" Jeremy asked.

Kate answered. "I've been there once. It's just on

the edge of a national park to the north of Budapest, very close to the Slovakian border in an area with a lot of caves, some of which are tourist attractions.

"You fly to Budapest and rent a car, and it's an hour's drive toward the town of Preska in Slovakia. You pass the castle and go through a couple of villages just before you cross the border.

"The castle was a ruin when I was there a dozen years ago. It was built in the fifteen-hundreds on a bluff high above the river. After the war, the Soviet government wanted more electrical power from Hungary, so they threw up a hydroelectric dam from prewar plans. The new lake flooded the river valley and two or three villages, but that wasn't anything the Russians cared much about. It's now a big producer of electricity."

Jeremy asked, "What's your ex-husband's connection to this old castle? Mickelwaite doesn't exactly sound like a sixteenth-century Hungarian name."

"It goes back a long way. In the sixteenth century, Hungary had two competing kings for a time. After a long period of squabbling, one of them, King John the First, lost out. My ex, at least in his own mind, is descended from a duke loyal to King John. The king who won the fight awarded the land to this duke to keep him loyal, and he built the castle on the most prominent place he could find. At that time it would have been relatively easy to defend.

"Henry bought the place from an old man who'd

lived in it a long time. You can't really say 'in' because it was a ruin, but he had a shabby lean-to
against one of the few walls that still stood. It had no
power or water and the old guy was delighted to find
an American who thought he was part of the family,
and an admiral to boot. You never saw such a
suck-up.

"The old man told us Vlad the Impaler used to
live there, too. My ex fancies himself a tough guy, so
that appealed to him."

JEREMY PECKED AT HIS iPHONE.

"I'll leave tomorrow afternoon. Air France has a
nonstop that gets in early enough for me to drive to
the castle and look it over.

"I'd better not," he said, holding his hand over
his glass as Eddie picked up the bottle to offer a refill.
"I have work to do tonight if I'm going to have the
background I need tomorrow. There's a man in the
suburbs I'd like to see first."

Kate said, "You may want to spend the first night
in Budapest, then drive the last leg in the morning.
There are several villages around the castle on the
Slovakian side of the border, but you wouldn't call
any of them a town, and the natives aren't friendly.
They're very possessive of their history, and not at all
happy that the castle is just across the border in Hun-

gary and not in Slovakia. It was a postwar accident of military geography."

"Ah. That will make it even more interesting. Let me think about it. Maybe I can use the time to pick my old professor's brain, if I can get to him. He's pretty frazzled dealing with the death of his friend, who was going to be leader of his political party."

"Just send me your schedule," Eddie said. "Mark and Kate, please meet me at the school tomorrow morning at seven. We'll try to track down where the submarine went after it landed."

17

ZOLTAN THE SPY

JEREMY SILENCED THE ALARM THEN TURNED TO Juliette. He slid to her side and put his hand on her thigh, then moved it up under her nightgown to cup her breast. She smiled and opened her eyes.

"*Tu es un vieux satyre*," she said. *You're a randy old man.* "Now?"

"Better not. I have a busy day. I just didn't want you to forget me."

"That's not likely. Get me up when you leave." She turned on her side and was immediately asleep again.

JEREMY LEARNED a quick morning routine when he was a young infantry commander. Toast. Coffee.

Maybe a hard-boiled egg from the refrigerator. Five-minute shower, two-minute shave, dress. He had packed a carry-on when he got home from the Grants' dinner the night before, and now took a stack of 50-euro notes from his desk drawer. He carefully counted ten of them and put them into an envelope, which he sealed.

In half an hour he patted Juliette on the shoulder to say goodbye and let himself out the front door of the 18th-century townhouse, touching its ancient lion's-head knocker for good luck. Normally he would turn right toward Canal Saint-Martin and the métro, but today he turned toward the dead end of Impasse Molière, where a narrow sidewalk between two townhouses much like his opened into bustling Avenue Jean Jaurès. Across the street, a Renault auto-repair shop offered parking space at stiff prices to a few lucky neighbors. Juliette's celebrity had kept their time on the waiting list very short.

Jeremy had lived in Paris for twenty years without a car, and never considered buying one. But when Juliette's racy Aer Lingus–green Mercedes convertible had come into his life, he discovered he liked it. Driving to an interview gave him time to think ahead about the questions he'd like to ask – and how he would deal with the predictable evasions, outright lies, and obviously faked loss of memory that eventually happened whenever he interviewed anyone who had been in power in the Soviet satellite countries. Like the man he was on his way to see.

He did not look forward to this meeting with Zoltan Kozorsky but, after flipping through the notes he'd made in researching his books, he decided Zoltan was his best chance of finding at least a little information about the resurgence of the destructive nationalism of wartime Hungary.

What Jeremy wanted to know was straightforward, if not simple: Why would Max Molnar, a successful American businessman, be talking to Viktor Nagy, a well-known Hungarian revanchist and at the same time a Russian oligarch with immense holdings in the timber industry and deep ties to the Kremlin?

Zoltan was a hardheaded man, and Jeremy knew he'd expect to be paid for his information. But if history was a guide, whatever he said would be accurate and as current as he could make it. He hadn't survived for more than two decades after the collapse of the Soviet empire by stiffing his clients.

———

RATHER THAN DRIVE directly to the Périphérique and the A3 autoroute, which were not an easy drive at the best of times but now would be backed up with heavy rush-hour traffic, he drove down Avenue Philippe Auguste to Place de la Nation, then east through the calmer park abutting the Château de

Vincennes. By the time he found a parking spot near the police station of Nogent-sur-Marne, he had decided how he would question Zoltan.

When the Soviet Union collapsed into a chaotic pile of underdeveloped and impoverished Central European countries, all looking for their own way forward, Zoltan had been a young commercial secretary in the Paris embassy.

Jeremy, then an army colonel on the way to the stars he eventually wore, was liaison officer to the French army. He had spotted Zoltan for what he was – a spy, and a good one.

But as the former satellites struggled to feed their people, spies were a luxury. Zoltan lost his job in the anti-communist purge that followed and decided to stay in Paris, where he earned a meager living writing about the nascent European Union for newspapers in Hungary and, of course, selling information gleaned from other émigrés to people like Jeremy and his successors. Somewhere, he had found the money to buy a trim townhouse two blocks from the police station.

He had ultimately landed a spot teaching European history in a high school and worked contentedly until his retirement, a year before the last time Jeremy had interviewed him.

JEREMY SPOTTED Zoltan from the end of his block. He was bent over, picking dead late-season blossoms off a rose bush, one of a half-dozen that stretched across the front garden just inside the black wrought-iron fence. Behind the roses, the tangle of perennials run wild showed clearly that Zoltan's priorities lay more with the orderly roses.

"Bonjour, Zoltan," Jeremy said. Zoltan spoke English well and comfortably but they always spoke French. It was their way of keeping their conversation on neutral ground, of avoiding the roles of victor and vanquished.

Zoltan straightened, pressing a hand against his back. Jeremy thought he looked less robust, his face gray under the familiar shock of black hair, but said nothing. We're all going to get there sooner or later, he told himself, grateful that it seemed to be later in his case, because he was at least ten years older than Zoltan.

"Mon Général." He seemed pleased. Probably doesn't get many visitors now, Jeremy thought.

"To what do I owe this visit? What brings you to the pedestrian banlieue?"

"I won't insult your intelligence by telling you it's a social call," Jeremy responded. "I'm trying to find out something that's happening in your native land and you seem like just the man to help me."

"Is this for a new book? I liked the last one."

"It may turn into a book, but for now let's just say it's a favor for a friend."

"A favor for a friend. I've done a few of those. But why doesn't this friend just call up his station chief in Budapest and put the question? Or is this something that has to be handled through the back door?"

"You always were quick, but you know I can't answer that one. Even if I knew the answer, and I'm not sure that I do."

Zoltan rubbed his back for several long seconds, then finally said, "Well, come in and we'll see what we can do."

THIS IS what my place would look like if I lived alone too long, Jeremy thought as he followed Zoltan through the door.

"Pick any chair in the living room," his host said. "Just move the junk to the next chair. I'll put on the kettle."

The newspapers Jeremy moved were in four languages, and none was older than a week. Zoltan's reading habits had not changed, but his interior decorator certainly had. When Jeremy had last been there, Zoltan's living room had had the sentimental decor of the émigré, designed to be a nostalgic reminder of home. The Eastern Europeans were second only to the Russians in their desire to re-create the look they had left behind. Jeremy remembered that Zoltan had even displayed a red lantern or two.

And now the room was pure Western Europe, heavy with the influence of Scandinavia by way of Ikea.

ZOLTAN RETURNED with a plate of cookies and a cup of the little cylindrical sweetener packets restaurants offer, grudgingly, to their customers who aren't satisfied with sugar cubes.

"I can't guarantee the provenance of these cookies," he said. "And the sweetener is the fake stuff. I can't use sugar anymore, so I don't even keep it around. The tea will be ready in a minute."

"You've redecorated since the last time I was here. It's very different."

"I got rid of all that old-country crap when my last girlfriend left. She was always pining for the Carpathians. I live in France and I've been a citizen here for years. And besides, I'm not really pleased with the things that are going on back there.

"We used to be independent, proud. Now we have a right-wing government that wants to get in bed with the damned Russians, of all people."

"As it happens, that's why I'm here," Jeremy said.

"I'm trying to find out something about an American businessman who, all of a sudden, is interested in Hungarian politics.

"He's made contact with a man you and I know well, who has his hand in both Hungary and Russia. Viktor Nagy."

The kettle whistled and Zoltan got up. "I'll get the tea. I can definitely help you."

"SOMETHING'S HAPPENING up in the northern mountains, in the caves," Zoltan said, his face somber, as he brought the tea into the living room.

"Viktor and I are not friends. He never thought I was serious enough about restoring Hungary to its properly elevated place in Central Europe, and turning its allegiance to the East, to Russia, and away from the immoral cesspool of Europe. Those are his words, not mine."

He paused. "I suspect that's what worries your friend. Oh, one more marginal country moving back into the Russian orbit wouldn't normally be a concern. But now that Russia has dismembered Ukraine to show it means business, everybody on this side is suddenly astir. Poland and the Baltics are in a panic. The Russian bear belches and Eastern Europe shits.

"Make no mistake about it, you are I are on the same side of this. I've seen what it's like to live under the Russian boot and I don't want anything to do with it again."

Jeremy sipped his tea. "It's good, even with the fake sugar." He put the cup back in its saucer. "As I said at first, I'm not sure of all the reasons behind my friend's sudden concerns, and the opinions I have may be all wrong.

"This all started as a flap over a little submarine that was stolen from its maker in Miami. That may be all there is to it, but I doubt it, because the thieves blew up the man's sailboat. When he survived that they sent a couple of Russian hoods to the hospital to kill him. They didn't succeed."

"That hardly sounds like a simple theft," Zoltan said. "These things take on a life of their own. At first it's a theft, or an insult, or even an auto accident, then before you know it, it's soldiers and armor facing each other across the border in some godforsaken place. Ukraine is already in play, and Poland is on the edge and, my friends tell me, terrified."

"Right," Jeremy said. "Figuring out what's behind things like this usually depends on knowing who's involved. And the pot started to bubble about the same time Viktor Nagy came into the picture. What can you tell me about him?"

"Most of what I know now is by way of reputation. When I was in the embassy here, he was in Budapest running internal security. I've long since quit trying to pretend I wasn't working on external threats.

"After the wall fell, he moved to Paris. That was sometime about 1990. A mutual friend told me Viktor was depressed at the thought of living under capitalism, but he knew the Americans weren't about to let in a spy like him, so he came to Paris. I understand he has never learned French."

"Did he go back into business?"

"He never left it. Espionage was just one of his trades. The other was business, more like wholesale grand larceny.

"Like all of us, he had to report back to Moscow. He got close to the minister for forestry, and when Yeltsin started to privatize the state-run businesses, he and his friend were able to buy immense tracts of timberland on the cheap. It didn't hurt that there was oil under some of it."

Jeremy asked, "So he's rich?"

"If the Russian oligarchs had a board of directors he would be on it, somewhere down the table. He's not prominent enough to attract many enemies, and he curries favor with Putin's circle. And they know his main interest is Hungary, not Russian politics. To them he's a reliable connection to one of the important lost provinces of the Soviet Union, and they want it back."

Zoltan picked up the pot to refill their cups.

"Are you in his circle now?" Jeremy asked.

"Not the way I view it. I can't speak for him.

"I've only met him twice. Once was about five years ago, when he was trying to gather a sort of ex-spies' chamber of commerce. I don't think that ever got off the ground, but he did tell me he had visited Moscow a couple of times, and once he met Putin. He didn't tell me what they talked about. That time he invited me to dinner downtown.

"It was different the last time. He just dropped in, like you did. I don't mind that because it breaks up my day. This was just under a year ago, one day last autumn. I remember because I had just turned on the heat and was having trouble getting it adjusted right."

Zoltan paused.

"Now we're getting to the point of your visit. He brought a friend, a man named Max, no last name. Max spoke Hungarian with an American accent. He wore a very expensive suit, and his hair looked like he had just left the coiffeur around the corner. It was a forest of little ringlets."

Jeremy asked, "So you never heard a last name?"

"No, but Viktor said I could trust this Max implicitly, that he was a true Hungarian patriot who had been in California for a long time. I learned later it was Max Molnar, the Silicon Valley billionaire."

"And this Max, what did he want?"

"He wanted a spy. He wanted someone to join his group to handle intelligence, and he thought I was uniquely qualified to provide information about Europe. Max hates the European Union. He is a nationalist, and that's all."

"Did his group have a name?" Jeremy asked

Zoltan replied, "He told me the final name hadn't been decided, but temporarily they call it Arrow Cross."

"Arrow Cross! That's the name the Hungarian Nazis used toward the end of the war."

"And that's why I turned him down flat. I didn't put it this way, but the last thing I want is to be caught between an old communist and a new fascist who agree only that they hate the EU and liberal democracy in general. It didn't work before and it won't work now."

Jeremy was silent for a moment. This is like going back home and finding the Ku Klux Klan running for Congress, he thought. Aloud, he said, "Is Max completely nuts or a big thinker?"

"I asked much the same question, although it was pretty clear they would lie to me," Zoltan said. "But it was Viktor who answered me, not Max. I got the clear idea that he was the political chief. In fact, Max let slip that he'd been out of circulation for several months. I don't know why, but I got the idea that he wasn't in Hungary or California."

Zoltan took a sip of tea and put the cup aside with a grimace. "Cold."

"Viktor told me Hungarian politics is in a state of

confusion," he went on, "and he and Max are trying their best to encourage that.

"If you start at the center of the political spectrum, the current government is more or less center-right. I happen to believe there's not much center there, though, and the government is becoming pretty authoritarian. You should see the newspapers.

"In any case, they didn't talk about left-right-center. They talked about the internationalists and the patriots. As you can imagine, they put themselves very firmly in the patriot camp."

Jeremy interrupted. "Let me guess. The internationalists are pro-EU, pro-American, or at least neutral. The patriots are nationalists."

"That's it," Zoltan said. "And they believe their duty is to swing the population into their camp. They seemed pretty confident they could do it."

"Tell me more about the castle. I've heard about it, but not in much detail."

"I don't know much, either. It belonged to an old Hungarian family but passed out of their hands after they all left the country before World War Two.

"Max said one of the descendants, a prominent American Navy officer, found out about it and bought it from the old hermit who had squatted there for twenty years. But he didn't have the money to restore it, so he went to his friend Max, and they went into partnership.

"It's still under construction, but the Arrow Cross

do military drills there from time to time, and I've heard that the Russian ambassador has visited."

"That would put it in a whole new light," Jeremy said. He got to his feet. "I have to go." He laid the envelope on the table between them and turned toward the door. "I'll probably be back. It's obvious this is more than just a random burglary."

Neither mentioned the money.

18

FAMILY HISTORY PAYS OFF

Saint-Yan

Mark and Kate took the métro to the Pyramides station and walked the two blocks to Gran'Langue. They arrived ten minutes early and found the door locked.

"So we wait," he said. "My guess is he'll be right on time."

As they were chatting, Paul Fitzhugh unfolded himself from the driver's seat of a sleek black Peugeot standing at the curb and walked toward them.

Kate reacted first. "Paul. Are you going with us this morning?"

"I sure am. We're at the point where Eddie brings in a second person, either Aurélie or me. She's in class today, so it's me. He should be here any minute now."

Mark said, "I understand you go 'way back with Eddie and Icky."

"That's true. I got wounded during Desert Storm and sent back to the States, and Eddie kind of adopted me. When I got out of Walter Reed he offered me a job and I've been here ever since. I'll never leave."

"What do you do?"

"Officially I'm facilities manager for the school, but unofficially I'm a man of all work. I drive Eddie's mother – he and she share this car – and I back Eddie up when one of Icky's projects needs help. And we're friends."

"Is Jeremy a friend, too?"

"To me he will always be General Bentham, so I'd say we're not close. But I have a lot of respect for him."

As they chatted, Eddie walked up behind them and asked, "Are you ready to move? We're going to take a little day trip down to the center of France, to the business airport where Max Molnar's plane arrived the day after Pegasus was stolen. I don't expect anybody will tell us he saw a submarine being taken off a plane, but we might pick up some bits and pieces that will help us put the whole story together. Get in."

Paul guided the Peugeot up Avenue de l'Opéra, circled around the opera house toward Rue Lafayette, and headed for the northeastern suburbs.

"WE'RE on the way to Le Bourget airport," Eddie said. "In the States it's best known as the airport where Charles Lindbergh landed. Now it's famous as the site of the Paris Air Show, and it's a bizjet airport. We're going to pick up a Cessna and fly down to Saint-Yan, which will take about an hour."

"WHEN YOU SAID Cessna I thought you meant a little puddle-jumper," Mark said as they boarded the sleek two-engine jet.

"I used to like the low and slow flight of the prop planes," Eddie replied, "but they're just about history now. This one is much more practical. It's good for short runways – although at six-thousand feet Saint-Yan's is not really short – and it only needs one pilot. Take a look up front and you'll see that it has a glass cockpit a lot like an airliner. Our pilot, Frédéric, tells me it almost flies itself.

"If I need to go outside of France I charter something larger, but that's not often. It's damned expensive, and I like the train, but for something like this the Cessna is ideal. In an hour we'll be talking to the man we're going to see, and we couldn't do that any other way."

The pilot was the last through the door. He

pulled it closed and turned to shake hands with Eddie, who asked, "How soon can we get away?"

"I have clearance. If we can get the bird moving in the next couple of minutes we can get right on the runway."

At that, Eddie urged the others to take their seats. He and Paul took the first row of seats, facing toward the rear, and spent most of the flight talking softly, their heads together. Mark and Kate could not make out much of the conversation but did hear several references to Molnar and drive times to Hungary.

As THE LITTLE plane started its descent, Eddie turned to them. "Now for a brief guided tour," he said. "This is the Charolais region. It's a big agricultural area and is mostly known for the famous beef cattle – we have more than four million of them. You'll probably see a herd or two of white cattle grazing in the pastures alongside the runway. It's a small airport, which is one of the reasons Molnar's people chose it."

"Or maybe Molnar himself," Mark retorted.

"There's a good chance you're right about that. We'll be landing to the north, pretty much parallel to the Loire River. You can see it off to the left, snaking through the countryside."

Mark put his arm around Kate and pulled her

close so he could whisper in her ear. "This is truly beautiful country. Can we come down here for a long weekend? We could rent a little farmhouse and take walks in the country."

"I'd love that." She turned and kissed him enthusiastically, then glanced quickly to see if Eddie was watching.

THEY CIRCLED to land into the wind on runway 33, which meant Frédéric had to taxi the entire length of the runway back to the terminal. Eddie told him to be ready to leave in three hours.

The long taxi gave them a chance to survey the airport. The stripes on some of its paved areas had faded almost to invisibility with weather and age, but the skydiving club looked well-kept and active, and the main building, with the control tower on top, had recently been painted.

Eddie said, "I asked Aurélie's father to make a couple of calls yesterday and he found the name of someone who may be able to help. He won't be happy about it, but he wouldn't be comfortable turning away a *commissaire de police* from Paris."

"A policeman in Paris has influence this far away?" Mark asked.

Paul answered. "There are several different levels of police in France, but there is one National Police, and they carry a lot of weight wherever they go. Also, Philippe is pretty well known. He was the Paris chief for a while a few years ago. A lot of people think he should still have the job."

Eddie said, "We're going to be talking to the station manager, and by now he will have interviewed the people who were working the day the Gulfstream arrived. I'll do all or most of the talking, since I'm told he doesn't speak much English. Your job is to look intelligent and interested."

Eddie asked for Monsieur Aubrey. A few minutes later a scowling, rotund man chewing an unlighted cigar emerged from an office behind the counter of the small terminal. He and Eddie exchanged greetings in French so quick Kate could not follow it, then Eddie turned and introduced each of them in turn, speaking more slowly.

M. Aubrey led them through a security door to a conference room barely large enough for all of them, where Eddie began to question him. It was obvious that he was reluctant at first, but within fifteen minutes they were chatting like old friends. M. Aubrey picked up a notepad and wrote a name on it, then left the conference room for a minute and returned with a single sheet of paper. With that, Eddie seemed satisfied.

M. Aubrey shook hands gravely with each of them, then steered them back into the lobby and shook hands one more time with Eddie, who led them out the front door to a café next to the parking lot.

Lunch wouldn't be served for an hour, so the café was almost empty. A businesslike waiter brought each of them a tiny, dense espresso. Mark put a sugar cube in his, sipped, flinched at the bitterness, and added another.

"That short meeting was worth the flight," Eddie said. "We would never have got that much information on the phone.

"He says the Gulfstream arrived late Sunday afternoon when the airport was effectively closed, with just a skeleton staff on hand. Working backwards from the flying time, that means the sub was stolen at about the same time you were waiting for the firemen to fish you out of Biscayne Bay.

"There was a truck waiting for them. It backed up to the side of the plane and something sizable was transferred. They had customs papers showing the cargo as pre-cleared machinery parts, and the staff here didn't challenge it because this plane brings stuff in several times a year, at least. That's important. The cargo would have been inspected at an airport where the plane and crew weren't known.

"We'll find out more about the truck. He said it was a rental from a couple of towns away."

Paul asked, "Did he see the driver?"

"More than that. They have his name, because

he had to register before he could go onto the ramp. He was young, and he had an Eastern accent.

"But there was another man, an older man who waited in the terminal then got into the truck after it left the security zone. Monsieur Aubrey said he seemed to be about sixty years old, handsome, with gray hair, clean-shaven, about six feet tall or a little less. He favored his left leg."

Kate gasped and covered her mouth.

"That's my ex, or at least it could be."

Eddie said, "That wouldn't surprise me."

Mark asked, "How did you get him to give you all that information? Just an introduction from Philippe Cabillaud wouldn't have been enough."

"You're right," Eddie said. "And that's where you came in, and it's why I got you out of bed so early this morning.

"I let him think you were CIA agents with a serious interest in this case, which I suppose isn't completely untrue.

"Late in the war, the Resistance was very active in this part of France, and just before D-Day they got a lot of support from the American government. The stories have been passed down to the current generation, who remain grateful. Don't believe it when people say the French are anti-American. They're not.

"And, it didn't hurt that my father was an American military spy here just before the invasion, which is usually worth a few points in a case like this. It sure was today."

"That must be a story," Mark said. "will you tell us about it some day?"

"After a few drinks some night. For now, let's go rent a car."

Paul drove the dozen miles to a combination truck-rental and furniture-storage business on the national highway to Vichy. Its office was tiny, with one middle-aged woman acting as receptionist, sales clerk and cashier. But she knew they were coming, and as they walked through the door she called out toward the shop in the rear, "Pierre!" Mark thought she looked remarkably like the airport manager.

Pierre Aubrey the nephew and M. Aubrey the uncle were as unlike as any two men could be. Pierre was a trim young entrepreneur wearing jeans and a black t-shirt. His baseball cap advertised John Deere and he insisted on speaking English.

"Mr. Grant, my uncle tells me you need to know about the truck I rented. I'll tell you what I can."

He said something to the receptionist in quick French. Then he turned and said, "My mother found the file."

When he had the rental agreement in hand he put it on the desktop and pointed at the various pieces of information, written with a fountain pen in a precise script.

"The renter, you'll see here, was Jacques Belfort,

from Paris. His age is twenty-six, he has a French identity card and a clean driving record. He looked reliable to me. He paid with a debit card on HSBC bank, one of the largest. It was authorized without challenge for a maximum of a thousand euros."

"A thousand," Paul said. "How long did they plan to keep it?"

"It was rented for a week. He actually brought it back day before yesterday, clean and undamaged. It only cost him a few hundred euros."

Eddie asked, "How many kilometers did he drive?"

"Let's see," the young man said. "The total was three thousand three hundred kilometers, or just under two thousand miles."

"That's a long way," Eddie said. "Was he the only authorized driver, or did someone help him?"

"He didn't ask to have anyone else put on the lease, but unless they have an accident when an unauthorized driver is in charge, we don't worry about it. He took another man with him, though. He was older, middle-aged, with gray hair. He waited in the car outside. I let them park it here while they had the truck.

"I've made copies of the rental contract and his driver's license and identity card. My uncle said you'd want them."

THE CESSNA WAS WAITING for them, door open, and within a half-hour they were at 20,000 feet. Eddie looked in the magazine rack until he found a map of Europe, which he spread on the table between them all.

"They drove a thousand miles each way, more or less," he said. He looked at the scale on the corner of the map and made a compass of his thumb and forefinger, with the thumb on Saint-Yan. With his forefinger he sketched a circle.

"They could have gone basically anywhere from Germany to central Spain," he said as he rotated his hand over the map. But the area we're most suspicious about is Hungary, and the castle is just the right distance away. And that's where Max Molnar and Kate's ex have overlapping interests."

Kate added, "They left Sunday afternoon and returned Wednesday afternoon, seventy-two hours. The drive is about eighteen hours each way. They could have arrived there Monday afternoon, delivered the sub, then started back Tuesday. Two men could share driving and just stop for a few hours at night."

Mark said, "Tell us more about the castle. Why on earth would they want a submarine there?"

"I really have no idea, but you could use it there. Let me set the scene for you. When Hungary finally unified, more or less, the winner gave this land to a nobleman, both in gratitude and as a way of keeping him loyal. I'm sure you remember the old maxim about keeping your friends close, but your enemies closer?

"There weren't a lot of permanent friendships among the wealthy landowners of that time. Politics consisted mainly of intimidating your neighbor by having a bigger army – more like what we'd call a militia today – and a bigger, better-defended castle. Also, you arranged marriages between your children and theirs.

"This castle was built out of the local stone. It's in an area known as the Aggtelek Karst, an area of limestone and underground rivers that dissolve it to make caves and sinkholes. In fact, one of the world's largest cave complexes is nearby, and that part of the country is honeycombed with them.

"The stone is shallow and easy to cut, so it's the building material you see in most old buildings.

"The castle was built in the fifteenth century, overlooking what must have been a beautiful river valley. But like I said the other day, the Soviet government put huge pressure on the Hungarian satellite government to generate more electricity, so in the late fifties a hydroelectric dam was built a mile or so downstream. The resulting lake flooded the valley and raised the water level so much that the castle is now only twenty or thirty feet above the water. There's an even bigger dam a few miles upstream."

"It must have been spectacular before the lake," Mark said.

"It's still attractive. People drive from Budapest to camp, swim, boat, and fish in the warm months, so the revenue from tourism helps the small towns. If the castle is ever rebuilt, it will give the little villages around it a big economic boost, which is something they can use, because the economy is in pretty bad shape."

Eddie asked, "Have you explored the castle? Is there anywhere they could hide the sub?"

"I'm sure there must be," Kate said. "But I was there a decade ago. It was still mostly a ruin, and I have no idea how much work has been done since then. It has at least one basement, but the stairs had collapsed and I saw no good reason to explore. Someone had been there, though. I saw a couple of new-looking ladders."

"But if there's still a lot of construction going on, Pegasus and Icarus could be stored somewhere away from the castle," Eddie replied. "We need to find the man who knows."

19

JACQUES BELFORT

"We can't go any further without having some idea where to find the sub," Eddie said as he picked up his phone and called Icky.

"Icky, I don't want to approach Philippe on this. It should come from you so he won't be angry that we're getting into his business, but we really need to talk to the young man who picked up the sub from Max Molnar's plane. Will you make that call?"

He described Jacques Belfort, then texted the copy of Jacques's driving license and rental contract he'd photographed at the rental agency. Icky promised to ask for Philippe's help immediately. He had no idea how quickly he would get it.

WHEN PHILIPPE CABILLAUD KEYED "JACQUES BELFORT" into his computer terminal, the screen flashed red. He sat up, then rubbed his eyes to help him see why he'd received such a high-level alarm.

Jacques Belfort, the screen said, was clean except that he had a girlfriend on the "Fiche S" list, the watch list of people who might be involved in terrorism. But she didn't fit the same mold as the terrorists who'd been active in France recently – she was Hungarian and Catholic. She was *fiché S* because of her membership in the Arrow Cross, the descendant of the Hungarian neo-Nazi group that governed the country under German tutelage near the end of the war.

The Hungarian authorities made it known she had moved to Paris, and they were concerned she might take unwelcome action against Hungarian diplomats or visiting politicians. The Paris police tracked her for two weeks and then interviewed her in the living room of Jacques Belfort's apartment in the nineteenth arrondissement. They could not agree among themselves that she was dangerous, but decided to include her on the list as a precaution.

Philippe didn't hesitate. He dispatched two officers to sit outside Jacques's apartment house, then when they arrived he picked up the phone and dialed the number on his screen.

He heard the double beep for what seemed like an eternity, but at last someone picked up the phone.

"Is that Jacques Belfort?" he asked.

"*C'est moi*," the voice on the other end answered. Jacques had obviously been taking a nap and was having trouble waking up.

"This is Commissaire Cabillaud of the National Police," Philippe said as authoritatively as he could. "I need to talk to you urgently about a package you picked up from a private airplane at the airport of Saint-Yan several days ago. Please wait there and I will come to you."

"Sure," Jacques said. "I'll take a shower and wait for you."

Philippe told the waiting policemen to be alert. "The trap is set. If he comes out he will be in a hurry. I will be there in twenty minutes."

The officers took up their stations on either side of the entrance. Five minutes later, Jacques burst through the building's shiny blue door wearing a backpack and carrying a suitcase.

Both officers were well over six feet tall and muscular, so stopping a beardless student posed no challenge. When Jacques turned to the right, the first policeman stepped away from the building façade and held up his hand.

"Wait there," he commanded. Jacques stopped but immediately started to argue. That stopped when the second policeman grasped his wrist from behind him and snapped handcuffs on it, then reached for the other wrist. The suitcase fell to the sidewalk.

"I can't tell you anything," Jacques said.

"Silence!" said the policeman who had hand-cuffed him. His partner stepped aside to call Philippe, who told them to take Jacques to the local precinct station and to put him in a conference room, not a cell, and to take off his handcuffs. "With a little luck he will be our friend," Philippe said. "Don't antagonize him any more than necessary."

As Jacques sat handcuffed in the back seat, the driver said, "You'll be talking to Commissioner Ca-billaud. He's a good man and an honest one, and he wants this to be as easy as possible for you. If you know what's good for you, you won't lie to him. He doesn't take that at all well."

PHILIPPE SAW A TALL, spindly young man – so young he was struggling to grow a wispy beard. Even if he succeeded it would never be an impressive one, for his uncombed hair was so light it was almost invisi-ble. The washed-out knit shirt, which once had been green, the lank hair, and the white painter's pants gave him an air of insignificance.

"A *nul*," Philippe murmured, mainly to himself, but he was pretty certain he could bring Jacques around to his side quickly. He did, but not for the reason he expected.

"I am Commissaire Cabillaud, who called you

earlier," he began. "You should not have run. I do not think the prosecutor will have any interest in you, but we will not know that for sure until this conversation is finished. I hope you understand what I am trying to tell you."

Jacques nodded, mute.

"Last Sunday you picked up a package at the airport in Saint-Yan and drove it away in a rental truck, along with an accomplice. The package did not belong to you, so I suppose you could be guilty of theft or of receiving stolen goods, but I am not interested in that.

"I need three pieces of information from you. First, what was in the box? Second, where did you take it? And third, who were you working for?"

Philippe sat calmly in a plastic chair on one side of the conference table, which even in its early days had been ugly. Now its Formica was peeling away, revealing random brown splotches. Jacques paced from one side of the room to the other, pausing to look out a window that admitted scant air and light and gave a view of the back of the adjacent building.

"Much of that I can't answer. I did it out of love. My girlfriend asked me to do a favor for her brother and drive a large wooden crate to Hungary for him. I'm a student and I should have been studying, but he offered me two hundred euros plus my expenses and I needed the money."

"Did you meet the brother?"

"Yes, he came from Budapest last week. He is the manager of a construction company in the north, but this was part of his other work, his political work. He is a leader in the Arrow Cross party."

"The Arrow Cross? I thought that group was dissolved after the war along with all the other Nazi groups."

Jacques replied, "It's not a legal party, more a splinter group. They're opposed to the current government and are really upset about all the immigrants coming through Hungary. I guess they don't remember how the western countries supported us after the war."

"So you delivered the package to Hungary. Where?"

"I took it to a little town in the north of the country, near the border with Slovakia. The leader of the movement is rebuilding an old castle there to be his national headquarters. I had a passenger on the trip, an old American who called himself the admiral. He was an unpleasant man.

"Anyway, the castle is nothing but a huge construction site, so I took it to a farmhouse across the lake from the castle. We left it in the farmer's old barn, then turned around and headed back to Saint-Yan. We turned in the truck and came back to Paris. The admiral drove, but I'd had all of his company I could stand. I persuaded him to buy me a ticket on the train." He paused and eyed Philippe uncertainly. "Are you curious about why I'm telling you all this?" he asked. "Two days ago I wouldn't have said a word. But when I got home last night I found a note from my girlfriend saying goodbye – she had moved back to Hungary. She only stayed with me so I'd do this job for her. As I think back over the two days her brother was here, I have doubts that he's actually her brother. I came home from class one day and found them looking pretty disheveled. My guess is he's her lover. Her main lover, or maybe just another sap like me."

Philippe asked, "And what was in the crate?"

"I never saw inside, you understand, but I think it was an underwater boat, a small submarine of some sort. The admiral said the Arrow Cross needed it to gather intelligence."

"Is the admiral going to be the chief of Arrow Cross in that area when the castle is finished?" Philippe asked.

"He's somebody important, but I don't think he's the leader. My girlfriend told me the big boss is a man named Max, who's part Hungarian and part American. He lives in Paris part of the time. Anyway, he's a rich right-winger who fancies himself the leader of Hungary. She says he is very charismatic in private, but isn't ready to go public yet, although he's an open secret."

"Even I have heard of Max Molnar, and I don't

follow Hungarian politics," Philippe said. "And he does live in Paris part of the time."

Philippe left Jacques drawing a map of the farm where he'd left the sub while he went to print a map of Hungary. When he returned, Jacques showed him the layout of the farm, with the barn fifty yards behind the house, then pointed out on the larger map how to reach it from the nearby town. It was a dozen miles from the castle on the other side of the lake.

He scanned and sent copies of both maps to Eddie and to Icky.

"There's nothing more I can do now," he told them. "I don't think Jacques will tell his friends about our conversation, but I can't be completely sure. I can hold him for forty-eight hours for receiving stolen goods while we check out the story, but the prosecutor won't be interested. That's all the time you have."

20

BUDAPEST IN THE AFTERNOON

BUDAPEST

As the Air France cabin crew bustled down the aisles checking seat belts, Jeremy Bentham got a good look at Budapest and the surrounding plain of the Carpathian Basin. He could pick out Buda Castle overlooking the Danube and remembered that Dr. Westerhof's apartment was in the hills behind it, about a mile from the river. He would go there as soon as the plane landed, stopping only to leave his bag at the hotel.

He had waited until just before the Airbus left Paris to call the professor, who he knew was preoccupied with reorganizing his political party. In the past he had found Dr. Westerhof to be crusty and aloof, but today he was invited to drop by as soon as he landed.

At West Point, Jeremy had initially thought the professor was German, but despite the Germanic name he was Hungarian and a strong patriot whose zeal had grown during his last years teaching in the United States. When the Middle East had blown up he had retired and returned home to Budapest, dragging his unwilling American wife with him. They had bought a prewar apartment in the hills on the Buda side of the Danube, overlooking the city, and she had made peace with the move. In recent years they had spent more time in Paris than in Budapest.

Dr. Westerhof offered him a glass of wine as they stood on his balcony.

"So tell me how I can help you. We haven't really talked since you were researching your books. I read them all and I compliment you on them."

"You could probably see your own influence in them. The time you spent talking to me was a very important part of my research.

"Here's the current problem. A small, very specialized submarine was stolen from a contractor's shop in Miami. At about the same time, he and his chief engineer came very close to being killed. A diver put a bomb on the hull of their sailboat but he was clumsy and they escaped before the explosion. It was a very close thing.

"We've tracked their submarine to France. It was picked up at a small airport in Charolais and driven somewhere a thousand miles away, more or less. The

distance exactly matches a point on the Hungary–
Slovak border where an old castle is in renovation.

"A man we think has an unfriendly connection to
the chief engineer is the owner of that castle. We believe a Hungarian-American businessman, Max Molnar, may be deeply involved in it."

"Max! You should have told me his name first.
I've met him, but more important, I know his reputation. He's tied up with a right-wing splinter political
group that wants to overturn the government and
take us out of the EU and NATO."

"Is that Jobbik?" Jeremy asked.

"Jobbik is mainstream next to his group. People
don't know much about the splinter Jobbiks, the little
outfits that are trying to gain seats in the parliament.
There's one thing they have in common, their desire
to leave the EU. If there's another, it's their view on
Jews, and as a Jew I'm sensitive to that. And on top
of that, both the governing party and Jobbik are financed by Moscow. These are people whose fathers
and grandfathers fought the Russians in the Second
World War, then lived under the communist boot for
forty years. It's inconceivable!"

Jeremy replied, "Well, that makes a little more
sense of what I heard in Paris. We suspect Max
Molnar is behind this. It appears that his corporate
jet brought it from Miami to a little airport near Paris
and then a confederate drove it to somewhere in
Hungary. We don't know where, but the mileage they

drove would include the northern Hungarian mountains in the border."

"That's an interesting place," the professor said.
"Max's new outfit is working up there, at least according to the rumors, and I'm told they have
training that involves the Russians. It's a depressed
area, the mines and factories no longer provide work
for the men, and they are receptive to all kinds of nationalist adventures, such as bringing Slovakia back
into the grand Hungarian Empire.

"I'm not up on it, but I have a friend who is.
Would you like me to ask?"

Without waiting for an answer he picked up the
phone and dialed. When the friend answered, he
barked, "Klaus. Meet me at The Goulash in fifteen
minutes. A friend from America wants to buy us
dinner and pick our brains."

Jeremy nodded in agreement.

"Klaus was my doctoral student," the professor
explained, "my last one, at Ohio. He's younger so he
gets around more than I do, but he doesn't have
much money, so when I ask him for help I always buy
dinner. Of course, I don't have much money either,
so that's where you come in," he said with a fleeting
grin.

"It will be my pleasure," Jeremy said.

As THEY WALKED toward the restaurant, Dr. West-erhof turned to Jeremy. "I should warn you that Klaus is a flamboyant personality. His body matches. He was pretty badly crippled as a boy. You'll see."

Jeremy opened his mouth to reply but the professor silenced him with a wave. "The accident that broke his back is what will make him valuable to you. The personality part of it will make itself obvious soon enough.

"He was caught in a landslide that killed one of his friends. It happened while they were exploring the cavern below Max Molnar's castle. His friend's body was never found, and it took Klaus days to crawl and swim out. All the movement turned his broken back into a lifetime disability."

"That's too bad," Jeremy said. "Did he learn to compensate for it?"

"He lives life pretty much to the fullest. He never married, but I don't think that's the fault of the broken back; he's just an unusual personality. That's the best way to put it. An unusual personality. You'll see. He alienates a lot of people.

"But he speaks English like an educated American. If you close your eyes, you won't be able to tell the difference. It's from childhood practice and then five years teaching in the States, until his job disappeared in the recession. He'll probably never mention it to you, but he's not very fond of the U.S. right now.

"And Klaus is not his original name."

"I thought it might not be. It's pretty German."

"He was originally Kolos, but his students thought that was strange so he changed it to Klaus. They were undergraduates and weren't really clear about the difference between Germany and Hungary, anyway."

The professor pushed through the heavy door of the restaurant. "I thought you told Klaus to meet us at The Goulash," Jeremy said.

"We call it that because it's so strange that a place named The Left Bank wouldn't serve French food. But if you like goulash, it's good. I'm not a fan. I prefer schnitzel."

"Let's sit against the back wall over there," the professor said, pointing at a garish red-velvet booth across the large room. "They sort of look for me there, and service can be a little casual otherwise."

They chatted, reminiscing on old friends they'd had in common at West Point.

"Klaus and I have known each other a long time," the professor said as he finished his first glass of lager. "But we've never been friends. At my age, and with my faithful but unhappy wife not in the best of health, I could use some. May I call you Jeremy? And I will be André."

Jeremy was touched. "Of course, André. There's no one else I'd rather have as a friend." They touched their glasses gently.

"Except maybe your TV star?"

"Juliette is not at all the same thing. The friend stage with her barely lasted beyond dessert," he said with a smile.

***

"Before Klaus arrives I need to mention something more serious. I know from your books that you have looked deeply into the history of Eastern Europe after the war, but I'd like to warn you about something that happened before the war – Weimar."

"I know it was a difficult time," Jeremy replied. "It was chaotic, with political murders all too often, and the military plotted with like-minded civilians in favor of a very authoritarian type of rule."

"It's the authoritarian part of it that concerns me now," André said. "Hungary isn't a police state, or even close to it, but its government is authoritarian, and its press has been subverted. The risk is authoritarianism descending into dictatorship, as it did in the thirties.

"I'll be dead before it happens, but you may not be. I don't have children, so for me it's the end of the line, and that's fine. But for you younger people, the risk of another little Austrian corporal is not zero.

"In fact, it's much riskier now than it was in the thirties. The power of big business is much greater now than it was seventy-five years ago. We learned in

2008 that capitalism is not self-regulating; far from it. What will you do to keep power in the hands it should be in? And that's not the plutocrats and oligarchs."

BEFORE JEREMY COULD ANSWER, a stir at the front door caught his eye. The maître d' was in a shouting match with a short man whose face turned more and more red as he watched. The Left Bank was not a quiet place – it had tile floors and hard walls that amplified the conversation of a hundred diners into a buzzy din, and the shouting match at the door was now evident to everyone.

"Oh, shit," André said, getting to his feet. "That's Klaus, arguing again with the headwaiter. They threw him out a couple of weeks ago when he insisted on smoking a really foul cigar. I need to stop this."

He hurried to the door and stood between the two angry men. Jeremy saw him put his hand on Klaus's shoulder but Klaus abruptly brushed it away, and then said something curt. He finally followed André toward the booth, but it was clear he was still angry. He marched, rather than walked, and continued to talk to André's back.

As the two men moved across the floor toward him, Jeremy had time to appraise Klaus. He had an obvious handicap – his right shoulder was tilted up at a sharp angle, and his trunk was twisted hard to the left, so that he seemed to be moving crabwise across the restaurant. He was sloppily dressed and had at least two days' growth of beard – more in some places. Clearly, he was as careless about shaving as about dressing. Jeremy hoped it was more precise when it came to information about the caves.

A dozen feet away, André stopped and turned to Klaus. Jeremy did not understand the language well enough to make out what was said, but the effect was immediate. Klaus looked for the first time at Jeremy and the scowl on his face relaxed. He nodded in agreement then followed André to the table.

Jeremy, normally the most even-tempered of men, thought the argument at the door had been rude and stayed in his seat as André made the introduction.

AN HOUR and several beers later, Jeremy's view of Klaus was beginning to soften. When the apology finally came it seemed genuine and, Jeremy believed, showed that Klaus understood himself.

"I am sorry about that scene at the door," he told both Jeremy and André. Then, turning as directly to Jeremy as his twisted body would allow, he said, "As you saw, I can be a remarkable asshole sometimes.

André knows I don't get along with the sniffy twit at the door, in his penguin suit. Not long ago, a close friend gave me a perfectly good Havana cigar he bought from his cab driver while he was there. I lighted it up just to take a couple of puffs and the headwaiter tossed me out on my ear."

"It was a terrible cigar," André interjected. "I've never smelled a worse one."

"How could I have known my friend had been cheated? Some Cuban cab driver sold him a box of dime cigars for a dollar. I think they were made out of the sweepings from a horse stall.

"Anyway, I hope we can get along. André tells me you need help with the caves along the Slovak border. That's my home territory, even though I grew up in Budapest. It's where I got this body, exploring the cavern under the old castle ruin while I was visiting my mother's brother one summer. My best friend's bones must still be there. I haven't heard of anyone exploring it since, and I don't blame them.

"It was so dangerous that the government put steel bars over the entrance to keep curious boys like me from going back in there. It's the only entrance I know about, although the cavern connects to a river that runs through the main chain of caves. There are miles of them under a national park that's only a few miles away.

"When I explored it, the cave was dry. It was only when the Russians made the government put a hydropower station on the river and create the lake that the water rose high enough to cover the entrance.

"There's another thing. I could frankly use a job right now."

Jeremy said, "And I could use some help. But let's have dinner before we drink any more, and we can talk while we eat."

André said, "Could I ask you to excuse me? I still have political problems to sort out. Jeremy, will you call me tomorrow?"

BY THE TIME dinner was done, Jeremy and Klaus were on first-name terms and had agreed to make a scouting trip to the castle the next day. They'd also agreed on a wage that Jeremy thought Icky would accept without too much argument. Most of it would be paid when the job was done.

"We should drive tomorrow afternoon," Klaus said. "We can approach the castle soon after sunrise the next morning. It sits on a rocky peninsula with bluffs on two sides. One drops to the lake, but the other is less vertical and has the forest at its base. We will be able to approach that side through the trees.

"We'll stay with my Uncle Andor, who lives on his farm a few miles out of town. He will be glad of the company, and there aren't any Holiday Inns anywhere nearby. And, the locals won't know we're in town. I think that might be important.

"Uncle Andor is the last of my family, and he's sort of an unofficial historian of the town. They call him The Mayor. I know a lot about the area, and he knows the rest."

JEREMY CALLED Eddie as soon as he had finished dinner. He saw an opportunity, if the team moved fast.

"I've just finished talking to a really odd duck, a friend of André Westerhof. He's strange, but he knows the area around the castle and explored it when he was a boy. In fact, he was hurt pretty badly exploring the cave that runs under the castle. I've hired him as a guide.

"I still don't see yet why Max Molnar wants the sub, but his castle is a good place to practice whatever he plans to do with it. It's on a big lake, which we knew, but Klaus tells me there's an underground part of the lake that may be connected to the cave network under the national park that's nearby.

"We need to explore it. Can you send Kate over here with some diving gear?"

"I'll talk to her, but there shouldn't be any problem. They're both divers."

"I know, but with his broken arm Mark won't be of much use. And anyway, I suspect Kate is the better diver, and I know she's the test pilot for the sub. I hope we'll get it back in time to use it.

"I'm going to meet Klaus around noon tomorrow. Air France has a flight that arrives from Paris about the same time. If you can get her on it, with some scuba gear, we can get the tanks filled here and be on our way. We need to get there by late afternoon, so we can meet his Uncle Andor."

"Consider it done," Eddie replied. "I'll update you in a couple of hours."

Jeremy caught a cab near the restaurant and had it leave him at the end of the Chain Bridge, whose stone piers and graceful suspension spans reminded him of the Brooklyn Bridge. The original did not survive the war and the new one, he had once learned as part of his book research, dated from 1949.

He sauntered across toward his hotel, mixing easily into a polyglot crowd of locals and tourists, all casually dressed for the warm summer night. At the center, halfway between the two stone arches that anchor the bridge into the Danube bedrock, he stopped to look at Buda Castle, gleaming on the hill above.

A dozen yards away, a group of Middle Eastern men sat smoking and chatting quietly on the sidewalk, their backs propped against the bridge railing. He tried to make out what language they were speaking but couldn't hear well enough to decide if it was Arabic. It was certainly not Hungarian or German.

As he concentrated, a dark van stopped with a loud screech of brakes and four men jumped out the side door shouting insults. The four were dressed alike in brown shirts, each with an armband bearing the distinctive angular symbol of the Arrow Cross. They climbed over the traffic barrier, rushed the refugees, and beat them with what looked like police batons.

After less than a minute the men poured back into the van as quickly as they'd left it. As it passed him, Jeremy got a quick look at the driver, then turned toward the refugees to see if he could help. None appeared to be badly injured, but they were obviously terrified.

The pedestrians around Jeremy immediately separated into two groups. One group moved away from the men as quickly as they could, without looking at them. Another group, speaking mostly French and German, stopped to offer aid. Jeremy helped an old German man stanch the blood flowing from a cut above one refugee's eye.

"We got rid of the Nazis once, and I'll be damned if we'll let them come back," the old man said before he turned to help another refugee.

"Has someone called the police?" Jeremy asked him.

"Probably, but if they come at all it will be a

while. They're Hungarians, too, and the Hungarians don't want the refugees. We Germans don't want so many of them, either, but we don't beat them up in the street. Not very often, anyway."

FIFTEEN MINUTES LATER, Jeremy leaned over the railing to look at a ferry passing below. He'd checked the map and learned that at least a dozen ferry lines moved up and down the Danube within Budapest, and he was trying to see how many of them he could identify. His phone chirped.

"All set," Eddie said. "Kate anticipated something like this, so she brought some gear from Miami, and Paul borrowed tanks from the *pompiers*. Mark and I will come, too, so we'll have teams of two, just in case. We won't travel together.

"One more thing. Jacques Belfort finally opened up and told Philippe where he left the sub. We were right when we guessed it was going to the castle. I've just sent you a map.

"They didn't have space for it in the castle itself because of the construction work, so they put it in a farmer's barn a few miles outside of town. He's a sort of local satrap Max knows."

Jeremy said, "That will make our job easier. Are we going to just pick it up and head back?"

Eddie's brief silence gave Jeremy the answer before he heard the words. "Icky has something else going on there. He wants us to locate the sub and check it out, but not bring it back just yet. He says it shouldn't take more than a day."

Jeremy said, "I think I'm beginning to understand what's going on. I'm on Chain Bridge right now, and just a minute ago a gang of stormtroopers wearing Arrow Cross outfits beat up a group of refugees. André Westerhof told me that happens here from time to time, although not usually in the midst of tourists.

"But this was odd: Two of the thugs were speaking Russian. I'd swear the driver of the van was the guy whose picture you showed me, the one who drove Max Molnar away from your office. The one who used to work for Mark. And the other two thugs were speaking pure American English."

Eddie was silent for a moment and then said, "I'll call Icky."

21

A BRIEFING FROM THE PROFESSOR

BUDAPEST

At nine the next morning Jeremy picked up a rental car and went to see the professor, who told him Klaus had called late the night before, giddy with delight that he had been invited to join the team.

"But I have to tell you I'm a little worried. He asked a lot of questions about who you work for and what your purpose is. I don't really know the answers so I couldn't tell him anything, but I don't trust him. And you shouldn't, either.

"I don't think he will sell you out before he's paid. He needs the money, but I suggest you wait until the entire job is done to give him any serious amount."

Jeremy said, "I'll be careful. Almost all of his

payment will come from Paris after we're finished. I'll know a lot when we see how his uncle greets us."

"THERE'S one other thing that's a little curious," André said. "I spent last night and this morning trying to salvage what's left of my political party after Vasily, and I found out he was working on something to do with the damned castle. It seems that no matter what I do or where I go, I can't escape it, or its neo-Nazis, or that wretched Max Molnar."

"How was he involved with the castle?"

"Not really involved, but he had made several calls to the national records center. It seems he wanted to find out who the legal owner of the castle is. The old general secretary told me Vasily had Max in his sights for some real estate violation."

"We know who owns it, don't we? It's Henry Mickelwaite, the ex-admiral. Kate thinks he may have done some sort of a joint-venture deal with Max, but he's been the one hundred percent owner since their divorce was final, and that was several months ago."

"That may be what she thinks, but the fact is she's still on the title as joint owner. I have no idea what difference it makes, but Max obviously thinks it could be important."

Jeremy, baffled, scratched his head and said, "I'll ask her when we get a chance, and when Klaus isn't around. I'm sure she will know exactly how it stands. She's not one to leave loose ends."

22

DINNER WITH UNCLE ANDOR

AT NOON PRECISELY THE HOTEL DESK CALLED TO announce that Klaus had arrived.

"We're stopping at the airport to pick up a colleague," Jeremy said as he pulled away from the hotel. "Then we need to stop and have some dive tanks filled. André found an industrial gas supplier who will do it while we wait."

Klaus was surprised the project was moving so fast. "I didn't know you wanted to look underwater," he said. "That could be dangerous. There are stories …"

"We just want to be prepared for anything," Jeremy said. "If we recover the submarine we may want to look around a bit."

Klaus was even more surprised to learn that the passenger would be a dark-haired woman hardly as tall as he was, but he was ostentatiously flattering as he kissed her hand and welcomed her to Hungary.

Kate and Jeremy lifted the larger of her equipment cases into the trunk and placed her wetsuit case on the back seat. She squeezed in behind Jeremy despite Klaus's protestations that she should take the front seat.

"You stay there. My legs are short and, anyway, Jeremy needs his navigator close at hand. It's a more important job than being a passenger." Klaus beamed.

After the tanks were filled, they drove north for an hour. Klaus kept probing to learn more about Kate, but she deflected all his questions about her background, except to say that she had been diving for more than a decade and had grown up around boats. She didn't mention the admiral.

They drove past the entrance to one large cave complex, whose parking lot was full of cars bearing European Union license plates. After another half-hour they turned off at a sign advertising a resort with access to the lake and soon entered a tiny village, where Klaus asked Jeremy to stop on the main street in front of a store that seemed to sell mainly beer and cigarettes. He stayed inside the store less than five minutes and returned with a sack.

"At the next intersection we could turn right and go straight to the castle, but today I suggest we continue straight ahead and go see Uncle Andor first," he said. "He lives another five miles out of town, on a farm that's been in our family for generations. Then we can come back and see the castle if there's time, or we can do it in the morning."

Jeremy asked Kate, "What do you think?"

"I think Klaus is right. We need a local contact. He can probably look at the map Eddie sent you and tell you the best way to find out if the sub is still there. Then we can figure out how to get it back."

"Okay," Jeremy said. "Straight ahead it is."

"Go ahead two miles," Klaus said. "On the way we'll cross the river that leads to the lake. You can see the castle from my uncle's farm. Cross the bridge, then take the second right, downhill. After three miles we'll come to his lane on the left."

"Whoa!" Jeremy said, and pulled the car to the curb. "That sounds a lot like the directions on the map. Let me look at it."

He pulled his phone from his pocket and held it up so Klaus and Kate could see the screen.

"We're here, in the town," he said. "Here is the right turn. We're going straight ahead across the bridge. Here." He pointed. "Then we take the second right, then a while later we turn into a farmer's lane.

"Klaus, your Uncle Andor has the submarine!"

UNCLE ANDOR's lane turned out to be a deeply rutted mile-long road that had once been gravel. On a tractor it would have been a comfortable ride, but it was a challenge to Jeremy's rented Opel.

"My uncle and his neighbors always argue over who should maintain this road," Klaus said. "It's the only way in to his farm, so he usually loses, but he holds out as long as he can. It feels like he maybe waited a little too long this time, though."

They pitched and bucked for ten minutes before the old farmhouse came into view to their left, at the edge of a dense hardwood forest. An unpainted barn stood in a pasture to its right. "That's the only place on the farm big enough for the sub," Klaus said. "If we had some way to carry it we could just drive in and get it, but it would cause a war with Uncle Andor. If we handle him right he will offer it to us."

As they drove the final hundred yards he told them, "Don't be fooled by his age. He was born during the war, so he's in his mid-seventies, but looks older. He's had a hard life.

"My mother was much younger, a late-life surprise for my grandparents. They died when she was hardly twelve years old and Uncle Andor raised her like a daughter. They had a falling-out later and she moved to Budapest, where I was born, but he was always kind to me.

"He was an enthusiastic and faithful communist from the day the Russians rolled in. He was too young for revenge against the Arrow Cross fascists after the war, which he will regret until the day he dies. He thinks the people who rule Russian now have broken faith with true communism, and he hates our own government for sucking up to them.

"And he's a tough old bird. There's a group of hooligans in town who try to bother him from time to time. He keeps a double-barreled shotgun over the door and showed me once how one barrel is loaded with birdshot and the other with buckshot. One dose of birdshot was all it ever took to run them off."

He added, "He doesn't speak much English – actually, none. I'll translate."

Neither Jeremy nor Kate volunteered that they understood some Hungarian, but Jeremy asked, "Would it help if I spoke to him in Russian? I know a lot of people here speak it."

"For God's sake, whatever you do don't speak Russian," Klaus said nervously. "The only Russians he knows now are the oligarchs who come to the old satellite countries to launder the money they've stolen. He won't have anything to do with them."

ANDOR'S HOUSE looked like a poor house in poor country. It hadn't seen paint for years and the porch across the front sloped ominously downhill toward the right. But the single chair and trestle table sitting next to the peeling front door looked firm, and the small refrigerator next to them was new and shiny.

"That's his beer refrigerator. I asked you to stop in town so I could bring him some more," Klaus said.

As the car stopped, Uncle Andor stepped onto the porch and waved.

"Does he know we're coming?"

"Just me," Klaus replied. "Let me get out first. He can be a little quick with the shotgun."

He walked to the porch and embraced his uncle. The two whispered for a minute, then Klaus signaled Kate and Jeremy to join them and made the introductions.

Both understood enough to know Klaus was introducing them as his friends from the United States who were anxious to learn the history of the old castle from the mayor, who knew stories no one else did. The old man beamed at the flattery. He smiled and shook Jeremy's hand, but most of his attention was reserved for Kate. She put out her hand but he grabbed her by the arm and hugged her close.

Klaus translated. "He says you look like my mother, his sister, and he wants to welcome you to our family home. He hopes you will come inside and sit a while, perhaps even stay the night. And I didn't even have to ask."

The interior was dark. A single bulb shed some light in the kitchen, but the only illumination in the living room was from the windows, which hadn't been recently washed.

Uncle Andor took the only real chair in the room, an antique leather recliner a decade or two beyond its best days. He straightened a white coverlet on a sofa facing out the window and pointed to indicate Jeremy and Kate should sit there. Klaus, who had obviously been through the same process many times before, pulled up an old piano stool. There was no piano in sight.

Jeremy tried to offer him space on the sofa but he refused. "I've used this seat since I was a boy. I don't see any reason to change now, but thank you."

"So, you are here to ask about the castle?" the old man said.

"Yes, we are very interested in it. But we are more interested in the large box you have in your barn," Jeremy said.

"How did you learn about it?" He didn't seem surprised at the question.

Kate picked up the conversation. "Uncle Andor, we are here because that box belongs to me, or more precisely, to me and a friend. It was stolen in Miami almost a week ago and the men who took it tried to kill me and my friend. They almost succeeded."

Andor looked angrily at Klaus and spoke so quickly that neither Kate nor Jeremy could understand. Klaus translated, "I am sorry, but he is angry that I did not tell him about the bomb. He does not like Max Molnar, the man at the castle, or the stormtroopers with him."

Andor interrupted. "Max Molnar and the gray-haired man who supervises the castle work have gone to Budapest with their driver. They asked to put the box here because there was no place to secure it in the castle, and they were afraid the stormtroopers doing work there would steal it. But the Arrow Cross men are camping in the woods, and Max has gone to Budapest to meet with some politicians." He spat out the word.

KATE LOOKED AT JEREMY. They had two days to re-cover the sub and accomplish whatever it was that Icky wanted done, so Kate decided to try for more.

"Uncle Andor, the box contains a small submarine. It is not a weapon, but is designed to gather information. I have no idea why Max Molnar would want it, but I cannot see how it would be of any use in a lake this small. Do you have an opinion?"

"I wept when the Soviet Union collapsed. Klaus has different political views from mine, far different, but neither of us likes having another authoritarian government. Especially, I do not like having one that kisses the backside of the thieves and murderers now in power in Moscow.

"I can only guess that your submarine is something Max thinks he can trade for information or political power. Any of the Russian oligarchs who have built country homes in Hungary would surely pay for it, if it would help him curry favor with the Russian government. Or if that failed, they would probably try to sell it back to your government."

Kate said, "It doesn't belong to the United States government. It belongs to me and my friend, and it will do us much harm if we aren't able to get it back."

THEY SAT in silence while Andor pondered what she had said. The sound of a clock ticking came through the door of a bedroom, and somewhere outside the front door a dog barked.

Andor turned to Klaus and asked, "What do you think?"

"All I know is what Professor Westerhof has told me. He trusts Jeremy completely. They have been friends for many years. I don't want you to do something that would cause problems with Max Molnar."

"That puppy! The man with the curls! After years of raking in ill-gotten profits he now wants to be the savior of the Hungarian people? Don't make me laugh. The man's a Nazi, and his friend is strange. He always laughs at the wrong time."

He turned to Jeremy and Kate.

"I will lend you the box, and I don't know what's in it, except that it belongs to you. You have to promise to return it by noon Saturday. If you don't, and Max Molnar returns, there will be trouble. He has great influence among the police because many of them are sympathetic to Arrow Cross."

Jeremy responded immediately. "We accept that condition. How can we carry it?"

"I have an old truck, and there is a hoist in the barn. That's the way Max and his people unloaded it after they brought it here from France."

"Thank you," Kate said, as she got up and kissed the old man on the cheek. "What you've done will help many people."

WHILE THEY WERE TALKING the sun had gone down behind the trees and the living room was almost dark.

Andor got up to turn on a table lamp. "You must stay tonight," he said. "Tomorrow you can take the box and you will have the entire day to test it or whatever it is that you need to do. I shot a fat rabbit this morning and was planning to make a stew. I will add some vegetables and there will be plenty for all of us."

Klaus turned to them and said in English, "We should stay. We lived on Uncle Andor's rabbit stew when I visited here as a teenager. He grows all the vegetables himself."

It was then that Andor revealed more about himself than he had intended. "All from my own garden," he said in accented English, and then put a hand over his mouth. "Oops. Now you know that I understand some of what you say. At least it will be easier now. Klaus told me I should not speak English, but I can try. If I make a mistake he can translate."

"Missus Kate, will you help me choose some potatoes and carrots from the cellar?"

She followed him into the kitchen, where he reached down to open a trap door in the corner. One at a time, they backed down a narrow wooden staircase into a dark, humid chamber redolent of rich earth, where they picked out a handful of vegetables for the stew. But what Andor really wanted was to ask questions.

"Your friend Jeremy – is he really a general?"

"He was, Uncle Andor, but now he is a writer. He is well known for his books about Eastern Europe after World War Two and is thinking about writing another one."

"And you. Do you really own this submarine?"

"Legally, I suppose not, but I built part of it so it feels like mine. My close friend Mark started it and owns the little company where I work. There are just the two of us."

"If he is your close friend, why is he not the man with you, rather than General Jeremy?"

"I would give anything if he were here, but he was hurt when our boat exploded. He had to stay in Paris. He will come later."

DINNER TOOK ALMOST two hours to prepare, but it was memorable. The savory stew was full of succulent chunks of tender rabbit and seasoned with herbs from his own garden. The aroma of fresh country bread filled the house. First, it would accompany dinner and then, spread with his own fresh butter and fruit jam, it would be dessert.

They discussed plans for the next day. By now conversation had shifted almost entirely to English, except when Andor's limited vocabulary brought it to a fumbling halt, and then Klaus translated. Jeremy and Kate both noticed that Andor paid close attention to Klaus's translations.

Something Andor had said still bothered Jeremy. He finally asked, "You said the Arrow Cross men are camping in the woods. What did you mean? Are they just camping out, or something else?"

"They change volunteers every month or so, and the new group came last week. One of their first missions is to spend three days and two nights in the forest up the mountain behind my farm. They do military training during the day, then at night they sit around campfires and talk of how they will bring back the heroic times of old Hungary. They listen to their teacher, a different soldier each time. Midnight is the high point. By then, with the drums and the campfire and the speeches, they're really worked up."

"Could we go back there and watch them?" Jeremy asked in reply.

"I have done so but it is dangerous and I don't think you would learn much. They tell stories of the glorious past and practice how they will attack the refugees, whom they always call the invaders. I do not see how you would learn anything worthwhile, and it would be risky."

Jeremy replied, "I saw them attack a group of refugees on the Chain Bridge last night. They didn't hurt anyone seriously, but with better weapons they would be really dangerous. You're probably right. We have to get up early anyway, so let's forget it for now."

"We will get up around seven in the morning and I will take you to the box," Andor said. "The truck is already in the barn, so you will be able to leave in a short time. I think you should get off as early as possible, so that my curious neighbors don't wonder too much about what my truck is carrying around with someone else driving it."

At first Klaus objected to the early start but his Uncle Andor was obviously not accustomed to being contradicted.

"I will go with you to the barn tomorrow but not to the castle," Klaus said. "I cannot afford to be seen there with you, and frankly it scares me. I will go with you as far as town, where I will see some friends, if they are up at that hour." He looked accusingly at Uncle Andor.

"Why don't you take the rental car? We can handle the box." Jeremy said.

In fact, they would not have to unload the sub alone, and the location had already been chosen. While Andor was cooking and Kate chatted him up, Jeremy had taken a half-hour walk so he could call Eddie, who was waiting with Mark at a site on the lake no more than a mile away. They had found a secluded cove where the sub could be launched, directly across from the castle but hidden from its view. They had brought provisions and planned to spend the night in their rental car, taking alternating watches.

"WE GO to bed early in the country," Andor said at nine o'clock, after Klaus had washed the dishes.

"Jeremy, you will sleep on the sofa. Missus Kate will have the bedroom. Klaus always sleeps on a pallet next to the sofa, and I have a chair in the kitchen I sometimes use when I cannot sleep. I will sleep there tonight."

"The sofa will be fine," Jeremy said. "I need one more trip to the outhouse and I'll be in for the night." He stood and walked out the door, but instead of stopping at the ancient privy he walked past it toward the barn. When he was completely out of earshot from the house, he pulled out his phone to dial Eddie.

In the instant before he pressed the button, he heard the dim sound of drums coming from somewhere up the hill. So Andor was right, he thought. They are up there dancing around the campfire and plotting more ways to attack the poor and the weak. We need to know more.

EDDIE ANSWERED on the second ring. When Jeremy filled him in on Andor's news about the midnight bivouac, Eddie said instantly that he and Mark would try to find it.

"I've made one or two midnight approaches and I'm just fifty-fifty so far. We'll be careful."

"Please do. I'll be back in Andor's bunkhouse with Klaus so you can't call me, but we should see you in the morning. If you get in trouble, call anyway." He turned to walk back to the house.

Jeremy and Kate set their phones' alarms for six-thirty a.m. and by ten all the lights were out.

Shortly after midnight Jeremy felt, rather than heard, Klaus struggle up from his pallet and creep out the front door. He's going for a piss in the woods, Jeremy told himself, and went back to sleep.

"CHANGE OF PLANS," Eddie said to Mark. "Andor told Jeremy that Max's trainees bivouac up in the hills behind his farm periodically, and tonight's the night. You and I need to see what's going on. Are you up for a walk?"

"Sure. I can do anything except chin myself. And I grew up hiking the mountains, or what passed for mountains."

Eddie took the iPad and pointed to the blinking blue dot. "Here's where we are. Let's take the road we came in on but follow it uphill until we're close to Andor's place. Then we'll hide the car and go the rest of the way on foot. Jeremy said he heard their drums when he went out to call us, so the party may already have begun."

They made a quick dinner of sandwiches they had bought at Budapest Airport, then took the car out with Eddie driving.

Mark watched the map carefully. The road

turned sharply left and headed downhill soon after they entered the dense hardwood forest.

He said, "The map says we're behind Andor's house and the road is starting to go down the hill, so we're probably driving away from the camp. Let's hide the car here and see what we can find further up the hill."

The headlights picked out a narrow lane on the left and Eddie pulled in, then found an opening between two groups of trees where he could park. They each took a flashlight; Mark stashed his laptop in the trunk.

The drum was closer, and clearly up the hill.

"It's hard to judge distance in the forest," Eddie said, "but my guess is that we're a half-mile or so away from the drum. That's consistent with what Andor said – they're out of sight, so they can have their bonfire without anyone seeing it from the road. So let's go see what we can find. We shouldn't use the lights any more than we have to, and we need to watch out for guards."

BACK ON THE PAVED ROAD, Mark whispered, "This is like where I grew up. Somewhere around here there will be a trail up the hill, probably cut for logging."

They walked a hundred yards before they found a rough trail.

"This is probably a logging road, and it will lead generally uphill with some switchbacks if the slope gets too steep," Mark said. He shielded his light and flashed it briefly to look at the ruts. "This hasn't been used in a long time. We should see where it goes."

Their eyes adjusted slowly to the dim starlight, and within minutes they began to make out the shapes of trees and the patches of lighter sky above, which contrasted sharply with the inky blackness of the ground beneath their feet. They walked up the hill in silence as the drum continued its monotonous boom. After they had switched back twice it was noticeably closer.

Eddie moved to Mark's side and whispered, "We should pick up the firelight pretty soon. We need to stay really quiet."

The path turned sharply to the right and a glow appeared through the trees. Mark whispered, "The road will take another turn before long. When it does, let's cut straight through the trees. We just need to get close enough to count heads and hear some of what they're saying. We don't want to sit around and sing campfire songs with them."

IN TWENTY-FIVE YARDS the road did make a switchback. Eddie and Mark moved off into the forest, treading carefully. The drumming had stopped. As if on cue, all the nocturnal insects of the forest started to make their own noise. The sound seemed to come from everywhere. When the drum went silent it affected their navigation the way an airport light going out on final approach would leave a pilot blind and disoriented. With more hope than confidence, they pushed on straight up the gentle hill, counting on dead reckoning to keep them on course.

As they crested the hill, Eddie stuck out his hand to pull Mark back – fifty yards downhill was the bonfire in its ring of stones. All the vegetation in the clearing had been trampled and a stack of firewood stood to the side. It was clear this campsite had been used many times before.

They lay down to watch. Four young men dressed in brown shorts and shirts, each with the Arrow Cross symbol on a band around his left arm, sat rigidly upright on two rough benches that faced the fire. They were lucky -- they had approached from the side, and the young stormtroopers were focused on the speaker, who paced back and forth between them and the fire, shouting and shaking his fist. They hadn't been seen.

Two of the four were obviously Slavic, and listened attentively to their leader's oration in Russian.

The young man closest to them picked up the drum. It boomed, and the four stood quickly and saluted their leader with a motion that struck Mark as half Boy Scout, half Nazi.

The leader turned to the drummer and started to speak in imperfect English. "I told the comrades, as I now tell you, that all of us have been chosen to bring Great Hungary back to its rightful hands. Together, we will bring Europe back to the brotherhood and friendship of the past, away from the sin and evil of the West."

He then lapsed back into Russian and ranted on for ten minutes. The drum boomed again in a steady rhythm.

Eddie carefully took two quick pictures with his phone, then touched Mark's shoulder and indicated with his head that they should leave.

IN A HALF-HOUR they had retraced their steps down the mountain and were driving toward their campsite on the lake.

"That reminded me of the stories I heard about the Hitler Youth," Eddie said.

"They are obviously being trained for something like that. This is ground zero for Max's political movement. Maybe we can find out more when we get into the castle tomorrow. Right now let's try to get some sleep."

Reveille came quickly. The sun was just visible behind the trees when Uncle Andor came loudly out of the kitchen roaring "Everybody up. It's time to move."

Klaus objected. "Uncle, it's hardly five. I thought we were going to sleep another two hours."

"I got up early to listen to the radio, and it said the water in the lake will be very high today. The wind is coming up. It will be rough."

Andor turned to Jeremy and Kate to explain.

"There's a much larger dam up the river that releases water every week or so to refill our lake and make room to store new water. We had a lot of rainfall this summer. When they release more water than usual the lake comes up over the banks and would make it hard for you to do anything. The wind will also be very strong today. The water will be choppy.

"It's better to move early. Coffee is on and I will cut some bread. Breakfast in fifteen minutes. Missus Kate gets the bathroom first. We men will wash up at the tap out back."

As Jeremy was rinsing his face in the very cold water of Andor's tap, he wondered what had really caused the change in plans. In any case he approved of it because his time in the military had taught him the benefits of an early start.

After breakfast, Klaus took Jeremy's rental car and headed off to town. The other three walked to the barn with Kate's boxes of diving equipment.

Klaus had offered to take them in the car, but she refused because she did not want him to get a look at Pegasus.

"Did you hear Klaus get up last night, about midnight?" Andor asked as they walked across the meadow.

"I did," Jeremy said, "but I didn't think anything of it."

"He's my family, but I don't trust him where politics is concerned. I don't sleep well, so when I heard him creep out I followed. He went about fifty meters away from the house and made a call. I'm pretty sure it was to Max Molnar, and I'm equally sure that Max is on his way back to his castle right now. That's why it's important for you to move quickly. And be very careful."

Kate was amazed, but Jeremy had been suspicious ever since he saw how quickly Klaus had changed his attitude in the restaurant when he learned there was money to be made.

ANDOR TURNED out to be remarkably strong. The plywood box was heavy, but not so heavy they couldn't hook it to the hoist and lift it to the back of the ancient flatbed truck. They tied it down with the least-rotted rope they could find, then covered it with the same old canvas tarps that had been on it before.

Jeremy took out the map Eddie had sent, the one
that had told him the sub was in Uncle Andor's barn,
and said, "We have picked a cove a couple of miles
away, in the opposite direction from town. Can we
get there by going back to your road?"

"There is a better way," Andor said. He pointed
out a barely visible track through the pasture.
"Follow that path for a half-mile and you will find a
good road. Turn right and follow it one mile to
where it crosses a very old road that hasn't been re-
paired for seventy-five years. The cove will be down
that road a hundred meters off to your right. You
will be there in a half-hour.

"I will walk back to the house. Go with God, and
watch out for Max Molnar."

IN FACT KLAUS was supposed to meet Max in the village, but not for two hours, so he drove into the
country to kill time. When he returned, he saw them
waiting next to the truck at the meeting point, but he
recoiled in fear and passed them by when he saw
Max pass a large pistol to Tom.

Max would not recognize the rental car, so he
drove by and kept going up into the mountains, on a
winding road that led through the forest. He figured
he would give Max enough time to leave, then find
lunch in the village before returning to his uncle's

home. The two fifty-euro notes Jeremy had given him as a deposit gave him a warm feeling of security.

WHEN HE DIDN'T SHOW up, Molnar was furious. He had brought Tom Farkas back from Budapest, skipping a political meeting it had taken him three months to set up, and he would not be foiled.

"That pipsqueak won't stand in our way again," he hissed at Tom. "Let's go out to the old man's farm and make him tell us where Klaus has gone. It was bad enough that he signed on with the Americans, but to disappear now ... I won't have it. And while we're here, we should bring the submarine back to the castle. With the driver there will be three of us. That should be enough to handle one old farmer and a box."

23

INTO THE CASTLE

"Look at the water level," Mark said as Eddie knelt on the bank and splashed water on his face. "It must be up two or three feet since last night."

"Water levels in chains of hydropower lakes like this fluctuate as upstream dams release water," Eddie said. "This one will probably go down when they open the gates. Let's hope it doesn't get much higher, though. Kate will be looking for an underwater entrance to the cavern under the castle, and the deeper the water the harder it will be to see it."

His phone buzzed. "It's Jeremy. Let's see where they stand."

"We're on the way," Jeremy told him. "Our cover may be blown. Klaus made a call late last night and his uncle thinks it may have been to Max Molnar. So whatever you're planning for the castle, we need to do it fast – in and out. Kate and I will be there in a few minutes."

"Where's Klaus?" Eddie asked.

"He went into town. If Andor is right, he's probably meeting Molnar. How did you do last night?"

"It was what we expected," Eddie said. "One instructor, obviously military, telling four young men, all of them still in their teens, how they were going to be great national heroes by protecting the Hungarian people from the threatening hordes of Arabs flooding into their homeland. They were a mean-looking bunch, and dangerous even if they are young and not very well organized. The interesting thing was, the instructor was Russian, not Hungarian. The stormtroopers seemed to be a mix of Russians and Americans."

"I heard Americans in the group that attacked some migrants on Chain Bridge the other night," Jeremy said.

WHILE EDDIE TALKED TO JEREMY, Mark was looking intently at the map on his iPad.

"Take a look at this," he said when Eddie's call ended, pointing at a narrow black line, a country road that led from the main road they had driven in on to their location. He pointed to the blue dot. "Here we are. When we got here last night I thought we were at a boat ramp, but it's actually an old road that continues into the lake."

His finger traced a path across the lake. "Here, on the other side, is the castle. And just to the right, there's another black line marking another secondary road. It looks like a continuation of this one.

"Remember what Kate told us about her ex's fixation on treasure under the castle? He said there was a story about an entire convoy of German trucks hurrying out of Poland ahead of the Russians. The way he heard it, they drove into the cave, then the entrance was dynamited to keep the Russians away from whatever it was they were transporting."

Eddie said, "This part of the world is full of tales about stolen Nazi gold and paintings and God knows what else, but if this one were to be true, this road could have been the way they got into the cavern. There are a lot more rumors of Nazi treasure than there is Nazi treasure. And if the Nazis did dynamite the entrance we're in trouble because Kate won't be able to get in, regardless of the water level."

"But it doesn't really matter if there actually *is* Nazi treasure," Mark replied. "What matters is that Mickelwaite may have believed it's there and convinced his pal Max that he might get some of his money back. It could be just one strand of an elaborate fairy tale. Or a scam. From what Kate tells me, they both have egos that have gotten them into trouble in the past."

"Maybe, but the odds are all we're going to find is a spooky old cave full of bat shit," Eddie said.

THE FIRST THING Mark and Kate did was knock apart the plywood crate. The sleek little submarine sat in the truck bed, glistening in the sunlight.

"So this is Pegasus," Eddie said with a low whistle.

Kate jumped up onto the truck, reached behind the helicopter's small hangar at the front of the sub and plugged an iPhone into a small control panel mounted flush with the top.

"Let's see if it will power up," Mark said. To Eddie he said, "Give me a hand up. And can you come up and be my other hand?" Eddie made a stirrup and lifted Mark onto the truck, then followed.

"I'll do the checkout while you two re-mount the wings," Kate said.

Together, the men bolted the first one quickly to a bracket on the side of the fuselage, repeated the process on the other side, then fixed the top and bottom vertical tail fins on their brackets.

In the meantime she was going through a series of tests.

"Electrical looks okay, fuel level is good but it could be better, hydrogen is low but will come back up when we're in the water."

Perplexed, Eddie asked, "Does it run on hydrogen?"

Mark said, "The main fuel is very high-energy torpedo fuel, but we boost it with hydrogen we take out of the water. It makes the fuel go farther and gives us a lot more speed and power.

"Pegasus at full throttle is so powerful no one could remain on his back. In open water he runs like a scalded cat. He can vault out of the water and land a hundred feet away."

Kate said, "So far nothing has failed. I have just a little bit of tweaking to do, mainly to tell it that we're looking for a recess in a rock wall. That'll just take a minute."

"Do we have the stirrup assembly?" she asked no one in particular.

"Is this it?" Jeremy said, picking up a tangle of webbing.

"Sure is. Gimme." She threw it over the fuselage just behind the wings, saddling it like a horse.

"Let's just get one final snapshot of the software. Who knows what might happen?" She took a USB drive from her pocket and inserted it into a recess to the right of the control panel.

"That's it," she said after thirty seconds. She retrieved the thumb drive and tossed it to Mark, then jumped down from the truck.

"Keep that somewhere safe. I'll change while you put it in the water." She ducked behind the truck.

"Mark, would you bring me the wetsuit when you get Pegasus in the water?"

With Mark contributing his one hand, Eddie and Jeremy slid the sub off the bed of the truck and placed it gently in the lake. Mark tied a line to a ring on the end of the right wing and knotted the other end around a tree.

A dense line of trees and scrub underbrush hid the car and truck from the lake, but when Mark pulled two bushes apart he could easily see the castle on its promontory more than a mile away. The day had dawned clear and bright with almost no clouds – a great day for a picnic, a lousy one for a clandestine insertion.

"You're going to have to do the crossing submerged," Mark called back to Kate. "If anybody's watching from the castle you'll be visible on the surface, but all this water flowing in will make it so muddy you should be invisible if you're submerged even a few feet. You won't have much visibility."

"I was planning to do that," she said. "The only better time would be at night, but then I might have to use lights to find the cave opening depending on how much crap is in the water. We'll just have to play the hand we're dealt."

He carried the yellow case behind the truck, where he found her wearing only the bottom half of a string bikini, holding the top in her hand. She reached for his good hand and put it on her breast.

"That will have to do for now. But later …"

—————

WHEN SHE CAME out from behind the truck her wet-suit was zipped and her mask pushed up on her fore-head. She had tied back her hair.

Eddie lifted the two air tanks to her back. She fastened the straps, then tested the airflow. Mark handed her the Ka-Bar knife Antoine had given her their last night in South Florida to replace the one the Miami police had taken for evidence. She strapped it around her waist and clipped on a toolkit and her phone's waterproof container. "Ready. And coil up that line and tie it to my left stirrup. A sailor never knows when she'll need to tie something. Let's go for it.

"Remember, guys, I'm going to try to get under the castle while you go in and figure out what's going on in there. If you run into problems head for the deepest part of the castle. Klaus says that opens into the cave below, and that's where I plan to be. If I can, I'll come in to help. We'll need Pegasus to haul out anything of interest you find.

"Jeremy saw just four stormtroopers on the Chain Bridge in Budapest and that's all Eddie and Mark saw singing kumbaya around the campfire last night, so we have to hope that's all there are, plus

Max and maybe Farkas. If they all show up at once we'll have to get out through the cave.

"If I can't get in I won't be much help to you, so I hope you'll have an alternate escape route in mind."

Jeremy said, "Klaus told me at dinner that the water sometimes rises to the ceiling of the original basement, which is now an abandoned sub-basement. There are openings in the wall to allow water to flow in and out freely and a watertight bulkhead in the ceiling, like the hatch of a submarine, to keep the water from rising into the new basement above.

"He didn't know why they just didn't fill it in, but maybe they're using it for storage. Anything in it would be very well hidden.

"Eddie and Mark, take your car and go around the far end of the lake to the castle. We have a lot less time than we'd hoped, so you'll have to get in and find out what's going on there, then get your butts out, and quick. If you don't connect inside, your meeting point with Kate is a little cove about two hundred yards south of the castle.

"I'll take the truck and go back to see Uncle Andor. With Klaus gone, I think I can get more information out of him. If I do, I'll call you. Worst case I'll come find you."

The shallow water foamed as the propeller spun up briefly, then dropped back to idle. "Bye, guys," Kate said. She pulled down her mask, gripped the breathing mouthpiece firmly, and turned the little sub gently out into deeper water. In seconds, her head sank out of sight.

EDDIE AND MARK left to drive the long way around, across the narrow road atop the dam rather than back through the village, so they wouldn't be visible from the castle most of the way. Jeremy took Uncle Andor's old truck and headed back to the house – he still had questions for Andor and looked forward to posing them while Klaus was not there to hear the answers. The old man knew more than he had told – or been willing to say in front of Klaus.

As he crested the hill in Andor's back pasture he knew something was seriously wrong. In the distance, halfway down Andor's potholed driveway, a box truck drove away in a hurry, bouncing and swaying down the lane, kicking up a great cloud of dust behind it.

Nobody in his right mind would drive that truck that fast down that road, Jeremy said to himself. He waited, partially hidden behind the crest of the low hill, until the fleeing truck disappeared around a curve.

He had intended to drive all the way to the house but decided instead to put Andor's truck back in the barn, safely out of sight. He was confident Max

Molnar had been in the escaping truck, and that he had come to retrieve the submarine. Why else would he bring such a large truck? And the submarine was obviously very important to Max and the people around him, which made it all the more probable that he had come himself rather than trust it to a subordinate.

As Jeremy pushed the old and creaking barn doors closed, he spotted a rusting double-bitted ax leaning against the wall. He picked it up and started the hundred-yard walk to the house, trying to make as little noise as possible.

He needn't have bothered. Even before he walked through the front door, he could smell the metallic odor of fresh blood. Inside, the living room looked like a slaughterhouse.

Under the window to his right lay the body of a man wearing an Arrow Cross uniform. The body was still warm but Jeremy felt no pulse. Andor had chosen the buckshot side of his double-barreled shotgun and the pellets had blown entirely through the man's body, spreading blood and bits of tissue on the faded wallpaper behind it. The blade of a large knife, covered with blood, was just visible under the body. The body was one of the young men he'd seen on Chain Bridge.

The shotgun lay on the floor a dozen feet away, in another pool of blood. But there was no sign of Andor.

Jeremy hefted the ax and began to search. It didn't take long. His first stop was the bedroom, where he found Andor lying on the bed at the end of a trail of blood.

At first he thought it was too late, but he found a feeble pulse, then confirmed that the old man was breathing, although his chest hardly moved. One hand was clenched around a wadded-up corner of the sheet, which he had pressed to his abdomen. Jeremy pulled back his shirt and found the source of the blood – a gaping stab wound that Andor had stanched with the fabric. He had staggered to his bed and managed to drag himself up onto it. The soaked sheet and the trail from the living room meant he had lost a lot of blood.

To survive, he would need medical attention very soon. But how do I call an ambulance in rural Hungary? Jeremy asked himself.

Klaus had to be the answer. Just maybe, Jeremy thought, just maybe he will respond to his uncle, even if he's really on the other side.

KLAUS ANSWERED on the second ring.

"Your uncle's been hurt," Jeremy told him. "He's been stabbed and has lost a lot of blood."

"Max. That bastard."

"It looks that way. Andor killed the man who

stabbed him, then managed to drag himself to his bed. He needs to be in the hospital. Can you call someone?"

"I'm already on the way back," Klaus replied. "There's a doctor in town. We were friends in school and I think he will help without telling anyone. But we must be very careful. A lot of the people here re-spect Max and his men, and they like the money his work brings. I will be there in ten minutes."

Jeremy turned back to Andor. He was breathing better, but Jeremy knew from his combat first aid ex-perience that he needed blood to replace what he had lost – in fact, he should have it immediately.

WITH ANDOR BREATHING REGULARLY and help on the way, Jeremy began to think about his next step.

Kate, Eddie and Mark were in serious danger. There was no way to know how much Klaus had told Max, and Andor could not tell him anything. He was reasonably sure that Max had been unable to pull any information from the tough old man.

What leverage did he have? No one out here in the Hungarian countryside would be annoyed at the notoriety this near-murder would bring, but the gov-ernment might.

And if Klaus were correct, the Hungarian gov-ernment had no love for Max. Governments, especially the authoritarian ones, have no sense of humor about revolutionaries.

Max and his men were obviously the advance guard of a pro-Russian movement – the Russian government wanted above all else to sow discord and distrust among the European nations.

The Budapest government, on the other hand, authoritarian as it was, wanted mainly to be left alone to trade with both sides, while at the same time reaping the considerable rewards of being a member of the European Union. If membership stopped, so would the money from Brussels.

And Hungary was the major beneficiary of EU subsidies. Jeremy racked his brain for the number and decided the last one he'd read was almost four billion dollars a year, a great deal of money for a small country with serious economic pressures.

The EU was already annoyed at the newspaper closings and other authoritarian steps the government had taken. André Westerhof had shown him the front page of one of the main newspapers as they'd waited for Klaus, and pointed out the stories that cast the government in a positive light. Of the ten stories on the front page, seven were in praise of the government and the prime minister.

He reached for his phone and dialed Icky. The conversation was short; in five minutes, Icky had promised to call a contact high up in the Hungarian intelligence services.

"He's a loyal guy, but he and his people don't like the guys who are trying to turn Hungary into a satellite again," Icky said.

"Will you be there a while?"

"I have to go warn Kate and the others. She's underwater so I won't be able to get her on the phone, although I might reach the others. I just won't know until I try. I'll leave as soon as Klaus brings the rental back. If I take Andor's truck I might get arrested for stealing it. Everybody knows whose it is, and nobody knows me."

24

ROUGH WATER AND HAND GRENADES

KATE HAD HER HANDS FULL. THE LAKE THAT HAD been so placid and calm when she started out had in the space of a few minutes turned turbulent and threatening.

The upstream dam had opened its gates wide. The surge of water moving past the castle added a strong current that slowed her progress and threw her off course. The whirls and eddies that resulted when the current curled around the boulders on the bottom made it hard to maintain a straight course. And the silt thrown up by the strong flow made it hard to see.

Damn, she said to herself as the sub bucked again. I wonder if it would be smoother on the surface?

She turned the nose up and leveled off close

below the surface, confident that the waves and the silt would make her hard to see from the shore. She stood on the stirrups and put just the top half of her mask out of the water to take a quick look, then ducked back under and turned the nose down quickly. She was less than a hundred yards from the cliff and could see an armed watchman on the castle wall above. A Zodiac cruised slowly along, far to her right, and it looked like the two men in it were carrying assault rifles.

So she had no choice. With the water rising, the gate to the cavern under the castle would be even deeper than she'd expected, which was good because it would make her invisible from the watchmen in the Zodiac, bad because it would make the cave opening harder to see. As long as the rough water didn't interfere with the passive sonar, though, she should be able to find it.

Once she was inside the cave, the rising water would pose its own problems. She had no idea how high the roof of the cavern was and thus whether she'd be able to evacuate Eddie and Mark back through the lake.

Right now, she thought, what we need is a hellacious storm that will run those guys off the lake and make me invisible, but there was no chance of that. If the upstream dam hadn't been releasing water, it would have been a perfect day to go boating. Even the wind was light and variable and the day was sunny; everything was working in favor of the other side. Oh, well, she thought. I'll just have to make my own storm.

She checked her depth meter. At a hundred yards from shore the water was almost a hundred feet deep: plenty of safety room if she had to evade the guards in the boat. At that depth a bullet would have no effect and she would be fully invisible. As it was, the silt would make her invisible below about ten feet.

Suddenly she heard the muffled sound of a racing outboard motor, growing louder and closer. She'd been seen, and the boat was coming her way. Showtime, she thought. Let's get this under way. She'd calculated that Eddie and Mark would be getting into the castle about now, so it was time for her to move into the cavern.

She stuck her head up one last time and saw the inflatable bearing down hard on the place she'd been minutes before, about fifty yards to her left. The guards' attention was fixed on that spot so they didn't see her, but she saw the tiny plink of a bullet from the parapet. A second later she heard the sound of the rifle shot. Time to get underwater and find a better location.

She headed for the bottom in a tight spiral, like a military pilot landing in a war zone. The warning light blinked as she passed under twenty feet from the bottom and she stopped the descent at ten, not knowing how many rocks might be sticking up around her.

She could just make out the shadow of the boat as it crisscrossed above her. A hundred feet to her left, toward the castle, an explosion made the water boil. She leaned forward and hugged the sub before the pressure wave passed over her and made it buck and pitch. Close call. It was time to get further away, so she headed up the coast toward the cave.

SHE GOT A BETTER view of the inflatable boat the second time she surfaced. It wasn't a French Zodiac, because it had a square nose, and it didn't appear to ride in the water like it had a vee bottom. It was probably a Russian or Ukrainian model made for export, then, which meant the fabric of the inflatable chambers was thinner than that of the more expensive Zodiac. And, it meant the boat had only two inflation chambers, not the three or five of larger milspec boats. Even the baffles inside the chambers wouldn't be enough to protect them from her Ka-Bar. Antoine told her he had sharpened it just for her. She had checked, and he was right – it would make quick work of the flimsy canvas pontoons.

She let the sub come to rest on the bottom and sat to think about the best plan of attack. Slashing only one side of the boat would be better than slashing both and sinking it entirely, she decided. If the boat sank, the two guards would have no choice but to swim for shore. But if it just tipped on its side and rode low in the water, they might stay with it to wait for rescue, thus taking two or three people away from the contingent waiting for Mark and Eddie in the castle.

SHE PUSHED the sub off and started a slow ascent. The boat was circling where the men thought she was, so she turned and headed toward it, careful to stay out of range of another hand grenade until the last second. She held her breath as she ascended slowly to the point she could make out the two guards silhouetted against the sky.

She saw one of them lean far out and point off to the port side, then make a pitching motion with his right hand. She hoped the grenade was a Russian model with a long fuse time, seven seconds, and not a NATO grenade with, at most, a five-second delay. Whichever it was, she was too close to it and had to get away – but it offered her the opportunity she needed.

"Go, Pegasus," she murmured as she pulled the sub into a tight circle that brought her in line with the Zodiac's stern. As the grenade went off fifty feet to her left but well below her she goosed the throttle and tilted the sub up, at the same time pulling the Ka-Bar from its scabbard.

She corrected her course to duck under the flashing propeller and passed down the length of the little boat at high speed, slashing its right pontoon from end to end. She turned sharply and dived straight toward the bottom. At twenty feet she jinked right to return to her original course, out of range of the grenades.

There were no more grenades. She couldn't stop to watch, but even without seeing it she knew what was happening on the surface. The right side of the little boat had collapsed, turning it on its side and dumping its crew into the lake. If they were lucky, the two guards had managed to hang on to the surviving pontoon. If not, they would need to swim. In either case, they were out of action. Even if they were strong swimmers it would take a half-hour to get to shore. More likely, they would wait for rescue, which would give her still more time to find Mark and Eddie. Anxiously, she hoped they would wait.

Two down, an unknown number to go. She hoped Jeremy's head count had been correct.

———

A HALF-HOUR BEFORE, Eddie and Mark had turned down a narrow track into the hardwood forest that ran halfway up the steep hill Klaus had described. At its peak, the castle was obviously a construction site. The ground floor walls appeared complete, but only part of the building had a roof. A catwalk that looked temporary ran around the top of the wall.

"That's where the guards make their rounds," Eddie whispered to Mark. "If Max came back from Budapest early, they've probably started patrols again."

They surveyed the terrain. They would be protected for all but the last thirty yards of the gentle climb. A driveway curved uphill from the paved public road at their left. At its highest point, just in front of the castle door, stood a large box truck.

"Well, Max is back. We can't just waltz in through the front door," Eddie said. "It has to be Plan B."

When they had surveyed the area the evening before, they had spotted a double freight door around the corner and down the hill from the front door, which seemed to lead directly into the basement. A gravel driveway leading to it had been widened recently, which told them something larger than usual was expected.

"That's where they plan to put the sub," Mark whispered now. "But it would be tough to get it into the water from here. What do you suppose they have in mind?"

"Either they'll find an easier place, like the one

we used, or they'll use that truck to take it somewhere else. It could be anywhere."

Mark looked again at the door, then at the steep drop-off to the lake, and replied, "You're probably right. But let's go see what we can find."

"Good. But that looks like a tough door. The last time I had this problem, Paul opened it with a credit card. This one doesn't look like it's going to be so easy."

"Hey, I'm an engineer. I fix things, and I can pick locks. Piece of cake."

THE LOCK DIDN'T SURRENDER AS QUICKLY as Mark hoped, but in less than a minute he turned the knob, opened the door, and looked in.

Eddie held him back, miming with two fists that he should go first because he had two good arms.

He jumped quickly through the door and two paces to the left, hoping to avoid a guard if one had seen the door open. In a few seconds, as his eyes adjusted to the weak light, he signaled for Mark to come in and close the door.

"All clear," he said. "Let's get some light on." He switched his light on and Mark did the same. The room was about half the size of Mark's shop, but otherwise very similar. An empty worktable stood in the center.

"Farkas!" Mark spat out the name like a curse. "This can only be the work of Tom Farkas. This shop is laid out exactly like mine. He must have photographed every inch of it."

Eddie said, "So he's probably been working for Max a long time?"

"I'd bet my life on it. To set up something this complex you'd have to order the equipment far in advance, and then spend weeks setting it up and testing it. Some of our equipment is special-order stuff from Germany. I bet they just finished the work, or the sub would be here now."

"Let's go around the perimeter and see if they left any clues. We have to find out why they want the sub," Eddie said.

Halfway down the first side, Eddie found a powerful waterproof flashlight.

"Underwater flashlight," he said. "No surprise. But at least we can turn off ours and save the batteries."

A few feet further down the bench, Eddie stopped again and asked, "Do you have a Geiger counter in your shop? That's what this looks like."

"I've used them in the past, but don't have one now. We don't use anything radioactive."

Mark bent to look closely at the small aluminum box.

"That's what this is, for sure. You put that wand next to something you want to measure and the radiation level shows on the meter. You can also hear the clicks on a speaker.

"There should be something to calibrate it. Shine the light down here." He squatted to inspect the lower shelf.

"Here it is," he said, holding out a short, round can for Eddie to take.

Eddie twisted the lid off the can and turned on the Geiger counter. A burst of rapid clicks that sounded like a newspaper being torn in half sounded in the room, and he pulled the wand back quickly.

"Well, it worked. But why would they want a Geiger counter? It's not a good sign. We need to find out what's going on here."

The powerful light probed in and under every cabinet and counter in the room. Two-thirds of the way down the left wall they found a worn leather briefcase.

"That's the cherry on the cake," Mark said. "Farkas used to carry that briefcase to work. He kept his laptop in it. Let's see if it's there now."

He worked quickly to pick the flimsy locks on the old briefcase. "Empty," he said. "Except…" He reached into the pocket that lined the top and pulled out a thumb drive identical to the one Kate had given him. He put it with its mate.

"I bought a half-dozen thumb drives like this a year ago," he said. "This means we have three versions of the software to compare. We can see what he's changed."

"FIRST, let's figure out where we are," Eddie said. "Klaus told Jeremy the original basement was so low that it flooded after the dam raised the water level and created the lake. So Max just layered it – the castle was a ruin anyway, so he built an entire new basement above the original one.

"In effect, he raised the top of the hill by ten or twelve feet. It must have been a massive earthmoving job."

Mark said, "The door to this room is about a dozen feet lower than the front door, so we must be in the new basement. The concrete here looks pretty new."

"And Klaus said there is a watertight port between the two basements."

"I know those," Mark said. "Every ship has several bulkhead doors."

"So let's find it and start there," Eddie replied. "We know there are people upstairs, but let's not challenge them unless we have to. It looks like this is where the work is done.

"I wasn't sure before, but now we know Tom Farkas is in this. Max Molnar by himself is bad enough, but Farkas has tried once to kill you and had to be part of the plot to bomb your sailboat and kill both you and Kate. So they won't be nice if they find us.

"The Geiger counter worries me. If they're planning something radioactive, I need to let Icky know." He looked at his phone. "Zero bars. We have no hope of getting a signal while we're inside. The signal was OK across the lake, so it's probably good here, once we get outside."

"We need to find out what else is in this new basement and look for the old one at the same time," Mark said. "Let's start with the door at the end of the shop."

Eddie pointed the powerful light down the length of the shop and picked out a steel door on the far wall.

"That doesn't look as tough as the outside door," he said. "Can you open that one?"

Mark leaned over the lock and twisted it gently. "This one's easier," he said. "It's designed to keep people out of this room, so I can just take the knob off." The screwdriver he always carried on his keychain made quick work of the knob. In less than a minute they turned off the main light and their own lights and pushed the door open. The room behind it was dark.

Eddie tapped Mark on the shoulder and signaled that he would go left and Mark should go right, then they crept through the door and spread themselves against the wall. Eddie ran into a cabinet of some sort and stopped. They both listened intently for any signs of life, and when there were none Eddie turned on his light.

The room was a duplicate of the other one, but instead of a shop it was fitted out as a dormitory. To their right, the wall had two double bunk beds, and to the left there was one. A trestle table sat in the center.

"It's like a warship, or a really cheap college dormitory. Six bunks, a mess table in the middle," Mark said. He pointed the powerful light into the corner behind Eddie. "It's a kitchen."

A sign above a sink full of pots and pans carried a picture of clean and sparkling dishes. A legend in German and English said sternly that the kitchen must be kept clean at all times. Another line in Cyrillic script seemed to say the same.

Mark said, "This place is built like the lower decks of a very old British warship. Six men can live down here pretty much independently and prepare their own food."

"Like in a firehouse," Eddie added.

———————

"JUDGING from the size of this basement, the access hatch to the original basement has to be in this room, since it wasn't in the shop."

The light swept around the room. In one corner, it found a smaller room that had been built out from the concrete walls, and next to it an alcove with a curtain over the entrance.

"Let's check the room first. It's probably the bathroom."

"Good guess," Mark replied from inside the room. "Two showers, three washbasins, couple of toilets. Enough for six men."

The alcove, on the other hand, was empty but had what looked like a manhole cover in the floor.

"There's our hatch," Mark said. It was round, with a wheel in its center to pull back the levers that held it tight to its steel frame.

"There will be another wheel like that on the other side. It should be safe to open – when we came in the water level in the lake wasn't nearly this high, but the room below might be already wet."

Eddie stopped him. "There's just one thing that's still bothering me. What was the Geiger counter there for? There's nothing radioactive on this level, so maybe it's down there. We'd better go back and get the counter before we go below."

HE RETURNED with the counter in hand. "I didn't bring the sample because I figured we don't want to confuse it. Let's open the hatch and stick the wand down there to see if it reacts. Then we'll find a way down."

Eddie grasped the wheel with both hands. The hatch popped up an inch before he had completed a full revolution, and he pulled it open with one hand.

"Easy," he said. "They must have bought a good one." He peered into the darkness.

When he turned on the light it revealed an empty room. The floor appeared dry but the air current that blew up at them was cold and moist.

"Underground air," Mark said. "This room is connected to the caverns. Maybe the info Klaus gave us isn't completely useless." He reached down holding the wand and the Geiger counter's monotonous click didn't change. "Nothing here."

Eddie put his leg down the hatch and found the steps of the metal ladder. In a few seconds his head disappeared beneath the floor. Mark, still hampered by having only one fully operational arm, followed slowly.

AT THE BOTTOM, Eddie wheeled to look at the entire basement. It was much older than the room above, made of large cut stones mortared together. And it was much larger.

"This is a monster," Mark said. "I suspect this room saw some gory stuff in the fifteenth century."

They walked clockwise around the room, starting at the end under the shop. When they got to the far end, they found an opening cut roughly into the stone just above their heads. A wide slot, barely six inches high, had been chiseled out at the base of the wall.

"What the hell is that?" Mark asked.

"Just putting it all together: the high water, the pressure hatch above us, the stories Klaus told – I'd say it's an opening that lets water into the room when the lake level rises. These stone walls were never made to withstand water pressure, but the concrete room above will handle it easily.

"So the smart thing to do would be to just let water flow in and out of this room as the lake rises and falls. That way there would be no hydrostatic pressure on the walls. Whoever thought of this knew his hydrodynamics."

EDDIE ASKED, "Is there anything in here to stand on? We need to see what's outside. That's where Kate will come from if she's able to find her way into the original cave."

Mark walked back toward the dark end of the room. He returned with a board in hand, his light tucked under his arm.

"This isn't what you're looking for, but we need

to keep that hatch closed in case Max and company figure out where we are. I can't do it with one hand, but if you'll put this two-by-six through the wheel, they won't be able to pull the hatch open more than an inch or two."

Eddie scampered up the ladder and put the board in place. He pushed on the hatch to check and found that it would open only two inches. "They could shoot through that opening, so we need to stay away from it," he said.

"Did you see anything else?"

"Yes, there's something covered by a tarp in the far corner. We should go look at it next."

THE SOMETHING LOOKED like a small pile of debris roughly covered by a tarp. Eddie pulled the cover away to expose a plywood box. The international sign for radiation danger had been carelessly painted over with thin white paint.

"Do you have the counter?" Mark asked.

"Back there," Eddie replied, pointing with the light back toward the window as he stood to retrieve it. He placed the wand next to the box and the counter chirped only a little faster.

"It may be stupid to break open a radioactive box. We have to know what's there," he said. "Let's hope I don't breach the radiation shield."

MARK HELD the light while Eddie reached for a rock. He hit the edge of the box hard three times, until the nails gave way, then pulled the sides apart. A silvery cylinder ten inches in diameter and eighteen inches long shimmered in the light. The Geiger counter chirped steadily, indicating that it was radioactive – more than the background but not enough to be dangerous.

"Here's a label," Eddie said. He turned the light on the black lettering under the radiation symbol and read quickly.

"Mark, this is a radioactive cesium source, made in America. They used to be in every medical lab in every advanced country, and they're supposed to be guarded like Fort Knox, but a lot of them still go missing. There are thousands of them out there. I read somewhere that one disappears in the United States every day."

"Kate will know what to make of it. But can it explode?"

"No, it's not an A-bomb. It's too weak for that. But if you put this together with some conventional explosives in the front end of your sub, sail it down the Danube and blow it up under Chain Bridge, it would poison Budapest for years. This is part of a dirty bomb. Cover it up again, and let's get as far away from it as we can.

"Now we know why Max wanted Pegasus and Icarus."

———————

"I FOUND some cinder blocks in the other corner," Mark said. "Let's take a couple of them to make a little platform so we can reach that window."

Eddie carried two blocks and Mark carried one, which they stacked into a small pyramid. Eddie stepped up onto it and pointed the light out into the darkness.

"Klaus was right about it – it's a cave, for sure. Just the other side of this wall there's a ledge about four feet wide, then the ground slopes down to the water three feet below. The ceiling of the cave is five feet above the window and rough. It would be a dangerous place to be if the water level rises a lot more. The light reaches the other walls straight across and to the right, just barely, but to the left there's nothing to see but darkness."

Mark stepped up and surveyed the cave. "The entrance has to be on the right. We know from Klaus's description that it was above water before the lake was filled but is now under water most of the time. The water has risen several feet in the last day, so the entrance must be at least that far below the surface, maybe more."

He clicked off the light and waited for his vision

to adjust. "It's really dark out there. There's not even any phosphorescence, but you don't usually see that in freshwater lakes anyway."

He started to step down, then stopped.

"Wait!" He turned toward the cave entrance and squinted. "I see a dim flicker of light below the surface, near where the entrance must be. Kate must be trying to get in right now."

25

KATE FINDS A WAY

KATE WAS, IN FACT, EXTRAORDINARILY FRUSTRATED AT the moment. She had found the cave entrance with no real difficulty, but it was closer to the surface than she hoped, which raised the possibility that she'd be seen from the parapet above.

The entrance seemed to be about twenty feet wide, which squared with Klaus's tale about trucks driving through it. It had been covered at some point with a protective screen that seemed to be mainly chain-link fencing over widely spaced bars, like a jail cell.

She went to the bottom of the fencing and pulled at one corner. It yielded easily, so that wouldn't be much of a problem, but when she reached behind to test the bars they felt solid. She knew that after so long in the water some of the bars must be heavily rusted, so she pulled away as much of the screen as she could and began to yank at them. In ten minutes she found an area where she could open a hole by twisting them up out of the way.

To verify she had room for the sub to pass through, she had to turn on the light above her mask. The glow, dim in the murky water, showed her the hole she'd made was barely large enough to slip the sub through, but it could be done, and then she would be in the underground lake – if she moved very carefully and avoided the dangerously sharp ends of the old bars.

Tired from the rough crossing and her work on the fence, she paused to catch her breath. She counted slowly to thirty, then wrapped her legs tightly around the fuselage and locked her ankles together. Pulling hard, she rowed the nose of the sub through the hole she'd made. Then she crouched low and grasped the bars above her to pull herself the rest of the way. She was in the underground lake.

Well, she thought, first job done. I'm either safely away from Max's goons or I've got myself into a trap that will be very hard to get out of. I can hardly wait to find out.

When she turned the turbine on again the low whine gave comfortable reassurance that she was still in charge of her own fate.

EDDIE LEFT Mark at the window with instructions to watch for Kate.

"Watch for?" he replied. "It's like the inside of a black cat out there. There's no way I could see her."

"Then just listen hard. If you hear anything, make a sound. Not a loud one, because we don't know who else is lurking in the dark. Maybe something only the two of you would recognize."

That brought all sorts of possibilities to mind, all of which Mark forced into the background.

"I'll think of something," he said. "What are you going to do?"

"If they're planning to make a dirty bomb they'll need explosives. We have the sub, so that delivery method is out unless they take it away from us somehow. But if we can find the explosives we could put them somewhere inaccessible."

"Like under twenty feet of water?"

"Something like that. I'll take the light and go back down the room to see what I can see."

Mark leaned as far out of the window as he could, listening hard. The only sound was the gentle lapping of the water at the base of the earthen shelf below them. Once he thought he heard the sound of something breaking the surface, but it didn't repeat.

Then came a sound he knew. Faintly, as though it were coming from a long way away, he heard the low whine of the turbine.

He ducked back into the room and turned toward Eddie. "I think I hear the sub. I'm going out to be sure."

"Okay. I'll be at this for a few more minutes. But be careful: that mud shelf could be slippery."

He looked closely at the slot at the base of the wall and saw immediately that it was too small to squeeze his body through. He'd have to go through the upper opening.

Climbing over the broken stone window ledge would have been difficult if he'd had two good arms, and with only one it was nearly impossible. But he made it and slid slowly down the rough outside of the wall. He looked up and could see the barest glimmer from Eddie's light coming through the opening he'd just slithered through.

The shelf was treacherous. To keep from sliding into the water he sat down with his back to the stone wall and dug his heels into the mud, listening intently for the sound of the sub's turbine to repeat. The lake was dead black. With no outside light, whatever wavelets there were splashed against the shore unseen. If there's no light, he asked himself, do the waves really hit the shore?

He saw a dim glow far in the distance and stuck out his arm to measure its direction – about ten degrees to the left. But it disappeared and, disappointed, he sat back to watch some more. Two minutes later he saw it again, this time at 45 degrees. It was making a circuit of the cave. Kate was using the sub's sensitive passive sonar to find the edge of the lake.

His greatest desire was to shout out to her, but prudence told him to stay silent. She would hear him, but so might others, and it wasn't impossible that someone had followed her into the cavern. So he stayed silent, shifting from side to side to keep his butt from going to sleep.

The light appeared again, this time directly to his left and notably closer. Now it would be safe to alert her. As he was about to call out to her, Eddie's light lanced out from the window and trapped her in its beam, surprising everyone.

"Kate!" Eddie and Mark called out in unison. "We're over here."

KATE LET OUT a whoop and raised both arms in the air.

"I'm on the way." Eddie turned the light down to the bank so she could see it to approach.

When the sub nosed into the soft mud at Mark's feet she handed him one end of the rope she had brought and tied the other to a ring in the sub's nose. Mark pulled in the line and reached to touch her extended hand.

"Cold," he said. "Are you okay?"

"Now I'm perfect. You can warm me up later. Eddie, I'm glad to see you, too."

"Me, too," Eddie said. "Kate, we've discovered something pretty big here. We've been in the old sub-basement Klaus told us about, the one that floods when the lake level rises. In fact, it looks like it will start to get really wet in there in less than an hour.

"Anyway, we found a transportation container for cesium-137. We were suspicious when we found a Geiger counter in Max's shop – which, by the way, is set up exactly like yours. The counter showed quite a bit of activity on the outside of the container. Not enough to be dangerous, but enough to make clear we were looking at the core of a dirty bomb.

"My guess is that their plan is to build a radiation bomb inside Pegasus' hangar bay by packing in explosives and putting the cesium container on top of it, then sending it somewhere they want to cause chaos. There would be few if any deaths but there would be a lot of radiation, which would shut down the area around the explosion for years and kill tourism."

Kate said, "So, Job One is to make sure the bomb doesn't get assembled or delivered. I used to work with cesium-137. We used it to measure liquid flow in pipes and to calibrate pumps and stuff like that. It's nasty – it's really a semi-liquid metal, and if it's exposed to water it explodes. In the container you found it will be packed in mineral oil.

"But how about the explosives. Eddie, did you find any?"

"About five pounds of C4. It was in a homemade explosives safe sunk below the floor level and with a wall between it and the cesium so it wouldn't blow radiation into the room if it went off. It would just take half a pound to bring down an airliner, so they wouldn't need that much for this little bomb, but it may be just a case of overkill. No pun intended."

Kate asked, "Do you think you're done here? I ran into a couple of guards on my way here, and their poor crippled inflatable is clearly visible from the castle, so by now they may have people on the way to intercept us. I need to go back and look, but I think we're going to have to escape by going further into the cavern, and the sooner the better."

Eddie said, "Klaus told Jeremy he thinks there's an underground river that connects with this lake. Even if we don't find the connection right away, there should be enough coves and inlets around the lake to give us a hiding place until the heat dies down. With luck, Jeremy will have the cavalry on the way by now.

"We don't know what else he found back at Andor's house. But just the information we got about the Russians visiting and bivouacking here, plus Jeremy's own observations of the Russian goons on the bridge, should make it possible for Icky to get some sort of action from the police or the intelligence apparatus. We can't depend on that, so let's get out of here. Now."

Kate replied. "I agree. You guys give me about ten minutes to go take a look-see at the entrance, then I'll come back and get you." She pulled her mask down.

As SHE TURNED the sub back toward the entrance, she asked Eddie and Mark to keep their lights off until she returned.

After she left, Eddie asked, "Can she find her way back without it?"

"Pegasus is like a movie cowboy's old horse. Just tell him to go home and that's where he'll go. On the surface it would be GPS and down here it's inertial guidance, but the result is much the same."

Mark thought she would travel submerged by a few feet. "It will be quieter that way, and smoother, and the passive sonar will work better. If there's somebody following us, she will see him before he sees us."

KATE DID NOT RUN into anyone before she got to the old and rusted fence. She tied Pegasus to it and swam through the opening she had made, then to within six feet of the surface. From inside the murky soup of the silty water it appeared that the day was still bright outside.

She climbed slowly up the screen until her head was just below the surface, then stuck it up just long enough to survey the area. To her chagrin, she saw another inflatable boat lurking fifty yards offshore. Like the first, it had two crewmen. It chilled her to see that one of them was struggling to get into a wetsuit.

She ducked underwater again and reached for the edge of the chain-link fencing she had stripped back from the hole. She pulled it as tightly as she could over the steel grate, twisting the wire of the fencing around the bars using a pair of electrician's pliers she had in her waist toolkit.

Folding it back in place and fastening it tightly at a half-dozen places took ten minutes. Three minutes later she was back with Eddie and Mark and discussing their escape.

"I've re-fastened the fencing over the grill, firmly enough that they'll have a hard time undoing it unless they have tools, but we should assume the worst and get out of here pronto."

She reached for the coil of rope attached to her stirrup. "We'll cut this line in half and tie each half to one wing of the sub. You'll get in the water and hold on for dear life. I'll ride on the surface, as slowly as I can, and you figure out how to stay out of the way of the propeller."

"Should we tie it around our waists?" Eddie asked.

"No. If you lose your grip you'll flail around in the time it takes me to stop. This way if you lose your grip on the line I can just turn around and pick you up."

Eddie said, "Before we leave, I think we should do something more to be sure they can't make a dirty bomb. Kate, do you have any idea how deep the water is in this lake?"

"It dropped off pretty sharply right inside the entrance, so I guess it's at least thirty feet deep or maybe more. I could go out and measure it if you like, because I think you're on the right track for a really good idea."

Mark interjected, "If we dump the C4 in the water, they can probably replace it. It's common enough. But if we put the cesium under thirty feet of water, they will have a very hard time finding it because water is a good insulator against radiation – and it will be a lot more difficult to replace than a few pounds of explosive."

"That's the best plan," Kate said. "Why don't you go back and bring the cesium container to the window and hand it to me."

Eddie scrambled back through the rough slot in the wall and in 30 seconds handed the container to

Kate, who took it a hundred feet out into the center of the lake and dropped it. She returned quickly, then took the rope from her stirrup, cut it in half and handed a piece each to Mark and Eddie.

"Tie these onto the rings at the ends of the wings. I'll pull slowly out into the lake. You wrap the lines around your wrists and just wait for me to pull you off, like water skiers."

In two minutes, Mark and Eddie floated behind the submarine as Kate drove it slowly toward the back of the cave. For the first few seconds, they had trouble keeping their heads out of water, but they soon learned to follow the lines without difficulty. Mark found he could do it with one arm, although he had a tendency to turn on his side and be ducked underwater. He soon gave up trying to keep his cast out of the water.

They heard a tiny chirp from the submarine. Kate said, "We are getting close to the back wall of the cave. I have to slow down some to look for the opening. You may have to tread water for a while. It looks like we have about eight feet of water under us. Come up closer to the ends of the wings so my turns won't get you too near the propeller."

She turned to the right and patrolled slowly down the wall none of them could see. After five minutes, she felt a gentle, cool breeze that brought with it the smell of the forest above them.

"We found it!" she said. She pulled the nose of

the sub very close to the wall. Mark and Eddie found firm ground below their feet, leaving them standing on the rocky bottom only waist deep.

Kate turned on the light above her mask. It revealed a steep and rough stone wall with an opening five feet above the water.

She parked her mask atop her head.

"I had hoped the opening would be below the surface of the water. This is going to be a tough portage. We'll have to drag the sub up to the hole and carry it across to the other side, but first we probably should take a look at what's there. Eddie, it will have to be you."

"TOUGH PORTAGE" was putting it mildly. He came very close to falling twice, the first time only a few seconds after he had found his first foothold, the second when he was almost to the mouth of the tunnel and lost his grip with one hand. He managed to hold on with the other and pulled himself up. Kate had prudently backed Pegasus away from the wall so he wouldn't fall on it – both for his safety and the sub's.

He peered intently into the tunnel and said, "It looks like the hole is plenty big enough to get the sub through, even with its wings in place. It seems to be about six feet high, so I have to keep my head down, but it's ten or twelve feet wide. Let me go see how deep it goes."

From the water below, Kate and Mark saw Eddie's light bouncing off the limestone. A few moments later his voice echoed back out to them. "It's about twenty feet long, and the water comes right up to the edge at the other end. If we can get the sub that far, we are home free. I hope."

"Do we have any idea where we are?" Mark asked. "We can't be too far below the surface, and we have to be pretty close to the castle."

"Remember, Jeremy said Klaus told him there is a big cavern system that runs close to the castle. Part of it is open to the public, but that part is a few miles away," Eddie said.

"It makes sense that there would be an entrance to this cavern. Someone must've explored it. My light would not stretch far enough to see if there has been any construction done, but there may be doors or stairways somewhere.

"Klaus said the government really clamped down on the spelunkers after he broke his back exploring. But if their security measures weren't any better than the gate Kate came through, we should be able to get out. That's assuming there are entrances and we're in the same cave system we think we're in."

Mark said, "It's going to be tough getting the sub through the opening and into the water on the other side. That's probably a river, so there may be currents to deal with, and we really have no idea which way to go. So let's get going."

Kate cut one of the lines in half again so they would have rope to tie to the nose ring of the submarine. She cut the other so they could use it to attach to a similar ring just ahead of the propeller.

Mark said, "With this many lines, two of us will be able to heave it up to the opening while the third stays below and uses the stern and wing lines to keep it off the rocks. The two of you should pull it up, because I wouldn't be much use lifting the weight, but I should be able to keep it straight."

Kate took off her dive tanks and fins and handed them up to Eddie, who put them to one side. She scrambled up the wall with the end of the nose line tucked into her toolbelt.

Mark backed away from the wall until the water was chest deep and tightened the stern line.

"Haul away," he said. "Slow and steady. You won't be able to stop until you have it all the way up."

AFTER TEN AGONIZING MINUTES, Pegasus rested firmly on the smoothest place they could find.

"Let's catch our breath, then get it to the other side as quickly as we can," Eddie said. "I have a feeling Max and his friends are scouring the area for us already. The diver Kate saw just before we left has had almost enough time to get here, and we need to be out of his range before he arrives."

26

A LAST MEETING WITH MAX

AFTER HAULING IT UP A SHEER ROCK WALL, CARRYING the sub a few feet on dry land was easy work, and in ten minutes they had laid it back in the water. Kate removed the lines from the nose and the stern and rolled them up. Eddie and Mark took up their positions at the end of the wing-mounted lines once more and Kate turned the little sub to the right, figuring that was the direction in which the public part of the caverns lay. The river would connect them even if they did not find a door in this part of the cave.

As they moved up the river, much more slowly now because of the current flowing against them, they began to hear noises from outside.

"I think I hear the sound of a big engine of some

sort, somewhere overhead," Eddie said. "It sounds like a helicopter."

"I hear it," Kate said. "It's a heavy one, could be military. Do you suppose Jeremy found us some help?"

They traveled in silence for another 15 minutes, with Mark and Eddie bobbing in the wake.

"Stop for just a minute," Eddie said. "I thought I saw a glimmer of light up ahead."

"I see it," Kate said. "It looks like a little vertical flash. We must be getting closer to the public areas."

Suddenly, the beam from a large flashlight blinded them. Eddie instantly released his line and moved away to the side.

Max Molnar held the large light, and Tom Farkas stood to his right with a deadly-looking Uzi sub-machine gun in hand. For the first time the trio were able to see the river: they were on a wide lake that narrowed ahead of them. Molnar and Farkas stood on a broad shelf three feet above the water's surface. The cave roof was at least twenty feet above their heads but sloped lower over the narrower portion of the river they were approaching. The cave outside the castle basement had looked dull and dirty, like a hole in the mud, but this part of the cave system was a colorful fairyland of yellow and ocher walls, with sheets of stalactites cascading from the ceiling down the walls.

"Well, well," Max said. "I thought we'd never

meet again, much less in a place like this. All I want is the submarine, Kate. Once I have that, and Tom confirms that it's still working, you can walk out the door behind us to freedom and go back to Paris."

Kate sat motionless, meeting his gaze. She had driven Icarus down the right side of the lake, where the water was shallow enough for Mark and Eddie to stand on the bottom, but she knew it was much deeper in the center of the river, to her left. She had no idea how the story would play out but had the sailor's instinct for deep water. It's the reason warships leave port before hurricanes strike – the deeper the water, the better their chances.

For Eddie, the water was chest deep; for Mark it came up to his shoulders. Kate slipped off her seat but had to hold the fuselage under one arm to keep her head from going under.

"How do we know we can trust you to let us go?" Eddie called up to Max.

"Too many people know you're here, for one. For another, I don't deal in murder. Never have, never will. I have big political plans, and getting caught up in a murder investigation would make those very difficult."

There was a sudden commotion behind Molnar and Farkas.

"What the hell do you think you're doing? You can't threaten my wife. I'll have you—"

It was Admiral Henry Mickelwaite.

"I TOLD YOU TO STAY AWAY," Molnar said curtly, but in an instant Mickelwaite was on him. Molnar reached behind him and took the Uzi from Farkas. He poked the admiral hard in the stomach with the barrel and said, "Back off."

When the admiral showed no signs of stopping, three shots rang out in quick succession and he tumbled off the ledge into the lake.

WHILE MOLNAR and Farkas were occupied with the admiral, Kate quietly opened the sub's hangar bay and launched Icarus. In the tight space of the cave its low hum was audible, but by the time Molnar realized what she had done it was invisible against the ceiling. He knew it was there somewhere, but he couldn't find it, even when he probed with his flashlight.

Kate started to move toward the admiral but Molnar commanded, "Stop. I didn't want to do that, but now there's nothing to keep me from getting rid of all three of you. No one would ever find your bodies in this endless cavern."

Kate rested her hand on the sub's control panel and turned to look at Mark, a question in her eyes. He nodded imperceptibly.

Eddie heard the muted whine of the sub's turbine and started talking to create a diversion.

"You probably won't be charged with murder for killing the admiral, Molnar. But if you kill us you'll be at the tender mercy of the Hungarian authorities, especially after the word gets into the American and European papers. Think carefully. All our futures depend on it."

"Mine, maybe. You don't have one."

As he turned the barrel toward Eddie, Kate shouted "Now! Get down!" and pushed the little sub forward. It circled away from her toward the deeper water on the left, the end of one wing poking briefly above the surface as it made a complete circuit, gathering speed.

At the same instant, an array of brilliant white LEDs on Icarus started to flash like a super-intense disco ball. Molnar and Farkas looked away from the water, seeking out the source of the dazzling light. Icarus had chosen its location well, behind a curtain of highly colored stalactites, which left only the pulsing light visible. Its body was protected by the stone outcroppings extending from the ceiling.

Mark and Kate knew what was coming next; Eddie had only the faintest idea. But Molnar and Farkas had no inkling, so when the sub sailed out of the water toward them, its turbine shrieking, they were taken completely by surprise. Molnar emptied the Uzi's clip in its direction, but by then it was moving on inertia alone. Less than ten seconds after Kate pushed the button, Pegasus smashed into the stone above the two men and exploded into flame. There was one short scream, then silence.

TWENTY SECONDS LATER, Eddie stuck his head gingerly out of the water. The high-energy torpedo fuel had burned itself out, the riverside ledge was a jumble of debris, and the admiral floated face down ten feet from shore. Kate and Mark surfaced, and she began to move toward the still body. Mark followed close behind her.

Kate felt for a pulse. "He's dead," she said sadly. "I'm sorry it came to this, but not really surprised. He just didn't know when to stop."

FOOTSTEPS ECHOED off the stone walls and Jeremy's head appeared around the corner. He saw Kate first and asked, "Is everyone safe?"

"Almost everyone," she said sadly.

Jeremy stepped onto the earthen ledge, followed by a Hungarian soldier. "This is Captain Havarti," Jeremy said. "Icky reached him and he just brought a squad in by helicopter. Three of them are over at the castle rounding up the Arrow Cross goons—Get down!" He ducked and pointed to a spot a dozen feet behind Eddie, where a diver had just surfaced. They all heard the sharp hiss of an air-powered underwater pistol. An instant later, its steel dart pinged off the rock wall behind Jeremy.

Eddie took a quick step toward the diver, who was trying frantically to reload the pistol. But when he saw Eddie move, he dropped the gun and reached toward his belt. Jeremy saw the blade glint in the brilliant strobe light Icarus was still throwing out and shouted, "Eddie, back away now!" He raised Uncle Andor's old shotgun and fired the barrel loaded with buckshot. At the same time, Captain Havarti raised his pistol and fired, his shots echoing Jeremy's.

The diver fell back, his body riddled with buckshot and bullets, only an arm's length from Eddie.

"Thanks. He's done for. That's the second time in my life a shotgun has got me out of a tough jam."

Jeremy tossed the shotgun aside and said, "Please keep your pistol out and ready, Captain. You could be all that stands between us and real problems if there are any more of these guys out there."

"I don't think there are," Kate said. "I only saw one man in a wetsuit just before we left the castle basement."

"I hope that's all," Jeremy said.

KATE SWAM quickly to Mark's side and put her arm around him. It was clear he would need help to get up the slick bank, so she and Eddie pushed him from behind. Jeremy reached down to take his good arm and pull him the rest of the way, then reached for both of Kate's hands and lifted her bodily onto the bank.

"Strong," she said. "I didn't know you could do that."

"Some of us older guys will fool you from time to time," he said with a smile, which broke the tension. Then he said, very seriously, "I'm very sorry about your ex, Kate. I know your marriage was over, but a long relationship like that leaves tracks."

"Thanks for that," she said. "He wasn't an entirely bad man, and I'll probably always tell myself it was him or us. All the same, it's a memory I don't look forward to holding."

WHEN ALL FIVE were safely on dry land, they started discussing their next step. The debris field was still too hot to approach. Some of the metal parts still glowed a dull red. Max's large light had burned up with Pegasus, so the brilliant and strobe-like flashes from Icarus were the only light. It was disorienting.

Eddie said, "Well, we've stopped something big, but we don't know exactly what." He filled the others in on the cesium transport container he and Mark had found in the basement. Jeremy caught the significance immediately.

"So our first impression is that they planned to use Pegasus to deliver a dirty bomb, and the center of a city would make the most sense. We're in Hungary, which to put it mildly is in political flux right now, so there's a good chance they planned it for Budapest."

Captain Havarti added, "I know what the western newspapers say about our politics, but things are much worse than you think. Max Molnar is not the only neo-Nazi dreaming of a return to the past. So far the government has been able to resist, but if something catastrophic happens, there's no way to tell if the government could stay in power.

"I'm a soldier; I serve the government. But if another Molnar succeeds in bringing down the government with the help of stormtroopers, there's likely to be a civil war. A lot of the same people who might join Max think Hungary should take over Slovakia, and they're entirely too fond of that autocrat who's in charge of Russia. They think we got a bad deal at the end of the war when a lot of good Hungarian farmland was moved into Slovakia with the stroke of a pen.

"They'd like to get it back, plus interest."

THE CAPTAIN SAID, "Let's take a look at the debris and see what's left. It should be cool enough by now."

Mark walked to the small pile of aluminum and steel and poked it with his foot. "Pegasus did a good job for us. I guess Icky will want us to build a new one right away. Kate, are you ready for that?"

"I'm ready when you are," she answered.

One charred body lay a few feet from the sub. Kate knelt and looked closely at the burned ruin that had been the man's face. "This does not look like Max Molnar," she said. "Where is his body?"

Eddie turned his bright light on the scene and looked around. "He's not here. Could he be in the water?" But only the admiral's body bobbed gently in the river's current.

The captain ran to the narrow door he and Jeremy had used to enter the cave. Eddie followed and found himself on the edge of a grassy field with a large helicopter idling in the center. The hardwood forest started not 50 feet from the cave entrance. Eddie spotted the castle two hundred yards away, visible above the treetops of the thick forest.

Havarti quickly organized a search party with the two soldiers remaining in the crew, leaving only the pilot to guard the helicopter. They spread into the forest and within a few minutes one of the soldiers found another door set into a rocky hillside, partially hidden by a thick stand of trees. It stood open, mute evidence of how Molnar had escaped.

Another look at the castle told the story. The truck was gone. They broke off the search and returned to the chopper.

"Nothing," Eddie said to Jeremy. "I suspect he got to the truck while the soldiers were inside rounding up the other Arrow Cross men. Captain Havarti will have the police put out a bulletin, but I'm sure he will rent another car or take a taxi to Budapest as soon as he finds a large enough town. We may not find him until the next time he wants to be found.

"So now we're back to the big question, or the next big question. What were Max's plans for the sub? Where did he intend to plant a dirty bomb?"

Mark said, "Pegasus will tell us his own story. We learned from Andor that Tom Farkas went to the barn and did some work on the programming. Kate downloaded the code, so we need to find my laptop and see what changes he made. That may tell us what Molnar planned.

"It's locked in the car Eddie and I used."

"You go check on that," Jeremy said. "I want to go to the hospital and check on Uncle Andor. He's a tough old man but he was badly hurt. I liked him, and besides, he may be able to give us more information."

CAPTAIN HAVARTI HAD OBVIOUSLY BEEN TOLD NOT to return until he had closed down Arrow Cross completely.

"I brought enough men," he said. "I'll take you to the hospital."

"Thanks, but I have a rental car and I'll need it for later. Why don't you finish searching the castle, then come to Andor's farm and meet us? We can talk over what we've found, and depending on what Mark and Eddie turned up, we may need more help from your government immediately."

"That's fair," the captain replied. "I'll meet you there in an hour or so. Call me if you find anything sooner."

Jeremy turned to Mark and Kate. "Can the two of you get the laptop and bring it to the farm with Captain Havarti?"

"We'll take a quick look at the program in the car then drive to meet you," Mark said.

MARK AND KATE walked to the rental car. Mark pulled his laptop from under a pile of sweaters and old rags in the trunk and they sat down in the front seat while it started.

"The quickest way to do this is to run the comparison program, don't you think? It will do the job in two or three minutes."

He plugged the thumb drive into the USB port and tapped the screen to open the program. As they waited, he took Kate's hand and said, "Where do we go next, friend and lover? Icky's going to want another Pegasus pronto."

"I think we need to spend a few days in Paris thinking about it. There's that perfectly good shop in Miami, but we could build one just as good in Paris in a month, less if we ship over all the equipment we've been using."

"I like that idea… Wait. Look at that." A red flag had appeared at the top of the screen. "They don't match," he said.

"Ah. Now it's trickier," Kate said. "If we're lucky the change will be in the geography module."

"I can't do this with one hand. You do it." He handed the laptop to her and she immediately started searching the navigation section to see if Farkas had coded in a destination. Normally, the sub would be expected to navigate itself, but it needed a target.

She looked intently at the screen as the lines of code scrolled by.

"Here it is. He did put in a target. Let's see what section of Budapest he planned to poison. My money's on the Chain Bridge and Budapest Castle. Making those radioactive would destroy the Hungarian economy. He must figure he could ride in on a white horse and be the savior of the nation."

"It's in Lat Long," Mark said. "Let's hope we can get Google Maps up out here."

"Well, the target is not Budapest. The longitude number is too low." She quickly copied and pasted the coordinates into the map's search bar, then waited. She turned the screen so he could see it.

As the left half of the screen painted slowly, the familiar sinuous form of the Seine appeared. Then the right half painted and they saw the locator mark – Pont des Arts, the famous pedestrian bridge connecting the Louvre Museum to the Institute of France.

"If you wanted to do maximum damage in Paris, that's where you'd put a dirty bomb," Kate said. "In the river, halfway between two of the most important institutions in the country. The Élysée Palace is only about a mile away, the American Embassy is closer, and Notre Dame Cathedral and the entire police and court system are just a stone's throw away."

"So Pegasus was for Paris."

"But here's the problem I see. After he left Eddie's office, Max Molnar went to see an old Hungarian secret service agent with a major grudge against capitalism. What's to say the cesium bomb is the only thing they were planning? Suppose, for example, they planned to shoot the French president? Or the Hungarian prime minister?

"It would be easy to point fingers. The markings Eddie showed me on the cesium container clearly show that it came from the United States. The debris would let Molnar point the finger at the CIA.

"Pegasus was intended for Paris. Its debris would point directly to the American government. Most people wouldn't believe it, but it seems that more and more people are willing to buy into conspiracy theories these days. It would cause a diplomatic crisis bigger than anything since the war and might cause the Europeans to shut down NATO completely. And who would *that* favor?"

"Russia, obviously," Mark replied. "And their Hungarian friends."

"We've stopped something really big."

MARK AND KATE were first to arrive at Uncle Andor's house. The body of the stormtrooper had been moved, but the living room still looked and smelled like a slaughterhouse. They decided to wait on the porch

After a few minutes they saw Jeremy's car bucking down the rutted lane. When it stopped, he got out carrying the satphone.

"It looks like Andor will live," he told them. "He must be one really tough old man to survive a wound like that."

"When do you expect Eddie and the captain?" Kate asked.

"Any minute. Eddie is finding us a ride home, or I should say Aurélie is setting up a flight for us. We should be ready to move soon after the helicopter arrives.

"It's been a long day. Klaus is staying with his uncle for now and plans to see him through his recovery. I bet neither of them would object if we sip a couple of the beers in that refrigerator. Who's for one?"

Jeremy took Andor's chair. Mark pulled a straight chair from the living room for Kate and took Klaus's piano stool for himself. Everybody took a beer.

"So Paris was the target..." Jeremy said after his first sip. "Say, this is pretty good stuff. They've been making beer in Eastern Europe for a long time. I think they've learned how to do it.

"Paris shouldn't be a surprise. It would make a much bigger splash than Budapest. I'm glad we found the sub and the cesium – or, I'm glad *you* found it. I was a passenger.

"I have the secure satphone, so Eddie asked me to call Icky and bring him up to date. We thought we should do it when the Hungarian Army isn't listening in, so I stopped on the road to call. I suspect the wheels will start turning very fast in Paris in just a few minutes."

Kate asked, "What do you think Max Molnar

will do now, General?" She was prompting him to approach the question purely from a military point of view.

"I've thought about that. First, Max Molnar has gone from the nationalist savior to the nationalist goat. He failed, and that's the worst thing a revolutionary can do. Usually it costs them their head, but Max is probably still alive, at least for now.

"First, he had to get out of Hungary. He's probably already long gone. In his shoes, I'd go to Budapest Airport and get on the first plane heading west, or charter one. In fact, that's what we're going to do.

"The one thing you can be sure of is that we civilians are now out of the loop. With an admiral killed by a Silicon Valley billionaire, this will be a huge intelligence and PR flap, and the French police will be out in force looking for Max. If he's smart he will turn himself in."

They heard the ponderous thump of Captain Havarti's helicopter as it approached, then bounced heavily in the meadow between the house and the barn. Eddie jumped out the door, ducked, and ran toward the house. The captain followed a few steps behind.

"I told everyone you arranged a charter to Paris," Jeremy said.

Eddie said, "Aurélie called Frédéric and chartered his Gulfstream. It should be waiting for us when we get to Budapest. Captain Havarti was kind enough to offer us a lift, and his men will return our cars."

"Mr. Grant was right to set this up quickly," the captain said. "The Max Molnar affair is already beginning to turn political. The secret service learned he was waiting on a plane to Frankfurt but couldn't get authorization to stop him because no one had filed a formal complaint, or so they were told.

"I offered to file charges myself but they weren't interested and told me to return immediately to Budapest. Which I will do, of course, but via the airport. And I'll wait until you are well on your way back to Paris before I talk to my superiors again."

"That plane has landed and he's gone to find some other way to get to Paris, or wherever he's going," Jeremy said. "Do you have any idea where he went?"

"No, I don't. I would tell you if I did, but we don't have much in the way of intelligence resources in Germany."

Eddie said, "Icky will alert the Paris intelligence people, and Aurélie has already called Philippe. He should turn up soon."

AN HOUR LATER, the chopper landed fifty yards from the charter terminal and they walked quickly to the luxurious Gulfstream, which sat idling on the tarmac.

Next to the little Cessna they had used to fly to Saint-Yan, it looked huge.

Aurélie was first down the stairway. She ran to meet Eddie halfway between the two craft, threw her arms around his neck and gave him an enthusiastic kiss.

"My hero!" she exclaimed. "You have saved Paris."

THE TONE WAS SOMBER in the cabin of the Gulfstream as it sped toward Paris. The team exchanged smiles and high-fives when Frédéric announced they had left Hungarian airspace, but the two deaths and the escape of Max Molnar cast a pall.

Eddie had called Icky from the helicopter. Icky had in turn had called Philippe, who told him the Paris police and the anti-terrorism prosecutor would take over.

"When we get to Paris we're going to be told to butt out," Eddie said. "The French government should handle it the rest of the way, but we might be able to move it along in the background."

Jeremy said, "No question. I've already had a text from my source Zoltan saying he wants to meet. He will call me with the time."

"I'm going to take advantage of the delay. I've told Juliette I'll meet her for dinner."

27

LOOSE ENDS

PARIS

The Gulfstream hadn't yet reached its cruising altitude when Jeremy's phone rang. The connection was bad, but he could make out that Zoltan had news for him.

"Zoltan, I'm in a plane on the way back from Budapest," Jeremy said over the sound of the engines. He paused. "I understand. I'll come to see you. Can you do it any sooner than that?"

He hung up and turned to Eddie, who sat across the aisle with Aurélie.

"Odd. Zoltan says he has something new and important to tell me, but not until tomorrow morning. There's some sort of embargo on it."

"Would you like me to go with you?" Eddie asked.

"Zoltan is a pro. He wouldn't ask for a meeting if he didn't think he had something important, and he did say we should meet alone. I think this is one I should do myself, but I'll call you as soon as I leave his house."

"We're pretty much out of this now," Eddie told him. "I spoke to Philippe a few minutes ago and he said the National Police already have a warrant to search Viktor Nagy's apartment and Max's as well if they can find it. There's nothing in his name on the Paris deed list, so if he has a *pied à terre* it will be in the name of a Luxembourg corporation or a front man."

"Unless Zoltan knows about another cesium bomb, we may be able to go back to normal. It would be nice if Mark and Kate could be tourists for a few days at least before Icky has them back in the shop building another submarine," Jeremy said.

Eddie replied, "Let's do a wrap-up tomorrow at our place and bring Icky in on the phone. Then we can all go our own ways, I hope."

A CALL from Budapest delayed Jeremy, so he didn't make it to Nogent-sur-Marne by eight o'clock, but he was only a few minutes late. Again, he chose to park a couple of blocks away and approach Zoltan's house indirectly. His conversation with Zoltan worried him

– he thought it more likely that there would be someone watching this time than during his first visit.

A curtain moved in Zoltan's living-room window, and the door opened before he had time to ring the bell.

"Come in quickly," Zoltan said urgently.

He did not offer tea.

"Viktor Nagy came to see me last night. He told me a story and he knows I will pass it on to you, but I had to promise I would not tell you until now," Zoltan said.

"So he was behind the bomb?"

"He didn't say that – he wouldn't – but he was the man behind the Arrow Cross party, and now that lies in shambles. He believes it's all Max's fault, but he says he's not angry, and that he and Max are going to South America for a while until things cool off here.

"I think his main worry is that this whole thing will mess up his relationship with the Russian government."

Jeremy said, "It might. I just heard from the Hungarian Army captain who rode to our rescue at the castle yesterday. They arrested three young men at the castle and, based on their questioning, the police picked up another half-dozen young Russian men who they think are soldiers but are operating as independent mercenaries, sort of like the ones in eastern Ukraine. They also arrested two Americans, who are definitely mercenaries working for a shady outfit in Florida.

"They suspect what Viktor thought was an effort to grab power in Hungary was in fact a Russian effort to do what they did in Ukraine and drive a wedge through NATO and the EU. It might have worked, too. The dirty bomb would have created just enough chaos to cover their tracks, especially if they could make it look like an American plot.

"The government is keeping it very quiet. Nobody wants it known that their friends have sent in hoods to work against them."

Zoltan said, "I've told you what Viktor told me. Now here's what I think – he's not going to South America, he's going to Russia. And he's not taking Max."

"Where do you think Max is?"

"I think Max is dead. Viktor is an east-bloc hood. He doesn't tolerate failure, especially when it embarrasses him. I think you'll find Max's body, although it might take some work. In the old days you'd never find it, but he doesn't have the staff here he had in Budapest. So you'll find Max, I'm sure.

"There's another thing. Remember, I told you Max had disappeared for several months. Viktor told me last night that he was in a training program in Siberia during that time, at a special weapons base that works with chemical and radiological weapons.

Did your trip to Hungary have anything to do with a dirty bomb?"

"Yes. We found a container of American cesium with the explosives needed to turn it into a dirty bomb. The target was the bridge between the Louvre and the French Institute. It would have turned the tourist areas into a wasteland."

BACK IN HIS CAR, Jeremy twisted through the streets of Nogent-sur-Marne until he was certain he had no tail, then he called Eddie.

"Viktor went to see Zoltan last night and said he was leaving the country."

Eddie said, "That's what happened, it seems. The police searched his apartment before dawn today and turned up nothing, except that he took a lot more luggage than you'd need for a week in the country. They found his car at CDG but so far don't know which plane he got on, if he even did. The car could have been a diversion. He could easily have got on a train for somewhere else in Europe."

Jeremy said, "He told Zoltan he and Max were going to South America. Zoltan doesn't believe him. He thinks Viktor is going to Russia and Max is dead. Zoltan said Viktor was angry enough to kill."

"We should know soon enough. It turns out Max has an apartment in the Marais that's owned by his company, Budapest Re. Philippe thinks the magistrate will sign off on a warrant any minute and they'll go search it. He asked me to go along. We're on the way there now."

"Better you than me. I'm going home to put my feet up for an hour then take Juliette out to a nice lunch and try to get life back to normal. Call if there's anything I should know."

THE ADDRESS PHILIPPE had given Eddie was on a tiny *impasse* off Rue Charlot, a thoroughfare in the Marais. For years, the Marais has been the primary Jewish area of the city, and on any day the sidewalks are a mix of men wearing the somber black garb and hats of the orthodox and the ever-present swarms of tourists, from solo Americans to groups of Chinese. More recently, it has become the city's center of gay culture.

Eddie and Aurélie left their cab at the corner and walked down the dead-end street until a policeman stopped them just long enough to learn Philippe had invited them.

Max's building was constructed in the old style – six floors of apartments surrounding a cobbled courtyard that in the eighteenth century would have been crowded with carriages, but now was empty. Not since the Citroen 2CV had there been a car small enough to use the minuscule driveway.

Philippe was in conversation with a police captain at the edge of the courtyard. He waved them over and told the captain they were to be allowed free run of the building. "They probably know more than anyone about the man we're seeking," he said.

The apartment was on the third floor and, as is the case in many older buildings, there was no elevator. The three walked upstairs and found the door to one of the apartments standing open, with police photographers and their lights inside. The scene was lit like a movie set, brilliant and starkly white.

"There's nothing so far, *monsieur le commissaire,*" an officer in rubber gloves and a white smock said. "It doesn't look like the apartment has been occupied for weeks, although the *gardienne* told us she saw Max Molnar come in earlier today, with two other men. She hasn't seen them since. They could easily have left while she wasn't watching the door."

"Did she give you a description of the other men?" Philippe asked. "I have some pictures."

"You can show them to her. She is outside in the hallway."

AN OFFICER BROUGHT in a slender middle-aged woman wearing the traditional smock of a domestic employee. Philippe showed her Victor's passport picture and asked if he was the second man.

"I think so, sir. He looked a lot like that."

"And the other man? What did he look like?"

"He was much younger, maybe thirty-five. He looked like a weightlifter. And he was very unfriendly."

"Did Mr. Molnar have a storage room in the building?"

"Oh, yes. All the owners have a *cave*."

A NARROW STONE staircase that curled tightly to the left and had no handrail was the only way to reach the *cave*. The *gardienne* pulled the string on the one light hanging from the center of the room. It cast a weak glow on the rough wooden storage lockers that lined the walls, each with its own padlock.

She led them to one locker, halfway along the wall. Philippe signaled for an officer to cut the lock. The old hinges complained as he pulled the door open to reveal a few shelves and an empty wooden crate, but no sign of Max.

"Madame, would he have access to anywhere else down here?" Philippe asked.

"There is an old pit where the owners used to store ice, before refrigerators. They would fill it up and cover it with sawdust, and have their servants take it up to their apartments for their iceboxes. We don't even lock it anymore because no one goes there."

She led them to a wider door in the corner of the room. It was fashioned from the same rude wood planks as the individual storage lockers, but it was secured only with a wooden peg. She pulled it open carefully.

"Be careful. The hole is just a foot inside the door, and it's two meters deep. Ten years ago an old man fell in it and broke both legs."

The room was dark. Philippe called for a heavy flashlight, which an officer hurried to put in his hand. He turned it into the room.

"Max," he said. A body swayed gently, suspended from a ceiling timber by a wire.

"Piano wire. It was the Nazis' favorite way to execute a traitor. This is someone sending a message." He reached out to touch the body. "Still warm. Viktor must have told him they were coming to get his luggage for their trip to Moscow, or wherever."

"It's a hell of a way to die," Eddie said. "I'm not sure even Max deserves this."

Aurélie dissented. "He planned to explode a radioactive bomb in Paris, and would have if it weren't for you. I'm not sure even this is bad enough for him."

TWO DAYS LATER, Eddie and Aurélie sat around the desk in his soundproofed office in the Luxor and waited for Icky Crane to come on the speakerphone. Jeremy had passed on the conference call. Mark and Kate sat together on a sofa under the one window. Philippe planned to participate but said he didn't have time to wait for Icky, and had asked Eddie to patch him in when the wrap-up actually got underway.

"Icky told me he had some more info about how the whole thing was set up," Eddie said. "There was a lot of money flowing from a source that won't surprise you. And it looks like Max diverted quite a bit of it for his own use, or maybe his and Viktor's."

THE SPEAKER CAME TO LIFE. "Hey, all. Is everybody there? It's Icky Crane."

Aurélie called the roll. "Eddie, I, Mark and Kate are here. Philippe is waiting to be patched in. Jeremy had a date with Juliette and said we could call him if we need him but he thinks the deal is done, at least for now."

Eddie connected Philippe, who started.

"We have found Viktor, although we'll never get to him. He used a false passport to fly to Madrid, then another one to fly first to Prague and then to Moscow. We think he's still there, although I suspect

Russian intelligence will ship him to the boondocks as soon as they've squeezed everything out of him they can."

Icky said, "That should take him out of action for the foreseeable future. Here's something interesting. Our station chief in Budapest says the murder of an admiral by a tech billionaire is all the talk of the town and seems to be turning the voters away from the extremes. An overnight poll last night put André Westerhof's Center Party within reach of a victory in the parliamentary elections.

"That would be welcome news to our government—"

"—and even more welcome to ours," Aurélie interjected.

"Right you are," Icky said.

Philippe added, "We've also solved the mystery of poor Vasily's murder on the Seine. The killer was the same man who put the ricin in your food – Boris. He will be our guest for a very long time, and I expect him to lead us to other members of the conspiracy. He was one of the Arrow Cross students a few months ago, and Max remembered him. It was Max who organized the bombing of Mark and Kate's sailboat, and the ricin. It wasn't Admiral Mickelwaite. He was just a follower."

ICKY TOOK UP THE STORY. "We've learned a lot in the last few days. I didn't bother you with most of it because it won't affect the outcome, but Raul and Antoine have been busy in Miami.

"Willimon did get one of the Russians to talk. The two of them are actually brothers, and they aren't Russian but Chechen. Chechnya had a couple of bloody wars with Russia but now is completely under Russian control. It's an important nexus between some of the nasty stuff the Russians like and the terrorist weapons the Middle Easterners want to buy."

Eddie added, "The Chechens are a problem along the Mediterranean coast, especially in Marseilles."

"I remember that you ran into a few of them when you were chasing Claude Khan," Icky said. "Willimon managed to break down the younger and weaker brother, who told him Max Molnar had personally hired them to bomb Mark's boat.

"Molnar already knew about the submarine, because Tom Farkas now worked for him, so he saw it as an excellent chance to kill two birds with one stone. He'd kill the admiral and get the castle, and he'd get the sub and use it to terrorize Paris and become prime minister of Hungary.

"It was a hell of a plot."

Kate asked, "Willimon got all that out of him?

I'd heard he was a good detective, but that's out-standing."

"There's another side to it, though," Icky said. "The younger brother told the older one what he'd done. So the older one sent word to Willimon that he'd talk, too. In fact, I was talking to Willimon just a few minutes before he was going into the interview room with the older brother.

"They talked for no more than two minutes, and according to the tape the Chechen said nothing. Instead, he strangled Detective Willimon with the chain connecting his handcuffs to the table. He's dead. So is the Chechen. A guard shot him, but too late to help Willimon.

"End of that story, I think."

Mark said, "I've lived in Miami a long time and I know it's weird and sometimes dangerous, but that's the worst story I've ever heard."

"THERE'S MORE," Icky said. "The next item of interest is the money. As is the case in most crimes, if you can follow the money it will lead to the criminal.

"Max Molnar didn't mount this operation on his own dime, or on Viktor's, either. In fact, it looks like they made money on it.

"The Russian embassies in Washington and Budapest wired hundreds of thousands of dollars to

Max, to his insurance company Budapest Re, and to some other places we haven't identified yet. It was immediately re-wired to secret accounts in Luxembourg, the Cayman Islands and Cyprus, the perennial laundry for Russian money. From there a good bit of it was wired to Budapest, where it was used to fund the construction of the castle. Some of that money is unaccounted for, and we think it went to Max and Viktor personally.

"And Kate, I have some news for you. Ready?"

"Sure. Go ahead."

"I found out that your ex was supposed to get your share of the castle when the divorce was final. Is that right?"

"Sure. I didn't want anything to do with it."

"Jeremy picked up something from Dr. Westerhof and asked me to check it out.

"It seems there were problems changing the Hungarian property records, and it still hasn't been done. In fact, your lawyer has struck out so far. Nothing he's tried has worked.

"In exchange for the money to rebuild, Max did a deal with Admiral Mickelwaite that gave him the castle if the admiral died. But when he found out about the delay in your divorce settlement he knew if he killed the admiral too soon you'd be the owner.

"That's why he bombed the sailboat. He figured he could steal Pegasus and Icarus and get away with it by hiding them in the Hungarian back country, but in order for him to get the castle you had to be dead, and you had to die before he killed your ex-husband, because if Admiral Mickelwaite died first their agreement would be null and void.

"So he called on one of his Russian footpads to plant the limpet, and when that failed he sent him to find you in the hospital and finish the job. Max left out some pretty important information his killer could have used – such as that you're a knife-fighting expert."

Kate said quickly, "Does that mean I own it now? That would explain why he lost interest in Mark when he saw me."

"That's right. It was supposed to be out-and-out murder for the title to the castle."

"And it nearly worked," she replied. "If Mark hadn't figured out that bump in the night neither of us would be here." She smiled and squeezed Mark's hand.

Mark spoke up. "Icky, I know you want another Pegasus soon, but we'd like to take a week as tourists, and then talk to you about it, okay? We have places to go and things to do. And we're going to start right now."

"We sure are," Kate said. "And somehow we'll figure out what to do with that damned castle."

ABOUT THE EDDIE GRANT SERIES

Finding Pegasus is the third in the Eddie Grant Series. All are loosely centered on Paris, where Eddie shares a home with Aurélie Cabillaud, now his wife.

In the first novel, *Treasure of Saint-Lazare,* Eddie and Aurélie reunite after years of estrangement and work together to identify and punish the criminals who killed Eddie's wife, child, and father.

The sequel, *Last Stop: Paris,* tells of their search for the kingpin after they pick up his trail at a society party thrown by a banker in his luxurious apartment on the Île Saint-Louis.

Finding Pegasus adds the new characters of Kate Hall and Mark McGinley.

All are available at Amazon in Kindle, audiobook, and paperback versions. You can see all of them on my author page. You may also join the low-volume mailing list on my blog, Part-Time Parisian.

If you enjoyed *Finding Pegasus,* please leave a review.

ABOUT THE AUTHOR

JOHN PEARCE has lived in Sarasota, Florida, for more than thirty years, but he is also a Part-Time Parisian, thus the title of his blog, PartTime-Parisian.com.

His interest in Paris began at the time he lived in Frankfurt, Germany, as a magazine editor and correspondent in banking and finance for the old International Herald-Tribune (now known as the International New York Times).

When he and his wife Jan sold a business in Sarasota they began spending part of each year in Paris, where John gathers information for his novels and together they enjoy the life of the arts and of food, mainly in the Fourteenth Arrondissement. While in Paris, John writes in the beautiful old Mazarin Library, which is part of the French Institute.

His first novel, *Treasure of Saint-Lazare,* was picked as the best historical mystery of 2014 in the Readers' Favorite Book Contest. His second, *Last Stop: Paris,* was finalist in the best Indie book contest sponsored by Shelf Unbound Magazine.

His fourth novel, whose working title is *Washington Square*, is already under way. The fifth is in the planning stages.

If you enjoyed *Finding Pegasus*, please review it on Amazon. And you're invited to subscribe to the Eddie Grant Readers Group, which you can do at PartTimeParisian.com.

Made in the USA
Middletown, DE
11 May 2020

93799160R10262